# SURVIVOR'S GUILT

Books by Robyn Gigl

BY WAY OF SORROW

SURVIVOR'S GUILT

Published by Kensington Publishing Corp.

# SURVIVOR'S GUILT

# ROBYN GIGL

KENSINGTON
PUBLISHING CORP.

www.kensingtonbooks.com

KENSINGTON BOOKS are published by

Kensington Publishing Corp.
119 West 40th Street
New York, NY 10018

All Kensington titles, imprints, and distributed lines are available at special quantity discounts for bulk purchases for sales promotion, premiums, fundraising, educational, or institutional use. Special book excerpts or customized printings can also be created to fit specific needs. For details, write or phone the office of the Kensington Special Sales Manager: Attn. Special Sales Department. Kensington Publishing Corp, 119 West 40th Street, New York, NY 10018. Phone: 1-800-221-2647.

Library of Congress Card Catalogue Number: 2021945739

The K logo is a trademark of Kensington Publishing Corp.

ISBN: 978-1-4967-2828-9

First Kensington Hardcover Edition: February 2022

ISBN: 978-1-4967-2830-2 (ebook)

10 9 8 7 6 5 4 3 2

Printed in the United States of America

*For Mom*

# CHAPTER 1

*April 4, 2008*

"HEY, STRANGER," DUANE SWISHER SAID, STANDING IN THE DOOR-way of her office. "How you doing?"

Erin McCabe looked up; brushed her long, copper-colored hair back from her face; and smiled. She and Duane had been partners in the law firm of McCabe & Swisher for the last five years, specializing in representing defendants in criminal cases.

"Oh, living the dream—one nightmare at a time," she responded, gesturing to the piles of papers stacked haphazardly on her desk among the empty Dunkin' Donuts cups.

"So has Judge Fowler incorporated casual Friday into his trial calendar?" he asked jokingly.

She smiled at his reference to the fact that she was wearing jeans and a Dixie Chicks T-shirt. "No. No trial today. Judge Fowler schedules his sentencing hearings for every other Friday, so I get to come to the office in jeans and see your smiling face." She reached down and picked up a brief in opposition to a motion to dismiss an indictment that she had filed in one of their cases. "And try to catch up on all the shit that's been accumulating while I'm on trial."

After pulling back one of the chairs in front of her desk, Duane plopped down. He stretched his legs out in front of the chair as he uncurled his six-foot-two-inch frame. Unlike Erin's casual Friday attire, Swish wore a charcoal-gray suit, with a light pink shirt, neither of which did anything to disguise that at thirty-seven he was still in great shape and only a few pounds heavier from when he was All Ivy at Brown. Swish, as everyone called him, both because of his last name and his prowess from three-point range on the basketball court, was not only her law partner, he was probably her best friend too. They made an interesting pair. Even though Erin was only six months younger, Swish, with his chiseled physique, dark brown skin, and well-trimmed goatee, made a commanding appearance. Whereas Erin, with her girl-next-door looks, dusting of freckles that ran across the bridge of her nose, and slim athletic figure, was often mistaken for being younger and less experienced, a perception that she wasn't afraid to use to her advantage in the courtroom.

"How's the trial going?"

"Remind me again why we agreed to take this case?" she asked.

He chuckled. "We got a big retainer."

"Right." She shook her head and inhaled. "Swish, these guys are definitely the gang that couldn't shoot straight. They set up an offshore gambling operation in Costa Rica, installed sophisticated encryption software to protect the website . . . and then talked about what they were doing on the phone like they were making dinner plans."

"So what's the defense?"

"The three guys at the top are arguing that they thought it was legal," she said, gesturing with her hands that she had little faith in the merits of their argument. "Our guy, Justin Mackey, claims that all he did was design and sell encryption software, and that he had no idea what anyone was using it for."

Swish shrugged. "Sounds like a plausible defense."

"He seems to think so, but I'm a little less sanguine. Unfortunately, even though he claims he didn't know what anyone was using the software for, he did a lot of talking on the phone and the wiretaps picked up some pretty damning conversations between him and one of the top guys. Plus, he liked to bet—a lot. Gonna be tough to sell that he didn't know what they were using his software for. And for someone who was supposedly into all this encryption shit to keep everything secret, he certainly didn't seem too concerned about talking about things openly on the phone."

"Any chance of a plea?" Swish asked.

"The State offered some decent deals early on, but no takers," she said. "My sense is these guys are protecting someone else."

"Even our guy?"

"Yeah. He clearly knows more than what he's letting on to me. That said, I'm not sure he even knows who he's protecting." She shook her head, allowing her frustration to show. She liked Justin. He was young, twenty-eight, lived with his mom, and seemed like a decent guy. As they prepared for trial and she had gotten to know him, her take was that he had just gotten in over his head, probably because not only did he bet a lot, but from what she had heard listening to the wiretap recordings, he also lost—a lot.

"How much longer do you have to go?" he asked.

"I expect the State is going to wrap up early next week. So we're in the home stretch."

"Any defense case?"

She cringed. "Not from me. I can't put him on the stand, they'd kill him on cross with the wiretaps."

"Sorry," he said. "Anything I can help you with?"

"No. I don't think so. If there's any silver lining it's that we're in front of Judge Fowler. Assuming Mackey gets convicted, I'm pretty sure Fowler won't revoke his bail prior to sentencing and, since it's Justin's first offense, I'm hoping he doesn't get more than eighteen months."

"Here if you need anything," he offered.

"Thanks. Anything new here?"

"I had the motion to suppress in the Creswell case in front of Judge Anita Reynolds down in Ocean County."

Erin smiled. Judge Reynolds had briefly presided over the case involving their client Sharise Barnes. Sharise's case had made Erin famous, or, more accurately, infamous, at least in much of

New Jersey. Then again, defending a transgender woman of color accused of murdering the son of a now gubernatorial candidate had a tendency to generate publicity, especially when Erin's own status as a transgender woman figured prominently in the coverage. "I liked Reynolds. I wish she had continued to handle Sharise's case," Erin said. "How'd the motion go?" she asked.

"She reserved, but I think she's going to grant it. I mean she should. They came into the guy's house without a warrant, after he refused to let them in, and then claimed they saw drug paraphernalia in plain view—in his bedroom on the second floor."

She laughed. "Yeah, you're right. I like your chances on that one."

He stared at her for several seconds. "I was with Mark at our game on Wednesday night and he asked how you were doing."

Erin flinched at the mention of Mark's name. She and Mark Simpson had dated for over a year, but she had recently ended their relationship and the wounds left behind were still open and painful. He had been the first man she had ever fallen in love with. And somehow, after a few false starts, he had gotten beyond the fact that she was a trans woman, and he had loved her for who she was—something that after she transitioned she assumed she'd never experience with a man or a woman. She knew Swish still saw Mark every week because they played on the same team in a men's basketball league. Trying to avoid where she knew this conversation was headed, she gave Swish her best "please don't go there" look, but she could tell from his expression that either her look didn't convey the intended message or even if he got it he was going to ignore it.

"Tell Mark I said hello," she finally said.

"Come on, E," he fired back. "I know it's none of my business, but Mark's a big boy—he can make his own decisions. If the roles were reversed, you'd be mad as hell that he was making decisions for you."

She closed her eyes and slowly drew in a deep breath. Even now, a month later, the look on Mark's face when she told him she was ending things was still vivid—it was not unlike how she felt years earlier when her wife had told her they needed to separate—a mixture of pain and disbelief. She opened her eyes. "Swish, you're right," she said. "It's none of your business."

Swish cocked his head to one side, his eyes widened, taking her in, then rose from his chair, his eyes never leaving hers. "Got it," he said brusquely before making his way out of her office.

*Shit.* She got up from behind her desk and walked over to one of the windows. Her office was on the outskirts of the business district in Cranford, perched in one of the second-floor turrets of a former Victorian home that had been converted into an office building twenty years ago. She loved Swish like a brother—not surprising given how much they'd been through together. Before they became partners, Swish had been an FBI agent, and probably still would be if he hadn't been forced to resign when he was set up to be the fall guy for a leak of classified materials involving the illegal surveillance of Muslim Americans after 9/11. When he left the Bureau he seemed to have a lot of options open to him, but to Erin's surprise when she had asked him to partner with her, he agreed and the firm of McCabe & Swisher was born. Of course, at the time, Erin was still living as Ian McCabe. It was only a year after they became partners that Erin had come out as a transgender woman, and the resulting fallout had almost crushed her. Some losses had been harder than others, none more so than her former wife, Lauren; her dad, Patrick; and her brother, Sean. The only ones who never wavered in their support were her mom, Swish, and his wife, Corrinne. Without them, she wouldn't have made it.

Still, as close as they were, it was too painful for her to talk to Swish about Mark right now. She needed to stay focused on the trial and find some way to separate her client from the other defendants, some way to convince the jury that Justin wasn't responsible for the huge offshore operations the prosecution had meticulously laid out over the last three weeks. Then, and only then, could she focus on her life again.

She grabbed her coffee off her desk and headed down the hallway to Swish's office. His office occupied one of the former bedrooms to the original home and, unlike the clutter and chaos of her office, his was always neat and orderly with everything in its place. There was never so much as a stray paper clip lying out on his glass desk.

"You got a minute?" she asked, standing in the doorway.

He looked up and nodded.

She took a few tentative steps into his office and stopped. "Swish, I'm sorry. I truly am," she said, biting her lower lip. "I know you're trying to be a good friend to Mark—and to me—but I'm just not in a good place right now. You know how I get when I'm on trial. I can't focus on anything else, and honestly, Swish, talking about Mark right now just hurts too much."

She could tell by his expression he wanted to say more, but it was a sign of how deep their friendship ran that he didn't. "You're right. Focus on what you need to do. We'll talk when the trial's over."

"Thanks," she replied, trying to paste a smile on her face. "I appreciate it."

# CHAPTER 2

AARON TINSLEY STUDIED HIS CLIENT'S COMPUTER. HE MISSED HIS days as a hacker, something he had started doing when he was fifteen. While the prospect of five years in prison for hacking into the NRA's e-mails had been a convincing enticement to get on the straight and narrow, it was still hard for him to wrap his head around the fact that at twenty-two he was now a white hat doing IT security. While his boss was a decent guy, a former hacker himself, and it did have the advantage of a regular paycheck, it meant his days were mostly filled with boring stuff.

Still, every once in a while, he came across something that provided him with the same thrill as hacking. Today was one of those days.

Up until about 6:00 p.m. last night, Aaron hadn't even known where Westfield, New Jersey was. But his boss had called him with what he said was a "special assignment" for a guy by the name of Charles Parsons who was having computer problems. *Must be real special*, Aaron had thought if they were willing to pay him double time to go out on a Sunday. Surveying his surroundings, Aaron had no idea how much Parsons's house was worth, but it was easily the biggest house he had ever been in. The home office he was working in probably had more square footage than Aaron's entire one-bedroom apartment in Queens.

As he searched deeper through the mostly unseen files on his client's laptop, he had to admit that he was enjoying the hunt. He examined the computer's registry, trying to find the hidden program he had begun to suspect was buried in the software code. Whoever had done this was a real pro. He was almost envious.

"I need to get on my computer. Are you almost done?" Charles Parsons asked, startling Aaron.

Aaron had been so engrossed in his search he was surprised to see Parsons standing in the middle of the room. Parsons, who was well tanned even though it was early April, appeared to be around six feet, with broad shoulders. Aaron couldn't even hazard a guess at his age, but his wrinkle-free face, contrasted with a shock of wavy gray hair, left the impression that Parsons was well acquainted with a plastic surgeon. Catching Parsons's annoyed stare, Aaron realized that he was still grinning in admiration for the cleverness of the hacker.

"What are you smiling at?" Parsons snapped.

Aaron willed his face into seriousness. "Sorry. Um, can we go talk in another room?" he said.

"What the fuck are you babbling about?" Parsons shot back.

Aaron powered down the laptop, closed it, and took Parsons by the arm, escorting him out of the office. "Mr. Parsons, please let's go into your kitchen."

"What the hell is going on?" Parsons said, yanking his arm from Aaron's grasp as they left the room. "I asked you to check to see if I have a virus, and you're acting like my computer has the bubonic plague."

Aaron sat on one of the stools in front of the marble island in Parsons's massive, well-appointed kitchen. "That's actually not a bad analogy," he offered, nodding his head. "Yeah, you have a virus, which it looks like you picked up from some porn website. That's easy enough to fix. Unfortunately, you have a much bigger problem. How long have you been running the encryption software?"

"Why? What's that got to do with anything?" Parsons asked, his eyes narrowing as he gazed suspiciously at Aaron.

"I'm not sure yet, but I think that may have a rootkit embedded in it. Which means your laptop, and probably any other computers you use that are running the same software on them, are infected with the same rootkit."

"What the fuck is a rootkit?"

Aaron shook his head from side to side. "In layman's terms, it's a program that allows whoever installed it to monitor everything you do on your computer."

"Wait, are you saying someone can see what websites I visited?" Parsons said, cocking his head to the side and rubbing his forefinger across his lips, his tone suddenly less defiant.

"Yes, but . . ." Aaron hesitated. "Well, it's much worse than that. It means that whoever is watching can record every keystroke you make. So that if you go to a website where you have a password, they can steal your password and lock you out. I think they've also taken over the microphone and camera to watch and listen to you. That's why I wanted to speak to you in here."

Parsons's stare conveyed disbelief. "Watch me? From my computer? You can't be fucking serious?"

"Yeah," Aaron nodded. "Unfortunately, I am."

"What's that got to do with my encryption software?"

"As best I can tell, the rootkit is embedded in it. So if you have the same software on your desktop, or any other computers, you probably have it on those as well."

Parsons's blank stare conveyed his failure to grasp the full impact of what Aaron was telling him.

"Look," Aaron said, speaking slowly now, "if this is what I think it is, it means that as long as you've had this software on your computer, whoever's responsible for it has seen everything you've done. Every e-mail, every transaction, every download—everything."

"But everything's encrypted. That's the whole purpose of the software. So only people with . . ." He stopped midsentence, panic spreading across his face with the realization that the encryption software was compromised. "Whoever this is, they can see everything?"

"Yeah, most likely," Aaron repeated.

"No. No, that can't be possible," Parsons said, his face suddenly ashen.

"When did you have it installed?" Aaron asked, enjoying the sudden shift in power as he watched Parsons's desperation grow. *Who knows,* he thought. *Maybe if I play this right and fix the problem, Parsons might pay me something extra under the table.*

"Um, I don't know—about a year and a half ago, I guess," he replied.

"And where did you get it?" Aaron said. "I mean, it's not something you bought at Staples."

"Some friends recommended it." When he saw Aaron's skeptical look, he got defensive. "I trust these guys. We do some business together and the business they're in requires secrecy, like mine. They said this software was the best."

"Any changes to it since then?"

"I got a new laptop about a year ago."

"Anything else?" Aaron asked.

"Yeah, about six months or so ago the guy who designed and installed the software came back and installed an update saying they needed to patch some potential security issue."

"Bingo," Aaron said, the final piece of the puzzle finally dropping into place. "It looks like whoever designed it built in a little something extra when they installed the update, because as good as it is as encryption software, it's even a better rootkit."

"I need this fixed now," Parsons said, growing angry. "I need access to my data. If someone has been watching me for six months, I need to secure things before someone steals my information."

Aaron didn't feel like incurring Parsons's wrath by telling him it was probably too late. The hacker had access for six months. Plus, they either already knew Aaron had been reviewing the computer's registry and that he had likely uncovered the rootkit, or they'd know soon enough. Not to mention that the only way to retrieve the encrypted data was to use the infected software. As Aaron weighed the options, he couldn't help but admire how thoroughly this mystery designer had fucked his client.

"You understand," Aaron started cautiously, "there are basically two pieces to the encryption software: One encrypts any e-mails you send and receive, the second encrypts any data that you're storing so no one can read it unless they have the same software."

Parsons nodded.

"Here's the problem," Aaron said slowly. "I'm assuming you encrypted and downloaded a lot of data you don't want anyone else to see." Aaron didn't wait for Parsons's response—his face told him the answer. "Assuming that's true, you can't access the information without unencrypting it, which requires you to use the program. So what we need to do is get you off the Internet so whoever is running this thing will lose access to your computer. Then we need to unencrypt all your data and get a brand-new laptop."

Parsons's head was bouncing like a bobblehead toy. "This can't be happening! Motherfucker!" he spat out, then started grabbing things and throwing them against the blue tiled walls. He started with the fruit in a ceramic bowl on the island, then the bowl, then anything he could get his hands on—a glass, a coffee mug. He finally stopped, his breath coming in short staccato bursts as he wrapped his hands behind his head, holding it as if trying to keep it from exploding. He looked at Aaron with the look of a cornered wild animal. "I need that data. I have to make sure . . ." He stopped. "There's a lot of important financial information that I've downloaded. I can't let that fall into the wrong hands."

Aaron scratched his head. "Where's the data now?"

"I have it on four external hard drives."

Aaron took a deep breath. "As I said, the easiest thing to do is get you offline, connect your hard drives, open and unencrypt the data on them, move it unencrypted to a new computer or hard drive, and then resave it using new encryption software."

"Can I do that on my own?"

"How good are you on a computer?"

He shook his head in disgust. "Can you show me how to do it? There's a lot of sensitive data, so once you show me, hopefully I can handle it from there."

"Sure. But in the meantime, whoever installed the rootkit has access to your data. So time is of the essence."

Parsons mumbled under his breath. "There may be another solution," he said. "I have an idea. I'll call you later. But in the meantime, go get me a new laptop and do whatever you have to do to get some new encryption software, so you're ready to show me how to do it as soon I need you."

Aaron let himself out through the front door and headed out to his car, happy to be getting out of the house. Any thoughts of making Parsons happy and getting a few extra bucks under the table had evaporated as he'd watched Parsons explode. This was not a guy he wanted to deal with any more than he had to. Get the job done and get out of town. He wasn't sure what Parsons was thinking when he said he might have another solution, but, by the look on Parsons's face, Aaron was sure he didn't want to know.

Parsons walked into his bedroom and pulled out the four hard drives, stared at them, now aware that someone else might know everything that was on them. Who the fuck would do this to him? He didn't trust his partners, but he couldn't imagine any of them would risk incurring his wrath by hacking him. He tried to remember the name of the guy who had installed the software and who had recommended him. He needed answers and he needed them now. He picked up the phone and dialed her number. Of all of them, she was the one who had always been loyal to him.

"Cass, it's me. I . . . we have a major problem. I just had an IT guy in here and he tells me our encryption software has some fucking rootworm or something in it."

"What the hell is that?" she asked.

Parsons hesitated, weighing what he wanted to tell her to avoid giving her too much information. "It allows someone to see what I'm doing on my computer," he replied.

"Charles, are you serious? This could be devastating."

"Listen to me. I don't need you to tell me how fucking bad this could be; I just need you to find the guy who installed this. Do you remember the little shit's name—McKay or something?"

"Mackey," she said.

"Yes, that's it. Justin Mackey. Tell Max and Carl to find him and bring him to the warehouse in Elizabeth. We need to have a little chat with him."

# CHAPTER 3

*I DON'T NEED THIS ON A MONDAY MORNING*, ERIN THOUGHT, STANDING at the entrance and scanning the nearly empty diner. This being New Jersey, the diner capital of the world, there hadn't been a problem finding an open one even at the ungodly hour of four thirty in the morning. After spotting Justin in the far corner, she slowly made her way over and slid into the booth opposite him.

Mackey had called in a panic forty-five minutes earlier, telling her that he had to talk to her. Although Mackey might not have been the brightest bulb in the luminary, he had never been an alarmist, so she managed to drag herself out of bed, splash some water on her face, throw on some clothes, and make her way to the Lido Diner.

She ordered coffee, too tired to be angry. He looked like hell, his eyes bloodshot and puffy, an indication that he had gotten less sleep than her. His stained T-shirt and jeans looked like he had grabbed them off his bedroom floor.

"I'm sorry," he said before she could ask him anything. "I would never have bothered you at this hour if it wasn't important," he said, running his hands through his uncombed hair. "I needed to see you to let you know that I have to disappear for a while."

"Disappear for a while? Justin, what are you talking about?"

"I'm not coming to court today, or probably for the rest of the trial. I have to get out of town."

Erin wasn't sure if it was the coffee kicking in or her client telling her that he was jumping bail, but she was suddenly awake. "Justin, you understand you're on bail. If you don't show up not only will the judge revoke your bail, but you'll be committing a separate crime: bail jumping. I know the trial isn't going the way you hoped, but even if you're convicted, I don't think Judge Fowler will give you more than two or three years tops. And because it's your first offense, you'll probably serve less than a year before you get parole. But if you run, you're really going to piss off the prosecutor and the judge, and assuming at some point you get caught, there's no telling what sentence you'll get."

"You don't understand, Erin. It's got nothing to do with this case," he said, nervously looking around the diner. "Despite what I'm charged with, I didn't design this software. Some guy named Luke, who I've never even met, designed all of it. He hired me and I just did what I was told."

Erin motioned for him to lower his voice. Between his emotions and the empty diner, it sounded like he was using a megaphone.

"It's Luke who did this, not me. It's not my fault."

"Stop! Justin, you've got to slow down. You're not making any sense. Who's Luke? What does any of this have to do with your case or with you disappearing?"

"I'm sorry. I'm just a little rattled."

As he took a sip of his coffee, Erin noticed that his hand was shaking.

"About a year and a half ago, I was a programmer at a start-up in the city. I was also betting and losing big-time. I owed my bookie a ton of money, like twenty-five grand, when he suddenly offered me a way out. They wanted to move their operations offshore and were looking for software to encrypt everything. It couldn't be anything off the shelf; it had to be unique. He told me if I could design or find encryption software that worked and install it, he'd write off my debt. So that's how I found Luke. He was looking for someone to handle installation of his own encryption software. He gave me the names and contact info for about a dozen of his customers in New York and New Jersey, and then paid me two hundred dollars a pop to go to their houses and install it. Truth is, I didn't care what he paid me—I just wanted access to the software so I could get out of debt to my bookie."

Justin paused, shaking his head. "About a year ago when I got indicted, Luke found out that I had used his software without his permission. He sent me a text and he was pissed. He told me if I ever used his software without permission again, he'd sue me. I told him I had screwed up and that I'd never do it again. Then about six months ago he contacted me and said I could make things right with him if I went out to the same people and installed an update he had developed. So I did. He even paid me to do it."

Maybe it was the early morning hour, but Erin was having trouble following this. "Okay," she said, "but what Luke is doing sounds perfectly legal. Why do you have to disappear?"

He looked up from his coffee at Erin and bit his lip. "Around midnight, I got a text from Luke. It said that one of the people I had installed the software for had discovered a hidden feature and Luke was worried I'd get blamed for it. He said they were going to come looking for me and suggested that since some of the people involved could be dangerous I should lay low for a while until he could take care of it for me. His message said that it might take a few months, but he'd straighten it out and I'd be okay."

"Do you know what he's talking about—a 'hidden feature' in the software?"

Justin cupped his hands on the sides of his neck and looked like he was on the verge of tears. "I'm not sure. But my guess is there was a virus or something in the update he had me install. Generally updates take a couple of minutes to install, but it took as long to download and install the update as it did to do the original software."

"Justin, this is crazy. Let's just call Luke and find out exactly what's going on."

"I can't. I have no way to contact him."

"You just told me you got a text message from him."

"It was from an unknown number; he always blocks his number and uses burner phones. But he puts enough info in the text so I know it's legitimate."

"How's he pay you?"

"PayPal."

"You have any idea where he is?"

"Not a clue. If I had to guess, I'd say somewhere on the West Coast because he's a software designer and his texts are always at weird times."

He slid his phone across the table to her with Luke's text open. She scrolled through it, trying to make sense of everything. *It's too early in the morning for this,* she thought.

"Okay," she said, "you said you only installed the software and updates on about twelve computers. Let's go to the prosecutor with this and, assuming there was some kind of virus in the software update, let the prosecutor's office figure out what is going on between Luke and these people. If you skip out now, it'll just be worse for you when the police find you. And, if these people are truly dangerous, you'll be protected."

He inhaled, appearing to weigh his options.

"No," he said with a sigh. "Some of these people have big bucks and they're pretty fucking scary—um, sorry, excuse my French." He stammered, seemingly embarrassed at having used the F-word in front of her. "I don't want to mess with them. I'm going to do what Luke suggests and lay low for a while and hope he can get me out of this mess."

"Justin, please think about this. If you run, you're only going to expose yourself to more jail time. And if these people are really dangerous, you're better off trying to work out a deal and getting protection. Just because Luke got you into this mess doesn't mean he's going to be able to get you out of it. Let me work this out for you."

He gave her a sad smile. "Thanks. I really appreciate everything you've done for me in the case. The truth is, I wanted to take the original plea deal, but the guys at the top wouldn't let me. So I was stuck. I know I didn't give you much to work with to defend me. Sorry." And with that he threw twenty dollars on the table to cover the two cups of coffee and walked out of the diner without looking back.

As she sat there staring into her coffee cup, a waitress came by holding a fresh pot. "Need a refill?"

Erin looked up and nodded.

"Don't worry about him, honey. You can do better," the waitress offered with a wink.

Erin, too tired to explain, simply said, "Thanks." She looked at her watch—five a.m.—too early to call Duane. Assuming Justin didn't show up in court, what was she going to say when the judge asked where her client was? She couldn't lie to the judge, but at least some of what Justin had told her was protected by attorney-client privilege. Then there was the fact that Justin genuinely believed his life was in danger. But what could she do? It wasn't like she could walk into a police station and give them anything to follow up on. *"What kind of car was he driving?" "I don't know." "Where was he going?" "I don't know." "Who was he afraid of?" "I don't know." "What did he do wrong?" "I can't tell you, he's my client."* Yeah, that would go well.

Erin finished her coffee, threw her jacket back on, and headed out into the brisk April morning. The sun wouldn't rise for another hour, but the purples and pinks of the morning twilight already dominated the sky. As beautiful as it was, it would have been even more spectacular had she been able to see it while jogging next to the Atlantic Ocean. She and Duane had just come off a very successful year, and she had used her share to purchase a two-bedroom condo overlooking the ocean in Bradley Beach. She had moved into it in January and soon came to love how deserted things were in the middle of winter. She was looking forward to the trial being over so she could head back to Bradley.

For now, however, because she had to be in Newark every morning for the trial, it was back to her apartment in Cranford.

She was only a mile from her apartment when she noticed the dark sedan. Unless her mind was playing tricks on her, she had seen the same car as she left the diner. Her apartment was on Riverside Drive, a one-way street that ran along the Rahway River. At this time of morning, it should be easy to figure out if she was being followed. The hard thing would be to figure out what to do if she was.

Reaching into her purse to retrieve her BlackBerry, she weighed her options. With the Cranford Police Headquarters three blocks from her apartment, she could always call 911 and then head straight there.

She checked her rearview mirror. The sedan was two and a half blocks back. She made the left onto Riverside, then, to continue on Riverside, she had to make a quick right. As she did, she accelerated, hoping that because of the quick turns and bends in Riverside, whoever was following her would momentarily lose sight of her car. That allowed her to make a right turn onto Central Avenue. As she did, she checked her mirror again and saw the sedan continue down Riverside, past Central.

She was relieved she had lost them, but had little doubt now that she was being followed.

She made a right back onto Springfield and then another quick right back onto Riverside, completing her square circle. Now she had to decide where to go. If whoever was following her knew where she lived, they might be waiting near her apartment. Fortunately, she knew a back way to get to the parking lot of her building without ever having to go down Riverside.

She made her way down the side streets, all the time focused on looking for a dark sedan. She momentarily thought about heading to the police department, but, like the quandary she faced with Justin, what would she tell them? She had no make or model of the car, no license plate, nothing to go on. Instead she pulled her car into the parking area behind her building and had her keys and phone ready as she hopped out of the car. After a quick 360, making sure no one was waiting, she bolted for the back door.

As she headed to the stairs to get to her third-floor apartment, the memory of an encounter on a different set of apartment

stairs came flooding back. That time the attacker had come prepared to kill her, and she'd barely survived—this time, not knowing why she was being followed, she wasn't taking any chances.

She made her way slowly up the stairs, listening for any noise
that would indicate someone was lurking in the stairwell. When
she got to the second floor, she opened the door enough so she
could peer down the hallway. When she was satisfied it was deserted, she walked down the hallway to the other set of stairs in
the building. As she had done before, she cautiously made her
way to the third floor and cracked the door to look down the hallway—nothing.

She quickly made her way down the hall to her door, unlocked
it, and pushed it open, her phone in hand in the event she had to
dial 911. She walked into her living room, looking to see if anything appeared amiss. When she was finally satisfied no one had
been in her apartment, she made her way to her bedroom window, which looked out on Riverside Drive.

There was no sedan in sight.

She double-checked the locks on her door, and then slumped
into her couch, the adrenaline slowly draining from her system.
After her heart rate returned to normal, she looked at her phone
still tightly clutched in her hand and dialed Duane's cell. He
picked up on the third ring.

"Hey, everything okay?" he answered.

"Not exactly," she replied.

An hour later, Duane was in Erin's kitchen, pouring himself a
cup of coffee. He had parked at the office and walked the two
blocks to her place on the hunt for a dark-colored sedan. He almost never carried his gun—as a Black man, he ran the risk of
being shot before he could even explain to a cop that as a former
FBI agent he had a right to carry a weapon—but he had taken it
this morning.

"Listen," he said. "The fact that you were tailed is bothering me."

"As soon as I lost them, they disappeared. Who knows, maybe it
was just my imagination."

"Neither one of us believes that," he replied.

He heard her moving around her bedroom, getting dressed for court, and he took her silence as a hint to change the subject.

"You know the prosecutor is definitely going to press you if Justin doesn't show up. Bail jumping is a crime. So if the judge asks, you can't say you haven't heard from him. And if you claim you can't say anything because the information you have is privileged, the judge may argue that the privilege doesn't protect him from committing the crime of bail jumping."

"But the truth is, he's already gone, and I don't know where he is," Erin called from the bedroom. "Besides, if he doesn't show up, he's already committed the crime, so it's past criminal conduct and protected by the privilege."

"Just be prepared for the worst," he offered.

She walked into the kitchen, wearing a navy blue business suit over a white silk blouse. "Will do," she replied.

"You mind if I give Ben a call and see what he thinks?" he asked. Ben Silver was one of the top criminal lawyers in the state and had represented Duane when he was under investigation by the Department of Justice.

"Not at all. My gut says I can't say anything, but I'd love to hear Ben's take." She rubbed her eyes, then put a hand on his arm. "I appreciate you always being here for me."

"It's what friends are for," he said, hoping his grin was reassuring.

"I know, but I've been a bit of a shit recently."

"You've been fine," he said.

It was a lie, but he could tell from her expression that she appreciated it just the same.

# CHAPTER 4

*E*RIN PACED THE DINGY HALLWAY OUTSIDE OF JUDGE PETER FOWLER'S courtroom, hoping against hope that Justin would suddenly step off the elevator. By nine twenty, when it was clear that wasn't going to happen, she had collared Assistant Prosecutor George Ramos and let him know they needed to speak with the judge about her client. At nine thirty, the clerk beckoned Erin and Ramos back to the judge's chambers.

At forty-four, Peter Fowler was still young to be a superior court judge, but despite his age, he had already been on the bench for nine years, having been one of the youngest judges appointed. Although he was a handsome and athletic Rhodes scholar, his nomination had almost been derailed when it came out during his confirmation hearings that he was gay. His appointment squeaked through and two years ago he had easily received tenure because he had proven to be an excellent judge who received high marks for his demeanor and legal acumen from prosecutors and defense attorneys alike—a difficult needle to thread. Most people in the know felt he'd soon be appointed to be an appellate judge, and there were rumors that he could be the first openly gay judge nominated to the New Jersey Supreme Court.

When they walked in, Fowler was pacing behind his desk. After motioning for them to have a seat, he rested his hands on the top of his desk chair and leaned forward.

"Ms. McCabe," he said, turning his focus to her, "I understand your client isn't in court yet and you have requested to speak to me with the prosecutor."

"Yes, Your Honor."

"What's going on?" he asked, his tone suddenly less formal.

Fortunately, on her way to court, she had spoken with Ben, who had already been briefed by Duane as to what was happening. Together she and Ben had put together a script of what she could tell the judge, and where she had to draw the line.

"Your Honor, I have reason to believe that my client will not be coming to court today"—she paused—"and possibly not for the remainder of the trial."

Erin could feel the judge studying her and gauging his response. "Interesting," he said. "The way you say that, it makes it sound like your client is unhappy with the service we've provided and has decided to take his business elsewhere." Before she could respond, he held up his hand. "Forgive me for being so glib," he said, looking down into his empty chair. "I assume if I ask you about the information you have, you will tell me it's privileged," he said, his gaze now fixed on her.

"That is correct, Your Honor."

"I see." He moved around his chair and sat down. "Well, this creates a bit of a dilemma." He turned his head to one side. "You realize bail jumping is a separate crime?"

"I do, Judge," Erin replied. "But, if the information I have is correct, then the crime has already been committed."

"Indeed," he said almost to himself. "Mr. Ramos, do you have any thoughts on the situation?"

"Judge, I just learned of Mr. Mackey's absence. If Ms. McCabe has information concerning his whereabouts, it is incumbent on her to disclose it to the court."

Fowler shook his head. "Perhaps she does, but I'm not going to go that route right now. That would open up a debate on the privilege, perhaps causing an interlocutory appeal and delaying this trial, which is in the home stretch. I don't see any need for me to do that." His head nodded slowly. "Unless Mr. Mackey has a justifiable reason for his absence—he's ill, for example—the trial can continue and whatever happens, happens. I'm assuming that if Ms. McCabe had information that would justify her client's absence she would tell us. Correct, Ms. McCabe?"

"Yes, Your Honor."

"So based on that, here's what we're going to do. Ms. McCabe, I'll give you another half hour. See if you can reach your client and talk some sense into him. At ten a.m., we will resume the trial whether Mr. Mackey is present or not. Outside the presence of the jury, I'll place on the record that Ms. McCabe has advised the court that her client has voluntarily absented himself from the trial, which under the court rules constitutes a waiver of his appearance. If at some point down the road your client comes to his senses, we'll deal with that then. Once I bring the jury in, I will give them a cautionary instruction that they are not to consider Mr. Mackey's absence for any purposes or speculate as to why he is not present." He looked at both of them. "Any problems?"

"No, Judge," they both replied.

"Anything you'd like to add, Ms. McCabe?"

"No, Judge," she said. "I appreciate Your Honor's courtesies."

He gave her a wry smile. "I haven't always been on this side of the desk, Ms. McCabe. I remember what it's like to deal with clients." He rose from his chair, signaling the conference was coming to an end. "Let my clerk know if anything changes. If not, we'll proceed at ten." Walking out of Fowler's chambers, she reached into her purse to retrieve her BlackBerry. She'd try again to get hold of Justin, even though she knew it was probably futile. But there was more at stake than just trying to convince him to come to court—she was worried about him.

Just as he had promised, when court resumed at ten without Justin, Judge Fowler cautioned the jury not to draw any conclusions or inferences from the fact that Mr. Mackey was not in court. From Erin's standpoint, this was akin to shining a giant spotlight on the empty chair next to her. *Whatever you do, don't think about the elephant that's not in the room.*

After the prosecutors had put on one final witness, they rested. The defense motion to dismiss the case was quickly denied, and one of the two lead defendants called a lawyer as a witness in an effort to bolster the defendant's argument that they had obtained a legal opinion that online gambling on a Costa Rican website was legal. Any benefit from his testimony quickly evaporated with the prosecutor's brief cross-examination that the lawyer was never actually retained and never provided an opinion it was legal. So much for the defense case, Erin thought when they rested.

Back in the office, Erin read through her notes and trial transcripts in preparation for closing, which she'd have to do tomorrow regardless of whether Justin was there or not. She planned to do her generic closing, reminding the jury of the presumption of innocence and that the State had the burden of proving each of the defendants guilty beyond a reasonable doubt. She'd address her client's conversations on the wiretaps as best she could: He was a salesman, she'd tell the jury, and while he also liked to make a few bets on sporting events, he wasn't part of a gambling conspiracy. He was just trying to make a sale by talking potential problems through with the customers. She, like her client, was a salesperson, tasked with selling her client's story to the jury. Over the course of most trials, she would convince herself that she was going to win, but she didn't have that feeling now. Still, she'd give it her best shot.

A movement in her office doorway caught her eye. Duane.

"Why are you still here?" she asked.

"Um, let's see: Fearful client demands you meet him at four in the morning, a mysterious dark sedan follows you to your apartment . . . need I say more?"

She looked at him sheepishly. "I'm not actually sure they followed me to my apartment. I lost them before I got there—remember?"

"Oh, and you think they don't know where you live and work?"

She snorted. "You sure know how to make a girl feel safe."

"That's why I'm still here."

"I'll be fine," she insisted.

"I know you will, because I'm following you home."

Despite her bravado, she was happy he was there. The events of the day had been unnerving, and Duane's presence helped her stay calm. Even though she had continued taking her Krav Maga classes, and had become good enough to earn her green belt, she knew from painful experience that all the training in the world didn't matter if your attacker had a gun.

"Give me another thirty minutes," she said. "I should be done by then."

"Will do," he replied, and disappeared down the hallway.

As soon as he walked away, she pushed her chair back from her desk, cupped her mouth with her hand, and chastised herself. Duane had a wife and three-year-old son, and yet here he was watching out for her, instead of going home to be with his family. She looked at everything spread out on her desk—there was nothing here that couldn't be spread out on her dining room table at home. Whatever summation she was going to come up with wasn't going to change if she did it at home or in her office. She got up and retrieved her trial bag from the corner of the office. She packed up everything she'd need and headed out into the hallway.

"Come on, Swish. Time to blow this joint," she hollered down the hallway.

# CHAPTER 5

*E*RIN THOUGHT HER SUMMATION WENT AS WELL AS IT COULD CONsidering that she didn't have a client in the courtroom. One of her tried-and-true tactics was to use her client as a prop in her closing, standing behind the client when she spoke to the jury about the sanctity of the presumption of innocence, hopefully forcing the jury to see her client as an individual, not as a defendant. But today, as she paced in front of the jurors making her argument, she suspected her client's empty chair provided a very different visual prop that she wasn't going to be able to overcome.

Judge Fowler waited for the jury to leave before he spoke. "Okay, folks, anything else we need to discuss today?"

Assistant Prosecutor Ramos rose to his feet. Ramos was short and stocky, and after fifteen years in the prosecutor's office he was considered a lifer—someone who would retire from the office at the end of his career. His low-key manner and quiet self-assurance appealed to juries, making him a formidable adversary. "Your Honor, I need to speak to Ms. McCabe privately, but then I believe we will need to speak to Your Honor in chambers."

Fowler stared at him quizzically. "It's been a long day for everyone, Mr. Ramos. Can't it wait until the morning?"

Ramos, who throughout the trial had been very accommodating, glanced in Erin's direction. "Judge, most respectfully, we need to do this now."

Fowler raised an eyebrow. "Very well. I'll see you in . . . How long do you need to speak with Ms. McCabe?"

"Ten minutes, Your Honor."

"Very good. I'll see you in ten minutes."

"All rise," the court clerk intoned as Fowler rose and exited his courtroom.

Erin followed Ramos into the small office the assistant prosecutors had access to when they were involved in a trial. The room was no bigger than a walk-in closet, with barely enough room for a desk and two chairs, one chair sitting behind the desk, one in front. There was a large calendar that hung haphazardly on the wall with notes of all kinds scribbled on it. On the desk was a computer that rarely worked, and when it did, it ran so slow that it was often faster for a detective or an assistant prosecutor to take the elevator down to the third floor and use the computers in the main office.

"You'd better sit," Ramos said, pointing to the chair in front of the desk as he positioned himself on the corner of the desk.

"What's going on, George?"

"Erin, I'm afraid I have some news about your client." He paused, leaving her momentarily confused. "The Port Authority Police found a body this afternoon in the trunk of a car at Newark Airport, and although there has been no official identification yet, based on evidence found with the body we believe it's Mr. Mackey."

Erin squinted, trying to process what he was telling her. "Are you saying Justin is . . . dead?"

"At this point we believe so. We should have a positive ID shortly. They were taking the body back to the morgue to run the prints."

She closed her eyes, shaking her head, replaying the scene in the Lido. "Shit." *He was so young.* She took a deep breath and looked up at Ramos. "Do you know how he died?" she finally asked.

"From what I was told, a single gunshot to the back of his head, execution style." He waited, allowing the news to sink in. "So, assuming it is your client, at some point Homicide is going to want to speak with you. You may want to think about the attorney-client privilege issue."

She winced, feeling like she had just been hit in the stomach—a bullet to the back of the head. Whoever it was that Justin had inadvertently pissed off played for keeps.

"If it turns out to be your client, we want to keep his name out of the press until after we get a verdict. If this leaks out to the press, everyone will be screaming for a mistrial."

Erin looked at Ramos in disbelief. He'd just finished telling her that her client may be dead—executed. At this point, a mistrial was the least of her worries.

A few minutes later, Erin sat stone faced as Ramos explained the situation to Fowler, who frowned as he jotted notes on a legal pad.

"Well, let's hope it's not Mr. Mackey," he said. "How long before you have an ID on the victim?"

"I would expect to hear very shortly." As if on cue, Ramos's phone began to vibrate. "Your Honor, this is my office, may I take the call?"

Fowler nodded.

Erin didn't even need to listen to the one-sided conversation. Ramos's body language said it all.

"I'm sorry, Erin," he said when he hung up.

Although the news was not unexpected, Erin nevertheless found herself stunned. Justin was a young guy, his whole life ahead of him—now he was gone, and for what? None of this made any sense. Who the fuck was this mysterious Luke, and what the hell had he gotten Justin involved in?

When she looked up, Fowler was crouching in front of her.

"Erin, I'm terribly sorry," he said, taking her hand. "I know we all occupy different roles in this system we call justice, but I hope none of us, particularly me, ever loses respect for the humanity of the people we deal with."

"Thank you," she said, squeezing his hand. "I appreciate it."

"Do you want me to have a sheriff's officer walk you to your car?" Fowler offered.

She could hear Duane's voice screaming in her head to say yes, but she politely declined. She just needed to be alone.

Around 9:30 p.m. Erin's phone rang. Looking at the display she saw that it was Mark calling. It was Tuesday night—game night for the basketball team he and Duane played for. Like Duane, he had played basketball in college, in Mark's case at NYU. Surely Duane would have told him that her client had been murdered. Part of her wanted to let it go to voice mail; the other part was desperate to hear his voice.

"Hi," she answered on the third ring, succumbing to her desire to hear him.

"Hi," Mark responded, caution evident in his voice. "I had a basketball game with Swish tonight and he mentioned what happened to your client. You okay?"

She wanted to lie and tell him everything was fine, thank him for the call, and hang up. But it was wonderful to hear his voice again.

"Actually, no," she responded.

"The game's over. I can stop by on my way home if you'd like."

So many thoughts ran through her head—*Yes, it would be nice to see you. Sure, let's talk. God, I miss you*—but instead she inhaled a shaky breath. "Thanks, Mark. I appreciate your concern, but not tonight. I'm going to try and get some sleep."

There was a long silence.

"Okay," he said finally, his tone conveying his disappointment. "I know it's been a tough day. I . . . I'll let you go."

"Thanks," she said, waiting for him to hang up. When he finally disconnected, she sat staring at the phone in her hand. *I'm an idiot,* she thought. Was she really trying to protect him, as she had convinced herself, or was she just trying to protect herself from her fear that sooner or later the fact that she was trans would destroy their relationship? A fear baked into her by a society that for the most part didn't see her as a woman at all—she was just some delusional male who liked to pretend to be a woman. Even her own father and brother had initially ostracized her after she came out, and the religion she was raised in told her that she was sinful for just being herself. It had taken her a long time to get over the guilt and shame and accept who she was, but she wasn't sure that beyond her mom, Duane, and a few others close to her, anyone else who knew her backstory would ever be able to fully accept her for the woman she was.

The following morning Erin resumed her routine of meeting her mother for breakfast. They tried to meet at least once a week to catch up, but with the trial, Erin had been so busy it had been a month since they'd last gotten together.

Although now sixty-six, Peg McCabe could easily pass for someone in her early to mid-fifties. She still worked full-time as a guidance counselor at Cranford High School and stayed in shape mainly by doing yoga. Whenever Erin looked at her mom, she hoped the old trope of a woman turning into her mother turned out to be true.

"I'm worried about you," Peg said as soon as Erin finished recapping the last few weeks.

"Why?"

Peg raised an eyebrow. "Let me see. You just told me your client was murdered. You had a case last year where someone tried to kill you—I don't know, Erin, call me crazy, but you're not exactly good for my blood pressure."

"Sorry," Erin replied, looking down into her coffee to avoid her mother's piercing gaze.

Her mother brushed her short brown hair back from her face and took a sip of her coffee. "But I suspect we're not here because you wanted to talk about your client," her mother said. "So what's going on?"

What was going on? Mark—Mark was what was going on. Hearing his voice again last night had brought back so many memories—good and bad—and she trusted her mom as a sounding board. She and Mark had been together for a year, but the longer they were together, the more strained it had become between Erin and his family. Mark's sister, Molly, was a doll, but as she and her civil union partner, Robin, liked to joke, as soon as Erin came along, suddenly having a lesbian couple in the family wasn't so bad. His brothers, Jack and Brian, were a different story.

Jack, the oldest of the siblings, would constantly tease Mark about being gay. "Well, you are dating a guy," Jack would taunt, and he and Mark had almost come to blows due to his refusal to stop referring to Erin as "he." When Mark had corrected him, Jack had looked at Erin and said, "Sorry, would you prefer I use 'it'?" Brian was never as blatant, but his laughing at Jack's insults let everyone know where he stood. Things had gotten to the point where Mark's mother had told Mark that Erin was no longer welcome in her home.

Finally, three weeks before Easter, with the Mackey trial about to start, Erin had told Mark that she wouldn't be the cause of him becoming estranged from his family. Despite Mark's protests, she called time on their relationship.

"It's Mark," Erin said to her coffee cup. "I broke things off."

Even with her head bowed, Erin could feel her mother's eyes on her.

"I'm sorry," her mother said. "Do you want to talk about what happened?"

"No," Erin replied, her voice quivering. "Or . . . maybe. It's not Mark exactly, it's more his family," she said. "Mark and his brother Jack almost got into a fight because Jack asked me if I preferred to be referred to as 'him' or 'it.'" Erin bit her lip. "Honestly, I'm sick of the nonsense. I don't want to deal with it anymore."

"I can understand that," her mother replied. "How does Mark feel about the way his family treats you?"

"He hates it. But his mother takes his brothers' side and she's made it clear that she doesn't want me there anymore—I'm too disruptive. Not to mention, in her mind, I'm not dating material."

"So Mark sides with his family?" her mother asked.

"No. No. Mark said he wouldn't see his family again until they came to their senses. But I couldn't let that happen."

"Why?"

Erin was taken aback. "Mom, I can't be responsible for that. It's his mother and brothers! I can't come between him and his family. At some point, he'd resent me for that."

"Sounds to me like he's better off without them," Peg replied, her tone matter-of-fact. "It also seems like you're making a decision that's not yours to make." Her mother held up her hand before Erin could reply. "Listen to me," she commanded. "You do guilt really well. It must be your Irish Catholic upbringing. But you're not being fair to yourself if you let bigots decide how you're going to live your life, and you're certainly not being fair to Mark if you aren't going to let him decide whether to spend time with you rather than his transphobic family." She grinned, and with a wink said, "Bet you didn't think I knew the word *transphobic*, right?"

"Mom," Erin started, but was cut off by her mother again.

"Don't Mom me. You know I'm right. When you came out to us four years ago, you knew there was a chance that you might lose your family once you transitioned. You also knew that your marriage to Lauren, who you loved, would be over. But you made the decision to do what was right for you. Your father begged you not to transition, but you put your own well-being ahead of what your family wanted. Why aren't you giving Mark the same opportunity? Doesn't he get to decide what's right for him?"

"It's not the same," Erin protested. "If I lost my family it was because of who I was, not because of someone I was dating. I'd be essentially asking him to pick me or his family."

Her mother shook her head. "No, you're not. From what you've told me, you haven't said, 'It's them or me.' At some point he may be faced with that decision, but if he is, who are you to make it for him?"

"I don't want to be responsible for him being ostracized by his family."

Her mother gave her a sad smile. "Erin, my dear, a little piece of advice—stop blaming yourself for other people's issues. You can't control what they do, honey. Life is short. Don't let go of your happiness without a fight."

"Thanks," Erin said, as the waitress arrived with their order, French toast for her, an egg white omelet for her mom.

After they finished breakfast and were getting ready to leave, her mother paused. "Do you have another minute? There's something I need to tell you."

Erin looked at her mom, thrown by the sudden change in her tone. "Sure. Is everything okay?" It was just one of those throwaway lines. Of course everything was okay.

"Honestly, I don't know," her mother replied with a sad smile. "About a week before Easter, I felt a lump in my breast. So I made an appointment and went to my gynecologist, hoping she'd tell me it was no problem. Unfortunately, that didn't happen. Instead she sent me for a mammo, and . . . well," she hesitated, "I'm going in tomorrow so they can do a biopsy."

Erin felt as if her chest had been placed in a vise. *Breast, lump, biopsy*—words often used in the same sentence, but not together in sentences pertaining to her mother. She forced herself to appear calm. "Okay," she said, "but chances are it's just a cyst or something, right?"

"Of course that's what we're hoping for," her mother replied, her rueful smile quietly dispelling Erin's optimism.

"Where is it tomorrow? I'll come with you."

"Thank you," she said with a small smile, "but your dad took the day off and he's going to come with me. They're going to do it right in the surgeon's office. Her name is Dr. Susanne Seiko. She seems very nice."

"Have you told Sean?" Erin asked, referring to her older brother, who was one of the most preeminent orthopedic surgeons in the state.

"Yes. When my gynecologist recommended the surgeon to me, I called him. After he checked her out, he told me she has a great reputation." She reached out and laid her hand on Erin's. "I didn't tell you at the time because you were in court handling the trial, and I didn't want to distract you with this."

Erin got up and slid into the booth next to her mom and hugged her. She felt awful that her mom had gone through all of this without her even knowing. Somehow in her zeal to represent her client she had allowed herself to lose track of what was really important in her life, the people she loved. "It'll be okay, Mom. It'll be okay," she repeated, as much for herself as for her mother.

# CHAPTER 6

"**Y**OU DON'T WANT TO DO THIS," CHARLES PARSONS SAID, HIS TONE commanding and defiant despite the precariousness of his situation.

So far things had gone exactly as she'd planned. She had known exactly where to hide and had waited patiently for him to come home. Then, after he went into his office, she knew she had him cornered. Now, as she pressed the gun up against his temple, there was no turning back.

"Yeah, I really think I do," she answered coolly, pressing the gun harder. Then, after a momentary pause, added, "Give me one good reason why I shouldn't," her tone matter-of-fact, as if she had just asked for a reason to skip dessert.

Parsons inhaled. "For Christ's sake, you're my daughter."

Her laugh was cold and empty. "Nice try," she said, then added in a tone both sarcastic and childlike, "Daddy." She pressed the gun so hard he winced. "But I said give me a reason not to do it, asshole. Not one more reason to do it."

"Look, you got what you came for. As it is I'll probably spend the rest of my life in jail. I would think you'd enjoy that more than killing me."

She snorted, even though the thought of him spending the rest of his life in jail, and what that might entail for someone like him, did cause her to ease up ever so slightly on the pressure she was exerting on the gun.

His right arm shot up, attempting to knock the gun away as he jerked his head to the side.

The explosion of the gun reverberated around the room as she was splattered with pieces of skull and brain. His body fell to the left, twitched several times, and went limp, part of the back of his head gone.

She closed her eyes and swallowed the bile that had risen in her throat. Despite everything he had done to her, the doubt had lingered—could she pull the trigger? Now it was over, and she didn't need a medical examiner to confirm he was dead.

Reaching down, she took his right hand and wrapped his fingers around the gun, then took stock of the scene before her. How would it look to the first cops on the scene? She had worried that the police would be suspicious if there was no gunshot residue on his hand or arm, but ironically, his attempt to knock the gun away might have left enough residue around his hand to support a conclusion he'd committed suicide.

She took off her latex gloves and put them in her pack, which already contained what she had come to retrieve. She removed her shoes and moved carefully, trying her best not to track blood and tissue around the room. Removing a black sweatshirt and a pair of black sweatpants out of her pack, she slipped them on over what she was wearing and donned fresh gloves before putting on a clean pair of shoes. As careful as she was, she knew her best hope was that whoever discovered the body would contaminate the crime scene and make her presence invisible. She looked around the room to make sure she had everything and nothing was out of place. Next she made her way to the kitchen, reset the alarm, went out the door that connected to the garage, and locked it behind her before making her way out the side door into the darkness of the backyard and disappearing into the night.

Later, as she headed south on Mountain Avenue, she pulled a cell phone from her purse. As she suspected, there were three missed calls from an unknown number.

"Hey, is everything okay?" said the voice at the other end, barely audible over the din of voices in the background.

"Yeah, listen, I'm sorry," she began. "Things were crazy at work and there was no way for me to call. I'm just leaving the office now."

"Oh. Okay." There was a slight hesitation. "I'm still at the bar if you want to come, or do you want to stop by my place?"

There was a small part of her that wanted to say yes. She hadn't intended to, but she had found herself having fun and enjoying their time together. But even if she didn't have to wash away the bits and pieces of him crawling on her skin, she had to stick to her plan, and that meant their relationship was over. "I'm sorry. I'm beat. I've had a really tough day." She paused. "I'll give you a call tomorrow or Sunday and find a way to make it up to you."

"Don't worry about it."

"I really wanted to see you tonight. But you know how it is—something happens on what you're working on, and it doesn't matter if it's a Friday night and you have a date."

"No problem. I get it."

"Thanks. I appreciate you understanding. I'll give you a call."

There was a long pause. "Okay. Sounds good." The doubt and hesitation were evident. "Get some rest."

"Thanks," she replied, clicking the button to end the call.

*It's better this way.* As it was they could never be together. Weird, what was she? Not a doppelganger; they didn't look anything alike. Stand-in, replacement . . . Whatever—she had served her purpose. This was no time to get sentimental. Time to move on.

"Whatta we got?" Detective Sergeant Ed Kluska asked as he sauntered into the room, smearing VapoRub under his nose to mask the pungent smell of the decomposing body.

"Charles Parsons. Age fifty-seven, hedge fund manager. Looks like he's been dead a few days," his colleague said.

Kluska gave him a look. "No shit, Sherlock. He's definitely a stinker."

Chris Burke held his tongue, as people usually did when Kluska spoke his mind. Kluska had a physique that made him imposing even when he didn't want to be. His bushy biker beard and shaved head had made it easy for him to go undercover when he was an up-and-coming detective assigned to Narcotics. The fact that he owned a Harley and could talk the talk was just an added bonus. But after a dozen years of living on the edge, waiting for some drug dealer to make him as a cop or take a shot at him as he banged down a door, he had moved to Homicide seven years ago. Hanging over his desk was the Homicide Unit's motto: OUR DAY BEGINS WHEN YOURS ENDS. Not that Homicide didn't have its share of risks, but he was no longer the one hopping fences and tackling suspects when they bolted. Now he spent most of his time putting together the pieces of investigative puzzles and playing "bad cop" in the interrogation room.

"Appears to be a suicide," Burke continued. "Single gunshot wound to just behind the temporal bone. Looks like he flinched a little as he was pulling the trigger. A Smith & Wesson .45 was lying next to his hand. Loaded with semijacketed hollow-point ammo."

"Well, at least he was serious about it. Who found him?"

"His assistant—Cassandra DeCovnie," Burke said, looking down at his notes. "She's out back on the deck. Dotson's taking a statement from her. Came over about two hours ago. She lives in Hoboken. Parsons was supposed to pick her up this afternoon to go to his brownstone in New York, and when he didn't respond to her calls asking what gives, she came here and discovered him. Between the smell and condition of the body, she got pretty sick. She also walked all over the place and has really fucked up the scene," he said, gesturing towards the bloody shoeprints near the body and around the room.

"Go figure. Next of kin?"

"According to DeCovnie, he has a daughter, Ann; she's a paralegal at McKenna & Ross in the city. She lives in Jersey City. Jersey City PD was sent over to notify, but apparently nobody was home. They'll keep us posted when they find her."

"Any note?" he asked.

"Nothing so far." He pointed to the laptop sitting on an easy chair. "The battery on that one seems dead. There's a desktop under the desk, but it was off, so didn't want to mess with either of them."

"Cell phone?"

"On the desk. Battery looks dead on that one too."

"Where's Forensics and the ME's office?"

"On their way."

Kluska gave him a quizzical look.

Burke shrugged. "It's a Sunday. What do you want from me? I called them. I guess they're busy."

"Oh for fuck's sake. Just make sure no one else walks around in here until Forensics gets here."

Kluska looked around the room, which seemed to have been used as a combination den and office. Two monitors graced the heavy oaken desk, a large flat screen hung on the wall, and the laptop sitting on the easy chair in the corner seemed new and high end—all the accoutrements of someone who could afford whatever he needed and a lot of what he probably didn't. Nothing seemed amiss, but Kluska knew that didn't mean much. All kinds of people commit suicide, but Parsons wasn't just some hedge fund manager; at one point he'd been a major domo on Wall Street, a minor radio and television analyst talking about investment strategies. But about six or seven years ago, he had disappeared from the public. There had been rumors of a federal investigation, then speculation that the investigation had gone away because of his political connections. Kluska was no real estate expert, but he knew that houses in this section of Westfield were worth $2 million plus. By the looks of this place, it was definitely on the plus side, not to mention Parsons apparently had a brownstone in the city. This guy had major bucks. But then again, with the shaky economy, maybe he had taken a big economic hit.

"Okay. Let's see what his assistant and daughter have to say. Look into his finances to see if there are any major money issues, and see if we can get anything on the gun. Take the laptop and phone—if we determine it's a suicide, we'll return them to the daughter, but only then. This guy must have an alarm company and surveillance cameras somewhere, so check and make sure there were no unwanted visitors. Have NYPD secure his brownstone to make sure nothing disappears out of there. Oh, and check with the feds and New York State to see if they have any ongoing investigations on this guy. He had some issues a few years back; maybe he was about to get jammed up."

"You want me to get a search team in?"

Kluska thought for a minute. Even though it was still technically a crime scene because cause of death was open, Tom Willis, the assistant prosecutor in charge of Homicide, would want a warrant. And since there was no probable cause a crime had been committed, better play it safe. "No. No reason to at this point. Restrict access to the house until we determine cause of death."

Burke laughed. "My guess is it's the huge hole in the back of his head."

"Funny, Burke. Maybe I'll ask to have you transferred to Forensics since you're so fucking brilliant."

"Come on, Ed, lighten up. Just busting your chops. And anyway, this one seems open and shut."

Kluska shook his head. "Hopefully, you're right and we can clear it quickly. But something doesn't smell right—pun intended—so let's make sure we dot our i's and cross our t's."

A young Westfield cop appeared in the doorway.

Kluska looked up. "Yeah," he responded with a touch more annoyance than he intended.

"There's a lawyer at the front door. Says he has to get in right away because he represents Mr. Parsons. What do you want me to tell him?"

"Fucking A," Kluska cursed. "Just what I need, some pencil-neck geek spouting the law. Tell him his client isn't seeing anyone at the present time."

The young cop hesitated, clearly not knowing whether to take the order at face value.

Kluska shook his head, realizing the young cop didn't know what to make of him. "Sorry, what's your name?" he asked.

"Jim Palladino," he replied.

"I'll talk to him," Kluska said, walking to the front porch, his body language displaying his irritation, where he found a man in his early thirties with thinning brown hair. Even though it was a cool night in April, the man was sweating.

"Can I help you?" Kluska asked, as he stepped through the front door.

"My name is Preston Harrison, and my firm represents Mr. Parsons." He reached out offering Kluska a business card. "I understand there is an issue and I need to get inside immediately to retrieve some of his legal paperwork and personal belongings."

Kluska took the fancy gold embossed card and looked at it, then took in Mr. Harrison, who was wearing a condescending smirk.

"Well, here's the thing, Mr. Harrison, I'm afraid I have some bad news for you. Mr. Parsons is deceased, and no one can go in the house right now."

"But I'm his lawyer. Ms. DeCovnie called me earlier to give me the news and she asked me to come and collect Mr. Parsons's records."

"She called you? Interesting. When did she call you? We've been here for almost two hours and she hasn't called anyone."

"I don't know what you're implying, Officer, but Ms. DeCovnie knows how closely my firm worked with Mr. Parsons, and she knew he would want me here immediately." The man made a move forward. "So, if you'd please step aside . . ."

Kluska blocked his way. "It's Detective Sergeant Kluska, not Officer. And I don't care how close you were to the deceased, you're not going inside right now."

Harrison's face reddened before he pulled himself up stiffly. "Then I need to speak to whoever is in charge. Where's your chief?"

Kluska tried not to laugh. "Look, dude, I'm in charge and you can't go in. Period, end of discussion."

Harrison reached into the inside pocket of his suit jacket and pulled out some papers. "This is a legal document, signed by Mr. Parsons appointing Ms. DeCovnie as his power of attorney. Now, I demand to be admitted to his home, immediately, so I can speak with Ms. DeCovnie."

Kluska turned to the young officer behind him, who was standing in the doorway watching the scene play out. He motioned him forward.

"Mr. Harrison, I ain't no lawyer, but I know a few things and one of them is that this power of attorney isn't worth the paper it's written on. It died with your client. So here's what I'm going to do. This is Officer James Palladino from the Westfield Police Department. I'm going to have him escort you to your car and then you're going to drive back to wherever you came from. If you give him, or me, any more grief, he'll escort you to *his* car, because I'll sign a criminal complaint against you for hindering an investigation. Capisce?"

The lawyer started to splutter, which only made Kluska smile.

"I'll call—"

"If you want to call the chief of detectives, the chief of police, the prosecutor, the governor when you get back to your office, you call whoever you like, be my guest. I don't care," Kluska said. "But for right now, I'm in charge of this scene and one way or another, you're leaving. I suggest you drive away nicely, but I have to admit, there is a part of me that's kind of hoping you don't. Your call, Mr. Harrison."

The lawyer stood for several seconds, appearing to consider what to do. Finally, he stuffed the papers back into his breast pocket. "You haven't heard the last from me, Officer . . . "

"Detective Sergeant Edward Kluska, Union County Prosecutor's Office," he said, handing Harrison his county-issued generic business card. "I look forward to seeing you again, Mr. Harrison."

Kluska watched as Harrison walked down the steps and headed toward his BMW, parked in the semicircular driveway in front of the home. Satisfied Harrison was leaving, he went back inside.

"Hey, Burke!" he called out.

"Yeah?"

"Add to your follow-up list to get me what you can on an attorney by the name of Preston Harrison. According to his business card, he's with the firm of O'Toole & Conroy with offices in Short Hills and New York City."

# CHAPTER 7

$F$IVE DAYS LATER, KLUSKA WAS THE LAST OF THE INVESTIGATIVE TEAM to arrive in a conference room at the prosecutor's office. He flipped the draft report on the conference room table and looked up at Sergeant Daniel Quinn, from the Forensics Unit, DQ to everyone. "You're all leaning toward it being a suicide," he said, pointing at the report.

Chris Burke and Eve Dotson shared a look. Finally, DQ said, "Yeah, that's what it looks like to us."

"Why?"

DQ looked down the table for help. "What do you mean, Ed? It's all in there," Burke chimed in, nodding toward the report. "No sign of forced entry. The alarm company has nothing suspicious. Nothing disturbed in the house. No outside surveillance cameras. The weapon is registered to him. His prints are on the weapon, including the trigger. The gun is where you'd expect it to be if he shot himself," he finished, looking back at Quinn.

Quinn gave Burke a quick nod in appreciation for his help, and then added, "There's some gunshot residue on the sleeve of his right arm. Unfortunately, we can't tell too much else from the scene because the woman who discovered the body contaminated it. So with everything we have, I agree with Chris, it all adds up to suicide," Quinn offered.

Kluska got up from the table and walked over to the dry erase board in the corner. "I'm not convinced," he said, picking up a marker. "You're right, there is residue on his right sleeve, but there's almost no GSR on his hand," he said, writing *NO GSR ON HAND* on the board. He looked at Quinn. "Any explanation for that, DQ?"

"Come on, Ed. You know GSR can be very unreliable," Quinn answered.

"Not buying it," Kluska replied. "According to Ms. DeCovnie, Parsons had no financial problems and she estimated his worth at around a hundred million dollars."

He turned back to the board and wrote, *WORTH APPROX $100M* and then underneath that wrote, *NO FINANCIAL REASON TO OFF HIMSELF*. He looked at Dotson, the newest member of the unit. "What do you make of the fact that there's almost no blood spatter or skull fragments scattered to the right of the body?"

Dotson hesitated. She had spent four years as a Maplewood police officer and had come to the prosecutor's office three years ago. She knew that as one of the few female detectives in the office, her assignment to Homicide had raised some eyebrows, and she didn't want to screw up on her first case. "Everything went in the direction of the shot. So it flew off to the left side," she said in a tone that was more question than answer.

Kluska turned to Quinn. "DQ, you agree?"

Quinn took a deep breath. "Normally with a contact gunshot you would expect to see some back spatter of blood and fragments."

*NO BACK SPATTER,* Kluska wrote on the board, then turned around to face the room. "And according to your report, in addition to his prints, we have two latents from the daughter on the gun. Why are her prints even in the system? She have a prior or something?"

"No," Burke replied. "Apparently because she works in the banking and finance department of a major law firm, she has to be bonded. They do an extensive background search, including submitting her prints to the FBI, state and local, and the N.Y. Banking Department.

*DAUGHTER'S PRINTS ON WEAPON*, Kluska jotted with flourish before heading back to his seat.

"So . . . you think he was murdered?" Dotson asked.

Kluska chuckled as he flopped back into his chair. "How the fuck do I know? I'm not saying you guys are wrong. But I told you when we started this guy had some juice, so let's turn over every rock before we come to a conclusion. I'm still not convinced that this guy offed himself." He picked up his copy of the autopsy report and flipped it open to a page he'd marked with a yellow Post-it. "DQ, on page three of the ME's report it says the entry wound was above the right ear and the bullet exited from the rear of the skull. Meaning the gun was pointed slightly toward the back of his head. Right?"

Quinn looked up from his copy of the report and nodded.

"Okay. If I were going to say nighty-night permanently, I'd hold my gun flush up against my temple and point straight. If I did that, with this type of bullet, we'd expect to see an entrance wound on my right temple and not the back of the head blown off. Agreed?" He didn't wait for them to agree before continuing. "I know in your report, based on what's in the autopsy report, you speculate that he may have flinched as he pulled the trigger, causing the gun to angle slightly, but let me give you a different scenario. Suppose someone else is holding a gun against his right temple. If he tried to knock or push the gun away, what then, Dotson?" he asked, swiveling to the young detective.

She tilted her head slightly as she processed his question. "That might cause the gun to move from the temple to above the right ear and change the trajectory of the bullet. Also, if someone was standing there, most of the back spatter would have landed on them." She looked up at the white board. "And it would explain why there's GSR on his sleeve, but not his hand."

Kluska nodded. "Exactly. Give this woman a prize," he said before turning to Burke. "Thoughts?"

"I agree it's worth looking at some more. But given the lack of any forced entry, it would have to be someone who either knew the place or he let in. Put that together with the prints and the daughter becomes the prime suspect."

"Yeah, so you don't think that's possible?" Kluska asked. "Look, it took until midnight on Sunday for the Jersey City cops to find her. She says she was in a bar alone on Friday night, waiting for a date who called to cancel because he had to work late. Not exactly a great alibi, and from what I hear, she wasn't all that choked up to hear her dad bought the farm. Not to mention that amount of money is a lot of temptation."

"But we don't even know if she is going to inherit it," Dotson chimed in. "From what she told Jersey City PD, she and her father were not on the best of terms. Plus, for what it's worth, she's adopted. Apparently he adopted her, shortly after he married her mother."

"Legally, being adopted gives her the same rights. So that doesn't help her. Where's Mom?"

"Deceased. Died when Ann was eight. She was raised by Parsons. Lived with him until she moved to Jersey City, where she lives in a condo he owned."

"So let's find out if there's a will and who's getting what. Burkie, talk to Willis and put together a warrant to allow the folks in Computer Crimes to go through Parsons's cell phone, laptop, and desktop. I want to know everything this guy was doing. I find it really strange that in walking around the house I saw that he had what looked to be some type of cameras in two of the bedrooms, but no outside surveillance cameras. Have Westfield PD pull surveillance videos from other houses in the area. Maybe they picked up something. And, Dotson, have a little chat with the daughter; let her know that her fingerprints are on the weapon and watch her reaction."

Over the next week they did what Kluska wanted done—begrudgingly at first, but they did it. Parsons's daughter, Ann, was brought in, and as Kluska watched her questioning through the one-way glass, there was something that he found troubling. He hadn't put it together yet, but she was definitely holding back about her relationship with her father.

At the end of the week Kluska walked into "the war room" on

the third floor of the Union County Prosecutor's Office. "So whatta you got?"

"Looks like you were right, Ed," Burke said as he logged in to the laptop on the conference room table. "Sybil Lucas and Barry Josephs up in Computer Crimes came up with some interesting stuff."

As Kluska took a seat, Burke moved the cursor and clicked on the arrow for the recording to play:

*"Surprised . . . ee me?"*

*"Wha . . . you doing . . . ?"*

*"Sit. . . ."*

*"As . . . say, payba . . . a bitch . . . Dad."*

*"You don't want . . . do this."*

*"Yeah, I . . . think I do . . . me one good reason why . . . shouldn't."*

*"For Chri . . . sake, you're my daughter."*

*"Haaaaaa. Nice ry, addy. But . . . said . . . a reason . . . do it, asshole. Not one mo . . . reason . . ."*

*"Look, you . . . came for. . . . I'll probably spend the rest of my life . . . jail. I . . . think you'd enjoy that . . . than killing me."*

The recording ended with the explosion from the gun.

"Where did we get this?" he asked Burke.

"According to Sybil, there was what appeared to be a small flash drive in the USB port of Parsons's laptop. When we got the warrant to search his computers and phone, I went up and asked her to take a look at what was on it. When she looked at it, she discovered it was actually a voice-activated recording device. It cuts in and out because a device like this has an optimum recording range of about ten feet and they must have been slightly beyond that."

"Shit," Kluska said. "We have a fucking recording of the murder."

"Yep!" Burke grinned. "And she says 'Dad' and 'Daddy,' and he refers to the killer as his daughter. Seems like a lock to me."

"Sybil come up with anything else?"

"Appears Parsons always backed up his data to external drives, so not a lot there."

"Interesting. What kind of websites did he go to?"

Burke shook his head. "She couldn't tell. He deleted his browsing history every day."

Kluska winced, wishing they had this information. "What about his e-mails? Anything there?"

Now it was Burke's turn to grimace. "All encrypted."

"What?"

"Can't read 'em. They've been sent and received using some type of software that makes them unreadable without the encryption password. Sybil said it appears that he had recently gotten a new laptop, and when he set it up he used e-mail encryption software, and without the password or software, the e-mails are gibberish."

"What about his old e-mails?"

"Apparently they're no longer stored on the computer."

"Anything else on there?"

"Our search warrant was limited to his e-mails and browsing history. So Sybil wasn't able to do a full scan and search of everything on the laptop."

*Shit. What was Parsons up to?* Kluska, who was unfamiliar with the world of high finance, didn't know if there might be legitimate reasons for all the secrecy, but his years in law enforcement had also left him jaded and suspicious.

"Have we looked at the hard drives yet?"

"We don't have them," Burke replied.

"We don't have them!" Kluska barked. "Where the fuck are they?"

Burke retreated, fearing Kluska's wrath. "Don't know. Didn't find them when we searched the house and the warrant didn't let us go into the safe. NYPD went through his brownstone in the city, but they didn't have a warrant, so who knows, could still be there."

*Fuck.* Apparently after Kluska's little discussion with Harrison, a few calls had been made to the prosecutor, and Willis had ultimately let DeCovnie and the lawyer go into the house to retrieve the will and financial records they claimed they needed for the estate. It would have been the perfect opportunity for that shyster to take the hard drives.

"Wait. If we don't have them, how the fuck does Sybil know he put stuff onto hard drives?" Kluska asked.

Burke shrugged. "I don't know. Sybil went on for about twenty minutes telling me about how she found fragments of deleted files left on the internal hard drive, and about some automatic download program being set up. It was all gibberish to me, but she can explain it much better than I can."

As Kluska mulled his concerns, Assistant Prosecutor Tom Willis walked into the conference room and took a seat. Willis had been with the office for twenty-five years. He still had a full head of wavy brown hair and had a reputation for being a womanizer, although he had so far managed to avoid any formal complaints.

"Heard we have a break. What's going on?" Willis asked.

Burke looked at Kluska, who motioned for Burke to play the recording. When it was done, Burke explained to Willis how the recording had been made.

"This is great. We have her fingerprints on the gun and now a recording where the victim IDs his murderer as his daughter. Look, I have enough for a complaint and an arrest warrant, but bring her in again and see if we can get a confession. I'll let you know when I'm almost ready, and we can pick her up. If she confesses—game, set, match. Even if she doesn't, there's enough for probable cause."

"Tom, a few things bother me," Kluska said. "I only heard the daughter speak once, when I watched her interview this week, but the voice on the recording doesn't sound like her. Plus, I still have a lot of unanswered questions about Parsons. There was a federal investigation about five, six years ago that disappeared. He encrypted everything. He apparently stored everything on hard drives we can't find. The woman who finds the body calls his lawyer, maybe even before she calls us. And the lawyer that shows up is more concerned with getting paperwork from inside the house than he is about a dead client. Some of these pieces don't fit."

Willis gave Kluska a dismissive wave. "You worry too much, Ed. I'll grant you the quality of the recording sucks, but it's all there. You should be doing a victory lap. You were right about it not being a suicide. Besides, I'm getting all kinds of shit from the front office to get this solved quickly."

"I hear ya, Tom. But as much as the front office wants this wrapped up, they won't be too happy if we shit the bed."

"Jesus, Ed. When did you turn into such a fucking old lady? We got this one. Bring her in."

Kluska glared at Willis. It was bad enough that he wouldn't even listen to what Kluska had to say, but to dis him in front of Burke, who was looking at the table to avoid eye contact, really pissed him off.

Willis pushed his chair back. "Let me know when you bring her in. I want to be here when we put the cuffs on her." A grin slowly spread across his face. "Cheer up, Eddie boy, this will be a feather in all of our caps." He rose from the table. "Especially mine."

# CHAPTER 8

September 2008

ERIN WATCHED HER BROTHER, SEAN, PACE BACK AND FORTH ACROSS
the surgical waiting room and wondered why he seemed to be the
most nervous person in their family. After all, he was a highly
sought-after orthopedic surgeon. Then it suddenly made sense—
of course he was worried, he knew all the things that could go
wrong, not to mention he was used to being the one in charge of
what was taking place in the operating room. Today he was a by-
stander—a mere mortal—waiting for news from their mother's
surgeon on how the mastectomy had gone.

For the last three and a half months, in an effort to shrink her
tumors, Peg had undergone neoadjuvant chemotherapy along
with taking other drugs, which her oncologist had hoped would
allow her to avoid a mastectomy.

Her mom's treatment, along with a lull in Erin's own trial
schedule, had allowed her to spend time with her mom, including two weeks that they spent together at Erin's condo in Bradley
Beach. Focusing on her mom had the added benefit of allowing
Erin to avoid dealing with her issues with Mark.

Unfortunately, by mid-August it was apparent that, although
the tumors were shrinking, a mastectomy would still be necessary
and today's surgery was scheduled.

Erin shifted her gaze from her brother and turned to her left.

There was an empty chair between her and her father, who sat bent over, his head bowed and his hands folded. Sean's wife, Liz, sat on the other side of him, gently rubbing his back as she quietly whispered that Peg would be fine.

Erin would have loved to have been the one comforting her father, but it had only been in the past year that they had begun to bridge the divide that had opened up between them when Erin had come out as transgender and then transitioned. For nearly three years, Sean and her father had refused to talk to her. It was only thanks to the persistence of her mother, Liz, and Sean's two sons, Patrick and Brennan, that they had started to heal. Erin knew her dad loved her, but she also knew he still struggled with the fact that she was a woman. A struggle made even harder when she had started dating Mark.

Watching Sean pace and her father quietly suffering, she was struck by the realization that her mom was the glue that held them all together. If something happened to her, would they all spin off into their own separate orbits, sporadically getting together when those orbits happened to intersect—perhaps Thanksgiving or Christmas? She tried to push those thoughts out of her head, afraid that even conjuring them up might somehow make the possibility more likely.

Erin tried to dwell on the positive. The five-year survival rate for her mother's type of cancer, stage IIIA, hormone receptor positive, was over 70 percent. And even though the effort to shrink the tumors wasn't totally successful, both the oncologist and surgeon had been upbeat in terms of the prognosis. Both had recommended a mastectomy of her left breast, then, depending on how many lymph nodes were involved, perhaps additional chemotherapy, followed by radiation and treatment with tamoxifen. It also helped that her mother's joie de vivre and her sense of humor remained unchanged.

Erin looked up at the wall clock—eleven fifteen a.m. Her mother had gone into surgery at seven that morning. The surgeon had told them to expect the surgery would take around three hours, and so, even though Erin had to pee so badly she thought her bladder was going to burst, she had stayed put, knowing that as soon as she went to the ladies' room, the surgeon would call them in and she'd miss the news. Finally, she couldn't take it any longer. "I have to run to the bathroom," she said quietly. "Wait for me if the surgeon comes out."

To Erin's relief, Liz stood as well. "I have to go too."

Erin gave her dad a small smile and patted his hand, trying to reassure him that everything was going to be fine.

"Oh my God," Liz said as they walked into the ladies' room, "I'm so glad you had to go. I should never have had that second cup of coffee. It went right through me."

After they had both finished and washed up, Erin said, "Thanks for being there for my dad."

"Of course," Liz replied, with a sad smile. She gave Erin a small hug. "He needs you, even if it's hard for him to show it."

"I know," Erin said, biting her lip. "At least he and I can talk now. One step at a time."

As Erin had anticipated, they came back to find Sean standing in the door to the recovery area, motioning for them to hurry up.

"Everything went well," Dr. Seiko said when they had all gathered inside. "The surgery took a little longer because we removed a few more of Peg's lymph nodes than we originally anticipated. Also, Peg made the decision that she wanted to have a mastectomy to her right breast prophylactically, both to reduce the risk of recurring cancer, and . . . well, from an appearance standpoint, she thought it might be easier in terms of breast reconstruction surgery."

Sean looked surprised. "My mom didn't say anything to me about removing her right breast."

"Is she going to be okay?" their father injected before Dr. Seiko could respond to Sean.

"Yes, Pat. The surgery went well. We're confident that we got all of the cancerous tissue, but we're also going to do the radiation, and, of course, she has to remain on the hormone-blocking medication. At this point, I'm very hopeful that your wife will make a complete recovery." Seiko then turned to Sean. "I don't have to tell you that your mother is a very strong-willed woman. She made the decision concerning what she wanted to do, and that's all I'm at liberty to say."

Her father exhaled as if he hadn't let out a breath since seven a.m. "Your mom and I discussed this. I wasn't a big fan, but you know your mother—when she makes up her mind, there's nothing that's going to change it. And she didn't tell you because she didn't want to get into an argument with anyone before the surgery."

"When will we be able to see her?" Erin asked before Sean could say anything else.

Seiko looked relieved. "They just brought her into recovery. I would say it'll probably be an hour, give or take. So if you want to grab something to eat, you have some time."

An hour and a half later, they gathered around Peg's bed in the recovery room. After blinking a few times, Peg looked to Erin. "I get your *Wizard of Oz* impression now," she said with a small smile, referring to the time two years ago when the family had gathered around Erin in recovery. "I do feel a little like Dorothy after a tornado, with you all standing around me."

"Listen, Auntie Em. Don't go trying to steal my lines." She leaned over and kissed her mother on the forehead. "How you feeling?" she asked softly.

They all took turns telling Peg how good she looked and how relieved they were that the surgery had gone well. Thankfully, no one mentioned the double mastectomy, although from the look on Sean's face, he wanted to.

They had hovered around Peg for about fifteen minutes when a nurse pulled back the curtain and said, "Okay, Margaret, time to get you to your room."

Peg cringed at Margaret—it was a formality she used only when she needed to use her full legal name. "Call me Peg, please."

"Of course," the young nurse replied, scribbling a note on Peg's chart.

As Peg was being wheeled out the door, she motioned for her

husband and Sean to come closer. "They said you could buy me a coffee and donut from the coffee shop. Think you guys can do that?"

"Sure," Pat said. "The usual?"

She nodded and squeezed her husband's hand.

After they had settled Peg into her room, she directed Liz and Erin to either side of her bed. "Liz, I know my son, and at some point he's going to want to talk to me about why I had my right breast removed. Honestly, as much as I love him and know what a great doctor he is, I don't want to discuss it with him. So, could you warn him off?"

Liz gave her mother-in-law a smile. "Of course, Peg. Whatever you need."

"Just so you both know, I don't have the BRCA gene. That's not why I did this. So, Erin, you don't need to get tested."

"That's good to know," Erin replied.

"But I did want to tell you why."

"Mom, you don't have to tell us," Erin interrupted, then glanced at Liz, who was nodding.

"But I want to tell you, because your father thinks I'm nuts," Peg said, looking as though she might start crying. "I have a friend who had one breast removed and then reconstructed, and she hated the fact that her breasts weren't a matched set anymore. One was old and droopy, and the other young and perky." Peg looked away, embarrassed. "She said she always felt like she was a car whose headlights were out of alignment, and wished she had gotten both breasts reconstructed at the same time."

Erin sat on the edge of the bed and took her mother's hand. "That makes sense to me. Why shouldn't you want to continue to look attractive?"

Peg's eyes welled with tears. "Your father didn't understand. He was pretty upset with me. He said, 'For Christ's sake, you have cancer and you're worried about how you're going to look!'"

Erin grabbed a couple of tissues and handed them to her mother.

"But I have to believe I'm going to recover, and when I do, I don't want to be embarrassed by the way I look." She looked up at her daughter and daughter-in-law. "Am I wrong?"

"No," they said in unison.

Later, walking to her car, Erin was drawn back to the conversation and her mother's desire not to be embarrassed by the way she looked. It was a desire Erin knew all too well. Erin was lucky. When she transitioned, her relatively small frame and the impact of the hormones had provided her with a body that took on the average contours for a cisgender woman. Yet, before she started living full-time as Erin, she had plastic surgery to give her face more feminine features. She didn't want to be embarrassed by the way she looked. There too she had been lucky, because unlike many trans women, she had the financial wherewithal to have done what she needed. But now, after listening to her mom, she realized society ingrained in all women, cis and trans, the need to meet certain expectations as to how they looked. It wasn't lost on her that neither she nor her mom had been immune.

After starting her car she retrieved her BlackBerry from her purse. As she scrolled through her e-mails and messages, she came across a text from an unknown number. She opened it.

**mccabe it's kluska from ucpo. want to meet with you off the record. let me know availability next week mon thru weds—early afternoon. important.**

Strange, she thought. She hadn't seen Detective Kluska since her days in the PD's office. Why the hell would he want to see her? And even stranger, why off the record? *What the hell*, she thought as she typed her response.

# CHAPTER 9

*F*ROM HER PERCH IN THE LAST BOOTH, ERIN HAD A FULL VIEW OF anyone coming into the Liberty Tavern. The place was deserted. She glanced at her watch. The lunch crowd had long gone, and the happy hour crowd wasn't due for another two hours. The only people in the place were a couple of guys sitting at the bar, who occasionally looked over their shoulders checking her out. *Don't get any ideas, guys*, she thought.

Kluska had asked to meet at two thirty p.m. Thirty minutes later, Erin was beginning to wonder how much longer she should wait when she saw him walk in. He stood by the front of the bar, temporarily blinded by the shift from bright sunlight to the bar's dim interior. Then, after about ten seconds, he started walking toward her. It looked like he had put on a few pounds—maybe more than a few—but he was still a hard guy to forget. He dropped onto the bench on the opposite side, causing the entire booth to shutter, and put a file folder on the table in front of him.

"Wasn't sure you'd recognize me. It's been a few years," Erin said, a grin spreading across her face.

"Jesus Christ, McCabe, I'm a fucking detective. You don't think I know how to go to your fucking website to find your picture?"

"Honestly, Ed, I just figured you got lucky and figured the two guys at the bar were too big to be little ol' me."

Kluska's mouth twisted. "You may be a skirt now, but doesn't mean I won't call you an asshole."

"Thanks. Good to see you too."

A waitress sauntered out of the kitchen. "You want something to drink?" she asked.

"Club with lime," he replied.

"You want another ginger ale?" she asked Erin.

"Please."

"Menus?" she asked.

"Not for me," Erin replied.

"No," he said.

"They do have a pretty good bar pie," he said, after she walked away, "if you're hungry."

She shook her head no. "Sounds like you come here often."

"Back in the day when I was still playing softball—and still drinking—this was a regular postgame watering hole. But I haven't had a drink in ten years and haven't played softball in about eight, so not for a while. Figured no one would recognize me this time of day. Besides, had to take it out of county, but not too far, in case I needed to get back in a hurry. Woodbridge was perfect."

"Sounds mysterious," she said as the waitress slid their drinks onto the table.

Kluska took a swig of his club soda. "Look, McCabe, I'll explain everything, but first I need a guarantee from you."

"Of course. You and I were always on opposite sides, but I always thought you were a good detective; if you're in some kind of trouble, just say so and this will be a privileged conversation."

He snorted. "Nothing that easy. I need it to be beyond privileged—I need it to be that this meeting never took place."

She gave him a quizzical look. Meeting him was one thing; lying about it was another. "Ed . . ."

"Humor me," he interrupted. "Could be my job on the line."

"Okay," she replied, both troubled and intrigued. "But if I don't like where this is going, I'm out of here."

He pointed to the manila folder on the table. "You hear about a murder in Westfield about five months ago, a guy by the name of Charles Parsons?"

She nodded. "Sure. His daughter pled guilty last week, right?"

"Yeah, that's the one. This is a copy of the discovery in the case," he said, putting his hand on the file folder. Before Erin could say anything, he motioned for her to wait. "Ann Parsons took a plea to aggravated manslaughter. Under the deal, she'll get a flat twenty, with an eighty-five percent parole disqualifier— so minimum of seventeen, maxes out at twenty. She gets sentenced in four weeks."

"Flat twenty doesn't sound like a bad deal. How old is she?" Erin asked.

"Twenty-five, I think," Kluska replied.

"So she gets out in her mid-forties, has a second chance at life. So what's going on, Ed, why are we here?"

Kluska took another gulp of his club soda and stroked his beard. "I don't think she did it," he said flatly. "There's something off here and I can't figure it out."

Erin's face scrunched, and her eyes narrowed. "Ed, you're the detective. Isn't that your job—to figure it out?"

"You ever deal with Tom Willis?"

Erin was trying to keep up with the conversation. "Yeah, I tried two murder cases against him back when I was with the PD's office."

"What did you think of him?"

"Honestly?"

"Yeah."

"Arrogant asshole," she said without hesitation.

"He hasn't changed. I told him before we arrested Parsons there were pieces that didn't fit, but he's convinced we got the right person. Or, he just doesn't give a shit because he's basically a lazy fuck, and if a piece of the puzzle doesn't fit, he'll just throw it away."

"Don't sugarcoat it, Ed, tell me how you really feel."

He gave her a dirty look. "As far as Willis is concerned, she's pled guilty; case closed."

"To be fair, Ed, that's the way it usually works. Isn't it? You don't typically keep investigating a case after someone pleads guilty," she said.

"Don't be a smart-ass," he fired back with a scowl. "I don't know why she pled guilty. But I've been doing this job for a long time, and I've learned to trust my gut—and my gut is screaming that she didn't do it. I want you to help her."

She leaned forward trying to gauge his motive. "Ed, clearly this is important to you, but what am I missing? If you're so convinced she's not guilty, why aren't you having this conversation with her attorneys?"

"I have my doubts about whose side they're on. She's represented by a couple of lawyers from Winston Drapper, hired by the executrix of her father's estate."

Erin knew Winston Drapper only by reputation. Based in Manhattan, they were one of the biggest firms in the country. Any attorney they had handling criminal cases was likely a former federal prosecutor or came out of the Manhattan DA's office. It was odd they'd be involved in defending someone in New Jersey on a state murder charge. Usually they handled criminal investigations involving Fortune 500 companies. Still . . .

"I don't know anyone there, but they're all supposed to be top-notch lawyers," she offered.

"Maybe, but they didn't do shit in this case. They got discovery and a couple months later they pled her guilty—no motions, no nothing."

"So why me?" she asked. "It's not like you and I have had a lot of cases together, and the ones we did, my clients were convicted."

Kluska's eyes flashed. "To start with, when I knew you as a PD, I always thought you were a decent attorney. Granted, you were brand-spanking new, but you had a presence in the courtroom that you can't teach. And I followed the case you had last year down in Ocean County. From what I read, you and your partner had to put up with some crazy bullshit. But the main reason is . . ." He stopped, his intense look replaced by something almost sheepish. "Look, don't take this the wrong way, but you've got more balls than a lot of attorneys . . . you know, just to do what you did," he said, motioning to Erin with his hands. "That took a lot of guts. Parsons needs someone she can trust, someone who will understand her, someone who's walked in her shoes."

Erin was now totally confused. "Ed, what the hell are you talking about?"

"Ann Parsons is a transgendered," he said, as if throwing down a gauntlet.

"What?"

"You heard me. She's just like you. Isn't that what you are—transgendered?"

She shook her head. "It's transgender—an adjective. I'm a transgender woman, not transgendered."

"Whatever. She was born a guy, like you."

Erin closed her eyes and made a decision not to get into a debate on Kluska's terminology. "I don't remember seeing anything in the paper about her being trans."

"There hasn't been anything. No one found out until after her plea. Once she pled, the estate moved to have her bail exonerated and Judge Spiegel had no choice but to remand her to the Union County jail to await sentencing. From what I'm told, her medical exam determined she was born a guy and they were going to move her to the male side of the jail." He shrugged. "I don't know all the gory details, but apparently she had sex change surgery a number of years ago, so she's being housed in the women's section of the jail."

Erin hoped her wince was noticeable. She hated the term *sex change surgery*. The phrase screamed like a tabloid headline—SO-AND-SO HAD SEX CHANGE SURGERY! But the fact that Kluska, a hard-boiled detective in the classic sense, was sensitive to Ann's situation surprised Erin. She decided she didn't want to appear pedantic by correcting him.

"Okay, assuming she's a transgender woman, I don't see how that plays into why you think I can help her."

Kluska looked exasperated. "Don't go stupid on me now! There isn't another fucking lawyer in the state that will understand her the way you can. She needs someone she can trust and who better than you?"

"You're making a lot of assumptions here. One, that she wants help; two, that she doesn't or can't trust her current lawyers; and, three, that even if I wanted to help there is something I can do for her. There's also the small detail that she already has counsel—it's not like I can just walk into the Union County jail and tell her I want to represent her."

"You find a quasi-legitimate reason to see her, and I'll get you on her visitors list. When you have a reason, text me at the number I texted you from."

He slid the file across the table, then downed what was left of his club soda. "Take this. Read it carefully. And, McCabe? I've never done anything remotely like this in my career. This blows up and my career is over. But I've never had a case where there's something so rotten that the stench makes me sick."

"Why are you so sure?" she asked.

"There's a recording of the murder. I've listened to it, I don't know, maybe a hundred times." He stood up. "I'm convinced it's not Ann Parsons on that recording. So was the detective who found the recording. She wanted to do a voice analysis comparison, but Willis shot that down." He looked down at Erin and raised an eyebrow. "Twenty years is a long fucking time, McCabe. Think about it. You're her only hope."

Erin waited until he was out of the bar to look at the file he had left on the table. Then she stuffed it into her pocketbook, put money on the table to cover their tab, and walked out into the sunlight.

# CHAPTER 10

WHEN ERIN GOT BACK TO THE OFFICE, SHE ASKED DUANE IF HE HAD time to review the discovery for a potential new client. She didn't tell him anything about the meeting with Kluska to avoid raising any red flags before he even looked at the file.

It was a little after five p.m. when Duane walked into her office and dropped the file on her desk.

"You want to tell me what's really going on here?" he asked accusingly.

"What do you mean?" she said with an innocent grin.

"Why are we looking at this case? It's not like I don't know who Ann Parsons is—the murder occurred in Westfield, all of about five miles from my house. She's already pled guilty to aggravated manslaughter of her father, and the sentencing takes place in about four weeks." He paused to frown. "Let's add to the equation that as a result of pleading guilty to killing her father, she'll lose any inheritance. Which means she probably has no money for a lawyer. And from what I see from a quick look at this file, she doesn't need a new lawyer; she needs a magician to make the evidence against her disappear."

All Erin could do was nod. She had read only Detective Chris Burke's summary report, but based on that, it was hard to disagree with Duane's initial analysis.

"Don't stand there glaring at me," she said. "Have a seat and let me give you a little background," she said, gesturing toward a chair. "But this has to stay between us, for reasons that will be obvious."

Once he sat, she proceeded to tell Duane about her strange meeting with Kluska and the information he had given her. When she was done, his expression matched the way she felt by the whole thing: dumbfounded.

"How well do you know Kluska?" Duane asked.

"Not well at all," Erin replied. "He was the lead detective in two homicide cases I tried when I was at the PD's office. Always came across as a straight shooter. I cross-examined him in both cases, which I lost, but other than that, I really had no other dealings with him. He was a detective, I was a PD, so we didn't run in the same social circles."

Duane leaned back in his chair, deep in thought. "I have to tell you, I don't think I've ever seen a detective go out on a limb like this for a defendant, especially after there's been a guilty plea."

"I don't disagree," Erin replied. "And even if we wanted to do something, it's not like we can waltz into the jail and say we want to meet with her. When I tried to explain all of that to Kluska, he just said for me to come up with a reason and he'd get me one visit."

"You don't think he's trying to set you up to do something stupid, do you?"

"What do you mean?" Erin asked in reply.

"Well, we have managed to piss off a few people in high places, including one gubernatorial candidate. Maybe they're using Kluska to try and get us to do something unethical."

There certainly was more than a kernel of truth to what Duane was saying—they had made some enemies in high places. But, like Kluska, she trusted her instincts, and hers told her that Kluska was sincere in wanting to help Parsons.

"I'll go through the file tonight," she said. "I saw two CDs in there. Did you get a chance to look at those?"

Duane shook his head. "Didn't get a chance, but it looks like one's a DVR with the video of her confession and the other is a CD with the audio recording of the murder."

"Okay. Kluska emphasized that he doesn't think the voice on the recording is Parsons's. Seems like a good place to start."

"What do you make of the trans thing?" Duane asked.

Erin shrugged. "I'm not sure it has anything to do with anything, other than Kluska playing on my sympathies."

Duane stood, his look betraying a certain caution. "According to the investigative reports, Ann was a graduate of Westfield High School. We both know someone who's a teacher there. Do you want me to ask him if he knew her back then?"

The thought had already crossed Erin's mind that Mark was a teacher at Westfield High, and had been for the last eight years. If Ann Parsons had gone there, when he was a teacher there, Mark might have some insights.

She was momentarily lost. "No," she said softly. "No, I got it."

Erin's apartment in Cranford was a small one-bedroom, so the table in her dining area doubled as a desk whenever she worked from home. The documents Kluska had given her were spread out on the table, and she had already spent time poring through them looking for any threads of evidence that might support Kluska's belief that Parsons didn't kill her father. So far, she hadn't come across anything that seemed to offer a way out for Ann.

One thing confused her, though—the results of the search warrant on Ann's home. All the usual things you'd expect an affluent twenty-five-year-old to have were seized: a laptop, a desktop, bank statements, and a cell phone. But Erin had noticed that when Ann had been arrested at the prosecutor's office, her cell phone had been seized. These reports showed that the phone seized from Ann's condo was a prepaid cell phone, a burner phone. According to the report from the detective who ran the analytics on the phone, it was purchased three days after the murder and only two numbers had been called, both of which came up as unknown numbers. Meaning Ann had made calls to only two other burner phones. Why in the world was a paralegal using a burner phone, unless she was involved in the murder of her father? But that didn't make sense either. If you were conspiring to kill someone, you'd get the burner phones ahead of the murder, not after. Unless she had used a burner phone before and "burned" it.

Putting those reports aside, she decided to move on to the recordings.

She popped the DVR of the interrogation of Ann Parsons into her player and watched Ann's confession play out. Two detectives, one male and one female, had brought her in, explaining that they had some new evidence they wanted to discuss. When they immediately read her her Miranda rights, she seemed taken aback. She asked if she was a suspect, and they responded that at this point everyone associated with her father was a suspect. Ann was there without a lawyer and Erin found herself almost screaming at the video for Ann to tell them she wanted a lawyer present, but she didn't.

The detectives bounced around for the next thirty minutes, talking about Ann's career and her relationship with her father before turning to the murder itself. For over twenty minutes Ann denied any involvement, explaining that she'd been at a bar in Hoboken waiting to meet someone. Unfortunately, that person had to work late and Ann left and went home. She provided the only phone number she had for her date, but told them she had tried the number and it was no longer in service. She also told them that after that night, she had never heard from the person again. In classic good cop/bad cop fashion, the male detective said they knew she was lying because there was a video of her coming out of the house the night her father was murdered. He then played the audio recording of the murder. Ann sat in stunned silence and then asked to hear it again. After they played it a second time, she rocked back and forth in her chair, chewing on her lower lip until finally whispering, "I did it." The female detective leaned across the table and said softly, "Ann, did you just say you shot your father?" Ann's head went up and down, indicating "yes." Finally, she asked for a lawyer.

After watching the interrogation, Erin listened to the audio. It was a short clip and she listened to it repeatedly, sometimes with headphones, sometimes without. She understood why Kluska felt the voice at the murder scene wasn't Ann's. Not only did the pitch seem different, the tonal quality was off. When Ann was being interrogated, she sounded hesitant and taciturn, while the voice from the murder audio sounded forceful and in command, someone unafraid.

Erin tried to flip her mind into trial mode, wondering how a jury might perceive the recording. The prosecutor would bring someone in to testify it was Ann's voice, and even if they could find a defense witness to say it wasn't, the quality of the recording was so bad that a jury might still come to the conclusion it was Ann. Perhaps they could find an expert witness to analyze the voices and speech patterns and opine it wasn't Ann. Even then, it wouldn't be easy.

It was just before eight p.m. when she finally took a break, admitting that it was looking pretty bleak for Ann. She looked down at her phone, wishing she had taken Duane up on his offer to reach out to Mark. *Get it over with.*

He picked up on the fourth ring.

"How are you?" she asked.

"Good," he responded. "You?"

"I'm good."

"I heard from Swish about your mom—how's she doing?"

"She's holding up. The surgery went well. She might need some more chemo and then radiation, but fingers crossed. I'm having breakfast with her tomorrow. Thanks for asking."

"Glad to hear that. Please give her my best."

"I will." She drew in a deep breath. "Listen, do you have a minute to talk?"

"Sure, I'm just driving home from the gym."

"Okay. Um, well the reason I called is to see if you knew a potential client of mine. Her dad had a home in Westfield."

"Who we talking about?" he asked.

"Ann Parsons."

There was silence on the other end. Finally he said, "I saw in the *Star Ledger* a week or so ago that she'd pled guilty to killing her dad."

"Yeah, she did. You know her?"

"No, not personally. She was supposed to be in my class her senior year, which was my first year teaching, but I was told at the beginning of the year she had a medical issue and would be homeschooled from then on. I know she graduated, but I never saw her."

"I presume they never told you what the medical issue was, or if they did, you couldn't tell me."

"You're right, I couldn't, but fortunately for me, they never told me." He hesitated. "I have no idea if there's any truth to it, but the rumor around school was that she tried to commit suicide."

Now it was Erin's turn to be quiet, wondering if it might be related to Ann being trans.

"You said she was a potential client, but she's already pled guilty," Mark said. "How are you involved?"

"Long story. Let's just say some people think she's innocent despite her plea," she offered, keeping it purposely vague for Kluska's sake. "Based on that, and the fact that she's trans, they asked me to take a look."

There was a long pause. "Erin, Ann Parsons isn't transgender."

"According to my sources, she is," Erin replied. "Why are you so sure she isn't?"

"Because I saw a picture of her when she was about five years old, and she was definitely a little girl."

"How'd you see a picture of her if she was never your student?"

"Now it's my turn to have a long story," he said. "Can I ask a delicate question? Are you seeing anyone? I mean, it's been six months, so I'd understand if you were."

She didn't know whether to laugh or cry. "No," she said softly.

"Okay, so here's another question: Have you eaten?"

"No," she replied. "But I'm hanging out in sweats and don't feel like getting dressed. I was just going to make myself a PB&J."

"Feel like Thai?"

"Thanks, Mark, but I really don't want to get dressed."

"Who said anything about getting dressed? It's not like I haven't seen you in sweats. I'm pulling up in front of Taste of

Thai now. I'll pick up some extra and be at your place in fifteen minutes."

"Thanks, Mark, but—"

"Great. See you then." He clicked off.

Her first thought was to call him back and tell him no. Her place was a mess, she was a mess—and, more importantly, she wasn't sure she was prepared to see him again. But she needed to find out more about Ann Parsons, and, if she were honest, she missed him. *The hell with it.* She wasn't changing, she wasn't putting on makeup, and she wasn't cleaning up. If he wanted to barge in, so be it.

Twenty minutes later her intercom squawked and she buzzed him in. She waited at the door, her hands suddenly clammy as she heard him bounding up the stairs. When he reached the landing outside her unit he stopped. It looked like he was carrying enough food to feed her entire floor.

Seeing him again made her heart dance. He hadn't changed. At six feet, he had jet black hair, disheveled in a way that suggested he combed it with his fingertips. Somehow he always managed to have just enough stubble to be sexy, without looking grungy, and his green eyes still sparkled. God, she'd missed him.

"Hi," he said, a goofy smile on his face.

"What did you get?" she asked, eying the bags and stepping aside so he could come into her apartment.

"Just a few things. I remembered you liked the chicken satay and the pork dumplings, so I picked up some of them." He walked into her kitchen and put the bags on the counter. "Let's see what else—there's some curried sea scallops, fried rice, noodle soup, and"—he reached into another bag and took out a six-pack of Sam Adams—"something to wash it down."

She looked at everything spread across the counter. "You do realize it's a school night, right?"

"Yeah, but to paraphrase one of my favorite philosophers, life moves pretty fast. If you don't have Thai food and a beer every once in a while, you could miss it." He gave her a sheepish grin and a shrug.

"Ferris Bueller. Really?"

"I'm impressed."

"You impress much too easily," she said.

He smiled and held her gaze, his voice suddenly turning serious as he said, "It's nice to see you."

"It's nice to see you too," she said softly. And before she could stop herself "I missed you" tumbled out.

"Missed you too," he said as he leaned over and kissed her cheek.

Feeling the color rising in her face and the tears gathering, she quickly turned and pulled some plates out of her cabinet, grabbed some silverware, and moved her papers out of the way so they'd have somewhere to eat. He opened two of the beers, and they passed the containers of food back and forth filling their plates.

"So tell me why you don't believe Ann Parsons is trans, and how you got to see a picture of her at five," she said after they started eating. "From what I'm told she's twenty-five. That would make you about sixteen or seventeen when she was five."

"Let me explain," he said between forkfuls of food. "You know that after I graduated NYU, I went to work on Wall Street at Lehman Brothers as an analyst. Part of my job was to work on pitch books, whether that was trying to get someone interested in buying a company or investing in a company. Toward the end of my time there, I guess it was around 1996, I actually got to go as part of a team that went to pitch Charles Parsons on making a substantial investment in one of our clients. I remember we were sitting in his office and he had photos all over the walls of him with powerful people. But sitting on the credenza behind his desk was a picture of him in a tux, a woman in a wedding dress, and a young girl around five, dressed as a flower girl. The guy leading our team, Chris Meehan, who was pretty high up on the food chain, says, all chummy, 'That's a beautiful picture. Is that your wife and daughter?' And Parsons, without even turning around and looking at the picture, gave Meehan one of the coldest looks I've ever seen someone give another human, and said, 'It is my daughter and it was my wife—she's deceased. Now, can we get down to business?' I'll never forget it. It totally threw Meehan off his game. So much so that after Meehan was about five minutes into his pitch Parsons turned to me, a second-year analyst, a nobody, and said, 'Perhaps you can explain why I should invest in your client, because obviously your boss here doesn't have a fucking clue.'" Mark took a swig from his beer. "That was the day that I decided I was done on Wall Street."

Erin sat quietly mulling over what Mark had told her. "So assuming Ann is twenty-five, she was born around 1983–84. Which means that if your estimate that Ann was about five in the picture is accurate, the picture would have been taken around 1988." She grabbed a pen and wrote a note on her legal pad, reminding herself to check and see if there was anything on Parsons's marriage. She squeezed her lower lip between her thumb and forefinger. "Not many kids were transitioning that young in 1988. I guess it's not impossible, but . . ." Her voice trailed off. "Did you get a good look at the picture? I mean, at that age, there's really little physical difference between boys and girls."

"Obviously I can't be sure. The child was dressed as a flower girl and my recollection is that she appeared like a normal five-year-old girl. I guess all I'm saying is that I'd be surprised if she was transgender."

"Were there any rumors about her at Westfield?"

"Other than she tried to kill herself, no. Why are you so sure she is trans?"

"Let's just say I was told that when she went through the medical intake at the jail they discovered she was a post-op trans woman."

"How could they tell?"

This was getting a little close to home. "Probably because, despite pending lawsuits, the jail is still requiring female inmates to have a gynecological exam, which includes a pelvic exam. That would reveal that she doesn't have ovaries and a uterus."

Mark nodded. "Got it."

The room fell silent, the only noise the sounds of them eating. After several minutes Mark asked, "Can we talk about us? Please."

"Okay," Erin replied cautiously.

He pulled his chair over so he was close to her. "The last six months have been really hard. I watched from a distance as you went through some tough times—your client was murdered, your mom was diagnosed with cancer—and you were alone. I'm not sure why you shut me out, I know you said you were protecting me from the slings and arrows of my own family. But the message to me was you didn't trust me enough to let me make that decision, or worse, didn't love me enough to allow me to decide."

"I'm sorry," she said. "It's not that I didn't trust you, I just didn't want you to wind up caught in the middle between me and your family. I really didn't mean to hurt you."

"It's okay," he said, reaching out to grasp her hand. "I'm not angry with you. If you don't want to be in a relationship with me that's your decision to make, but you don't have the right to make the decision as to whether I want to be in a relationship with you. Only I get to make that choice."

Silence filled the room. "Do you?" she finally asked, looking into his eyes and swallowing her fears.

"Do I what?" he asked.

"Do you still want to have a relationship with me?"

"Yes," he said, leaning forward and gently kissing her.

# CHAPTER 11

WHEN SHE HEARD MARK GET OUT OF BED, ERIN ROLLED OVER TO look at the clock—five thirty a.m. She listened to him quietly getting dressed in the dark while she played back the events of the night before and how their discussion had morphed from Ann Parsons to Mark's family and their relationship. After hearing his perspective, she was embarrassed because had the roles been reversed she would have been upset with him for the lack of faith and trust. The term *makeup sex* popped into her mind, and even in the dark she knew her face was flushed with the memory of how wonderful it felt to make love again.

"I'm awake," she said, propping herself on her elbow.

"Sorry. Didn't mean to wake you. I just need to get home, showered, changed, and to work by seven."

She flipped on the lamp on her night table and was disappointed to see he was already fully dressed.

"I'll give you a call tonight," he said as he came around to her side of the bed to kiss her.

She threw her arms around his neck and pulled him closer. When they broke their embrace, she said, "I'm so sorry. I—"

He put his finger to her lips. "Stop. Please. It's okay. We're good." He kissed the top of her head, smiled, and made his way out.

With one last look at the clock, she decided there was no point in trying to go back to sleep. She was taking her mom out to breakfast at seven thirty to see how she was doing post-surgery, so she rolled out of bed, put her sweats back on, and made her way back to her dining room table and Ann Parsons's file.

Lost in the aftermath of her rekindled relationship with Mark was the question of Ann's gender identity. The best she could come up with was either Ann's mom had allowed her to transition at a very young age or perhaps Ann had an undiagnosed intersex condition. Whatever it was, it certainly didn't impact her guilt or innocence.

After an hour spent reviewing the details with little new insight, she was just about to pack things up when she noticed a notation on the inventory sheet next to the entry for a desktop computer that had been seized from Charles Parsons's Westfield home: "Warning: Do not connect to the Internet—encryption software infected with rootkit." *Encryption software? What the hell is a rootkit?* she wondered.

She quickly searched it on the Web and was startled by what she discovered. She went back and checked the rest of the inventory. A laptop had been confiscated, and when she checked the examination report, it described the laptop as new, and the information that was on it had been downloaded three days before Parsons was murdered. She opened the calendar on her phone—timewise it fit. *Shit. Was it possible?*

Her mother was waiting at the front door when Erin pulled up. After her mom slid into the passenger seat, Erin gave her a hug.

"Thought you'd stood me up," her mother said.

"Sorry. I was working at home and I came across something that took me down a rabbit hole," Erin said, giving her mother an apologetic smile, and as she did, she took in how her mom looked better than the last time they'd been together when she came home from the hospital. Erin knew most of it was an illusion—the penciled-in eyebrows, a wig that matched the color of her normal hair—but some of it was real. Her mother's skin color actually looked like a color in the human palette as opposed to the gray pall she'd had during the chemo prior to surgery.

"How you feeling?" Erin asked.

"Semi-human," she said. "I'm starting to get some strength back."

"You sure you're up to going out?"

"Yeah, I just need to try and get some normalcy back. I also seem to have an appetite again. So I'm looking forward to my egg white omelet."

After they parked, Erin watched as her mother gingerly made her way into the booth in the diner. Her cautious movements revealed how much pain she was still dealing with.

"Maybe we should have waited a few more days," Erin said.

"Too late now," her mom responded with a wry smile.

Erin shook her head—was her mom strong willed or just stubborn? "How's Dad holding up?" she asked.

"Pretty good. He's been a rock, but I think at this point he's just mentally and physically exhausted." She gave Erin a small grin. "And how about you? For someone who fell down the rabbit hole, you look pretty . . . content." Her mother tilted her head slightly, and then her grin turned into a full-fledged smile. "Anything new with Mark?"

Erin blushed, preventing her from displaying plausible deniability.

"You're a terrible poker player," her mother said with a laugh.

"Thanks," Erin responded sarcastically.

"Coffee, ladies?" the waitress interrupted.

After Erin agreed, the waitress turned and looked at Peg, who nodded. As she filled Peg's cup, the waitress said, "This has got to be your daughter. Except for the hair color, she looks just like you."

"That's funny," Peg replied. "I always thought she looked more like her father."

Erin looked down into her coffee and tried not to laugh. After the waitress had walked away, she said, "You're too much."

"What?" she retorted. "Until four years ago, I never thought you looked like me."

Erin took a sip of her coffee and marveled at how despite everything her mother had been through she hadn't lost her sense of humor. Since Erin had come out, they had connected in a new way. Maybe it was a mother-daughter bond, or maybe it was just a shared love that they hadn't expressed as openly before. Erin knew her mother had initially struggled when Erin told her that she was transgender, wondering if somehow she was the cause. But over time, as they talked through things, her mother had come to accept that Erin hadn't chosen to be transgender; it was just who she was. And during the time after she transitioned, when Sean and her father had stopped speaking to her, her mother had never wavered in her love and support.

"I'm so worried about you," Erin blurted, causing her mother's eyes to widen. "When you got sick, it made me realize how important you are to me—to the entire family. I know you're going to be fine and live for a long time, but I want you to know how much I admire you, love you, and . . . need you. I'm not sure I would have survived without your love and support." Erin reached across the table and took her mother's hand. "Thank you. I know I don't say it often enough, but thank you for being you and for loving me unconditionally."

"You're welcome." Peg's smile was warm and compassionate. "I hope I'm here for a long time too." She paused. "That said, when I was so sick during chemo, and still had the surgery ahead of me with radiation still coming my way, there were definitely times when the thought of death wasn't so scary—the pain ending didn't seem like such a bad option. I mean it's not like we can avoid it—death, that is. At some point we're all going to die."

"Geez, Mom. Thanks for sharing those upbeat thoughts."

"What? You almost died a couple of years ago. Were you afraid?"

"That was a little different. I had a psycho pointing a gun at my head. I honestly didn't have a whole lot of time to contemplate the temporal nature of my existence."

"Fair," Peg said. "All I'm saying is that I think I've come to terms with my mortality. It's not the dying part that scares me; it's just not knowing what, if anything, is on the other side."

"Well, I'm glad you've come to terms with it, because I haven't."

Her mother squeezed Erin's hand. "Hopefully we won't have to worry about it for a while."

"Hopefully," Erin replied.

"So tell me, what's going on with you and Mark?"

After breakfast, Erin took her mom home, then made her way to the office. Walking in, Erin greeted Cheryl, their receptionist, secretary, and paralegal all rolled into one, and then asked if Swish was in.

"Yeah, he was here when I got in."

"Thanks," Erin responded, making her way to his office, where she found Duane editing an appellate brief. "You have a minute?"

"Sure," he replied, motioning her to a chair in front of his desk.

"It's about Ann Parsons."

"You come up with a defense?"

"No. But there are a few things that have piqued my curiosity."

"Uh-oh," he said.

She began with her questions on whether the voice from the murder scene belonged to Ann. Then she told him about her conversations with Mark, and why he had questions about whether or not Ann was transgender. Finally, she told him about the fact that the laptop was only about three days old when Parsons was murdered and that the prosecutor's inventory log indicated that a desktop computer taken from Parsons's house was infected with a rootkit in the encryption software.

"What the hell is a rootkit?" he asked.

She described what she had learned from a quick Internet search and a call to an acquaintance who was a computer engineer.

"Okay. But what's that got to do with who killed him, or more importantly, why it helps prove Ann didn't?" he asked, his squint conveying his skepticism.

"I don't know that it does—yet. But here's why I'm intrigued. When I met with Justin shortly before he was killed, he told me that the guy he had worked for installing the update to the encryption software had warned him that there were some very nasty people who were upset and might blame him. When I asked Justin what he might be blamed for, he speculated that there might have been something in a software update that might not have been kosher."

Duane stroked his goatee. "But Mackey had also told you there were a number of computers he had installed stuff on. Even assuming Parsons's was one of them, it doesn't mean Parsons was in on Mackey's murder. Am I missing something?"

"No. Not at this point, but there's enough there that I'm intrigued. I certainly haven't connected any of the dots—at least not yet," she said, her face a study in resolve.

"Assuming there are dots to connect," Duane added.

"Of course," she replied with an air of innocence.

Duane stared at her. "Oh, I've seen that look from you before," he said, shaking his head. "Let me remind you, Ms. Quixote, before you go off tilting against this windmill, we do not represent Ms. Parsons. So whatever it is that you're thinking about doing, we would be doing it gratis."

"Actually," she said, "I have an idea."

His eyes narrowed. "Why do I have a feeling I'm going to regret this?"

"I'm going to reach out to Justin's mother. She lives in Carteret, and perhaps she'll retain us on a contingency basis to sue whoever murdered him."

"I hate to rain on your parade, but who you gonna sue? Mackey was murdered over four months ago, and as far as you know, there are no leads. Four months in a homicide investigation is a long time. It's probably already on the cold case list."

"You're right, it's a long shot. But I'll be honest with his mom and keep her expectations low. What I am hoping is that it will provide us with a reason to speak with Ann in jail."

"I don't know, E, this seems like a waste of time."

"You're probably right. So I'll run with it for a few weeks and if I get nowhere, at least I know I gave it a try. That okay with you?"

"Sure," he replied, his tone conveying his resignation.

"Okay," she said, standing up to head back to her office. She paused on her way out and turned around. "Could you do one thing for me?"

"What's that?"

"I told you that when Mark and his boss met with Parsons, he told them his wife was deceased. Could you find out who she was and how and when she died?"

He sighed. "You're going to suck me into this, aren't you?"

"No, you're just a much better investigator than I am. You know, FBI Special Agent kind of stuff."

Duane snorted. "Right." Then with an impish grin added, "And how is Mark?"

Her smile said more than her words.

"He's good," she replied.

As she got to the door, she turned and said, "Oh, and thank you."

"For what?"

"For putting up with me. I know that over the last six months between Mark and my mom's situation, I haven't been fun to work with."

"Hey, with your mom, no worries, you get a free pass. With Mark . . ." he paused, his grin growing. "Glad it's working out."

# CHAPTER 12

MARTIN CONROY STORMED INTO HIS PARK AVENUE OFFICE OVER-looking the Waldorf Astoria, screaming at someone on his BlackBerry. "I don't give a fuck if he is the mayor's brother—tell him he's a fucking piece of shit and I'm going to bury him and his fucking client!" He launched his briefcase into the corner of the room and stared at the ceiling. "Look, I have to go. I have people here. Just make sure you tell him that if I don't get what I want, his client won't be able to get a job cleaning up dog shit."

He hit END, looked up, his demeanor suddenly shifting. "Cassie, my dear," he said obsequiously, walking over and giving Cassandra DeCovnie a peck on each cheek. He gave a quick head nod to his associate, Preston Harrison, who had followed him into the room. Then, with a quick tug on the French cuffs of his powder-blue shirt, he moved behind his desk, catching a glimpse of himself reflected in the glass of the de Kooning that hung on the wall behind his desk. At fifty-eight, he worked hard on his image as a high-priced lawyer. Today he wore a black pin-striped bespoke suit, with a pink silk Bvlgari tie and pocket square. He was tanned and his silver hair was slicked back. He found it amus-ing when people compared his appearance to that of John Gotti in his prime. A comparison he had been known to exploit when trying to intimidate his adversaries. He worked out every day in an effort to maintain his physique, which, although it had softened with age, still showed traces of the high school wrestler in his square shoulders and barrel chest—attributes his custom-made suit emphasized.

"You look lovely today," he said. "How was your trip to surrogate's court?" he asked, knowing he was going to provoke her.

DeCovnie glared at him. "A waste of my time," she spit out. "Two hours of waiting for the judge." Then, turning her icy stare toward Harrison, she added, "Only to have him speak privately with my attorney for thirty seconds and tell us we could go."

"Any updates from the prosecutor's office on when we can get Charles's computers?" Martin asked, turning his attention to Harrison.

"I spoke with Tom Willis, and he assures me that once Ann is sentenced, we will get everything," Harrison responded with an air of confidence.

"For Christ's sake, she pled guilty and he's been dead for five months! I'm the fucking executrix of his estate! I need those computers!" DeCovnie screamed.

Conroy glanced over at Harrison. "Preston, I need to speak to Ms. DeCovnie privately. Check my schedule with Angela, and have her set aside some time for us this afternoon."

"Why do you keep that little twerp around?" DeCovnie growled once Harrison had left. "He's useless."

Conroy laughed. "I could lie to you and tell you that it's because he's a Harvard-educated lawyer, which he is, or that I admire his legal acumen, which I sometimes do. However, the reality is much simpler—his father owns sixty percent of the largest privately held pharmaceutical company in the country. So it turns out that Mr. Harrison is very good for the firm's bottom line." His smirk suggested it was a trade-off he was content to live with. "So what's on your mind this morning, Cassandra?"

She rubbed the bridge of her nose with her forefingers and lowered herself onto a couch. "What's on my mind?" she asked incredulously. "Are you serious, Martin? The same thing that's been on my mind for the last five months! We are dealing with an unmitigated disaster. Need I remind you that we still haven't found

Charles's hard drives, hard drives full of shit that could destroy a lot of people—you and me included. The prosecutor's office won't give us access to his computers. Arthur is apoplectic that the distribution list may well be on them. Not to mention that on either the desktop, laptop, or one of the hard drives, there is all his encrypted information on our offshore accounts. Without that information, we can't get access to those accounts. Your associate, young Mister Shit for Brains, thinks I'm upset because I can't get access to the hundred million–dollar estate. And as nice as that will be, we both know that there should be five or six times that in our offshore accounts." She exhaled. "That's what's on my mind, okay?"

"Cassie," Conroy began, leaning back in his chair, "I am acutely aware of the risk that exists with Charles's hard drives missing. I know from speaking with Charles that after Max and Carl had their tête-à-tête with that Mackey fellow, Charles thought he had solved the hacking problem. He told me that the IT guy had helped him move the financial information to the new laptop. However, I suspect that after the hacking Charles was a little spooked, so my guess is he hid the hard drives somewhere until he could secure all the data himself—certainly he wasn't going to allow the IT person to do that. Of course, he didn't plan on winding up dead," he added without the slightest hint of regret. "But I understand that still doesn't answer the question of where are the hard drives," he said calmly, his demeanor belying the fact that those questions were eating at him too. But he had learned long ago that in both the legal arena and the business world the scent of fear, like blood in shark-infested waters, could be deadly.

She curled a leg up underneath her. Although she had long ago given up her modeling career, she still maintained her willowy figure, which was accented by the navy blue Chloe suit she was wearing. "I was never as convinced as Charles that Mackey's demise eliminated the problem. Max and Carl said that Mackey denied being the person responsible right up until the end." She inhaled and slowly blew her breath out between her lips. "As to where Charles might have hidden the hard drives, I don't have a clue. I've been staying at his brownstone on East Sixty-Eighth for the last month, and they're not there. I told you when I arrived at his Westfield house on that Sunday and found him I looked for the hard drives before I called nine-one-one." She lowered her head. "I still kick myself for not taking his laptop before calling the police. If I had, we could have had access to those accounts five months ago."

He smiled politely. He shared her regret that she didn't take it, but he never put voice to it. He had his own tinge of regret for not answering her call when she discovered Charles's body, which resulted in her calling young Mister Shit for Brains, as she so aptly called him. Of course, he found his absolution in the fact that he had been cavorting with several young women at the time she called and his phone was off and she should have been astute enough to take the laptop without consulting with him.

"What about Ann? Do you think she could have taken the hard drives?" she asked.

"There's no reason to believe that she would even know about the hard drives," Conroy said darkly, masking his concern that Ann remained an unknown risk. For now her guilty plea served his purposes, but he was all too aware that her usefulness had an expiration date.

Martin leaned forward in his chair, stroking his lower lip as he considered the problems he had inherited from his business associate. "I never understood Charles's insistence on keeping her around. As you know, he was hardly the sentimental sort. Yet, despite the fact that she was—*is*—a danger to all of us, he allowed her to remain."

DeCovnie bit her lower lip. "I don't have to tell you that Charles was rather twisted. So, let's just say he enjoyed her ambiguity. After she almost committed suicide, I think he always felt it was only a matter of time until she tried again. But, in the meantime, he just continued to have his way with her. He didn't lose interest in her until she had the operation, and by then it would have been hard for her to disappear without raising suspicions." She paused. "And, as you know, Charles also had an insurance policy to make sure she stayed quiet. She knew that if she ever stepped out of line, Charles would have exacted his revenge."

Martin raised a finger to his lips. "It appears in that regard, Ms. DeCovnie, you have learned well."

She shook her head. "I never threatened anyone. I merely suggested that if she took responsibility, everyone would remain protected."

"Well played."

DeCovnie uncurled her leg, stood up, and walked toward the window, twirling a strand of her pearls around her finger. "Any luck finding the other one?" she asked.

"Nothing. We have the best on it, Sun International Security. My firm uses SIS on all of our sensitive cases. They're mostly former intel types—discreet and thorough, with great contacts worldwide. If she's out there, they'll find her.

"But she seems to have disappeared off the face of the earth," she said.

He turned to face her. "Oh, she's still on the face of the earth."

"You still think it was her?"

"Yes," he replied without hesitation.

"She disappeared over eleven years ago. Why would she come back now?"

He rubbed his fingers across his chin, his eyes taking on a distant look. "Because revenge is a dish best served cold." His eyes narrowed. "That's why we need to find her before she finds us."

# CHAPTER 13

MARILYN MACKEY'S LIVING ROOM WAS SMALL, BUT IT DIDN'T FEEL cramped, even with a shadow box, couch, and upright piano. Erin couldn't help but notice that other than a picture of Pope Benedict and a statue of the Virgin Mary, the only things decorating the walls and the shadow box were framed pictures of Justin, a photographic portrayal of his life from boyhood until his mid-twenties. The last picture captured the Justin whom Erin had gotten to know—a handsome twenty-something guy.

Erin made her way across the room to the upright piano in the far corner. Sitting on top of the piano were several photographs of a young boy about ten and a girl who appeared to be about eight. There were others of the girl, starting when she was a toddler through about the age of ten.

Marilyn walked into the room carrying a tray with two coffees. She noticed Erin looking at the pictures on top of the piano. She slowly bent over and placed the tray on the coffee table. "Those are mostly of Justin's sister, Joelle," she offered. "The two of them were very close as young children, Justin being eighteen months older. Joelle was diagnosed with leukemia when she was ten and she passed two years later."

"I'm sorry," Erin replied reflexively. Making her way back to the couch, Erin could see the sadness that covered Mrs. Mackey's face like a shroud. Dressed in slacks and a sweater, she wore her gray hair back in a frizzy bun and a pair of thick, dark-framed glasses that accentuated her lack of makeup. Erin found it impossible to pinpoint her age but suspected that she was probably younger than she looked.

"Thank you," she said, taking a seat opposite Erin. "You never get over the loss of a child. There isn't a day that goes by when I don't think of her and wonder what if she had lived." She closed her eyes. "I'm not sure Justin ever recovered from losing his sister. Perhaps some of that was my fault—I know I was never the same after Joelle passed." Then almost to herself, she added, "Now they're both gone."

Erin suddenly felt small and full of doubt about the merits of her plan. When Erin had spoken to her on the phone about wanting to meet with her, she had sensed Marilyn's reluctance. There was nothing that was going to bring back her son, she had told Erin. Why would she want to sue anyone? Just looking at Marilyn, Erin could see that she had been hollowed out by the loss of her children. How, Erin pondered, could she ask this woman who had lost both her children to join Erin's scheme?

"Please help yourself," Marilyn offered, pointing in the direction of the coffee.

"Thank you," Erin said, taking a seat on the couch and adding some sugar and milk to the coffee in front of her. When she finished, Erin looked up and found Marilyn studying her. "Is there something wrong?" Erin asked instinctively.

"I'm sorry. I didn't mean to stare, but if Justin hadn't told me I would never have guessed."

"Guessed what?" Erin asked.

"That you . . . that you were a man."

Erin winced, but held her tongue. She was here for a reason and right now she needed to stay focused on why she was here.

"I'm sorry," Marilyn said on seeing Erin's reaction. "I didn't mean to offend you. I meant it as a compliment."

"Thank you," Erin mumbled. She took a sip from her coffee to allow herself time to concentrate. "Mrs. Mackey, can we talk about Justin's murder?"

"Please call me Marilyn," she replied softly.

"Of course," Erin said. "I want to pursue whoever killed your son."

"I'm confused. Why are you involved? Aren't the police handling this?"

"Yes, actually solving the murder is a police matter. But I have certain information that I'd like to explore."

"So what does that have to do with me? As I told you on the phone, nothing can bring my son back. So if you'd like to explore it, you don't need my permission."

Erin leaned forward. "Mrs. . . . Marilyn, I think I know who is responsible for your son's murder, but to put the pieces together I need to meet with a woman who is in jail charged with the murder of the man I believe ordered Justin's execution. To get in to meet with her, I need a client. Justin's estate is the client I need."

Marilyn snorted. "Are you serious? Justin didn't have any estate. After he died, his car was repossessed, what little money he had was used to pay his bills, and I'm still paying the funeral parlor for his wake. Fortunately, Father Muscatello didn't charge me for Justin's funeral. I don't know where he got the money to pay for you in the criminal case, but you're wasting your time if you want to get money out of me."

Erin shook her head. "No. I can assure you that I'm not looking for money from you. Legally, we would need to do a retainer, but it would be strictly what's called a contingency fee. What that means is that the only thing Justin's estate would ever have to pay is if we ever recovered any money, my firm would receive a percentage of the recovery."

Marilyn began to fiddle at the buttons of her sweater. "Why do I feel like there's more you're doing here than just trying to find out who murdered my son?" she asked, a catch in her voice.

Should she lie? Erin looked past Marilyn, to the picture of Justin on the wall, bringing back the image of a panicked young man sitting in the diner, skipping town in an effort to stay alive. She was still haunted by the voice in her head that whispered she could have done more to help him. No, she quickly decided. Marilyn deserved the truth. Maybe knowing that it wasn't just about Justin would allow her to give some meaning to Justin's death.

"There is more involved," Erin finally said. "But where it's going to lead, I'm not sure."

They sat for another twenty minutes while Erin explained her suspicions as to why Justin had been murdered. When she was done, Marilyn looked stunned.

"What you're telling me is that he was murdered for something he didn't know anything about?"

"Based on what Justin told me, yes, that's my belief."

Marilyn leaned forward and, covering her face with her hands, slowly began to sob.

Erin felt powerless, not sure if she should try to comfort her or give her space. Torn as to what to do, Erin reached into her purse, removed a package of tissues, and made her way over to where Marilyn was sitting. "Here you go," Erin said, gently tapping Marilyn's arm.

Marilyn removed her hands from her face and took the offered tissues. "Thank you," she said, wiping her eyes, and then gently blowing her nose. After several minutes, her gaze made its way to the pictures on the shadow box. "I want nothing. Money can't give me back my son. Do you understand that, Erin? My child is gone. I'll never see him again—ever. Never hear him laugh, never see him get married, maybe have kids of his own. That's been taken from me, even if you find out who's responsible."

She looked at Erin with an inscrutable expression that caused Erin to steel herself for a "no."

"But," she continued with a sigh, "if you can find the people responsible for taking Justin's life, maybe his soul will be at peace."

Duane had slowly grown into the role of being a full-time lawyer, but sometimes he still missed the excitement of handling an investigation—the who-dunnit, how, and why. When he left the FBI, he interviewed with several large law firms, but it always felt like they wanted him less for his talents, but more so they could check off a box on one of their diversity forms—Black lawyer, check. The opportunity to join forces with Erin seemed like a more natural fit. They had known each other for years, meeting when Erin was dating Lauren and he was dating Corrine, who were college roommates. Of course, when they met and became friends and then started the firm together, Erin was still Ian. Like everyone, Duane had been shocked by the news. Ian was such a regular guy—how could he be trans? There had also been a part of him that was upset that Ian hadn't told him before they became partners, but both Corrine and Lauren had urged him to give it a try. And as strange as it was to watch his friend morph into this new persona, she seemed so at peace with who she was that within weeks of her coming back to work as Erin, they had settled into a new normal. He shook his head and smiled, trying to remember who she used to be. It had only been four years since she transitioned, but trying to picture her as anyone other than Erin seemed impossible.

Funny, he thought, how much appearances matter. When word of her transition first started to spread, he had caught some major shit from some of his buddies about practicing law with a "trannie." Then after they saw her, and realized she was an attractive woman, the talk faded away. He knew that it wasn't fair, but women were judged on what they looked like, just as he was judged on the color of his skin. There was one difference: The way Erin looked she could blend in as a woman, but he'd always be judged for being a Black man in a white world.

"Hey, how'd it go with Mrs. Mackey this morning?" Duane asked when Erin appeared in his doorway.

Erin reached into her briefcase, walked over to his desk, and handed him a signed copy of the retainer agreement.

"Well you certainly didn't waste any time," he said with a small chuckle.

"Time is one thing we don't have," she answered quickly. "Ann Parsons is due to be sentenced in three and a half weeks, and if she's going to withdraw her plea, her only real shot is to do it before she gets sentenced." She shook her head. "I was going to say the retainer is only a foot in the door to get to see Ann, but it's really only like a toe in the door. We still have to parlay this into a jail visit with her."

"Why do you keep saying 'we'? This is your case, remember?" he said with an impish grin.

"You're right," she said with a small smile. "All you agreed to do was look into the death of her mother. Find anything?"

"You expected me to do that this morning?" he teased.

"Yes!" she shot back.

He chuckled. "Oh, in that case . . ."

"Duane Abraham Swisher!"

"Relax. I got it—and, unfortunately, I think it's only going to suck you further into this case. . . ." He motioned for her to take a seat, grabbed the legal pad that was sitting on the side of his desk, and began to read his notes. "According to the obituary in the *New York Times*, Nancy Parsons, age thirty-one, died on Tuesday, November 12, 1991. Survived by her husband of three years, Charles Parsons, and her daughter, Ann, age eight."

"Cause of death?" Erin interrupted.

Duane looked up. "Patience, Ms. McCabe, patience," he said before returning his attention to his notes. "According to the *Times,* she died suddenly at their home on the Upper East Side. Through my sources at NYPD, I was able to get a copy of the police report. Found by the maid at the bottom of the staircase at one p.m. According to the maid, Mr. Parsons had left on a business trip the previous night and Mrs. Parsons had told her not to come in until the afternoon. The ME placed the time of death at between eight and nine a.m. Ann was in school at the time of the fall. No sign of foul play, no bruising inconsistent with a fall, so the ME ruled it an accident, speculating that her heel caught on the carpet on the steps and she broke her neck in a fall down the stairs."

Duane handed her a copy of the obituary.

Erin squeezed her lower lip between her thumb and forefinger. "I know it's a copy of a faded black-and-white photo, but she looks like she was a beautiful woman."

"Here's a better picture," he said, offering a color photo.

"Where did you find this?" Erin asked.

"A lot of searching and a little bit of luck. It's from February 1991 at the Grammy Awards."

The picture showed Parsons with a broad smile, standing in a black tuxedo, with his arm around the waist of his wife, who looked resplendent in a sea-green gown. She appeared petite, with a short blond bob and eyes that matched the color of her dress—she was stunning.

"You have the kind of money Parsons did, you get invited to a lot of places."

Erin handed the photo back to him. "Strange. She's so young and beautiful, full of life, and less than a year later, she's dead."

He nodded. "There's more. I did some further digging. Nancy Parsons, nee Slater, was born April 6, 1960, in Jersey City, the only child of John and Mary Slater. Her father was killed in Vietnam in 1968 and her mother died of breast cancer in 1979. In 1981 she married her high school sweetheart, Dennis Cooper, who was then a corporal in the marines. Looking at Ann's date of birth from the arrest report, she was born one month after her father was killed in the Beirut barracks bombing in October 1983."

"Jesus," Erin mumbled.

"In 1984, Nancy took a job with the New York Giants and 1986 became the assistant coordinator for the luxury boxes. That is where she apparently met Charles Parsons, whose company had a luxury box at the stadium. Again according to the *Times*, they were married in June of 1989 at the Plaza Hotel in New York, and in December of 1989, Charles adopted Ann and changed her name from Ann Cooper to Ann Parsons. So Parsons was her adoptive father and not her stepfather."

"Doesn't sound like there's much there. What do you think?"

"Actually, there is one more thing. It's tenuous at best, but worth looking into. I checked the obits to see if anyone died the same day under unusual circumstances in the general vicinity."

"And?" Erin asked.

"A Dr. Philip Davies was the victim of a hit-and-run accident around six thirty that morning while jogging in Central Park, something he did every morning. His office was six blocks south of where the Parsonses lived."

"Okay?"

"Turns out that on page three of the Metro section of the *Times* for the day the obits ran, there was an article reporting that the police considered the death of Dr. Davies to be suspicious. He was a pediatrician scheduled to meet with detectives in the Nineteenth Precinct later that morning—which, in case you're wondering, is the precinct for the Upper East Side of Manhattan."

She leaned back in her chair. "You're right; it's all very tenuous. There have to be a couple hundred thousand people who live on the Upper East Side. Not to mention this all happened seventeen years ago. Assuming there were dots to connect, I don't know how you're going to do it."

"How *I'm* going to do it?" he asked. "Remember, you only had one favor to ask me: Run down some info on Nancy Parsons's death. I got that for you. This is your wild goose chase, not mine. We have paying clients whose files need work."

"You're right," she said. "This is my mess." She slowly got out of the chair. "Can I take what you have?"

He put his notes, the police report, the copy of the photo, and copies of the *Times* articles back into a manila folder. "Sure," he said, handing it over.

"Thanks. This is all great stuff," she said. "I'll keep you posted if I find anything new."

With a big smile, she headed back to her office.

*Oh, that's so unfair,* he thought. He turned to face his computer screen to look at his e-mails. *I have enough to do without getting involved in this . . . this whatever it is. We don't even represent anyone. She's already pled guilty, for Christ's sake. It's insane.* He shook his head. *Ah, fuck it!*

He marched into Erin's office. "That was low."

"What? What did I do?" she asked, sounding bewildered.

"Don't give me that crap. You know what you did. You played the chick card."

"Swish, I don't know what you mean. I agreed with you. This is my mess, which you wanted no part of right from the start. You did what I asked. I'm not upset," she said.

"See, you just did it again. You're trying to make me feel guilty for not getting involved!"

Her eyes widened. "Now you're the one who's not being fair. I think you're right—this is a wild goose chase, which I'm sure has nothing to do with Justin's murder."

He stared at her for the longest time. "You know, if I hadn't known you before—"

She waved a finger in the air. "Don't you dare go there, Mr. Swisher."

He closed his eyes and plopped down in one of her chairs. "What do you need me to do?"

# CHAPTER 14

$E$RIN WAS ACCUSTOMED TO MEETING WITH CLIENTS IN JAIL; JUST part of the milieu in which she worked. And, because she was an attorney, those meetings usually took place in a room set aside specifically for lawyers to confer with their clients. Today was different. Ann Parsons was not her client, and so, like everyone else hoping to visit, Erin had lined up at the Union County jail at seven a.m. to make sure she got her visitor's pass to see Ann when morning visiting hours started at nine a.m. She had waited in the visitor's waiting area with all the other spouses, friends, and relatives waiting to visit. As she sat in the waiting room, she thought of Kluska, who had once again stuck his neck out, this time to get Erin on Ann's visitors list. Why? What was his motivation?

At exactly nine a.m., the correction officers began bringing the inmates into the visiting area. Erin had studied all the pictures she could find of Ann. She would only have a few short minutes to connect with Ann and convince her to keep talking. What Erin couldn't glean from the pictures, mainly height and weight, she had found in the arrest reports. As a result, Erin had a pretty good visual of Ann. Twenty-five years old, five feet six, one hundred fifty pounds, shoulder-length black hair, brown eyes, round face—a fairly average woman in most respects—certainly not as striking as her mother had been. And yet when Erin saw Ann enter the room she turned out to be smaller and thinner than expected. *Jail will do that to you*, she thought.

"Ms. Parsons?" Erin asked.

Ann looked up from the table, her expression conveying confusion over this stranger who knew her name. "Yes," she answered tentatively.

"My name is Erin McCabe. I'm an attorney and I was wondering if I could speak to you about a civil case I'm handling." When Ann's expression shifted from confusion to concern, Erin added, "The case I'm handling doesn't involve you directly. I've just been led to believe that you may have some information that could be helpful to my client."

"I don't know you. How did you get in to see me?"

Erin had suspected she might have to lie a little—now was as good a time as any to begin. "Because I'm an attorney investigating a case, and you potentially have information that may be helpful," she said, hoping Ann didn't have a sensitive bullshit detector, because if she did, there was a chance Ann could decide to just get up and ask a guard to leave.

Ann lowered her gaze. "Who did you say your client was?" she finally asked.

"I didn't say," Erin replied with a small smile. "May I sit down?"

Ann's gaze betrayed her wariness, but Erin decided to use her silence as acquiescence. Dropping into the orange plastic chair opposite Ann, she said, "I'm representing the estate of Justin Mackey in a potential lawsuit against the people responsible for his death."

Ann's eyes narrowed. "Look, Ms.—I'm sorry, what's your name?" she said softly.

"McCabe. Erin McCabe. Please call me Erin."

"Er . . . Erin, I don't know a Justin Mack, and definitely don't know anything about his death. I honestly have enough problems and really don't need any more right now."

"His name was Mackey, Justin Mackey, and he was about your age," Erin said slowly, her face conveying the loss she still felt over Justin's death. "Ann," Erin continued, shifting consciously to using her first name, "I promise this will not get you in trouble. I know you don't know anything directly about his death, but you may have information that could be helpful. Can you give me five minutes?"

Ann looked nervously toward the guards and shrugged.

*Focus on Justin's mom,* Erin thought. Ann had lost her mom at a young age; maybe that was a way in. "Justin's mom was devastated when he died. So she's hired me to see if I could sue those responsible for his death. I feel so bad for his mother. She's now lost both her children. Justin had a sister who died at the age of twelve from leukemia."

Ann was back to looking at the table; it was impossible to tell if she was getting through.

"Justin worked with computers," Erin continued. "And in particular with a type of software called encryption software. Unfortunately for Justin, he got mixed up with some people who were involved in illegal gambling operations, as well as, I suspect, more serious types of crime." There was still no reaction from Ann. "The day before he died, Justin came to me in a panic. He had installed some software on computers for some rich and powerful people. I suspect one of those people was your father."

At that, Ann looked up, but her face still betrayed no reaction.

"The day before he was murdered, Justin got a call saying some of Justin's clients were pissed because they had discovered a problem with the software. Justin didn't know what the problem was, but he suspected that the guy who designed the software—the one who called him to warn him—had embedded a virus in it. If I could find this guy, the guy Justin worked for, it would be a good start."

"I don't know why you think I would know these people," Ann said, picking at a scab on the top of her hand. "I wasn't involved in my father's business at all."

Erin frowned. "No, I understand. I'm just wondering if you know a guy by the name of Luke."

"No, I'm sorry. I don't."

"Justin sometimes referred to him as Lucas," Erin added.

"No. I don't believe so," Ann replied.

Undeterred by Ann's answers, Erin continued. "Justin didn't

know everything these people were involved in, but he knew they were dangerous." She stopped and waited until Ann looked up. "A day after Justin met with me, he was murdered. Assassinated with a bullet to the back of his head and stuffed in the trunk of a car."

Ann's eyes widened, but rather than opening up, Ann seemed to withdraw even further into her silence.

"Ann, I'm sorry. I'm sure this is a very difficult time for you. I understand what it's like for people awaiting sentencing. Almost all I do is defend people charged with criminal offenses, which is why I was representing Justin in the first place. I only took on this case for his mom because someone murdered her son in cold blood and I'm trying to prevent them from getting away with it."

After what seemed like an eternity, Ann spoke. "It's horrible what happened to your client. I'm very sorry for his mom's loss. But my father is dead. I've admitted to killing him." Erin immediately made a mental note of her choice of words. *I've admitted,* not *I killed.* "So even if he was somehow wrapped up in what happened to your client, I don't know how I can help."

Erin had to be careful. She didn't represent Ann, so there was no attorney-client privilege. Right now, Erin could be compelled to testify about anything Ann said.

"Ann, what would you think if I told you that there are people, me included, who don't think you killed your father?"

Ann laughed uncomfortably. "I'd think you didn't know what you're talking about," she said, looking away and picking at her hand.

The next move was critical: Go at Ann too strong, and she'd lose her for good. Not strong enough, and Ann would call her bluff and the game would be over. Somehow Erin had to find a way to thread the needle—time for one more piece of creative speculation based on a theory Duane had put together. Suppose Ann's pediatrician had found out she was being abused and had warned her mother. If Parsons was a child abuser, he could also have been into child pornography, which could tie back into encryption software. So use the theory, but alter the content and attribution a little. "Justin told me that he thought some of the people using the encryption software were involved in the child pornography business." Ann bit down on her lower lip, but said nothing. "Including your father," Erin added. "I think that's why Justin was murdered."

Ann closed her eyes, but said nothing. Finally she looked up. "I'm sorry. I can't help you."

Erin had one last Hail Mary to throw. Normally, as a lawyer she could give her client a business card, or even write her information on a piece of paper, but today she was just a member of the public visiting an inmate. No exchanges were allowed.

"Maybe after I leave, you'll think of something that could be helpful. If you want to check me out, I know they have computers in the library here. Not sure how much time you get on them, but if you search my name, you'll get my firm and contact information." Erin winced a little. "You'll also see a lot of stuff online about me and some of the cases I've handled." Erin paused for effect. "I guess I should warn you, I had a case last year that got a lot of press, so a lot of the links deal with the fact that I'm transgender. I hope that doesn't bother you."

For the first time, Ann made eye contact, her brow furrowed. She tilted her head ever so slightly, as if to get a better look at Erin. "You had that case with the prostitute. The one who was charged with murder? That was you. You were all over the papers."

"Yeah, that was me," Erin replied, holding eye contact with Ann. "I guess, depending on your point of view, that case either made me famous or infamous."

Ann lowered her head. "I want . . . I need to think about things," she mumbled.

"That's fine," Erin replied, hoping she had struck a chord.

"Can you . . . would you maybe have time to come back Friday?" Ann said to the table.

"Sure," Erin responded, trying not to sound too excited. "I'll see you Friday at one p.m. Thank you for your time, Ann."

The unprotected bottom of the metal legs squealed across the linoleum floor as Erin slid the plastic chair back and slowly rose from the table. "I'll see you on Friday." She turned quickly and made her way out of the visiting room, trying to get out before Ann could change her mind.

Duane had already been through the prosecutor's office's analysis of Ann's e-mails; now he was poring over their review of six months of Ann's cell phone and landline records, looking for common threads: frequently called numbers, long phone calls, anything that might offer a clue as to what Ann had been up to in the weeks and months leading up to her father's murder. Like the prosecutor's office, he had come up with nothing. Ann's life appeared, at least from her phone records, to be as bland as white bread.

Still, he made a note of one number that she'd called twice, a week apart, both times shortly before nine a.m. on a Monday. There was also the fact that there were no calls to any number belonging to her father. They could have seen one another in person, Duane mused, but not a single call in a six-month period seemed odd.

Then he went looking for her alibi. In her first statement to the police, she claimed that she was in a Hoboken bar waiting for a date the night he was killed, and that her date had called to cancel because he had to work late. He grabbed the phone records and ran his finger down the list of calls until he got to the Friday night of the murder—nothing incoming, nothing outgoing. So had she lied about the call, or did she have another phone? Erin had mentioned a burner phone that had been seized during the search of Ann's condo. He pulled out those records, which showed she had used it only after her father's death, not before. No help there.

He pulled out the analysis of her bank records. For someone whose father was worth an estimated $100 million, apart from living in one of his million-dollar condos, she certainly didn't appear to be some spoiled little rich kid. Based on her bank statements, she lived a very frugal lifestyle and didn't appear to have access to any of her daddy's wealth. She made sixty-five thousand a year as a paralegal in the banking and finance department of McKenna & Ross. According to the police report, on the fifteenth of every month she took out $2,000 in cash and gave that to her father to cover utilities, condo fees, and general upkeep. Figuring in taxes that meant she was giving almost half of her take-home pay to her father in cash, which made no sense. Two thousand dollars was pocket change to Charles Parsons. Why would he make her do that?

He had read the reports; this should have been an open-and-shut case. So why were there so many pieces that just didn't seem to fit?

He decided to follow up on the phone number Ann had called twice, which came back to a cell phone listed to a Marsha Kramer in Brooklyn. A quick Internet search revealed that she was a paralegal in the banking and finance department of McKenna & Ross. The investigator's instincts kicked in and he quickly thought through what he would say to her before picking up the phone and dialing Marsha Kramer's work number. Hopefully, she'd agree to meet.

# CHAPTER 15

"Ms. Kramer?" Duane asked the young woman sitting at the table.

She looked up, seemingly taken aback by the large Black man hovering over her.

"Duane Swisher," he offered.

She continued to stare at him, saying nothing. "Thank you for coming, especially on a Friday morning," Duane said with a small smile. "Can I get you a coffee?" he inquired, noticing she had nothing in front of her. "I'm going to grab one. They sometimes frown on people sitting here without buying anything."

She looked around the Starbucks, and finally nodded. "A vanilla latte, please."

"Got it," Duane said, trying again to give her a reassuring smile, as well as trying not to read too much into the look she had given him.

As he waited in line, he viewed her from the corner of his eye. She looked to be around the same age as Ann, mid- to late twenties, with black curly hair that framed her round face. He wasn't sure if he was unnerving her or if it was something else, but from the way she was gripping her bag in her lap, she appeared to be on edge. So nervous in fact, he was concerned that she might leave before they even had a chance to talk.

"Here you go," Duane said, sliding the latte over as he took a seat. "I appreciate you taking the time to meet with me," he began. "I know this is your morning break—"

"Can I see some proof that you are who you say you are?"

Duane nodded; reached into his jacket pocket and removed his credentials, which showed him as a former FBI agent, along with a business card; and handed them across the table to her. She examined the photo, then looked up at him. "I thought you said you're a lawyer. This says FBI Special Agent."

"You'll see that it says I've resigned in good standing. I was an agent. Just a lawyer now," he said with a wry grin.

"Am I in some kind of trouble?" she asked.

Duane's poker face didn't reveal his surprise at her question. *Why would she think she might be in trouble?*

"Not with me, you're not," he said. "As I explained on the phone, a woman whose son was murdered has retained my firm and we believe that Charles Parsons, Ann's father, may have been involved in some way. So we're just trying to follow up on some leads. My partner, Erin McCabe, has spoken with Ann already." As he spoke, Duane kept his focus on Marsha, trying to read her facial expressions and body language, looking for any tells that he could utilize.

"Are you saying Ann may have been involved in another murder?"

He had learned as an agent that if your subject gave you an unexpected opening exploit it. "No. I'm not suggesting that at all," he replied, then leaned forward as though he was sharing a confidence. "Honestly, between us, I know Ann pled guilty, but I don't think she killed her father."

Her eyes studied his face, seemingly looking for signs of a trap. She took a deep breath and he watched her shoulders relax. "I don't think she did either," she finally said, barely above a whisper.

"Well, it's nice to know that I'm not alone," he said. "Why do you think that?"

Her eyes glanced around the room. "I've worked with Ann for over three years now, and I didn't even know who her father was until it was in the newspapers. She's a really quiet, nice person. I can't imagine her hurting anyone."

"Was she upset when he died?"

Marsha seemed to stiffen again, and she reached down and began fiddling with the zipper on her purse. "Um, I don't know. We really didn't talk too much about it. She was out for about a week after he was killed, and she was arrested a few days after coming back. I haven't seen her since."

"From what I've been told, her father was a bad guy," Duane said, trying to keep the conversation going.

Her expression suddenly turned suspicious. "I'm not sure why you want to speak with me. I don't know anything about Ann's life."

Duane's instincts were all telling him she was hiding something, but for the life of him he couldn't figure out what. "The reason I reached out to you was that according to Ann's phone records, in the two weeks before her father's murder, Ann called you two Monday mornings in a row shortly before eight a.m. Do you recall why?"

The slightest of smiles formed on Marsha's lips and she seemed to momentarily relax. "Actually, yeah. We were working on the same transaction, and the partner on the file is a real stickler and wanted us in the office by eight a.m. On both occasions she called me to tell me the PATH train was late and she'd be in about thirty minutes late." She paused and her smile broadened. "The second time it happened, when she got to work, I said, 'Ann, I didn't hear anything about PATH being delayed this morning.' And she kind of looked at me and sheepishly admitted she'd been out late the night before on a date. I remember thinking to myself, 'Well, good for you.'"

"She tell you anything about the person she was dating?"

"No. I was surprised she told me as much as she did. Like I said, she's quiet, really reserved—this was the first time she ever mentioned seeing someone."

"She did tell the police she'd been stood up by a date the night her father was murdered. What's weird is that I've been through all her phone records, and other than you, she wasn't calling anyone. It's almost as if she had another phone."

Marsha pursed her lips and, as she had earlier when she ap-

peared nervous, began to play with the zipper on her bag. Her reaction was everything Duane was hoping for, so he went all in.
"Do you know if she had another phone?" he asked.

She looked at the table for a long time. When she looked up
her face was pained. "I don't want to get in trouble!" she blurted.

*Be careful. You're not her lawyer,* he warned himself.

"I don't want to get you in any trouble. What are you concerned about?"

She closed her eyes. "Suppose, hypothetically, that Ann gave
me something to hold for her."

"Okay," he responded.

"And suppose the police never interviewed me or asked me if I
had anything belonging to Ann."

"So far it doesn't sound like you've done anything that you
could get in trouble for," he replied.

She reached down, opened the zipper on her purse, and took
out a black cell phone and held it in her hand.

"Um, so the day Ann was arrested, she was upset—no, not
upset, nervous. She told me that she had to leave work early because the police wanted to talk to her again about her father. She
said she didn't know what it was all about, but she seemed concerned about it. She said everything was okay, but . . . then she
reached into her desk and took out this phone." Marsha paused,
looking at the phone she held in her right hand. "She handed
this to me and asked me to hold on to it for her, and that if anything happened to her to please throw it away. I asked her what
she was worried about, and she just repeated that if she died or
got arrested just throw it away." Marsha looked embarrassed. "Obviously I didn't, because I worried it might be tampering with evidence. So I held on to it, thinking that at some point the police
would interview me, and I'd give it to them, but they never did."

"Have you contacted the police to let them know you have it?"

She shook her head no.

"Didn't the police come and search her work space?" Duane
asked, dumbstruck that the police hadn't spoken to her coworker.

"I was told they came to the office, but I was at a closing that day and no one's ever contacted me." She put the phone on the table and pushed it across to him. "I don't want it. You're a former FBI guy, you take it."

He looked at the phone sitting on the table. *What the fuck?*

She abruptly got up from the table. "Please, I don't need any problems and I don't want to get into trouble," she said, her eyes wide, the fear evident in her face. "I need to get back." She quickly turned and walked out, leaving her vanilla latte and the cell phone sitting on the table.

After Marsha left, Duane considered how to deal with the gift he had just been handed. Had there still been an active investigation of Parsons's murder his obligation would have been clear—Ann's phone would have been evidence. But Ann had pled guilty—the investigation was closed. No one could allege that he obstructed justice, and if what Marsha said was accurate, she hadn't violated any laws either. At this point, the safest thing to do would be to take it to an expert and have it examined. He knew just the right person for the job—someone beyond reproach who testified for both law enforcement and defendants alike. He took out his own phone and scrolled through his list of contacts. *May as well try to reach her now*, he thought as he called her number.

Connie Irving walked out of her office into the waiting room. She was dressed casually in jeans and a sweater. Her shoulder-length black hair hung in tight curls. "Mr. Swisher," she said with a warm smile, walking over to where Duane was standing and giving him a hug. "It's been a while. Four years?"

"More like five," Duane responded, quickly calculating how long he'd been out of the FBI. Like Duane, Connie Irving was a former FBI Special Agent. Unlike Duane, Connie had voluntarily left the FBI, deciding to capitalize on her expertise in cell phone technology by forming her own company, Irving Cellular Forensics, which offered consulting services, primarily to lawyers. "Thank you for making the time to see me on no notice," Duane continued.

"Well, you're lucky on two fronts: first, that I was here—I just got back from Seattle yesterday—and secondly, I'm still so pissed off at the Bureau for railroading you that I'm only too happy to see if I could help you."

"Thanks," he replied, feeling a twinge of satisfaction that there were other agents who knew he had been set up and forced out.

"Coffee?" she offered.

"No. Thank you. Already reached my limit for the day."

"Then come with me and you can tell me what was so urgent." She led him into the pristine office and gestured to a couch and chair by a sleek bay of windows.

Her walls were lined with her awards and pictures, mostly from her fifteen-year career as an agent. There was one of her shaking hands with FBI Director Mueller as he was handing her a commendation and another with her and Attorney General Ashcroft.

They spent several minutes catching up and discussing mutual acquaintances from their days at the Bureau, but then she turned to business. "Duane, I don't want to rush you, but I'm squeezing you in and I have a conference call in about fifteen minutes."

"That's fine," he replied. "That's about all the time I have because I have to try and reach my partner before eleven a.m." He explained as quickly as he could what he and Erin were doing and how he had come into possession of a cell phone. He removed the phone from his jacket pocket and laid it on the coffee table.

"Can you check the call history for me?" he asked. "Secondly, assuming there are calls in the history, can you get me any information on the location of the phones when the calls were made? Depending on what you find, I may need you both for chain of custody on the phone and as an expert witness."

She nodded. "Call history is easy if it hasn't been deleted. Even a burner phone keeps an internal call history. That's why you burn them when you're done." She reached down and took the phone off the table. "Follow me," she said, leading Duane to a door on the right-hand side of her office. Inside was a room lined with worktables, computers, and other electronic equipment.

"Well, now I know why your office doesn't look like you do any work there. This is where the magic happens," Duane said with a chuckle.

Connie laughed as she went to a bin containing a tangle of cell phone chargers. When she found what she wanted, she plugged it into the phone.

"Give it a minute or so to charge, and then we'll take a look at the call history." She pulled out a stool and sat down. "As for cell tower location . . . that I can't help you with. Between us, when I was with the Bureau, we would occasionally get it without a search warrant, but sooner or later the courts are going to find you need a warrant or a subpoena to get that information. Now that I'm outside the Bureau, there's no way to get it absent a subpoena."

She swiveled her stool around and picked up the phone. Soon enough, the screen powered up. She hit a few buttons and scrolled down. "Interesting," she said, mostly to herself. "When was the murder again?"

"April eleventh."

"There's only two numbers ever called on this phone. One number was called every . . . what day of the week was the eleventh?"

"A Friday," he replied.

"So it looks like the one number is called every Sunday afternoon at around four p.m. The other was called more random, but it was called three times the night of the eleventh, between seven thirty p.m. and nine p.m. There's also one incoming call from an unknown number at nine forty p.m. on the eleventh." She turned back to her computer and typed in the phone number. "I can't be sure without doing a more thorough search, but it looks like both numbers being called are burner phones."

She took out a pad and wrote down the two numbers, then tore the sheet off the pad and handed it over. "I'm going to have to get on my call, and you said you have a call to make. Give me a day or so and I'll send you a complete breakdown of the call history."

"Thanks. If we ever do get in this case, what are you charging these days?"

"Five hundred an hour; three thousand for a report; minimum five thousand to testify."

He whistled. "No wonder you left the Bureau."

She shrugged. "When I saw what people with less experience than me were charging in the private sector, I decided it was time

I took care of myself. I have two kids to put through college some-day, and it's sure as hell going to be a lot easier to do that on what I'm making now than what I was making as a fed."

"I hear you," he replied.

"Keep me posted on whether you get in the case or not. If you do, and the call history helps your defense, you'll turn over my re-port in discovery and the prosecutor's office is going to demand the phone. Once they have it, I guarantee they'll run the cell tower information, which they'll be obligated to give to you in discovery."

"Thanks," he replied with a grin.

As he walked back to the subway he called Erin and filled her in on getting the phone from Marsha Kramer and his visit to Connie Irving. Erin agreed with him that the calls on the night of the murder were interesting, but not necessarily exculpatory for Ann.

Walking down the steps to the Number 2 subway, he thought about Connie's comment that he had been railroaded out of the FBI. He had long harbored those thoughts, but never said them out loud to anyone other than Ben, his lawyer; Corrine; and Erin. He was surprised that others perceived it that way. One of the proudest days of his life had been when he walked across the stage on graduation day at Quantico and received his credentials as an FBI Special Agent. For a long time he had tried to convince himself that race had nothing to do with why he had been targeted as the person who leaked information about the profiling of Muslim Americans by the FBI following 9/11. But he was no longer so sure. He remembered the first time he had met their client Sharise Barnes and told her that he was a former agent. When she asked him why he wasn't still an agent, he had told her that they thought he had broken the rules. She had given a full-throated laugh and said, "Why, they didn't realize you were Black when they hired you?" He had loved being an agent, but maybe it was time to recognize that the love was unrequited.

Connie Irving was in the middle of her call when two men walked in. Each held a 9mm pistol with suppressors attached.

"Hang up," the taller of the two commanded.

She lowered the phone from her ear and placed it back in the cradle.

"Just do as you're told and we'll be gone in a minute."

The adrenaline focused her senses on his choice of words and the suppressors attached to their pistols.

"The guy who was just here gave you a phone, right?"

If she lied, she'd be shot on the spot. At least giving them what they wanted might spare her.

"Yes," she replied softly.

"Where is it?"

"Locked in the file cabinet in my work space, which is next door."

"Let's go," he said, gesturing with his gun. "And don't try anything stupid."

She opened the door to her workspace. She needed to do something—once they had the phone it would be too late.

"Where's the file cabinet?" he demanded. She pointed to one in the corner, next to her worktable.

"Give me the key."

"It's a combination lock," she said, a catch in her voice.

"Open it. And remember, I have a gun pointed at the back of your head."

She worked the dial slowly—right, left, right—and then gave a slight tug on the door.

"Step away," he ordered.

She stepped to her right, allowing him to move forward. He shifted his gun to his left hand and took hold of the handle with his right. That's when she struck.

Her fist caught him squarely on the Adam's apple, causing him to drop his gun as he tried to raise both hands to his throat. As he did, she grabbed his head and spun him around so he was in front of her. His partner, initially caught off guard, opened fire.

# CHAPTER 16

*E*RIN PACED THE WAITING ROOM, ANXIOUS FOR VISITING HOURS TO start. She kept turning over in her head what Duane had told her about Ann's second burner phone. What did it mean? Without cell tower information, they couldn't be sure where Ann was the night Parsons was murdered, only that she was making calls around the time he was murdered. The cell tower information could either back up her alibi or put her at her father's house in Westfield. Of course, there was a third possibility: Ann wasn't the one who had pulled the trigger, but was coordinating with the person who did. However you cut it, two out of three didn't look great for Kluska's theory of her innocence. Maybe, Erin thought, she had allowed herself to fall into the trap of making the facts fit her desire that Ann be innocent, rather than allowing the facts to dictate the answer.

And yet, based on what Duane had just learned, there was also the second number that Ann called every week. The regularity reminded Erin of her calls to Lauren when they were dating in college: seven o'clock every Sunday evening, like clockwork. In the dark ages before cell phones, a set time had been the only way they could make sure they'd connect via pay phones. Erin flinched, surprised by how even now, years after their divorce, revisiting her relationship with Lauren could still sting like peeling back a scab to expose a wound.

*Refocus,* she thought. What was the best way to play this with Ann? Confront her directly, or take a more subtle approach? She was still undecided when the corrections officers started leading the inmates into the visiting area. One after another, they filed in and began taking seats. Soon, the last inmate walked through the metal-barred door. The CO standing at the door gave the signal to the control room to close and lock it.

Ann hadn't come.

Erin approached the CO. "Excuse me, I'm visiting with Ann Parsons and she isn't here."

The CO looked at Erin indifferently. "Lady, if she isn't here, she either didn't feel like seeing you, or she's on lockdown for some reason. Nothing I can do about either situation."

"Hi, Connie, what's up?" Duane answered when he saw her number displayed.

"Mr. Swisher?" a male voice responded.

"Yes. Who's this?" Duane asked, startled by the male voice.

"My name is Detective Barry, NYPD."

"Is Connie okay?"

"No. Ms. Irving has been shot."

"Shot! What the hell are you talking about? I just left her twenty minutes ago. Is she okay? Where is she?"

"She's on her way to the ER at Bellevue. She asked me to call you, because she said it had to do with a phone you wanted analyzed."

Duane breathed again, taking comfort that Connie had been conscious and able to communicate. "I'm on my way."

"Good. Ask for me when you get here."

Even on a good day, the ER at Bellevue was a madhouse—today wasn't a good day. Duane, who had been right outside the PATH station when Barry called, had gotten to the hospital in fifteen minutes. Twenty minutes later he was still waiting for Barry to show his face.

"Swisher," a short, stocky, balding white guy in a rumpled suit called out from the door leading into the medical section of the ER.

"Yo!" Duane hollered back, rushing over.

"Barry," he said, offering his hand.

"Swisher," Duane replied, shaking his hand. "Is Connie okay?"

"I think she'll be okay," he said in a voice honed by a Staten Island upbringing and thirty years of a two-pack-a-day habit. "They stabilized her—she lost a fair amount of blood. Glad you got here so quickly. They're about to take her up for a CT scan, but from what the doc told me, she's got two bullets in her. Husband's on his way. Follow me."

Duane followed Barry through the maze of the ER. Barry seemed to know instinctively when to zig and zag between the rows of cubicles until he came to the one he wanted. "Ms. Irving? Mr. Swisher is here. Can we talk?"

"Duane?" she said weakly.

"Yeah, it's me. Can we come in?"

"Please," she replied.

Barry pulled back the curtain. Connie was propped up with the head of the bed elevated. The left shoulder of her hospital gown was pulled down, exposing the packing over a shoulder wound. In her right arm there were two IVs, one with blood, the other saline.

"Hey, you okay?" he asked.

She gave him a weak smile. "Peachy," she replied, turning to gaze at her left shoulder.

"What the hell happened?" he asked.

"Apparently you weren't the only person interested in that phone. About ten minutes after you left, two guys came in looking for it."

She related that they knew that he had just left a phone with her. When she saw the suppressors on their guns and that they weren't concealing their faces, she figured her life expectancy was down to minutes. Fortunately, her FBI training had kicked in and allowed her to take advantage of their carelessness.

"Apparently, two of the bullets that hit the guy I was using as a shield passed through him and lodged in me—one in my left shoulder, the other in my right thigh. And as much as that sucks, my shield bore the brunt of it. Detective Barry here tells me he didn't make it."

Duane glanced at Barry, who nodded.

"What about the other guy?"

"Took off as soon as he realized he shot his partner," she said.

"Connie, I'm so sorry. I had no idea."

"It's okay, Duane. I didn't think you walked me into a trap. Just remember this when you get my bill," she said with a grin.

"By the way," she continued, "I thought of something after you left. You said the woman you may represent is accused of killing a guy named Charles Parsons. That name struck a chord. Do you know an agent by the name of Celeste Roberts?"

"Name rings a bell."

"Good woman. She's with the Bureau's Child Exploitation and Human Trafficking Task Force. I seem to remember the task force looking at a guy by the name of Parsons right around the time you left. Worth a call."

They spoke for a few more minutes until the orderly came to wheel her up to Radiology for a scan.

After Connie was wheeled out, Duane and Barry headed to the cafeteria for a coffee and so Duane could give a statement. When they were done, Duane left a message for Erin as to what was happening.

Now that he was finally alone, his mind turned inward. *How the hell could I be so fucking stupid?* He had been followed to his meeting with Marsha, then to Connie's office. His failure to pick up on the tail had almost cost Connie her life. He lowered his head, looking into his third cup of coffee. He still blamed himself for the death of a witness in another case. She'd been thrown off a roof shortly after speaking with him. The image of her flailing her arms, desperately trying to fly as she fell, still haunted him.

If, as they suspected, Mackey's murder was tied to Parsons, he should have seen the risk. These guys played for keeps and he and Erin were poking the bear. *No more fuckups.*

He made a few calls before he finally got hold of an agent he knew who was still assigned to the Newark FBI office, who connected him to Special Agent Celeste Roberts.

"Roberts," she answered brusquely.

"Agent Roberts. My name is Duane Swisher. I'm a former agent. Connie Irving suggested I give you a call."

There was a short pause. "Swisher . . . I remember you. How you doing, and how the hell is Connie? I miss that woman."

"I'm fine, but I'm at the hospital because Connie's up in radiology right now. She was shot."

"Shot! What?"

Duane proceeded to explain to Roberts what he knew about what had happened to Connie, and about the case he and Erin were looking into. When she heard that the murder victim was Charles Parsons, she interrupted him. "Parsons from Westfield?" she asked.

"Yeah, that's the guy."

"Interesting," she said almost to herself. "Off the record?"

"Sure."

"Even off the record, you know I can't say too much. Besides, I didn't even work that case—my recollection is that Jodi Collins had the lead. But what I remember is that back in 2001, right after the Human Trafficking Task Force was formed, there was an active investigation on Parsons and a number of other folks connected to him. I don't know the details, except the rumors were that it involved kids. One thing I do recall is that just when everyone here thought the bad guys were going to be rounded up and charged, the plug got pulled and the case disappeared. Collins and a few others who worked it were furious. I thought she was going to resign."

"She still on the job?"

"Yeah, but she's as straight as they come. She probably wouldn't even confirm to you that there was an investigation of Parsons." She hesitated. "Listen, if at some point you really need to talk to her, let me know. I can probably run interference for you."

"Just out of curiosity, why are you helping?"

There was a long silence. "Connie's good people. If she told you to call, that's good enough for me. Besides, I told you, I remembered you. In this office, those of us who were here at the time all know about you because we all know who leaked—and it wasn't you. So you're a cautionary tale around here. If you could be scapegoated, any one of us could be next."

It was almost seven p.m. by the time Duane got back to the office to fill Erin in on what he knew. After her scan, they had taken Connie to surgery to remove the bullets. Surgery had gone well, and she was in stable condition and expected to make a full recovery. The shooter was still at large, but the dead man had been identified as Max Gallagher. The phone Duane had gotten from Marsha Kramer was now in an NYDP evidence locker.

When Duane finished, Erin leaned forward in her chair and rested her head in her hands. "My brain hurts," she said. "Who's willing to murder to get Ann's phone? And, more importantly, why? She pled guilty, for Christ's sake. Who thinks she's still a threat?" She bit her lower lip. "Maybe we should just call it a day."

Duane leaned back in his chair. He didn't have all the facts yet, but, like Kluska, his gut was screaming at him that there was a lot more here. Plus, whoever was behind this had tried to take out Connie. He locked eyes with Erin. "No. Now I'm pissed. I'm in."

She turned her head slightly, her eyes narrowing. "Okay," she said. "So, what's it all mean?"

"Not sure," he said with a sigh, "but clearly someone is worried about what might be on Ann's phone. I guess it could be the person she called three times that night?"

Erin ran through the various possibilities in her head. "Well, if we're still going with Ann's innocent, those calls could have been her calling the date who stood her up."

"Yeah, but why use a burner phone for that?"

"To keep Daddy from knowing she was seeing someone?" Erin said. "Her regular cell phone was on his bill, so he could see everyone she called."

Duane nodded. "Good point."

Erin exhaled. "Unfortunately, if she doesn't want to see me anymore, this is all academic."

"Tell that to Connie Irving," Duane responded. "Bet she doesn't think it's academic."

"Touché," Erin replied. "But the fact remains, without Ann as our client, I don't know where we go."

"It's not just Ann. There's more." Duane filled her in on his call with Celeste Roberts and how unusual it was for an agent to share any information, even on an investigation that had been closed for years.

Erin frowned. "What if, as you speculated, Parsons was an abuser and what if he had abused Ann? She's not the biggest person in the world—and Parsons was a big guy—well, suppose she was terrified of him and wanted to take him out. Maybe she'd hire someone to do her dirty work."

"That could explain the calls the night of the murder," Duane said.

"It could also explain why she's taking the hit—she was involved and she's protecting whoever else was involved."

He snorted. "You realize, there's a lot of 'what-ifs' in there. Two minutes ago you speculated that the calls were consistent with her date not showing."

"Shitty coincidence getting stood up the night your dad gets murdered," she said.

"No kidding," he said.

The room was silent, the only noise coming from Cheryl, making copies down the hall.

"I think I need to meet with Detective Kluska," Erin finally said.

"I was thinking the same thing. He's our only shot at you getting back in to see Ann. Any way to contact him without the risk of exposing him?"

She smiled, took out her BlackBerry, scrolled for a few seconds, and then started typing away. **Softball team is having a reunion tomorrow at 11 a.m. Hope you can make it—usual place**. Before she hit SEND, she read it to him. "That's innocuous enough, right?"

"Yeah, I have no idea what it means. But you realize tomorrow is a Saturday. Wherever the usual place is, it could be crowded."

"Nah, it's a bar. That's when it opens. Won't be anybody else in the place for at least an hour. We'll be done in half an hour."

The next day, Erin waited for Kluska in the same booth at the back of the Liberty Tavern. Two glasses of orange juice sat on the table, the one in front of her was half empty, the one across from her, full. She still wasn't convinced he was coming, because about an hour after she had texted him, he'd replied, **Really? It's a fucking Saturday!** to which she'd replied, **Hate to break it to you but beauty sleep won't help you. Be there.**

At ten after eleven, he walked in the door. This time he didn't hesitate, just headed right toward the back booth. She smiled—in his jeans and Grateful Dead T-shirt Kluska could still do undercover work in any biker bar in the country.

He plopped down opposite her. "Nice message. I guess you get some credit for not being stupid."

"Nice to see you too," she responded.

"McCabe, I put my career in jeopardy the first time I met with you, but that was my choice. This time it's not my choice, and I'm really not happy about being here."

"So drink your orange juice, listen to what I have to say, and you'll be out of here in twenty minutes."

Kluska scowled. "Nobody talks to me like that."

"I just did. Get over it. Do you want to help her or not?"

His shoulders tensed and his hand curled into a fist. "Go ahead," he muttered through clenched teeth.

"This time I need your assurance that this meeting is just like our first—it never happened."

Kluska gave a jerk of the head she took as a nod.

She told him about her meeting with Ann; what Duane had found out about Nancy Parsons; Ann having a second burner phone that they had secured; the two numbers that had been called; and the attempt to steal the phone, which almost cost Connie Irving her life. Then she told him about her second visit to the jail, when Ann didn't show.

"So what am I supposed to do?" he asked.

"How'd you get me on her visitors list to begin with?"

His look betrayed his reluctance.

"Jesus, Ed, you really think I'm going to sell you out? I'm telling you stuff you don't even know. Come on, in for a penny, in for a pound," she said.

He rubbed his chin. "I have a friend who's a captain at the jail. Said I knew a lawyer who needed to interview Parsons on a civil case before she got sent off to state prison, and asked him to put you on her list as a favor."

"So call him and tell him that when I went back at her request, she didn't show, so I was wondering if she was on lockdown. If she's on a disciplinary detention, it can't be more than seven days, and I'll still have a shot at seeing her. If she just blew me off—well, then, I'm not sure either you or I can help her."

Kluska picked up his glass of orange juice, downed it, and banged the glass back down on the table. "I'll let you know." He slid out from the bench, turned, and walked out, leaving Erin to wonder what he meant.

# CHAPTER 17

WASHING THE DISHES FROM SUNDAY BRUNCH, ERIN SNUCK A LOOK at her mom, who was sitting at the kitchen table pretending to read the paper. Despite her mom's assertion that radiation wouldn't be so bad, the last week had been hell. Peg's skin had become so raw around her armpit that it hurt just to wear clothes. A salve had helped, but moving her right arm caused her to wince in pain. More troubling was the fatigue. Over the last few days, just getting dressed and going downstairs seemed to leave Peg exhausted. Sean assured Erin that it was not an unusual side effect of combined chemo and radiation therapies and said hopefully their mom's stamina would slowly return once radiation was over, but Erin wasn't so sure.

It was hard seeing her mom like this. Erin longed for her old mom, the one who took charge in every situation and who always brightened a room with her wit and wisdom. Now it was hard for her mom just to get through a meal.

After brunch her dad had gone into the den and fallen asleep. He too was battling exhaustion, but his was from worrying and trying to care for Peg. He had asked Erin to come over the last two Sundays to help her mom with things around the house.

When Erin was finished with the dishes, she poured herself another cup of coffee and retook her seat.

"Thank you, dear. I appreciate the help," her mom said with a weak smile.

"No problem," Erin replied. "Would you like another cup of coffee?"

"No. I'm good. And thank you for doing the wash. I just haven't had the energy the last couple of weeks," she said with a sigh. "Your father tries, but housework was never his forte."

"You know things must be rough when Dad's happy to see me," Erin said with a chuckle.

"Don't say that," Peg said. "Your father has gotten much better with you."

"I guess," Erin replied, the memory of the hospital waiting room not far from her mind. "I know he still struggles, especially when he sees me with Mark."

"Speaking of Mark . . . ," her mother said.

Despite herself, Erin stiffened.

"What's going on?" her mom asked.

Truth be told, Erin had spent most of the morning trying not to think about what was going on. At that very moment, Mark was at his mom's talking to her and his brothers about the fact that he and Erin were dating again, and none of the possible outcomes made Erin feel warm and fuzzy. The most likely outcome being that Mark was going to be ostracized by his mom and brothers. His sister, Molly, and her partner, Robin, would be fine with them, even happy for them, but Erin dreaded the tensions that would result from the family being cleaved apart like that. And as much as Mark tried to convince her that whatever happened wasn't her fault, whether it was trans guilt or Irish guilt, some part of her felt responsible.

"Did you break it off again?" her mother asked, interrupting her thoughts.

"No," Erin responded. "No, just the opposite. Mark is with his family telling them that we're back together again."

Her mother gave her a sad smile. "Whatever happens, trust that it will be for the best."

"That sounds very Zen," Erin suggested.

"Cancer will do that to you."

Erin could find no witty reply, so they sat there in silence. Finally, Erin said, "I'm meeting Mark at around one to head to Patrick and Brennan's soccer game. Would you like to join us?"

Peg sighed. "Thanks. But as much as I'd love to see my grand-sons, I don't have the energy yet. Besides . . ." Peg hesitated. "Per-haps it's best if you and Mark had some time to yourselves so you can discuss . . . things."

"Yeah," Erin replied, her voice barely a whisper.

As it turned out, Mark texted her just as she was leaving for her apartment to say he was still at his mom's and would meet her at the field, leaving her in limbo as to what was happening. Sensing things weren't going well, she suggested she would just meet him after the game. At least this way she could try to enjoy watching Patrick and Brennan play.

Now, Erin stood on the sidelines as Liz cheered on her sons. Patrick, now fourteen, was a freshman in high school, while twelve-year-old Brennan was in seventh grade. Erin adored both of them, and had been a fixture at their soccer games. Then she transitioned . . . and things changed.

Like everyone else in her life, her brother, Sean, had been stunned when she first came out, but to his credit, unlike most of her guy friends, Sean at least seemed to understand the situation. And yet, after she'd had facial surgery and started living as Erin, Sean had stopped communicating with her entirely. His explana-tion to their mother had been that he needed to protect Patrick and Brennan; because the boys had been so close to their uncle, Ian, he wasn't sure how they'd react to the news their uncle was now their aunt, Erin. Erin had been devastated. Protect the boys from her? What was she, contagious? As if being near her was somehow going to impact the boys' sexual orientation or gender identity.

Amazingly, it had been Patrick and Brennan who had brought them all back together as a family. About two years after she had transitioned, Erin had gotten an e-mail from the two of them inviting her to their soccer game—an invitation that came with-out their parents' knowledge. They had found her law firm online and from there got her e-mail address. She had made it to several of the games before they lost in the State Cup Tournament. The boys, realizing they weren't sure when, or if, they'd see her again, had run back to the field to see her and let her know they loved her. Once Sean had witnessed his sons' love for their aunt, and how comfortable they were with her, things had started to get better.

When she was growing up, soccer had been Erin's entrée into the male world, even if she'd never felt comfortable in it. Her love for the sport had somehow allowed her to transcend her feelings and adapt to a world in which she often felt out of place. And maybe because it was a sport that rewarded speed and agility, rather than brute strength, she had excelled, first in high school and then in college. But when she went off to law school, she had stopped playing, only restarting last winter when she'd joined an indoor coed league. Then one of the women on her coed team mentioned that she played in an outdoor women's league and invited Erin to start training with them so that when they needed extra bodies she could fill in. The irony was, she'd only been invited to play because of Lauren, her ex-wife, who had suggested Erin as a replacement.

*Lauren*, she thought. Erin and Lauren had fallen in love in high school, and for a while that was enough for her to try to be Ian— a guy's guy whose love for Lauren would surely keep the feelings of being a woman at bay. But try as she might, she just couldn't keep up the façade of being a man, and as that façade crumbled, so did her marriage. It was no one's fault—Erin simply couldn't be the man Lauren had married, and Lauren wanted to be with a man. They still cared deeply about each other, but Lauren had moved on, with a new marriage resulting in the pregnancy that had ultimately led to her recommending that Erin take her place in the coed league. Strange, the twists and turns life takes.

Now she faced a different dilemma. Unlike Lauren, Mark loved her for the woman she was—unfortunately, his family didn't.

"Everything okay?" Liz asked, startling Erin from her thoughts. "It's not like you to be distracted during a soccer match," she said with a half smile.

"Well, the Cobras are winning five nil," she said, referring to the Princeton Cobras, Patrick and Brennan's team. "So it's not like I'm on the edge of my seat."

"Worried about your mom?" Liz asked.

"Yeah, absolutely that's part of it. I never considered that she was a mere mortal before she got sick. I guess I just assumed Mom would always be part of my life, and the realization that things change and someday she won't be here has upended me."

"Peg's a force, for sure," Liz said, studying Erin before continuing. "But you, more than most, should understand that things change. It's life. It doesn't necessarily make things easier, but maybe if we all understood how temporary our journeys are, we'd be better people and cherish life more."

Erin paused, reflecting on what Liz had said. Would it make people behave more selfless, or would the realization that death was a constant companion simply reinforce our baser instincts? "Maybe. But I think most people don't consider we're only passing through. Seems like we're programmed to think we'll be around forever."

With the score lopsided, the Cobras had switched players around to give the team members a chance to play in new positions. As a result, Patrick, who usually played forward, was playing as a defensive midfielder, and Brennan, normally a midfielder, was on defense. Erin, who spent most of her soccer career as an outside midfielder, understood the challenges involved in playing a new position. Watching her nephews, she was impressed with how easily they had adjusted to the challenges of a new situation just like they had adapted so easily to her.

"It's more than your mom, isn't it?" Liz asked.

"Yeah, it's the whole situation with Mark and his family." She looked at Liz a bit wistfully. "A part of me thinks we could be as happy as you and Sean, but then I don't know how that's possible if he loses his family in the process. So I'm torn. I just . . . wish I could be in a relationship where my being trans wasn't an issue."

Liz moved closer and gave Erin a hug. "Sounds to me like it's his call. And, if you love him, whatever decision he makes, all you can do is know that it's for the best."

"I know," Erin mumbled. "I know."

\* \* \*

"What is so fucking urgent that I had to get here as soon as I landed at LaGuardia," Conroy complained as soon as Cassandra showed him into the library of Parsons's brownstone on East Sixty-Eighth.

"Max is dead," she replied stone faced. "Carl shot him."

"What?!" he screamed. "What are you talking about? Dead? How? Why didn't you call me?"

"Stop shouting at me," she snapped. "It happened Friday. Can you just shut up and listen for a change?"

She proceeded to tell him the whole sordid story, how, on Arthur's order, Carl and Max had followed Duane Swisher from a meeting with a paralegal colleague of Ann's to the offices of a Connie Irving, a forensic phone expert. Arthur, worried about what information might be on the phone if it was Ann's, had directed them to get the phone from Irving at any cost. What they didn't know was that Irving was a former FBI agent, with the skills to defend herself.

"Okay. But who the hell is Swisher?" Conroy said, throwing his arms up. "And why the fuck is Arthur worried about him?"

"It's touching that you're all choked up about Max's untimely passing," she said dryly before folding her arms across her chest.

"What the fuck do I care about Max? He's just some thug that Charles, and now Arthur, used to do their dirty work. Get back to my question, what the hell is going on here?"

Her eyes narrowed and her jaw tensed. "Swisher is the law partner of Erin McCabe, a criminal defense attorney who visited Ann Parsons in the Union County jail. Before you start screaming, 'Why is Ann being visited in the jail by some criminal defense attorney?' the answer is we don't know, nor do we know how she got on Ann's visitors list. We also learned that Ms. McCabe was representing Justin Mackey when he met his demise, and I should mention that Ms. McCabe is transgender. Given the nature of the information, I did not feel safe discussing this on the phone, or by text or e-mail. Thus, my request that you get here as soon as you got back from fucking some fourteen-year-old girl in California."

He walked over to the only window in the room, pulled back the curtain, and looked out. "She's sixteen," he said tightly. "I don't know why you want to push my buttons, but—" He stopped. "Why did Arthur decide to have this Swisher guy followed?"

"Arthur had both of them followed. On Friday, McCabe went back to the jail to visit with Ann, and it was only thanks to a friendly corrections officer lodging a complaint that Ann was ineligible for visitors. At the same time, Carl and Max followed Swisher to a Starbucks, where he met with a woman who, as I said, worked with Ann. The rest I told you."

Conroy wrapped his hand around his mouth. "I go away for a few days and Arthur decides he's fucking in charge. This is bullshit. Did Carl at least get the phone?"

She shook her head. "NYPD has it."

He laughed. "Well, that isn't necessarily bad news. It'll probably sit untouched in some evidence locker for decades."

He walked back across the room and dropped back into the leather chair. "And now that Arthur has totally fucked things up, what does he suggest for dealing with this situation?"

"Kill them both," she said.

Conroy snorted. "Jesus. First Charles, and now Arthur—their solution to every problem is to kill somebody. Hasn't Arthur learned? Killing Mackey certainly didn't solve Charles's problem and I'm not sure killing these two interlopers is the right solution—at least for now."

"Okay. Then what do you suggest?" she asked.

"As long as Ann is compliant, there's little that McCabe and Swisher can do. And remember, we do have an ace in the hole when it comes to Ann. Perhaps word should get back to her that if she doesn't continue to play ball, we can exact revenge in many ways. In the meantime, keep an eye on these two and, if necessary, Arthur's solution is always available to us."

Erin parked her car in front of her apartment. Before she got out of her car she looked and saw she had a message from Kluska. **The game that was cancelled last Friday has been rescheduled for the same time this coming week. No need to register before the**

**game, your team is already checked in**. She nodded, slid her phone back in her purse, and headed to her place.

Opening the door she heard Mark in the kitchen. "Hey, smells good. What are you making?"

"Short ribs," he replied, walking out of the kitchen and handing her a glass of red wine.

"Are we celebrating something?" she asked, an air of optimism in her voice.

"How the Cobras do?" he asked.

"They won, five to nothing," she responded, confused by his question.

"Good. We're celebrating the Cobras' victory," he said, clicking his wine glass against hers.

She made no effort to take a sip. "Mark, please talk to me. What happened?"

He took her hand and led her to the couch. "You told me once that when you told your dad you were trans, the way he reacted made it one of the worst days of your life."

She nodded.

"It was like that—not good," he said. "All I can hope is that with time, like things have gotten for you with your dad, it will get better for me and my family."

She put her wine glass down on the coffee table. "I'm sorry," she said, leaning over and hugging him. Her tears slowly spilled out of the corners of her eyes.

He held her tight, then slowly released her and took her face in his hands. "It's okay," he said slowly. "We're okay. As long as we have each other, we can handle this." He kissed her on the forehead. "Have faith. I love you."

# CHAPTER 18

KLUSKA'S MESSAGE HAD BEEN CLEAR, BUT SHE STILL WORRIED THAT something would go amiss, so Erin was relieved when she got to the visitors sign in and her name was on Ann's visitors list. It had been a relatively quiet week. Connie had called Duane after she had gotten out of the hospital, to confirm that both numbers were burner phones. The only good news Connie had was that, because Max Gallagher and his partner were attempting to steal the phone, she was close to convincing Detective Barry to have NYPD do a cell tower search.

Thankfully, when the gate rolled open this time, the fifth prisoner in line was Ann, who immediately made her way over to Erin's table and slid into the plastic chair. Erin's smile died at the first words out of her mouth.

"I only came to tell you that I don't want to talk to you," Ann said flatly. "I wasn't able to see visitors last week because I got written up. I'm sorry, I can't help you." She started to get up.

"Do you know a Max Gallagher?" Erin asked quickly.

Ann hesitated, hovering in midair. "Why?"

"He's dead," Erin shot back.

"Dead?" Ann dropped back into her chair. "I don't understand."

"He was killed trying to steal your burner phone that my partner discovered you had given to Marsha Kramer."

Ann visibly stiffened. "I . . . I don't know what you're talking about."

"Ann, I'm trying to help you," Erin said, speaking quickly, and hoping that what she was about to say came close enough to the truth that it would earn Ann's trust. "You only called two numbers on that phone. One we think was the person you were supposed to meet the night your father was killed. The other, we're not sure who that is, but you called them every week at the same time, so it's likely someone you're close with. I know in your statement you said you gave your father money every month for rent and expenses, but I don't believe that. You withdrew two thousand every month in cash and I suspect you sent it to the same person you called every week." Now Erin decided she needed to bluff. "We're just waiting on the cell tower information, and once we get that, we'll have a better idea of who it is."

Ann shifted uncomfortably in her seat, squeezing her hands together. "No. Please don't do that. How did you get my phone?" Ann said defensively. "What's it got to do with your case?"

*Time to tell the truth,* Erin thought. "We're investigating the murder of my client, who I believe your father had murdered. At the same time, I'm trying to help you too, because I don't believe you murdered your father. I don't know why you pled guilty, but I suspect you're trying to protect someone else."

A look of panic grew on Ann's face as Erin spoke. "You . . . you don't understand. You have to leave. They know everything I do here. They—"

"Who's they?" Erin interrupted. "Who are these people you're afraid of?"

Ann's eyes pleaded with Erin. "I can't," was all she got out.

Erin pursed her lips and sat back in her chair. "You realize that once you go to state prison, whatever they promised you is not going to happen." At this point Erin knew she had to wing it. "Ann, I'm not your lawyer, so nothing you tell me is privileged. But you don't have to retain me to represent you for the privilege to apply. All you have to do is tell me you want to talk to me because you're considering representation—then we're safe. It seems to me that you're lying and willing to spend twenty years in prison to protect someone else based on promises that were made to you, promises I guarantee will be forgotten the moment you're sentenced for killing your father."

Ann stared down at the table, her lip quivering.

"Must be something really big if you're willing to forfeit ten million dollars. That's a lot of money to walk away from."

It was a throwaway line, just something Erin was thinking to herself that she happened to say out loud, but Ann suddenly looked up, and Erin realized she may have struck a nerve.

"All I have to do is say I want to talk to you about representing me to make what I say privileged?"

"That's right," Erin replied.

"How do I know I can trust you? Maybe they sent you here to test me."

"Did you use the jail computer to do a search on me?" Erin asked.

"Yes," Ann responded.

"Then you know why you can trust me."

Ann stole a glance at the corrections officer standing by the gate. "We need to make this fast," she said, turning back to face Erin. "I want to talk to you about possibly representing me."

"Sure," Erin replied.

"I know that because I pled guilty I lose the money I was to inherit, but can the person handling my father's estate give that money to someone else in my place? Someone we both agree on."

"I'm not a trust and estates lawyer, but generally, no. The executor is obligated to follow your father's will. So depending on what the will says, if you don't get it, it either goes to someone else pursuant to the will, or it goes back into what is called the residuary of the estate. They can't just give it to whoever they want," Erin said. "Do you know who it goes to if you don't get it?"

"Yeah. It goes to a charity set up by my father, the Parsons Foundation. Under his will, other than what he left me, the foundation gets everything." She hesitated. "But the foundation can give it to whoever it wants, right?"

"Ann, I'm not an expert, but from the little I know from being on the board of a charitable organization, a charity simply can't legally give away ten million dollars to someone unless the donation is in keeping with the charity's purpose." Erin could sense Ann was looking for more. "Look, it's no secret that private foundations have very little oversight, so it's possible they could spend money and make it look charitable when it's not—but it's not legal. So it would depend on who's running the foundation and how much they're willing to bend, or ignore, the rules. And I guess from your perspective, it depends on how much you trust the person from the foundation who promised to bend or ignore the rules."

Ann picked at her hand. "So if they don't do what they promised me, there's no way I can legally force them to do it?"

Erin knew there was little she could do to blunt the blow she was about to deliver. "I'm afraid not," Erin replied.

Ann stared at the table. When she looked up, Erin noticed a look of resolve she hadn't seen before. "Buy a burner," she said in a whisper. "Then send a text to the number I called every week. The message should say, 'Felipe it would be a good time for a vacation.' Got that?"

Erin nodded.

"You should get a return text that says, 'good idea going to take a week off.'"

"Okay, then what?"

"I'll call your office collect on Monday at 10 a.m. to see if you got the right response." Ann paused. "In a few seconds, I'm going to start yelling at you. I need you to say something like, 'Well, if that's the way you feel, I won't be back.' Then walk out in a huff."

Before Erin could respond, Ann pushed her chair back from the table and jumped up. "I don't know how many times I have to tell you, I don't need or want your help. Please leave me alone."

Erin slowly rose from her chair. "I don't understand you. But if that's the way you feel, don't worry, I won't be back." She turned quickly, shaking her head as she walked toward the exit of the visiting room.

* * *

It was just after 3:00 p.m. when Erin got back to the office. She removed the new phone from its packaging and plugged it in to charge it. Then she took her notepad out of her purse and studied what she had written down as soon as she had gotten out of the visiting area. *Strange*, she thought.

"Sorry, I was on a call," Duane said as he walked into her office. "How'd it go?"

Erin proceeded to explain what had happened and Ann's fear that she was being watched, resulting in Erin agreeing to storm out of the visiting room to give the illusion she was angry with Ann. Erin was convinced that Ann was protecting someone, most likely whoever was on the other end of this phone. The *who* and *why* were still murky.

"What do you think?" Duane asked when she was finished.

"Not sure, but my guess is that the executrix promised Ann that if she pled guilty Ann's ten million dollar inheritance would go to someone else. If your hunch is correct, and Ann wasn't paying cash every month to her father, it's probably the same person she sent the cash to and called every Sunday."

"Even if that's all true, why spend twenty years in jail and forfeit ten million dollars for a crime you didn't commit?"

Erin shook her head. "I wish I knew."

She looked down at the phone and saw it was charged enough that she could now send the message. She typed it in, double-checked both the number and the message, then hit SEND.

"Let's see what happens," she said, placing the phone down on her desk to continue to charge.

The Lincoln Town Car crawled through traffic as it headed uptown. Sitting in the backseat, Martin Conroy tucked the notes to the speech he was delivering tonight into the inside pocket of his suit jacket. He'd be brief—commenting on his firm's commitment to the arts and how wonderful the Center for Children's Theater & Arts was in developing young talent. But his mind wasn't focused on his speech, or even on the event, where he'd have the opportunity to schmooze with some of the firm's well-to-do clients. Instead, his life was slowly being consumed by the shitshow created by Charles's death.

He'd always assumed he'd survive Charles—actually he had planned on it. Sooner or later Charles's years of alcohol and drug use would exact the ultimate toll. And when the time came, he'd have control of everything. Unfortunately, he hadn't anticipated Charles's demise would happen when it did, leaving him scrambling to effectuate his plan. In a weird way it actually helped that the remaining members of the unholy alliance, Cassandra and Arthur Hiller, were polar opposites. Arthur's solution for everything involved some form of mayhem. As opposed to Cassandra, who seemed hell-bent on running around screaming the sky was falling without offering any practical solutions. So it fell to him to take care of things, which was fine with him because it allowed him to cover his tracks.

For now, he agreed with Cassandra that finding Charles's hard drives was a priority—the information on them could be devastating. But for him, getting Charles's laptop was the key—that's what he needed. As long as it was clear to Ann that if she crossed them there would be severe consequences, and not just to her, Martin was convinced the meddling from the new lawyers would amount to nothing more than a distraction. Why Arthur had sent Max and Carl on their fool's errand was beyond him. There were certainly times when he regretted the day he had allowed Charles to bring Arthur into this business. But even in college, Charles had shown a penchant for running with a dangerous crowd.

When he and Charles initially met at Columbia as freshman in 1964 they had only one thing in common: avoiding Vietnam. He was a prep school kid who had grown up on the Upper West Side. His admission the result of his status as a legacy, not his academic credentials. Charles, on the other hand, was there on an academic full ride. He was a math whiz from Staten Island, whose father was a New York City cop, his mother a bartender at a shot and beer joint, a block from their home. But a perfect 800 on his math SAT had garnered him admission. His prowess with numbers also led him to begin a gambling operation on campus. In its second week, a weird combination of NFL and AFL results left Charles owing over $5,000 he didn't have—fortuitously, Martin did, and their partnership was born. By sophomore year the operation was earning them more than what a tenured professor was making, with the added benefit of being in cash. They had also discovered they had something else in common, an attraction to "younger" women who, after a few drinks, were too inebriated to resist their sexual advances.

After college, when Charles had become a whiz on Wall Street, and Martin had finished law school and joined his father's firm practicing in the rough-and-tumble world of New York real estate, they parlayed their various extracurricular activities into extremely lucrative side businesses—all tax free.

*Where were the fucking hard drives?* It wasn't just access to the financial information for the offshore accounts that he needed—he'd get that from the laptop—but the information on the other drives had the potential to destroy him. Some of what Charles had on the drives Martin knew about and had been able to exploit when he represented Charles as federal investigators were closing in—it was amazing how influential politicians could be after seeing a recording of them cavorting with a sixteen-year-old. But knowing Charles and his penchant for exploiting the weaknesses of everyone in his circle, Martin was sure that he only knew the tip of the iceberg. He could only imagine who and what Charles had secretly recorded to use when the need arose. Among Charles's collection he was sure there were videos of him, Arthur, and Cassandra that would be devastating if they fell into the wrong hands. *Focus*, he thought. He needed to stay focused.

# CHAPTER 19

S HE OPENED ONE EYE AND LOOKED AT THE CLOCK—EIGHT A.M.—
then rolled over and threw one arm over Mark, who was still
sound asleep. She loved the fact that all he ever wore to bed was
boxers. That way she could snuggle into him and allow herself to
become intoxicated by his smell; maybe it was the soap he used,
but it reminded her of how the woods smelled after a rain
shower—earthy, but also clean and fresh. She found it strange
that as much as she loved Lauren, she didn't remember that she
had a unique scent. But from the first time Mark had kissed her,
there was something about the way he smelled that turned her
on. She didn't know if it was him, or maybe just the new hormones coursing through her veins. As she soaked in his scent,
part of her felt guilty, probably always would, that he had chosen
to be with her even if it resulted in him being alienated from his
family. But she couldn't deny that she had been thrilled when he
told her that regardless of what happened with his family he
wanted to be with her.

Last night they had walked to Il Gabbiano's for dinner and
shared a wonderful David Bruce pinot noir. Then they had
walked back to her place, enjoyed some fresh coffee, and wound
up making love until they both fell asleep, exhausted.

She found it amazing that in the four years since she transitioned the feeling of what it was like to inhabit a man's body had

almost totally faded from her consciousness. She had grown accustomed to her new body and the pleasures that lurked, sometimes in very unexpected places. For a man, the pleasure of making love was explosive. As a woman, the pleasure was like the curl of a slowly swelling wave that broke with a rush on the shoreline and then slowly receded. She closed her eyes, and relaxed, content in a way she had never known.

"Hey, sleepyhead," she heard as a gentle kiss landed on her forehead.

She opened her eyes and realized she had fallen back to sleep. "What time is it?"

"Nine thirty," Mark said as he pulled her closer.

"How's the weather?"

"Looks nice out."

"Want to go for a run?" she asked.

"Only if you promise not to run me into the ground."

"Promise," she said, giving him a kiss. Mark kept himself in good shape playing on Swish's team in a men's basketball league, but Erin was a runner, and had been since college. She had started so she'd be in shape for soccer season, but over time, running had morphed from a way to stay in shape to a form of therapy. Initially, as she was trying to hold on to her life and marriage to Lauren, and then, after they separated and Erin had started to transition, she ran just to try to keep from falling apart. There had been so many days that she had used the pain of a hard run as a diversion from the pain of losing her wife and the estrangement from her father and brother.

As Mark climbed out of bed, she rolled over and picked up the burner phone from the nightstand. She had one text message.

She clicked on the icon and opened the message: **no I can't too busy at work**

Rubbing the back of her neck, she tried to figure out what it meant. It wasn't the response Ann had told her to expect, but then again, maybe she was being tested. She put the phone back on the nightstand, stretched, and hopped out of bed to change for their run.

* * *

One thing Erin liked about running in the section of Cranford where she lived was that once you crossed Orange Avenue there was very little traffic because all the roads were constructed with dead ends, so there was no access to any of the main roads. It was like being in a real-life maze where nothing led you out, and you had to find your way back to the start. She picked a six-mile run that would take them up and around Nomahegan Park. They headed up Riverside Drive, with Erin content to let Mark set the pace. Life couldn't get any better than this, she thought, easily matching him stride for stride as they glided up the winding street snaking along the Rahway River.

As they went, neither of them noticed the car parked on the side of the road, the windows tinted to obscure the two men watching.

"I agree with you," Swish said as they sat in his office Monday morning. "If Ann's worried about people watching her, she would never give you the right response."

"So what do you make of the second message I received yesterday?" Erin asked. The second message had been unexpected. On Sunday, she and Mark had gone out to brunch and then to her nephews' game. He had dropped her off. Walking into her bedroom, she had noticed the burner phone on her night table and absentmindedly picked it up when she saw she had a new text message. She had opened the text: **besides the weather is nice where I am.**

"My guess is that it's a follow-up to let Ann know something. But what it means—well, I guess we'll find out in about five minutes," he said, glancing at his watch. "Assuming she calls."

Erin paced around Duane's office.

Duane's phone rang and he picked it up. "Thanks, Cheryl, put it through." He hit his speaker button. "Collect call from Ann Parsons," the operator said. "Will you accept the charges?"

Erin took a seat by Duane's desk. "Yes, operator," Erin replied. "We'll accept the charges."

"Ms. McCabe?" a muffled voice said.

"Yes, Ann. This is Erin."

"Did you get a response?" Ann asked.

"I did," Erin replied. "The first response was, 'no I can't too busy at work.' I also received a text yesterday. It said, 'besides the weather is nice where I am.'"

There was silence.

It probably was only about ten seconds, but it seemed much longer as they waited. "Can you visit me this afternoon?"

Erin looked up at Duane, who nodded. "Yes. I'd also like my partner, Duane Swisher, to come with me. Is that all right?"

"I have an appointment with the social worker at eleven. I'll add both of you to my counsel list. I have to go," Ann said quickly and hung up.

"Strange," Erin said.

Duane put his hands behind his head. "No. Not from her perspective. Keep in mind that call wasn't an attorney-client phone call. Meaning, it was on an open line, so legally, anyone could have been listening, and she believes people are watching her, so it makes sense. Keep it simple. Anything important can wait until this afternoon."

Unlike general visitors, during certain hours, attorneys could visit their clients in the privacy of a small room. Erin and Duane made sure they were there promptly at one p.m. to check in, leaving everything apart from their legal papers, a pad, and a pen in Duane's car.

They reflexively stood when Ann was brought into the room. Erin immediately noticed that Ann looked pale. The bags under her eyes betrayed a lack of sleep, and from her appearance, it looked like she hadn't eaten or showered since the last time Erin was there.

After the corrections officer left them, Erin did the introductions. Duane extended his hand across the small table. Following a small hesitation, Ann took it.

"Nice to meet you," Duane said, gently shaking her hand.

Erin and Swish each started to sit, but Ann remained rooted in place.

"Is everything okay?" Erin asked.

"I don't think I should be here," she said.

Duane spoke first. "Ann, I know we've never met, but Erin has described your concerns about being monitored and your worries about the safety of someone close to you. I want you to know that we're sensitive to your concerns, and, as a former FBI agent, I understand them. That said, the minute you put us down on your lawyers list, whoever it is that is keeping tabs on you was alerted. I understand why you might feel that the only way to protect yourself and the other person is to play ball with whoever is threatening you. But chances are those people can't be trusted. So meeting with us now, and being honest with us, is the only way to determine if we can help."

Erin glanced over at Swish. *Well played*, she thought. The FBI's loss had been her gain.

Ann slid the chair out from the table and slowly sat down. "I don't know how you can help. I've already pled guilty."

"Ann, let's start with the basics," Erin replied. "If you want to talk to us about representation, our conversations are protected by the attorney-client privilege. Is that why you're here?"

"Yes," Ann said, more to the table than to them.

"Okay. Then the first thing you should know is that if you did murder your father we can't get you anything better than the deal you already have. However, if you didn't kill him, then seventeen years, at a minimum, is a long time to spend in jail for something you didn't do."

"My lawyers said there was no defense. The evidence was overwhelming," Ann said, finally looking up.

"I don't want to mislead you—based on what we've seen so far, I'm also not sure it is defensible," Duane said. "But that's why we're here—to hear your version and figure out your chances."

"Ann, at the end of the day, you'll decide what you want to do, not us. As Duane said, all we can do is listen and give you the best advice we can. Think of it like getting a second opinion."

Ann sat motionless. Erin couldn't tell whether she was deep in thought or paralyzed with fear. "I've never killed anyone," she said, almost in a whisper. "I wanted to kill him. I can't tell you how many times I planned it. But I couldn't do it."

"Did you plan or work with anyone else to have him killed?" Erin inquired.

"No," Ann replied firmly.

"Where were you the night he was murdered?" Duane asked, perhaps more accusingly than he intended.

She sighed. "In a bar in Hoboken, waiting for my date."

"The date that never showed?"

She nodded, picking at her hand.

"Have you seen the guy you were dating since the night he stood you up?" Duane continued.

"She," Ann said.

"I'm sorry?" Duane responded.

"I had a date with a woman. I'm a lesbian."

"Had you gone out with her prior to the night of the murder?" Erin said, jumping in.

"Yeah, we had dated for two or three months." She looked back to Duane. "And to answer your question, no, I never saw her after the night she stood me up."

"Do you know who she is?" Erin asked.

Ann snorted. "I know the name she gave me. Terry Gore. But don't waste your time looking for her. I tried. Like everything else she told me, apparently her name was a lie too."

"Do you know anything about her? Where she lives? What she does?" Duane asked.

"Again, only what she told me, all of which turned out not to be true."

"Have you told anyone about her?" Erin inquired.

"I told my lawyers. They said they'd search for her, but with the little I knew, they said it would be like looking for a needle in a haystack."

"Did she ever meet your father?" Duane asked.

"Not that I know," Ann responded. "But I did take her to the house in Westfield once," she volunteered.

"Any particular reason?" Duane asked.

"She said my father was a celebrity, and she had never been to a celebrity's house."

"How long were you there?" Erin asked.

"He wasn't there so we spent the night," Ann replied, the color rising in her cheeks.

Noticing Ann's reaction, Erin probed a little more. "Do you go to the house in Westfield often? I mean without Terry."

"Occasionally." Ann closed her eyes. "But that was the first time I stayed overnight there since graduating college. It's . . . too painful to be there."

Duane looked at Erin. She shook her head, wary of the potential that Ann had been abused, which would mean they would need to move slowly to avoid the trauma of forcing her to relive her abuse.

"Why did you tell the detectives from the prosecutor's office you did it?" Erin asked, moving away from the obvious follow-up.

"I was afraid. I thought if I told them what they wanted to hear, they might let me go."

"Why did you plead guilty?" Duane asked.

She hesitated. "I wanted to protect . . . someone very close to me."

"Can you tell us who?" Erin asked, her tone gentle.

Ann stiffened and closed her eyes. "No. Not yet."

Erin decided not to push her on whom she was protecting.

Seeing Erin hesitate, Duane changed subjects. "If you weren't the one who killed him, do you have any idea why on the tape he says the person shouldn't kill him because he's their father?"

Once again she sat motionless for what seemed forever. "I presume because whoever shot him was his child," she finally offered.

"I'm sorry," Duane said. "I didn't realize he had any children other than you."

"I'm not his child," Ann replied.

Duane and Erin shared a look.

"We understand, Ann," Erin said. "We know that Parsons adopted you after your mother married him. Is that what you mean?"

"No," Ann replied. And for the first time since they started talking, her expression showed the relief of putting down an unbearable burden. "I'm not Ann Parsons."

# CHAPTER 20

*T*HEY DIDN'T SPEAK ON THEIR WALK BACK TO THE PARKING GARAGE. When they were finally settled in Duane's car, Erin felt like the nausea was going to overwhelm her.

"Are you okay?" he asked.

Shaking her head, she removed a package of tissues from her purse, then wiped her eyes and blew her nose.

"How can human beings be so cruel?" she spit out between clenched teeth, her anger consuming her anguish. "Swish, she was fourteen when he started abusing her—four-teen," she said, enunciating each syllable of her age. "Then he used her in porn movies. What kind of fucking monster was he? I've seen all kinds of shit over the last twelve years—defended rapists and murderers, drug dealers and pimps, but never, never . . ." She closed her eyes, fighting to maintain control, her mind spinning as if caught in an eddy.

Duane put his fist up to his mouth, in an effort to hide his own emotions. "I'm sorry, E. My suggestion is we try to focus on if, and how, we can help her, and not on the details of what she's been through. We can't fix what happened—we can only help her move forward. And the first step is helping her decide what she wants to do—and then trying to figure out legally what we can do."

Erin's head remained bowed, pain still carved into the lines of her face.

"Let's start with what she's not telling us," Duane said.

"Okay," Erin whispered, desperately trying to grab on to something—anything other than the images careening through her consciousness.

"We know there's someone out there she's concerned about who could get hurt, but she won't tell us who it is."

Erin nodded. "I also get the sense that she may have an idea of who actually murdered Parsons, but she isn't giving us anything to work with."

"Which means, she still may have been involved. In which case withdrawing her plea may not be such a good idea," Duane suggested. "And then there's the ethical problem."

"What ethical problem?" she asked, puzzled.

"If we're going to file a motion to vacate her plea, it has to be supported by her certification."

"Yeah, okay?"

"And what's the opening line to every certification you've ever drafted?"

She looked at him, perplexed. "I so-and-so hereby certify that . . ."

"Exactly. But she's told us that we are not allowed to disclose to anyone the fact that she's not Ann Parsons. So how do we prepare a certification for her that will have an opening line that says, 'I Ann Parsons hereby certify that' when we know she's not Ann Parsons? Aren't we suborning perjury?"

For the first time since they got in the car, there was a tinge of a grin on Erin's lips. "A little-known fun fact is that New Jersey is a common-law name change state."

"What the hell does that mean?" Duane asked.

"It means that you can legally change your name simply by consistently using another name as long as you're not doing it for a fraudulent or criminal purpose. Ann's been using that name for about eleven years. Sounds to me like that qualifies."

"Why do you know that?"

"I did a fair amount of research before I changed my name. The truth is, if you want to change your official documents, things like your birth certificate, license, and passport, you need a court order granting you a name change. But for what you're worried about, I think we're okay."

He smiled and shook his head. "Okay, issue number one solved. But to get the judge to vacate her plea, we need to provide a colorable claim that she's innocent. Just her saying, 'I didn't do it' might not cut it. She doesn't want us saying too much, but if we don't say enough, the judge will deny the motion."

Erin nodded. "As my supervisor at the Public Defender's Office used to say, if it was easy, she wouldn't need us."

"Speaking of the judge, what do you know about Judge Spiegel?" he asked.

"Good judge. Fair guy. When I was with the PD's office, I was assigned to his court for a while. I tried a couple of cases in front of him. Lost them both, but he gave my clients a fair trial. That's all we can ask for."

"Um, you appear in front of him since . . . ," he said, gesturing at her with his hands.

"Nope."

"Think he'll have any problems with the new and improved you?"

She shrugged. "You never know. But he's a bit of a free spirit. My guess is he'll be fine."

After starting the car and backing out of their parking spot, Duane began winding their way to the exit. Erin was staring out the passenger-side window when she said, "Where do you think the real Ann Parsons is?"

"Good question," Duane said.

"And did she kill her father?" Erin added almost to herself.

He headed toward Rahway Avenue. They were approaching the stop sign when he said, "Don't look, but pretty sure we have a tail."

"Really?"

"I noticed a black Ford Explorer on the way here was always about four car lengths behind us. And just now, when I pulled out of the garage, a gray Lincoln on the street pulled out a car behind us. The sedan that followed you, was that a Lincoln?"

"I can't be sure. My guess is a Crown Vic. But it could have been a Lincoln," she replied, tense. "But if the one you noticed on the way here was an Explorer, why do you think there's a connection to the Lincoln that just pulled out?"

"Because professionals use at least two cars to do a tail."

"So you're thinking it's not the same people who followed me?"

"That's my hunch," he responded.

"So who then?" she asked.

"My guess is Parsons's people." He turned, facing her. "How is it that you get cases where you manage to piss off rich and powerful people?"

She shrugged. "Just lucky, I guess."

"Yeah, well last time a lot of people died, and you came pretty damn close to getting killed. They've already gone after Connie Irving, so let's be careful. I don't want anyone dying."

"I'm all in favor of not dying," Erin added.

Conroy paced across his office, his anger with the two meddling attorneys starting to grow.

"So what do we know?" Conroy asked, pulling up one of his office chairs and taking a seat opposite DeCovnie, who sat cross-legged on the leather couch in his office.

"According to our source, she made a phone call to them at ten a.m. It was on an open line, so a friendly corrections officer listened in. They gave her two very cryptic messages and then she asked to see them. She then added them to her attorney list. When they got to the jail, they met for over two hours in one of the attorney meeting rooms. They left the jail and went back to their office." She twirled a strand of her hair around her finger. "What can they do now? She's already pled guilty. Isn't it too late?"

"They could move to allow her to withdraw her plea."

She rubbed the back of her neck. "I can't believe that's even a possibility." She inhaled. "I don't have to tell you—"

"You don't," he interrupted. "The question is, how do we handle it? Do we know where the brother is?"

"No. He hasn't shown up for work since Friday, and no one has seen him at his apartment either."

"Shit. Those messages must have been a way to warn him." His expression hardened. "We need to find him, now! If we have him, she'll do whatever we want."

He stormed to his desk and flipped open a file folder marked with the SIS logo. About an inch and a half thick, it contained credit reports, school records, newspaper articles, and background reports. On top was a picture of Duane Swisher from the firm's website, paper-clipped to a summary of an investigative report:

*Duane Abraham Swisher. African American, DOB 2/1/71, married to Corrine Swisher, née Butler, a psychologist at Scotch Plains–Fanwood High School. Lives at 3406 Chiplou Lane, Scotch Plains. One child, a four-year-old son named Austin. Attended Brown on a full academic scholarship. Played basketball at Brown, where he was All-Ivy two years. Columbia Law School followed by seven years in the FBI. Voluntarily resigned in good standing from the FBI five years ago and started practicing law in Cranford, New Jersey, with Ian McCabe. Licensed to carry a firearm Glock 45 9mm registered to his name.*

He opened a second file folder that had pictures of both Ian McCabe and Erin McCabe clipped to the summary:

*Erin Bridget McCabe, aka Ian Patrick McCabe. Caucasian, DOB 8/4/71, divorced, formerly married to Lauren Schmidt, no children. Lives at 35A Riverside Drive, Cranford, drives a 2003 Mazda Miata. Grew up in Union, New Jersey, attended Cardinal O'Hara High School, where he was an All-County soccer player. Graduated from Stonehill College in North Easton, Massachusetts, then Temple Law School, and clerked for the Honorable Miles Foreman in Monmouth County. Worked for the Union County Public Defender's Office for five years, then left to start his own firm and shortly after that he formed the firm of McCabe & Swisher with Swisher. Four years ago, he legally changed his name to*

*Erin Bridget McCabe and started practicing law as a woman. Both*
*McCabe and Swisher were involved in a high-profile case representing the*
*defendant accused of the murder of William Townsend, Jr., the only son*
*of state senator William Townsend.*

As he finished, his eyebrows went higher.

"I know I sound like a broken record, Martin, but we need those hard drives. We can't allow Ann to withdraw her plea."

"Cassandra, I am well aware of the problem. . . ."

He picked up the file folder for Erin McCabe, studying the two pictures. "However, unlike Arthur and Charles, I believe eliminating people often creates new and unexpected problems." He looked again at McCabe's folder. "We need to find a way to neutralize McCabe—both of them," he said with a small chuckle, letting the folder fall back on his desk. "She appears to be the key."

"How?" she asked.

Not trying to hide his malevolent grin, he picked up his phone and asked his secretary to get Ted Pendleton at Winston Drapper. When she did, he hit the speaker button.

"Ted, I have you on the speaker because I'm here with Cassandra and we have something we need to discuss with you."

"Martin and Cassandra—this is indeed my lucky day."

"Ted, it appears your client Ann Parsons has been meeting with another attorney."

The voice on the other end was tight. "What other lawyer? Parsons is to be sentenced in two weeks."

Conroy explained the new developments, and the suspicion that Ann was on the verge of withdrawing her plea. "In light of that, we'd like you to visit your client and see if you can talk some sense into her. At the very least, find out how McCabe got in to see Parsons. Maybe we get McCabe disqualified for engaging in unethical conduct."

"And of course, we'll make sure you are compensated for your efforts," DeCovnie interjected.

"Get there tomorrow," Conroy added.

"Martin, there's simply no way I can go tomorrow. I have a very full schedule and for me to trek into New Jersey—hold on, I'm looking at my calendar—I can get there on Friday."

"Rearrange your schedule. You were paid a hundred thousand–dollar retainer for this; don't make me request an itemized bill for your services. As I hope you can appreciate, stopping your client from withdrawing her plea is of the utmost importance to the estate."

Pendleton's sigh was audible. "Fine."

"Thank you," Conroy said. "Do a quick Internet search on Mc-Cabe. Her office is in Cranford, New Jersey. You may want to call her and see if you can put the fear of God in her. I know your politics, so if nothing else, I'm sure you'll get a laugh out of the results of your online search."

Conroy hung up his office phone, pulled out his BlackBerry, and scrolled through the contacts until he found what he was looking for. Luigi Rossi was one of the founders of SIS and a former member of the Italian Intelligence Services. Charles had introduced him to Conroy. Like Charles, Luigi had an affinity for younger women. In 2000, he and several others formed SIS and had been very helpful in keeping Charles from being prosecuted. Conroy knew that SIS was well versed in working in the gray areas, and certainly knew people who are willing to handle things across the line.

"Luigi, I need a favor," he said when Rossi answered. Conroy picked up a third file on his desk, this one with a logo from a different firm. "Get hold of your friend. I need a warrant placed into the system and with an APB issued for a David Rojas. Caucasian, five foot ten, a hundred seventy pounds, DOB May 17, 1988. Put his last known address as Kissimmee, Florida." He paused. "Wait. Change the DOB to 1986. We need the police to ultimately agree they have the wrong Rojas. When the arresting authorities contact your friend to see if they have the right David Rojas, I need to know immediately." He stopped, listening to the voice on the other end. "No. I don't want any harm to come to Mr. Rojas—not yet anyway." He clicked END and looked up at DeCovnie.

She looked perplexed. "It sounds like you're trying to get Ann's brother arrested. How does that help us?"

"Ah, my dear Cassandra. All we want is every police officer in the country helping us find Mr. Rojas. Luigi will have a friendly police officer enter information into a computer that there's a warrant for David Rojas, a very common name, especially in Florida, and if they pick up our David Rojas, it saves us a lot of time and resources. Once Ann knows that her brother is vacationing with us, we remove any thoughts of her withdrawing her plea." He tugged on his French cuffs, his eyes smiling with self-satisfaction.

# CHAPTER 21

"*T*HEODORE PENDLETON," HE ANSWERED.

"Mr. Pendleton, this is Erin McCabe. I understand you called looking for me," Erin replied.

"I tried to reach you three times this morning."

"Yes. So I've heard," she replied. "Unfortunately, judges take a dim view of me returning phone calls from their courtroom."

"Are you trying to be sarcastic?" he fired back.

"No. Not trying at all."

There was a noticeable pause. "I'm calling to warn you to stay away from my client unless you want an ethics complaint against you."

"Are we talking about Ann Parsons, Mr. Pendleton?"

"Who else would we be talking about? My other clients wouldn't hire some crazy lawyer in New Jersey who doesn't even know what sex he is."

Erin rolled her eyes and shook her head. "In that case none of your clients will have a problem with me. I know I'm a woman. Regarding my speaking with Ann, I have a signed retainer agreement with Ms. Parsons, so it appears she's my client too. What a small world."

"Do you have any idea who I am?"

"Sure," she replied, looking down at the sheet in front of her. "You are a very well-educated and politically well-connected lawyer, who also seems to have overlooked several defenses for our mutual client, including the fact that Mr. Parsons sexually abused Ann and threatened to kill her for almost a decade. There's also the fact that *she* didn't kill him."

"I don't know what little game you think you're playing here, McCabe, but you'll rue the day you fucked with me."

At the sound of the other phone being slammed down, Erin looked up at Duane, who gave her a thumbs-up and hit STOP on his tape recorder.

"That went well," she said with a sarcastic grin. "Think he'll file an ethics complaint?" she asked.

"Who knows? Seems like a big enough prick to do something like that."

"You think I have anything to worry about?"

"No, but it could get dicey if they start looking into how you initially appeared on her visitors list," Duane replied.

"Yeah, I've thought about that. Hopefully, I'm never asked, but if I am, the safest thing is to go with the truth—mostly."

When Duane continued to look dubious, she added, "I won't sell Kluska out. He came to me in confidence, and he could lose his job."

"I get it," Duane responded.

After the call with Pendleton, Erin read the drafts of the brief and certifications Duane had put together on the motion for Ann to withdraw her plea. Erin was the first to admit that he was a better writer than she was. His years in the FBI writing what were known as FBI 302s, which were the reports on various aspects of an investigation, especially witness interviews, had taught him how to write succinctly but thoroughly, a skill that many lawyers did not possess, Erin included. Erin always marveled after reading a legal brief that Duane had prepared because his arguments always flowed perfectly from one to the next. Her legal writing, on the other hand, suffered from what Duane joked was *verbosus advocatus,* a flaw that many attorneys had: If you have a good point to make, why say it once when you can repeat it five or six times.

The law required Ann to show that she had a colorable claim of innocence, that she had good reasons for withdrawing her plea, and that her withdrawal wouldn't unfairly prejudice the prosecutor in taking the case to trial or give her an unfair advantage at trial. On all points, Erin was impressed with Duane's brief.

Ten minutes later she walked into Duane's office carrying her redlined version of the documents and the burner phone.

"Great stuff, as always," she said. "I made some small changes to Ann's certification for you to look at."

"Okay," he said.

"There's something else. I heard the burner vibrate on my desk as I was coming to see you. What do you think this means?" she asked as she handed him the phone.

His eyes scanned the message: **It appears we're in for a warm spell here. Think I do need to get away on vacation.**

Duane handed the phone back. "My guess is that whoever we're communicating with is in trouble and wants Ann to know."

Erin took a deep breath. "Yeah. I suppose all I can do is tell Ann tomorrow about the message and see what happens."

Unlike their previous meetings, Ann started talking as soon as she sat down in the attorney meeting room.

"They're trying everything they can to stop me from withdrawing my plea," she said in a rush. "Yesterday, I got a visit from the big shot lawyer they gave me, a guy I haven't seen since the first day I was charged. After that first meeting, I only dealt with two of his associates. But yesterday he was here in person telling me what a great deal he got for me and how I'd be insane to withdraw my plea. I said to him, 'What if I'm innocent?' and he said, 'Ann, innocent people plead guilty every day of the week. If you don't take the deal, the chances are you'll spend the rest of your life in jail.' He also had nothing nice to say about you. Said you were only motivated by getting publicity and didn't care about what happened to me."

Seeing Ann fired up for the first time since they met and knowing she was about to douse those flames caused Erin to hesitate. "Ann, there's something you need to know."

Ann gave her a sidelong look. "What?"

Erin quoted the text message she had received the day before, trying to gauge Ann's reaction. It wasn't long in coming.

"Shit," Ann said with a sigh.

"Can you tell me what it means?" Erin asked.

Ann sat in silence for a long time. "It means I'm an idiot," she said in disgust. "They always win. I don't know what I was thinking." She folded her arms on the table and buried her head in her arms.

Erin chewed on her lower lip as she watched Ann. The only sound in the locked room was Ann's muffled sobs. Even though it was against the jail's rules for an attorney to have physical contact with a prisoner, Erin reached out and gently rubbed Ann's shoulder. "I'm sorry, Ann. But please, trust me enough to tell me what it means. Don't give up. Maybe there's something we can do."

Ann raised her head just enough so she could see Erin. "No. You've done all you could. It's my fault. I should have known better."

"Who is it that they're going after?" Erin asked.

Ann slowly sat up, her eyes puffy from crying, defeat etched into her face. "My brother," she said without emotion. "I have a younger brother in Florida."

"Is he the one you send money to every month?"

Ann nodded. "About nine years ago, Parsons discovered I had a brother and he used that to make sure I did what he wanted, warning me that he'd have my brother eliminated if I didn't. When Parsons was murdered, Cassandra DeCovnie took over and she's doing it now. She's the one who promised that if I pled guilty she'd make sure my brother would receive my inheritance. When you told me she couldn't do that as executrix, I knew there was no way she'd do it on her own. The message you sent him was my message for him to disappear, and his responses were to let me know that he had gotten the message and was safe. But now this message tells me that he knows they're closing in on him and he needs to get away." The pain swept across her face as her hands began to tremble. "I thought the messages we sent would help him get away, but if they find him, they'll kill him. I can't . . . ," she said, burying her head again in her arms.

"Ann, don't give up. Maybe there's a way. Where does your brother live?"

# CHAPTER 22

JAMAL JOHNSON PULLED DOWN THE WINDOW SHADE, HOPING TO CATCH a quick nap on the flight from Newark to Tampa. "JJ" to everyone who knew him hadn't hesitated when Duane and Erin had called to see if he could do them a favor. He and Duane had been friends since they had been on the high school basketball team together at St. Cecilia's. JJ, who was a year older than Swish, had been captain of the team his senior year, when the two of them led St. Cecilia's to the number two ranking in the country. He'd been one of the top recruits in the country and decided on Notre Dame with the goal of going pro, but an injury his freshman year had crushed his dreams.

Devastated by his injury, it was only the love and support of his family and friends like Swish that had gotten him through the initial months after learning his shot at pro ball was gone. Determined not to be bitter, he had gone on to get a master's in social work and had started his own practice while also working at a group home for LGBTQ homeless kids.

Relaxing before the plane took off, he thought back to how he had come to know Erin. They met before she transitioned, when she and Swish started their law firm. JJ remembered the day Swish had come to him after Erin had told Swish that she was trans. Swish had been lost and unsure of how to react. He had come to JJ for advice because JJ had shocked his own little corner of the world when he came out as a gay man his senior year of college. JJ had taken Swish out for a few beers and talked about what it all meant—personally and professionally. At some point, JJ had let Swish know that Erin had come to him months earlier for his guidance, knowing that she was about to rock her own portion of the universe with her news. And as proud as JJ was of Erin for being who she was, he was equally proud of Swish for standing by her when most of Erin's friends deserted her. JJ knew it hadn't always been easy for Swish. They hung out with a lot of the same guys, so JJ knew better than anyone the shit that Swish took from some folks over the fact that his partner was trans. Many of their friends shared a view of masculinity that left little room for gay men and even less for trans women. Even JJ, a gifted athlete, with his shaved head and multiple tattoos on his six-foot-four frame, wasn't immune from homophobic slurs questioning his masculinity.

Erin and Duane had been direct about what they needed. They were being watched and they needed someone they could trust to meet their client's brother, whose life was in danger, and safely bring him back to New Jersey despite the many pairs of eyes watching. Perhaps it was his second-level black belt in karate that made him less worried about running into trouble, or maybe, despite the risks, he just felt he owed them for all the pro bono legal help they had provided to the kids at the group home—help they often gave without asking. Sometimes it was representing the kids in juvenile court, other times just providing some legal advice, not to mention that Erin was a valuable resource for many of the trans kids JJ worked with. And despite coming from a place of privilege, she had a way of connecting with them that JJ admired.

He checked the burner phone for any messages, then turned it off and slipped it into the pocket where he also had a photo of Rojas. If all went well, his flight would arrive in Tampa at around one a.m., he'd then meet Rojas at a coffee shop, and be on the six a.m. flight back to Newark. From there, JJ was going to take David to a halfway house in Newark run by one of his friends, where he could stay until they figured out a long-term solution.

\*   \*   \*

Erin woke with a start, her pajama top soaked with sweat. She glanced at the clock on her night table: 4:30 a.m. *Shit, why didn't I think of this before?* She quickly reached for the burner phone, which was lying next to the clock. There was a text from JJ at 4:23: **all's well heading to check-in.** Trying to battle through the early morning confusion that was clouding her thought process, she forced herself to get out of bed so she could try to reason through her sudden epiphany. After changing her top, she made her way into the kitchen. She pulled open the refrigerator door, the interior light temporarily blinding her, and poured herself a glass of orange pineapple juice. She waited, allowing her eyes to readjust to the darkness, and walked into the living room and plopped down on the couch. Ann hadn't seen her brother in almost twelve years. He was nine at the time. How could they be sure that whoever was on the plane with JJ was Ann's brother? If Ann Parsons wasn't Ann Parsons, how could they know if David Rojas was David Rojas?

Maybe it was because her brain was still half asleep, but it took her several minutes before the answer came to her. *DNA,* she thought. They'd have to get DNA from both of them. Since they were siblings, their DNA would show if they had the same mother and father. Getting David's would be easy—they could take a blood sample at the halfway house JJ was taking him to. Ann's would be a little trickier.

As she sat there in the darkness, her mind wandered until it suddenly refocused on the big picture. Were they doing the right thing? As it stood now, Ann would be out before her forty-fifth birthday. If she retracted her plea and they lost at trial, Ann might never experience freedom again.

She finally decided to see if she could get another hour's sleep. She put her untouched juice on the kitchen counter and went back into the bedroom and sat on the edge of her bed. She picked up the burner and checked—no new messages.

After tossing and turning for over an hour, Erin finally gave up and hopped in the shower. Visiting hours for lawyers started at

8:00 a.m. so she decided to be there right at eight so she'd have plenty of time to go over the certification with Ann and talk to her about her larger existential concerns for Ann's future.

"You're here bright and early," Ann said after the corrections officer left the room.

"We have a lot to go over, and I'm hoping to hear by ten that your brother is safely in New Jersey."

Ann closed her eyes and nodded. "That would be wonderful," she said almost as a prayer.

They went through the certification word by word to make sure it was perfect. When they were done, Erin slid the original across the table to her and handed her a pen. After Ann signed it, Erin slid another copy of the document across the table.

"You see where the staple is?" she asked.

Ann looked puzzled, but nodded.

"The pointed end of the staple is exposed on the back page. I need you to puncture the tip of your finger so it bleeds, and when you get a good drop of blood, I want you to press your finger against the back of the paper."

Ann looked at her like she was crazy. "What?"

"You said you haven't seen your brother in twelve years, and thus we have no idea if the person flying back to New Jersey is actually your brother. The easiest way to make sure you're siblings is a quick DNA test."

"How long will that take?" she asked.

"Assuming he's safe and we can get him tested today, we should have the results by Monday," Erin responded.

"When's the motion have to be filed by?"

"Technically, we can file them any time before your sentencing next Friday. But realistically, I don't want to cut it that close. So assuming it is your brother, he's safe, and that you still want to go ahead, I'd like to file our motion on Tuesday."

"If my brother's safe, why wouldn't I go ahead?" Ann asked.

Erin steeled herself to talk about the other thing that had her wide awake this morning. "You realize that if you go to trial there's still a good chance a jury could find you guilty."

Ann nodded. "Yes," she answered.

"If that happens, you won't be looking at twenty years, you'll be looking at a minimum of thirty."

"So are you agreeing with that pompous Pendleton? I'd be insane to withdraw my plea. Is that what you're telling me?" Ann asked, the growing frustration evident in her voice.

"No, Ann. That's not what I'm saying. I understand doing twenty years for a crime you didn't commit is really unfair. But there's no guarantee you're going to win if we go to trial. I just need to make sure you understand the risk before we ask the judge to let you withdraw your plea."

Ann swiped away a tear as it rolled slowly down her right cheek. "Maybe this won't make sense to you—or maybe to anyone—but I have been used and abused by these people since I was fourteen years old. They've already taken my life away from me. I won't tell you that it doesn't matter to me whether I walk out of the courtroom a free woman or I'm led out in handcuffs to spend the rest of my life in prison. It does. But what matters more is that I am finally standing up to them and saying, 'Fuck you, I'm not taking it from you anymore.'" Her eyes burned with rage. "Erin, I can survive in a prison cell. But I can't survive in the prison they've put me in. It's not the walls that take away your freedom, it's not fighting back. As long as they had my brother, I couldn't fight back. But if he's safe, I want—no, I need—to tell my story. The world needs to hear my story, whether they believe me or not, because there's more than just me. Trust me, there's more. They need a voice too."

"I'm with you," Erin said. The realization that the course of Ann's life now hung on her skill as a lawyer slowly settled in on Erin. So far life had handed Ann a bag of shit—all Erin could hope was that she hadn't just added to it.

It was after ten when Erin got back to the office. She had received a text from JJ that they had landed at Newark and he'd call around ten thirty. When she went in to see Swish she told him about Ann signing the certification and her desire to move forward as long as her brother was safe. She also related her early morning epiphany and took a baggie out of her purse. In it was the paper with Ann's blood on it.

"You look serious. Everything okay?" she asked.

"Yeah, just spent the morning going over our finances with Cheryl," Swish replied.

"And?" she asked, knowing that her distaste for the business side of things let the burden fall on Swish.

"Well, so far we've had a pretty solid year, but we're going to be sucking wind if we get into this case and have to try it. In addition to not being paid for our time, we just paid out of pocket for JJ to fly down to Florida and fly back with David. And that's just the tip of the iceberg. We'll need to retain several experts, and they're all going to have to be paid before they get on board."

Erin felt her spirits drop. Sometimes in her zeal to right the wrongs of the world, she lost sight of the fact that even lawyers had to pay their bills. And Swish had a wife and a young son to support. All she had to do was take care of herself.

"I know. I'm sorry. Swish, we paid the firm's line of credit down to zero last year, so perhaps we can draw down on the line to pay the experts, and do a separate agreement making me solely responsible to pay it back. We can pay you out of the line of credit too."

His smile was warm and real. "No, E. That's not why I'm telling you this. I'm telling you because I have a fee coming in on the Coleman case, and I was going to suggest that rather than taking any of that fee, we use it to cover the expenses in Ann's case."

"Swish, that's incredibly generous of you, but you originated that fee and you have a family to support. You shouldn't suffer financially because I'm off tilting at windmills."

"Well, to use a different literary reference, 'All for one and one for all.'"

Before Erin could respond she heard the burner phone ringing.

She grabbed her purse and it took her a few seconds of rummaging before she pulled the phone out to answer it. "Hello," she said tentatively.

She was relieved to hear the deep baritone of JJ's voice greeting her back. He sounded weary, but calm.

"Hold on," she said. "I'm with Duane. I'm going to put you on speaker. Where are you?"

"David and I are at the halfway house my buddy runs."

"That's great," they responded almost in unison.

"We arrived safely and we're going to try and get some sleep. I'll give you a call this afternoon."

"Wait, JJ. Before you go—your buddy's halfway house, do they do drug testing?"

"Sure," he replied. "Why?"

"I need them to take a small blood sample from David."

JJ's tone reflected his confusion. "Why do you care if he's clean or not?"

"I don't," she said. "I do care that he is who he says he is."

# CHAPTER 23

*E*RIN AND SWISH SAT ON ONE OF THE BENCHES IN THE MIDDLE OF THE courtroom, waiting for the conference with the judge. The DNA tests on Rojas and Ann had proved they were siblings, so with David safely tucked away at the halfway house, they had moved ahead with the motion to substitute as counsel for Ann and withdraw her guilty plea. They shared a knowing look as everyone else in the courtroom ignored them, seemingly in hopes they'd go away.

Pendleton and his associate, Allison Bennett, sat at defendant's counsel table with Ann, who was trying her best to ignore them. The scene reminded Erin of a couple about to get a divorce—once close, now not even able to share simple pleasantries.

On the other side of the courtroom assistant prosecutors Tom Willis and Jay Carver seemed oblivious to everyone else as they read the motion to withdraw the plea.

"Counsel, the judge will see you now. Follow me," the judge's clerk said, opening the door that led back to Judge Alan Spiegel's chambers.

Judge Spiegel was standing behind his desk when they walked in. Alan Spiegel was just as Erin remembered him. He was in his mid-fifties, about five foot nine, with curly gray hair. He had a warm smile and greeted them in his shirtsleeves, his suit jacket and judicial robe occupying different hooks on a coat rack in the corner of his office. She smiled when she saw he was wearing one of his bow ties. She remembered him once saying some men wore bow ties because they were repressed, others to make a statement that they weren't afraid to be different. Although he never opined on his reasons, she always believed he fell in the latter camp.

He greeted each of the assistant prosecutors by name and shook their hands, and after doing the same with Pendleton allowed him the opportunity to introduce Ms. Bennett.

He then turned to Erin and Duane. "Ms. McCabe, it's been a few years. Nice to see you again," he said, smiling broadly. "And you must be Mr. Swisher. Nice to meet you," he said as he shook their hands. "All of you please have a seat, and thank you all for coming in on short notice. I received the motions filed by Ms. McCabe and Mr. Swisher on Tuesday, but"—he looked down at his notes—"with sentencing scheduled for tomorrow morning, I thought it might make sense to see what everyone's position is and whether we are going to need full briefing on the motions or if there is a consensus on how we should proceed."

"Mr. Pendleton, I received the letter you faxed over yesterday afternoon in which you indicate that you are objecting to the motion of McCabe & Swisher to substitute in as counsel for the defendant, Ann Parsons, due to allegations regarding Ms. McCabe's conduct. Obviously, to the extent you want to make a record, I would certainly need to hear this in open court, but at this point I'd like to see where we're going before proceeding in that fashion."

Pendleton leaned forward in his chair. "Judge, in thirty years of practice I've never encountered anyone who has behaved in the fashion of . . . *Ms.* McCabe. Without so much as a courtesy phone call, she blatantly went in and solicited my client. This hogwash in her motion about interviewing Ms. Parsons in connection with another case is nothing but a smokescreen to try and cover up her unethical behavior. While I can certainly appreciate Your Honor's desire to handle this informally, we need to make a record of what took place here, including having Ms. McCabe testify as to how she got on my client's visitors list, so that this can be reviewed by an appellate court and the Office of Attorney Ethics."

Judge Spiegel nodded, jotting notes on his pad. "Okay. But let me ask you this: Regardless of how Ms. McCabe came to meet with Ms. Parsons, I have before me a certification signed by Ms. Parsons that specifically states she believes you and your firm did not provide her with effective assistance of counsel, and requests that I allow Ms. McCabe and Mr. Swisher the opportunity to represent her going forward. Do you have something from her that contradicts this? If not, how can I ignore that?"

"That's easy, Judge," Pendleton responded. "It's clear that Ms. McCabe has exercised undue influence on Ms. Parsons because of this transgender thing they have in common."

Erin focused on Spiegel's face, trying to determine his reaction to Pendleton's position, but it remained inscrutable.

"Interesting. I've never seen the concept of undue influence applied in this context," Spiegel said. "Mr. Pendleton, are you aware of any case law that supports your position?"

"Judge, we only received the motion on Tuesday. But, if we're provided with the opportunity to research the issue, I'm sure we'll be able to supple Your Honor we ample authority in support of our position."

"Thank you," Spiegel said, turning toward Willis. "Mr. Willis, I also have a fax from your office stating you would oppose Ms. Parsons's motion to withdraw her plea. Does your office take a position on the substitution of counsel as well?"

"Judge, I think our position on that will depend on what Mr. Pendleton can develop on how Ms. McCabe first came to meet with the defendant and whether those circumstances should disqualify her from appearing in this matter."

"Well then," Spiegel said. "It appears we're not going to be able to resolve this informally, unless of course," he said, turning to Erin and Duane, "you wish to withdraw the motions."

Erin sported a small grin. "No, Judge," Erin responded confidently. "We're prepared to move forward in keeping with our client's request."

"Fair enough," Spiegel said. "Ms. McCabe and Mr. Swisher, in light of everyone's position, I see no point in asking you to respond at this point to either Mr. Pendleton or Mr. Willis since we will need to do this in open court and make a full record. Are you okay with that?"

"Yes, Judge," Erin replied.

"Good," he said. "Obviously, I will adjourn tomorrow's sentencing." Spiegel paused and turned his head slightly to the side. "I will wait until I see everyone's papers before deciding, but I will need more than what I have before me now to require Ms. McCabe to testify at next week's hearing. So far, I haven't seen anything concerning Ms. McCabe's actions that would cause me to contact the Office of Attorney Ethics. Obviously you are free to do whatever you believe you must do consistent with your own ethical obligations. If you believe that she did something legally or ethically wrong, that is fair game. However," he said, turning to face Pendleton, "personal attacks on her are not fair game. I will not tolerate it. Am I clear?"

Pendleton looked over at Willis and then back toward the judge. "Yes, Judge. Of course," he responded obsequiously.

"Good. Thank you all for your time." Spiegel stood and shook hands with each of them before they left.

*Damn it,* Conroy fumed. With Ann's motion to allow her to withdraw her plea only two days away, they appeared no closer to finding Rojas. Through his contacts at TSA, Luigi had discovered that Rojas had flown back to Newark Airport with someone named Jamal Johnson, but despite following Johnson since Sunday, and staking out where he worked, there was still no sign of Rojas. As much as he hated to admit it he had only two options: find Rojas pronto, or eliminate the new lawyers. He desperately needed either Charles's laptop or the hard drive where he backed up the financial information. If the motion went forward, there'd either be an appeal, if the judge denied Ann's motion, or a trial, if he granted it. Either way the prosecutor's office would hold on to everything. With only two alternatives to stop the motion, he needed to implement both—now.

Conroy called Luigi, and it was agreed that SIS would have some former special ops people that it contracted with pay Mr. Johnson a visit. Conroy had suggested that Luigi use resources who had no qualms about the techniques they employed to persuade Johnson to give up Rojas. Then he called Arthur. The call went better than Conroy expected. Arthur, whose default setting to resolving issues was to eliminate the source of the problem, had offered a plan that demonstrated a restraint that had surprised Conroy. Rather than killing both lawyers, just take out McCabe. Not only did she appear to be the one who had connected with Ann, but it would be easier to plant stories providing a potential motive for the killing. Conroy had to admit it just might work.

"Yes, Mr. Hiller, you wanted to see me?"

"Yes, Carl. I've just had a very pleasant conversation with Martin Conroy and he has finally come around to my way of thinking. The woman you've been following—McCabe—she has become an unwanted nuisance and we need her removed."

"When?"

"Tonight. Time is of the essence."

"What about the other lawyer—Swisher?"

"No," Hiller answered with a malevolent grin. "I need you to make McCabe's death appear to be a random act of violence against a trans woman. I want this to look like a hate crime."

Carl returned Hiller's grin. "Hate crimes are my specialty."

"Good. Assuming this goes well, see me tomorrow and I'll arrange a bonus for you."

"Will do."

After Carl left, Arthur poured himself a drink. He was enjoying that Conroy had come around to his way of thinking. He had told Charles many times that he didn't trust Conroy, but Charles had always dismissed him, reminding Arthur that he had known Conroy since college and much of Conroy's legal practice was built on clients Charles had referred to him. Charles would laugh and say, "I can destroy Martin with about four phone calls, and he's smart enough to know that too." But with Charles gone, Arthur's concerns about Conroy had come to the fore. Without Charles, could they trust Conroy? He knew Cassandra shared his concerns, as they had commiserated over the last few weeks over Conroy's dismissive attitude toward their worries over the laptop and hard drives.

After his second drink, he sent DeCovnie a text message.

**spoke with martin he has agreed to implementing my solution**

**both?** She replied?

**no just her**

**when?**

**tonight**

# CHAPTER 24

S HE READ AND REREAD THE TEXTS BETWEEN ARTHUR AND DECOVNIE. "My solution." What the hell was Arthur's solution? Whatever it was, it was happening tonight. But it wasn't happening to both. "Just her." Who was the "her"? Was it Ann? Was it unrelated?

No. If it involved DeCovnie, Conroy, and Arthur, somehow it was related. *Think, damn it.*

Just the fact that she could see the texts was a stroke of luck. Back when she had access to Parsons's laptop, she had been lucky enough to be monitoring his activity on a day that he sent DeCovnie a text message with a picture attached to it. Later, after he had logged out, she had logged in as him and resent the same message with the note, "Did you get this?" When DeCovnie dutifully opened the second attachment, it infected her phone in the process. After Parsons was murdered, everyone had gotten rid of their infected computers, but luckily, DeCovnie hadn't gotten a new phone.

After all these years, she still remembered Arthur as a violent, ruthless man, who was feared even by those close to him. Unlike Parsons, who presented an air of sophistication, Arthur made no such pretense. He was short and beefy and carried his Staten Island background as a badge of honor, along with the scars from the street fights he had survived. What he and Charles shared was a taste for underage girls. That and gambling was what brought them together and had made them both very wealthy men.

Knowing Arthur, it wasn't a leap for her to conclude his solution revolved around violence. She suspected that the only reason Ann was still alive was because they thought she might know where the hard drives were. So if they couldn't kill Ann . . . maybe they were targeting those who were speaking for her, Swisher and McCabe. But it wasn't both of them; it was "just her." Her guess? McCabe was going to be killed tonight.

She sat back, wondering how she should play this. This wasn't her fight. She had no idea why Ann had pled guilty, but that was Ann's problem, not hers. She had her own problems to work out, but she needed more time, and maybe if McCabe was killed, that might delay things even further. No, it was more likely that it would scare Ann into just allowing her plea to stand and ending the case in the next week. Besides, if DeCovnie and the rest of them wanted McCabe dead, that was reason enough to stop them.

But even if she was right, how could she stop them? It wasn't like she could go up to McCabe's door and warn her. She had to work in the shadows, hiding in plain sight. She opened her nightstand and took out the spare gun that she kept there. In her sock drawer she took out the suppressor, which was hidden in the back.

She walked into the bathroom and splashed cold water on her face. She had killed before—once in Fallujah, and then the second time. She stared into the mirror. Was what she was about to do murder? Did the ends really justify the means? Was what she was about to do forgivable because they deserved it? But wasn't she already a murderer? She had blown off the back of his head— although perhaps she wouldn't have pulled the trigger if he hadn't hit her hand. Or maybe that was just her conscience trying to assuage her guilt. Did she even have a conscience anymore? She paused, the realization of how cold blooded her thought process had become slowly sinking in. Maybe she had become just as evil as they were. After all, tonight she was preparing to shoot whomever Arthur sent to kill McCabe.

*But all I ever learned from love was how to shoot at someone who outdrew you,* she sang silently. *Hallelujah . . .*

\* \* \*

*Time to call it a night,* JJ thought, sliding the last chart into the filing cabinet. His last patient had left around ten p.m. and he had worked on his clients' charts for another forty-five minutes. He went over to the door in his office that led out to the hallway and locked it. His office was set up so that he had an entrance from the hallway into his waiting room, and then after the session finished, his client would exit through the door in his office. That assured confidentiality because the client in the waiting room never saw who was in his office, and the person in his office never saw who was waiting. He grabbed his cell phone and opened the door to the waiting area to turn off the light and lock that door.

Standing in his waiting room were two men, one bigger than the other. Both had their faces covered by ski masks. One had a slapper, the other the equivalent of a police nightstick.

*Shit, why do they want to rob me? I don't have any money.*

"Good evening, Mr. Johnson," the one with the slapper said, smacking it into his open palm.

JJ was startled that they knew his name.

"We just need one little piece of information. We just need to know where Mr. Rojas is, and if you'll be kind enough to tell us, we say thank you and have a nice night."

JJ hesitated, the realization that this wasn't a robbery taking hold as he quickly tried to piece together exactly what was happening. "Sorry. I don't know a Mr. Rojas," he said, hoping to buy some time.

The bigger of the two, who was holding the nightstick, shook his head. "You really are a stupid motherfucker, aren't you?"

JJ's decision was instantaneous—these guys were big and armed, so striking first was his only hope. And for a brief moment, his karate skills caught them off guard, allowing him to get in a few good licks before they realized they were in for a fight.

The first blow from the slapper stunned him and he took a hit from the nightstick in the ribs, but he managed to recover quickly and the three of them engaged in a weird dance around the room, each of them looking for an opportunity to strike. As he faced them with his back to the door, JJ reached behind him, feeling for the door handle, hoping to make his escape. Unexpectedly, the door flew open and JJ found himself enveloped in a bear hug from a third person. Before he could break free, he took several blows to his face. He managed to flip the guy who was holding him from behind but in the process took a glancing blow to the top of his head from the nightstick, causing him to drop to his knees, dazed.

"Look, dude, either you tell us where Rojas is or your friend McCabe is dead. Your call, cowboy. You decide if she lives or dies."

Struggling to catch his breath, JJ was stunned. Give up Rojas or Erin dies? *Fuck!*

She positioned herself strategically outside McCabe's apartment building so if they were coming for her, she could see them whether they approached on the Prospect Avenue side, or if they came down Riverside. She suspected it would be the latter— they'd be rushed and probably unfamiliar with the area. Riverside was one way, and unless you knew the area, you'd think Riverside was the only way in. She, on the other hand, had been here the day she followed McCabe from the Lido, so she knew to park farther down on Prospect so she could be back on North Avenue in less than a minute. From there the Garden State Parkway was only blocks away—the perfect getaway.

She watched a car slow down as it approached the front of the building. Time, like the car, slowed down as her heartbeat grew stronger. The car drove past Prospect and pulled into a parking space at the corner. She could make out the New York license plate. Her breath quickened when it parked. She tapped the gun in her pocket.

The doors of the Ford Focus opened and two men stepped out. She had seen enough men preparing to kill to recognize the dance—the movements precise and well choreographed as they scanned their surroundings and got their bearings. It was too far for her to make out who they were, but she had no doubt she had guessed right. They were coming to kill McCabe.

Her conscience swam up, but she pushed it down. She had been over this—there was no other way to stop it. This was justified. She had to do it. She had the element of surprise. All she needed to do was walk past them, turn, and shoot them in the back. Don't give them a chance. Shoot them in the back—cold blooded? *Oh shit, I've become them. Murder or self-defense? Ladies and gentlemen of the jury, you decide.*

She pulled out her burner and dialed 911.

"Cranford Police, what's your emergency?"

"I'm near the corner of Prospect and Riverside," she said in a whispered voice, cupping her hand over her mouth to make sure her voice didn't carry. "There are two white men next to a dark-colored Ford Focus with New York license plates parked at the corner. They both have guns."

"How do you know they have guns, ma'am?"

"They have them out. I can see them," she lied.

"Where are you and what's your name?"

"Oh my God, they've seen me," she ad-libbed. "They're heading toward me. Help!" She clicked END, hoping it was enough for them to send a car.

The two men shared a muffled conversation over the roof of the car, and then they started walking toward the building.

*Come on. Where's the cavalry?*

She touched her gun inside her windbreaker pocket. Maybe she'd need it after all—thankfully she had already secured the suppressor.

They moved slowly at first, marking out their exit strategy. They were crossing Prospect when she finally decided she had to make her move.

She headed down the walkway and turned onto the sidewalk in front of the building. *Still nothing.* She could see them eying her warily as she approached, and her hand tightened on the gun in her pocket. Then she saw the flashing light bouncing off the building farther down Riverside. The car was heading towards them, coming up Riverside the wrong way on the one-way street.

She was now face-to-face, looking directly at both of them. That's when it all came back—his smell, the harshness of his hands, the coldness of his laugh. Even now, more than a decade later, he was one of the faces that haunted her. Him, Charles Parsons, Martin Conroy, Arthur Hiller, Liam Fletcher, Max Gallagher—so many others. Others whose names she never knew. So many.

When they were a few feet past her she stopped. Her hand gripped her gun. Without even thinking she flipped off the safety. "Hey, aren't you Carl Shamey?" she said.

He whipped around on hearing his name, but when he turned, he saw the flashing police lights heading up Riverside Drive. He poked his partner, and they both headed back toward their car as quickly as they could. He scowled at her as he passed, clearly frustrated by his inability to place her.

As the police car pulled up alongside the Ford, she retreated into the shadows and watched in case things went south. A female officer got out and placed her hand on her weapon.

"This your car?" she asked them.

"Yes, officer. Is there a problem?" Carl asked.

"I hope not," the officer replied politely.

A second car came down Riverside with its lights flashing and parked on Prospect. An officer got out and positioned himself behind the two men.

"Can I see some ID please?" the first officer asked.

Carl reached for his wallet in his back pants pocket, moving his jacket in the process.

"Gun!" the second officer screamed. "On the ground face-down, hands out in front of you," he commanded, as both officers pulled out their weapons.

The two men did as directed while the female officer reached inside her vehicle and grabbed her radio. "This is car twelve,

Montinelli. Corner of Prospect and Riverside. Ten thirty-five two armed individuals. Request additional backup."

Satisfied things were under control, she turned and, as several curious onlookers began to gather, she walked in the other direction, ultimately making her way back to her car by a circuitous route. When she finally got behind the wheel, she sat lost in her thoughts. Maybe she wasn't a monster—at least not yet.

# CHAPTER 25

THE PHONE STARTLED ERIN FROM A SOUND SLEEP. AS SHE FELT FOR it in the dark, she squinted at the clock—12:12 a.m. Her immediate thought was that something happened to her mom, but when she found the phone she saw it was Duane calling.

"Hello," she mumbled.

"Where are you?!" Duane screamed.

She looked at the phone. Swish never screamed. "In bed; asleep. Swish, what's going on?"

"Check your place. Make sure you're safe."

"I'm fine," she said.

"Humor me—check!" he demanded. "And take the phone with you in case."

She reached over and turned on the lamp on her night table. Deciding this would go faster if she just did what he wanted, she hauled herself out of bed and roamed her apartment, flicking on lights as she went and checking to make sure the door was locked. "Okay, everything's fine," she said when she was finished. "Now, do you mind telling me what this is all about?"

"I'm on my way to Trinitas Hospital."

"Why? What's wrong?" she asked, suddenly wide awake.

"They came after JJ tonight and, from what he managed to tell me, he was beaten up pretty badly. In the course of it they told him if he didn't tell them where Rojas was you were going to be killed."

"Oh my God, did he tell them where David is?"

"No. He managed to fight them off. But he's convinced they're coming for you tonight. Until I can get to you, I'm going to call Mark and tell him to come over."

She recoiled involuntarily. "No! Don't involve Mark in this. Besides, I'm three blocks from police headquarters—they can be here in two minutes."

She walked to the front window to peek out and see if there were any suspicious cars only to find the strobe of police lights bouncing off the parked cars and the tree line on the other side of Riverside Drive. She pulled her curtains back and tried to peer down the street, but the side of the building blocked her view.

"Uh, Swish."

"Yeah."

"Based on what I can see, I'm guessing there are several police cars farther down Riverside. I can see their lights going. I'm going to throw on some clothes and see what's going on."

"No! Stay put."

"Swish, the cops are already here. Trust me, my neighbors are nosey enough that they'll know what's going on."

"E, please."

"Talk to you in a few."

Fifteen minutes later she called him back.

"It's a good thing you aren't dead, because I'm going to kill you," he said when he answered the phone. "Do you understand you were targeted tonight?"

"How's JJ?" she asked, ignoring his comment.

"He's pretty banged up, with a fractured right radius and probably a concussion. But feeling much better knowing that you're alive. What did you find out?"

"According to nosey neighbor number one, around eleven thirty the police arrested two men on the corner right down from my building. Both of them had handguns. According to nosey neighbors two and three those handguns had silencers. Swish, if you're at the hospital, what about Cori and Austin?"

"They're okay. There's a black-and-white sitting in front of my house. Pays to know some of the guys on the force. What about you? You okay?" he asked.

"Physically, sure. Mentally, I'm a hot mess. It looks like they were really coming for me."

"Yeah, no shit. Two guys with guns getting arrested about fifty yards from the entrance to your building after the guys that beat the crap out of JJ said that you would be killed strikes me as pretty compelling."

"Shit. How do I keep getting myself into these cases where people want to kill me? Is my karma that bad?"

"Or maybe your karma is pretty damn good given you're still here."

She sat there, trying to piece things together. After what had happened to Connie, she should have known that, even with Parsons gone, whoever was still lurking in the background was dangerous. Who that was, she didn't have a clue. If this all tied into what Justin had been involved in, there were a helluva lot of pieces still missing and she just wasn't smart enough to put it all together yet, but clearly they wanted her out of the way.

"You okay?" Swish asked, breaking the silence.

"Yeah. Maybe you're right. Maybe my karma isn't so bad."

"What makes you say that?"

"How come they got caught fifty yards from my building? It's not like I live in a neighborhood where the cops are doing random stop-and-frisks."

Now it was Swish's turn to be silent for a moment. "I don't know."

"Crazy," she said to no one.

"Please do me a favor, don't be alone tonight. Call Mark."

"Will do," she said, knowing she wouldn't. If someone was out to get her, she didn't want Mark caught in the crosshairs.

She knew it was probably crazy, but after she hung up from Swish, she changed her clothes, combed her hair, and walked the three blocks to the police station. Not surprisingly, at this hour of the day, no one was sitting at the front desk, so she hit the buzzer.

"Can I help you, ma'am?" an officer asked when he got to the glass.

"Yes. There were two men arrested over on Riverside Drive a little while ago. I was wondering if I could talk to one of the arresting officers."

"Why do you want to do that, ma'am?"

"Because I think the men they arrested may have been coming to shoot me."

At first, he looked at her like she was crazy, but slowly his expression changed. "Do I know you from somewhere? You look familiar."

"Don't know. Someone tried to murder me about two years ago. Maybe you saw me then."

"You're that McBride lawyer, aren't you?"

"It's McCabe. But yes, I am a lawyer."

"You must be one very unpopular lawyer if you think those men were coming for you and someone tried to murder you two years ago."

All she could do was shrug.

"Wait here," he said.

About ten minutes later Officer Gail Montinelli opened the door and motioned for Erin to follow. Erin gave a small smile, remembering Officer Montinelli as the investigating officer from a prior incident at her old apartment.

"Remember me?" Montinelli asked as they headed to an interview room.

"Absolutely," Erin replied. "You're the officer who responded to my 911 call and searched my apartment about two years ago when someone broke in."

"Good memory," Montinelli responded.

*Or maybe there just aren't a lot of female police officers in Cranford,* Erin thought.

Once they settled in and Montinelli had taken Erin's contact info, she laid her notepad and pen on the table. "So why do you think these guys were after you?"

Erin had decided on her way over to give an abridged version.

She explained that she was working on a high-profile case, and that a friend of theirs who was helping out had been beaten pretty badly in Elizabeth, followed by a warning they were coming to kill her. In fact, if Montinelli checked the phone logs, there should be a call from Elizabeth PD around midnight to do a safety check on Erin.

Montinelli picked up the pen and started taking notes. After giving Montinelli JJ's name and address, Erin told Montinelli about what had happened to Connie Irving, that two men had broken into her business and shot her shortly after she had met with Erin's partner. "Do you think that was related to this?" Montinelli asked.

"Yes," Erin replied. "But I have no idea if either one of the guys you arrested tonight were involved in what happened in New York. But it certainly might be worth doing ballistics on their weapons."

"Interesting," Montinelli responded. "Right now we have these two on illegal possession of handguns, which is a second degree with a minimum three years without parole under the Graves Act. But you and I both know that they'll probably be out on bail in less than twenty-four hours. Maybe if I can get an assistant prosecutor to ask the bail judge to hold them until we can get some ballistics done on their guns in our lab, we'll get lucky. Fortunately, we're one of the few counties that has our own ballistics lab, so we have a shot—sorry, no pun intended. We have a chance at convincing a judge to hold them while we do some testing." Chewing on her lower lip, she said, "Yeah, worth a look. Thanks for coming in."

"You're welcome," Erin replied. "Can I ask you a question?"

"Sure," Montinelli responded.

"How come you stopped them?"

"Wasn't a random stop. There was a nine-one-one call about two guys with guns. My shift had just come on duty and I was still at headquarters, so I went."

"Thanks," Erin said. "Can you let me know what happens? Especially if they get out on bail."

"Absolutely," Montinelli said. "As I'm sure you know, I'm just a patrol officer and a detective will be assigned tomorrow morning. But I'll make sure it's noted on the file to keep you in the loop."

"I appreciate that," Erin said.

They started to walk down the hallway. "Um. Listen, you seem to have more than your fair share of people trying to kill you. Please be careful, and don't hesitate to call me if you need anything," Montinelli said, handing Erin her business card.

"Thanks again," Erin said with a warm smile.

# CHAPTER 26

*D*AMN IT. SHE WAS EXHAUSTED, UNABLE TO SLEEP, HER MIND DES-
perately trying to calculate the chances that he would figure out
who she was. Why had she called out his name? It had been eleven
years. Her long blond hair was now jet black and spiky, and her body
was no longer that of a developing teen. After four years in the cru-
cible of the marines, one of which was spent in Iraq, her physique
had become hard and androgynous. Except she had called him by
name. Word would get back to Arthur, Martin, and Cassandra, and
they'd figure out it was her. Of course, they'd still have to find her,
but they would eventually. Money and power will out.

She wasn't ready to move to the next stage yet. Her plan was to
send the videos to the feds, but only after she had the money, and
she hadn't counted on it taking this long to crack the passwords
for the accounts. She still needed some time. Parsons had been
smart—or paranoid—and even though she had his hard drive
containing all the information on the accounts, he had used a
code to hide the real account numbers and passwords. Not to
mention that Parsons only had half of each password, it had taken
time for her to go hunting for the other half on Conroy's computer, which she was able to find, thanks to the rootkit.

She still needed more time to decode everything, time that
she'd have if Ann withdrew her plea. But she had gone and complicated things for herself by calling out Shamey's name.

*Idiot.*

\* \* \*

"Fucking idiot," Arthur spit out.

"I concur, Arthur," Martin said, walking over to the bar in Charles's brownstone where they were assembled. He scanned the selection before choosing a Glenfiddich forty-year-old single malt scotch whisky, which he knew ran about four thousand a bottle, and poured himself a glass. "Perhaps you should have realized that before you sent him out on this job," he said, after taking a long sip from his drink.

Hiller glared at him, but said nothing.

"Why were they denied bail?" DeCovnie asked.

Martin snorted. "Because I'm told the assistant prosecutor asked for seventy-two hours to allow the forensic unit to finish ballistic testing on the handguns seized from Carl and Seth. Which is not good."

"Why?" she asked.

Martin snorted again. "Because even though Carl was smart enough to know not to use the same gun he used when he shot Max because ballistics could get a match on the two shootings, unfortunately he had the other weapon under his seat. So when the police did an inventory search of the car after his arrest, what to their wondering eyes should appear but a second handgun!"

Conroy swiveled in his chair so he was facing Arthur. "There's more. Carl gave his attorney a message to give us. He said he saw Ann at the scene."

"Ann?" Arthur said. "Is he delusional? Ann's in jail."

"Not faux Ann, Arthur—the one, the only, the original."

"Oh my God, you were right," DeCovnie proclaimed darkly.

Martin took a long sip from his drink. He had found the tape of Charles's murder compelling proof that Ann was back, but he had apparently underestimated her and her desire for revenge. He had deluded himself into believing she had returned to kill Charles, and with him gone, she would disappear again. Carl's claim that she had been at the scene was beyond disturbing.

"What a fucking shit show!" Arthur bellowed. "I surmise that Luigi's goons did not find out where Rojas is?"

"You surmise correctly," Martin said. "All in all, not a good night."

"So what next?" DeCovnie asked.

"There remains the possibility that the court will not allow Ann to withdraw her plea. However, given where we are now, I believe preventing Ann from withdrawing her plea is no longer our best option. So after reexamining our alternatives, I've come up with a plan B," Martin said, then took another long sip of his drink.

"Plan B?" DeCovnie said. "We don't need a plan B, we need Charles's laptop."

"I agree. And if Ann loses the motion to withdraw her plea, McCabe will surely file an appeal, which will tie this up for years!" Martin added.

"So kill the whole lot of them and be done with it," Arthur suggested.

Conroy groaned. "Because this last hit on McCabe has worked out so terribly well for us," he said, raising his eyebrows.

"Then what are you suggesting?" Arthur asked, his growing annoyance evident.

Conroy stood up and walked over to the desk in the study and ran his hands along the expensive wood, admiring Charles's taste in furnishings.

"I don't like the delays any more than either of you," he said, sliding into the chair, "but I will confess a little secret. I didn't trust Charles, and so eight years ago, he and I took a vacation and went to all the banks and opened new accounts. We each had the account numbers, but we each had only half the passwords. We also agreed on a code, so that when we stored our part of the passwords, they were in a code that only we knew."

"So how the hell does that help us?" Arthur barked. "It sounds like we'll never get access to the accounts."

"Arthur, my point is, be patient. No one else can get into the accounts. So the accounts are safe. The concern is where are the hard drives, which I'm afraid may have many of the videos that Charles was inclined to watch and keep as leverage on us, as well as other well-connected folks. None of us want those videos to see the light of day."

"Damn it, Martin. There's five hundred and fifty million dollars sitting offshore, a third of which is mine!"

Conroy leaned forward, resting his arms on the desk. "We all want our share of the money, Arthur. But our adult websites are still very profitable, so none of us are starving. We've taken down all our sites from the dark web. Assuming faux Ann goes to trial, it will give us additional time to find her brother and prevent her from testifying at trial. Once she's guilty, she'll be sentenced to life," he said, a smile spreading across his face.

"But won't McCabe just file an appeal of her conviction, tying us up for years?" DeCovnie asked.

"Yes, but once she's convicted, we should be able to get the laptop back."

"Why?" Arthur said.

"I don't want to get all lawyer-like on you, but it has to do with the Rules of Evidence. The reason the prosecutor's office still has the laptop is that they need to show the jury where the recording device that recorded the murder was located and how it works. Once the trial is over, the issue of the chain of custody of the recording isn't likely going to be part of the appeal, and I have it on reliable information that the prosecutor's office will give us the laptop."

"Why can't we just get them to make a copy of everything on the laptop?" Arthur asked.

"Jesus, Arthur. That's the last thing I want at this point, some computer expert from the prosecutor's office seeing everything on there. No, absolutely not!" Martin replied, growing more aggravated.

"What if she is found not guilty?" Arthur posed.

"Then we expose her as a fraud and prevent her from inheriting from Charles's estate. Then we'll have her deported because she's not here legally."

"I still say she's too big a risk," Arthur grumbled. "She knows who we are. What's to stop her from trying to expose us as part of her defense?"

"Fortunately, other than using her in the porn movies, Charles mostly kept her to himself. He never shared her with us, not like he did with the original Ann."

"Damn it, Martin!" DeCovnie screamed. "Just because you didn't screw her, it doesn't mean she can't hurt us. Don't forget that I was the one who brought her to Charles. And I was the one suggesting that she should plead guilty to protect her brother."

"Please—I suspect that ten million dollars will be a powerful incentive to prevent her from opening up too much about her true identity. Not to mention that there's not a single document that proves she even exists. She's undocumented and Charles used his Florida connections to have all the documents concerning her foster care purged from the system. Besides, testifying about how Charles abused her is a two-edged sword. While it may generate sympathy, it would also provide a powerful motive for her to have killed Charles." He paused, taking another long sip of scotch. "There are risks in every direction. All we can do is get the money and be prepared to use our influence with the media to discredit Ann if we need to. No one will believe a transgender porn star who is in the country illegally."

There was silence in the room. "I'm not happy," Arthur finally said through his scowl.

"Arthur, I've known you for thirty years, and I've never seen you happy. Well, outside of when you're getting a massage from a fifteen-year-old girl."

"Fuck you," Arthur snapped.

Martin laughed and took another sip of his drink.

"Did you tell Pendleton?" Arthur asked.

"No. But as I indicated, it did come up in my conversation with our source in the prosecutor's office and I was told that it appears likely that the judge will allow Ann to withdraw her plea, and, if necessary, they can always put their finger on the scale if it appears close."

"What about the real Ann?" DeCovnie asked.

"I've already spoken with Luigi. We will find her and eliminate her," Conroy replied.

Arthur walked over to the bar, grabbed a glass and a bottle of

Knob Creek bourbon. He poured until the glass was almost full. He slowly crossed the room, the bottle in one hand, the glass in the other. "This is all Carl's fault."

"Can he be trusted to keep his mouth shut?" DeCovnie asked.

"No," Arthur said. "And he could certainly cause us more potential problems than Ann," he added.

"Well, Arthur, we finally agree on something," Conroy said, his eyes narrowing. "That is why I believe that, assuming Carl gets transferred to Rikers, we should arrange for him to commit suicide."

Arthur's dower expression didn't change. He simply nodded and said, "Agreed."

# CHAPTER 27

*E*RIN WAS SURPRISED TO SEE RICH RUDOLPH, A REPORTER FOR THE *Newark Journal,* sitting in the courtroom on Friday morning. Wearing a wrinkled white shirt, with his tie askew and the top button undone. Erin had gotten to know Rudolph, who covered the state courts, back when she was a PD. She wasn't sure who had tipped him off, but it likely meant there were going to be some fireworks at the hearing.

It was a strange tableau. Ann Parsons sat at counsel table with two attorneys she was giving the silent treatment to, complete with angling herself toward Erin and Duane, who were sitting behind her at the courtroom railing. On the other side were prosecutors Ted Willis and Jay Carver, backed by Detective Sergeant Ed Kluska. When she walked in, Kluska had acknowledged her with a simple nod.

"All rise," the courtroom deputy intoned as Spiegel bounded up to the bench.

"Good afternoon, everyone. Please be seated," Spiegel began. "I've received everyone's papers, including a cross-motion from Ms. Parsons's current counsel, Theodore Pendleton of Winston Drapper, to disqualify the firm of McCabe & Swisher from representing the defendant. I also note that although I requested counsel avoid personal attacks, I was disappointed to see that not all counsel took my admonition to heart. That said, the defendant in this case is a twenty-five-year-old woman. I have no evidence before me that she is suffering from any mental or emotional issues that would prevent her from deciding issues involving her legal position. So, given the Sixth Amendment right to counsel of one's choosing, and fully cognizant of the fact that, depending on what happens on the motion to withdraw her plea, the defendant may face a trial in this matter, I would like to question Ms. Parsons."

The courtroom deputy walked over; asked Ann to stand, place her hand on the Bible; and then administered the oath to her.

"Good afternoon, Ms. Parsons. You understand you are under oath?"

"Yes, Judge."

"You appear to have an abundance of legal counsel," he said with a small grin. "Up until now Mr. Pendleton and Ms. Bennett from Winston Drapper have represented you, but I have in front of me a motion by the firm of McCabe & Swisher to substitute in as counsel. Are you aware of that?"

"Yes, Judge."

"At this point, I'm not asking you about your plea—this is just about who represents you going forward. Did you authorize Ms. McCabe to make the motion on your behalf to be your attorney?"

"I did, Judge."

"And in that motion, you request that the firm of McCabe & Swisher be allowed to represent you. Is that still your position?"

"It is, Judge."

"Did anyone pressure you to request this change?"

"No, Your Honor."

"In their papers opposing the motion, your current counsel argues that Ms. McCabe unduly influenced you to make this request. Leaving aside any legal advice Ms. McCabe or Mr. Swisher may have given you, has Ms. McCabe or Mr. Swisher done anything to try and influence you to change counsel?"

"No, Your Honor."

"Explain to me in your own words why you want to change counsel."

"Judge, let me start by saying that I've worked as a paralegal for four years, so I know a little about how lawyers deal with clients, and I do not believe I have received competent representation. When I was charged, the estate offered to retain Winston Drapper to represent me. Other than seeing Mr. Pendleton at my arraignment and plea, I never spoke with the man until a week ago. I met primarily with a Mr. Thompson, who sometimes had Ms. Bennett with him. Mr. Thompson never discussed my relationship with Mr. Parsons or what defenses I might have to the charges. After he met with the prosecutor's office to discuss a plea, Mr. Thompson came to me and said he had obtained a good plea offer, and that I should accept it. Of course, once I pled guilty, the estate moved to exonerate my bail, which Mr. Thompson did not oppose on my behalf, resulting in me being sent to the Union County jail. So I'm not sure whose interest they were putting first—the estate's or mine—but I never felt like they had my best interest at heart."

Erin watched Pendleton as Ann spoke. He fidgeted in his seat and every once in a while emitted a "hmph" or an "argh." A few times, Allison leaned over to try to say something to him, but he shook his head and ignored her. Eventually, she gave up. When Ann said that the estate was paying Winston Drapper, Erin could tell from his body language that he was undecided as to whether to stand up and object. He actually started to rise from his chair and then stopped.

"Ms. Parsons," Judge Spiegel continued, "has anyone made any promises to you as to what might happen if you change counsel?"

Ann hesitated. "No, Judge," she replied.

"Has anyone made any threats to you concerning changing counsel?"

This time Ann's hesitancy was pronounced. Finally, she said, "Concerning changing counsel, no, Your Honor."

Spiegel tapped his pen on the side of his face, seemingly weighing his options. He jotted something down on his legal pad and then looked up. "Thank you, Ms. Parsons. You may have a seat."

He looked around the courtroom. "Does anyone have questions of Ms. Parsons limited to the issue of changing counsel?"

Pendleton rose to his feet. "I have questions, Judge."

"Anyone else?" Spiegel asked.

"No, Your Honor," Erin and Willis replied.

"I am aware that this is a hearing and there is no jury present. However, I am also aware that a member of the press is in the courtroom." He paused. "Welcome, Mr. Rudolph," Spiegel added with a warm smile. "While I certainly don't want to imply that the press is not welcome in my courtroom, given the somewhat un- usual nature of these proceedings, I'd like to see counsel at side- bar, because in fairness to the defendant, I'd like to know the line of questioning counsel is going to pursue to avoid prejudicing her position going forward. For the record, I also want to note that I am temporarily sealing this portion of the record, which I, of course, will reconsider when we're finished."

As they huddled at the judge's bench, the court reporter took her machine and moved around so she was sitting facing the lawyers. "Mr. Pendleton, give me an idea of what you want to ask the defendant that I haven't covered."

"Judge, her implication that my firm may have had a conflict of interest is outrageous. I suspect that was planted by Ms. McCabe and I'd like to question her about that."

Erin was ready to respond, but Spiegel simply shook his head. "Mr. Pendleton, first of all, I think there's an attorney-client privi- lege issue. However I rule on this motion, Ms. Parsons has the ab- solute right to consult with, and obtain advice from, counsel concerning representation. More to the point, I think Ms. Par- sons's point is well taken. While I understand that your firm does not represent the estate, clearly the estate's move to exonerate the bail was not in Ms. Parsons's best interest, and your firm, which was being paid by the estate, did not oppose it. Even if there is no actual conflict, and I'm not deciding if there was or wasn't, I'm satisfied that it's a legitimate matter for the defendant to be concerned with. I will not allow questioning on those issues. Next."

Pendleton's face grew red.

"I'd like to question her concerning what she knows about how Ms. McCabe wound up on her visitors list. Hopefully, Your Honor is going to allow me the opportunity to call Ms. McCabe as a witness on our cross-motion to disqualify her, and this will be relevant to that application."

"Ms. McCabe?" Spiegel said, turning to face Erin.

"Judge, I submitted a certification concerning my representation of another client and why that led me to wanting to speak with Ms. Parsons. I also provided a copy of the retainer agreement with the other client, which shows that I was retained prior to visiting Ms. Parsons. I think for me to go further than what I've already provided to the court and counsel in my certification would impinge on the attorney-client privilege for both Ms. Mackey, on behalf of her son's estate, and Ms. Parsons."

"Mr. Pendleton, let me assume that the circumstances surrounding Ms. McCabe's initial visit with Ms. Parsons appear to be unusual," the judge said, turning his head slightly and looking in Erin's direction. "Even assuming that, how is that initial meeting relevant to the question currently before me—should the defendant be allowed to withdraw her plea?"

"Judge, as we argue in our papers, we believe this 'other client' is nothing but a ruse for Ms. McCabe to see the defendant."

"I understand, Mr. Pendleton. What I'm asking is, assume it was a ruse—how does that impact what I have to decide today?"

"Judge, most respectfully, I believe that this whole transgender thing between McCabe and Parsons—"

"You mean Ms. McCabe and Ms. Parsons," Spiegel interrupted.

Pendleton looked at Erin. "Judge, I know when counsel was a public defender, he was Ian McCabe. If you read up on him, he changed his sex and uses that to get these cases. He had one in South Jersey a few years ago and now he used it here too."

"Mr. Pendleton, Ms. McCabe is entitled to be treated with the dignity and respect afforded to any member of the bar. We happen to have a law in New Jersey that protects her and Ms. Parsons from discrimination and I would ask you to be respectful and use the correct pronouns when referring to her." Without waiting for Pendleton to respond, Spiegel continued. "So if I understand, the reason you want to call Ms. McCabe to the stand is to question her about her status and its relationship to her being retained as an attorney in this case?"

"Absolutely, Judge. *Her* testimony will show not only how she got to meet with my client but how she used her status as a trans-gendered to wrongfully influence Ann Parsons. I will refrain from commenting on Ms. McCabe's mental health, but clearly anyone like Ann Parsons who believes that they want to live as a woman when they aren't a biological woman has mental issues that need to be explored."

Spiegel closed his eyes momentarily, as if gathering his thoughts.

"Mr. Willis, what is your office's position on Mr. Pendleton's cross-motion?"

"Judge, we are not taking a position. We do not want the issue of how Ms. McCabe came to represent Ms. Parsons to become an issue for appeal, and we believe the current record is sufficient to uphold the defendant's plea of guilty."

Erin watched Pendleton out of the corner of her eye as Willis spoke. His face dropped and he appeared surprised by the prose-cutor's position.

"Mr. Pendleton," Spiegel began, "I reviewed the portion of your motion dealing with Ms. Parsons's mental health and state of mind, and I see no merit to those arguments. Your argument is not supported by any medical evidence, and unless you have something else to add, I am not going to permit you to question Ms. Parsons or call Ms. McCabe as a witness."

Pendleton, still seemingly caught off guard by Willis's position, sputtered, "Ba . . . but, Judge, this is wrong. My professional cre-dentials are second to none and it's outrageous that I have to lis-ten to this . . . person," he said, gesturing to Erin, "unfairly malign me and my firm, when she suffers from delusions she's a woman"

"That's enough, Mr. Pendleton! You are perilously close to crossing a line. Ms. McCabe's status has nothing—I repeat, nothing—to do with this motion. Despite my cautioning you at our conference last week not to make personal attacks, your papers in opposition to this motion and in support of your cross-motion were replete with them. If I hear another word from you about Ms. McCabe's status, I will hold you in contempt. Am I clear?"

Pendleton stood silent, glaring at the judge.

"I asked you a question, Mr. Pendleton. Am I clear?"

"Perfectly," Pendleton responded.

"Good. Anything else you would like to question your client on?"

"No . . . Judge."

When Erin returned to her seat Swish leaned over and said, "Uh, the last part of Pendleton's argument was not exactly sotto voce. We pretty much heard everything."

She turned around and looked at Rudolph. Although his eyes were wide, they suggested that if he had heard anything, it would not be in his article.

When Spiegel was back in his chair, he looked down at his notes. "For the record, I've heard Mr. Pendleton at sidebar and I'm satisfied that the questioning he wanted to pursue will not assist the court in making its ruling; therefore, I am not going to allow it. I am directing that the sidebar colloquy be sealed and not be made bar of the public record, but that if my ruling on this motion is appealed, that portion of the transcript shall be filed separately with the Appellate Division under seal, so that court will have Mr. Pendleton's proffered questions.

"Turning to the motion, for the reason I will put in writing, I find that under the Sixth Amendment the defendant is entitled to counsel of her choosing and am therefore going to grant the motion of McCabe & Swisher to substitute in as counsel for Ms. Parsons. I am hereby relieving the firm of Winston Drapper of any further obligation in connection with this case. I will sign an order to that effect."

Spiegel looked down at Pendleton. "Thank you, counsel. While I hate to play musical chairs, as Ms. McCabe and Mr. Swisher are now counsel of record, please allow them to move up to counsel table."

Rising from the table in a huff, Pendleton stuffed his papers into his black leather briefcase, then turned and made his way out of the courtroom. Bennett, momentarily caught off guard, looked up at Spiegel.

"Thank you, Your Honor."

Spiegel gave her a rueful smile. "You're welcome, Ms. Bennett. Have a nice weekend."

"You too, Judge," she said, quietly gathering her things.

"Let's move on to the second motion. Counsel, I've read everyone's papers on this. I know your respective positions, and I thank all of you for your well-reasoned arguments. Do either of you have any legal arguments that you'd like to add?"

To her surprise Willis rose. "No, Your Honor."

Erin stood as well. "No additional legal arguments, Your Honor."

Spiegel began by reviewing the terms of the plea bargain Ann had entered into and the sentence she would receive if sentenced in accordance with the plea agreement. He then looked up at Ann.

"Ms. Parsons, please remain seated. I remind you that you are still under oath. You are aware of that, correct?"

"Yes, Your Honor."

Spiegel then went through with Ann what Erin had been over countless times. If she was convicted at trial, she could well spend the rest of her life in jail. She acknowledged she understood.

Then Spiegel paused and looked at her. "Ms. Parsons, earlier this afternoon I asked you if anyone made any threats to you concerning changing counsel, and after a long pause, you answered, 'Concerning changing counsel, no, Your Honor.' Do I have that correct?"

"Yes, Your Honor."

"Okay. Now I'm going to ask you a similar question. Did anyone threaten you in any way, directly or indirectly, to get you to plead guilty?"

"Yes, Your Honor," Ann answered without hesitating.

Spiegel lowered his head but kept his gaze fixed on Ann. "I want the record to be clear. You're telling me, under oath, that

someone threatened you directly or indirectly, and said threat resulted in you pleading guilty?"

"Yes, Your Honor."

"Who threatened you?"

"Cassandra DeCovnie, the executrix of Charles Parsons's estate."

Erin stole a glance over at Kluska, who was sitting directly behind Willis. He must have been a good poker player, because she
spotted no reaction. Willis, on the other hand, was not pleased—
he clearly understood this case was now going to trial. The people
in the front office were not going to be happy.

"Thank you, Ms. Parsons." Spiegel motioned for his law clerk.
They shared some whispered conversation, and Spiegel turned to
face them.

"As I said. I am going to write an opinion on this. But to be fair
to the parties and allow them time to prepare, I will tell you that I
am going to allow Ms. Parsons to withdraw her plea. If counsel are
available at the same time next week, I will issue my opinion and
order and then I'd like to have a scheduling conference to move
this matter to trial expeditiously. Mr. Willis, please get a copy of
the discovery to counsel as soon as possible. Is there anything
else? If not, we're adjourned."

As the sheriff's officers slowly moved behind Ann to take her
back to the Union County jail, Erin leaned forward. "I'll come see
you Monday afternoon."

"Okay," Ann replied, seemingly torn between being happy
and sad.

Erin smiled. "It'll be okay."

"Glad one of us thinks so," Ann said.

The officers cuffed Ann and led her out through a side door.

As Erin began packing up her stuff, she noticed Rudolph
speaking with Willis and Carver. Kluska had moved away, clearly
wanting no part of the conversation. When they finished, Willis
approached her and Duane.

"Well, if it isn't the X-Men: one ex–G-man and one ex-man."

He snorted and his gaze settled on Erin. "I'm impressed—if I didn't know better, I'd swear you were a real woman."

She rolled her eyes. "And if I didn't know better, Tom, I'd swear you were a real man."

His face flushed and he put his hands on his hips. "What's that supposed to mean?"

Carver placed his hand on Willis's shoulder. "Tom, it's been a long week. Let's go have a beer."

Willis continued to stare at her for several seconds. "I'm going to enjoy kicking your ass again. Mark my words, McCabe, your client made a big mistake hiring you and a bigger one withdrawing her plea. She's going down!"

Carver gently nudged Willis, and they slowly headed out of the courtroom.

"That was interesting. Any comment?" Rudolph asked, notebook in hand.

Erin smiled politely. "No."

"Erin, what about your client's statement to the judge that she was threatened into pleading guilty. Can you tell me more about that?"

"No, Rich. I have no comment on that at this time."

"There have been rumors about Charles Parsons for years, even talk that he narrowly avoided a federal indictment. Do you expect any of these allegations will play any role in your client's defense?"

"I really can't comment at this point on what our strategy will be. All I can say is that at the end of the trial I fully expect everyone will agree that my client is innocent."

"That's better than not guilty?" Rudolph asked with a chuckle.

"Rich, you're a veteran reporter. You know that under our system a jury can convict a defendant or find them not guilty. My comment was broader than my belief that the jury will find my client not guilty. It is my belief that at the end of the day everyone will know she's innocent."

"Thank you," he said, clearly taken aback by her response.

"Can I ask you something off the record?" he asked. "I promise it won't be in my story, but Pendleton's comments about you at sidebar were a little loud and hard to ignore. And then just now, Willis went after you. Do you get crap like that often?"

"Off the record," she said with a sad smile. "Yeah," she said. "It comes with the territory."

# CHAPTER 28

Whan Peg reached the booth, she leaned over and gave Erin a kiss before plopping a newspaper on the table and sliding into the opposite booth. "So," she said smiling, "were you going to tell me you were going to be all over the newspapers again?"

"Hi, Mom. Nice to see you too."

"Sorry," Peg replied sheepishly. "Hi, dear. It's good to see you."

"How you feeling?"

"Actually, for the first time in a long time, I'm feeling pretty good."

"That's nice to hear. You look good," Erin said, and she meant it. Her mother did look good. Some of it Erin knew was still an illusion—makeup, a wig—but there was an energy coming from her mom that had been missing these many months of treatment. "It's been a long road," Erin said.

Her mother's expression was wistful. "Yeah, it has been. Chemo, surgery, radiation—but I guess if you have to have cancer may as well have the complete experience."

"Geez, Mom. Really?"

Her mother shrugged. "So tell, Ms. Front-Page News, why haven't you told me about your new case?"

"Probably because you've had enough on your plate. Remember, you were going through the complete cancer experience," she said, placing air quotes around *complete*.

"It sounds like there's a lot going on in this case," her mother replied.

Erin blew out a long breath. "You don't know the half of it. But I can't share at this point, because everything's attorney-client privilege."

"Well, I hope at least no one's trying to kill you this time," her mother said, picking up her menu.

When Erin said nothing, her mother's eyes widened. "Erin McCabe, tell me your life isn't in danger."

"My life isn't in danger," Erin repeated.

Peg's eyes narrowed. "I hope you lie better in court."

"I never lie in court," Erin said.

"That's good, because if you'd lied as badly there as you just did to me, you'd be in a lot of trouble." Her mother scowled. "So, young lady, what the hell is going on?"

Erin suppressed a laugh.

"What's so funny?" her mother asked, frustration creeping into her voice.

"Nothing. I just love it when you refer to me as 'young lady.'"

"You're trying to avoid the subject."

"I'm sorry, Mom. I'm not trying to drive you crazy. It's just another one of my cases where there are powerful people on the other side who aren't necessarily happy with what I'm doing."

"How come you never represent the rich and powerful people?" Peg asked.

"I don't know. We generally don't run in the same social circles. Besides, given who I am, I'm not sure that I was cut out to represent the rich and powerful."

Her mother's look was a mix of pride, concern, and resignation. "Please be careful," she finally said.

"I will. Pinky swear," Erin offered.

"So, what's happening with Mark and his family?" Peg asked, changing the subject.

Erin snorted.

"What?" her mother asked.

"I thought we were moving away from the subject of people

who wanted to kill me." She laughed. "Sorry. Mark is good. We're good. His family, however, . . . not so much."

After she finished breakfast with her mother, Erin headed to Swish's house. Erin hadn't seen JJ since he'd been attacked, so she and Swish had decided to visit him together. Cori and Erin hugged and tried to chat, but with four-year-old Austin constantly pulling on his aunt Erin's arm to come play with him, it was hard.

As she and Swish got ready to leave, Cori put her arm around Duane's waist. "We have some news we want to share with you," Cori said with a big smile. "Austin is going to have a little brother or sister come the end of May."

Erin threw her arms around both of them. "Oh my God. That's wonderful news. I'm so happy for both of you."

When Erin and Swish were under way, she turned to him. "Now I feel really guilty about getting us involved in this case. Why didn't you tell me Cori was expecting?"

"Because I knew this would be your reaction. Remember, I told you after they went after Connie that my feelings had changed and we were in this together. Now, after what's happened to JJ and them coming after you, no, . . . we can't give up now." He smiled. "Besides I didn't buy an oceanfront condo in Bradley with my draw from last year. So financially, Cori and I will be fine."

"I wasn't just thinking about the financial piece."

"I know. Don't think I don't worry about them—I do, every day. But Cori and I have done everything we can to make sure they're safe and protected." He paused and stole a look in her direction. "I don't see you backing down, and you're the one they came after."

She snorted. "We both know it's different. If something ever happened to me, it would fall under 'shit happens.' But if something happened to you or your family because of a case I got you involved in, I'd never forgive myself."

"You can't feel that way, E. You seem to have a bad habit of trying to make decisions for the men in your life. I know what I'm doing and I can make my own decisions."

*Ouch!* she thought. "It's only because I care," she said quietly.

As they drove on in silence, she noticed he was staying on the local roads.

"Are we being followed?" Erin asked.

"No."

"Good. Last thing we want is someone paying JJ and Gary a visit at home," she said.

"You don't think they already know where he lives?" he asked with a raised eyebrow. When she didn't answer, he added, "Any idea yet who's your guardian angel that called nine-one-one?"

"No," she said. "Not a clue."

"So let's go back to your original feeling that Parsons and his gang are somehow connected to Mackey," he said.

"Okay."

"Mackey gets a text from Luke, some guy he thinks may be on the West Coast, who basically tells him to skip town because he's pissed off some mean, important people."

"With you so far," she said.

"So let's assume Mackey did put the rootkit on Parsons's computer. Let's also assume Mackey was telling you the truth and he had no idea what he had done."

"Makes Luke the guy we're looking for," she interjected.

"It also means that because he could see everything on Parsons's computer, Luke probably realized that the rootkit had been discovered."

"Which would be why Luke told Mackey to disappear. If Luke was privy to everything Parsons was up to, he likely had an appreciation for how dangerous they might be." She paused and closed her eyes, the scene in the Lido replaying in her head. "Unfortunately, for Justin, Luke's warning was too little, too late."

She looked out the window, remembering the pain etched on Marilyn Mackey's face. Life could be so unforgiving. She turned to face Swish.

"So perhaps Luke is my guardian angel." She closed her eyes. "That still doesn't explain what happened the other night. How does Luke, presumably on the West Coast, get two people stopped in Cranford, New Jersey, at eleven thirty at night? How would he even know they were coming for me?"

"Hate to continue to rain on your parade, but it also doesn't explain who killed Charles Parsons. Or why."

JJ's partner, Gary, opened the door of their duplex only a few seconds after Erin rang the bell.

"Well, if it isn't my two favorite lawyers," he said, his broad grin visible beneath a well-trimmed beard. He gave Erin a hug. "Hey, sweetness, how you doing?"

When Gary and Erin first met, they had hit it off immediately because, like Erin, Gary was a runner; in his case a serious runner, with the classic lean, lanky frame befitting a long-distance one. A math teacher at Science Park High School in Newark, he was also a competitive marathoner. In the spring, he had narrowly missed qualifying for the U.S. men's marathon trials. His best time of two hours and twenty-five minutes was just short of the time needed.

"I'm good, Gar. How about you?"

"Tired of playing nurse," he said with a full-throated laugh.

"After what happened to JJ, I'm surprised you're even talking to us," Swish said, giving Gary a guy hug as he came through the door.

"How's he feeling?" Erin asked.

"Already started bitchin' about not being able to play hoops. I told him he's lucky they broke his right arm, 'cause now at long last he'll have to learn how to shoot with his left," he said, before his voice took on a somber note. "Guess I'm just happy it wasn't more serious. He's a tough dude, and from the little he's told me, it took everything he had to survive. Think he's trying to protect me. As if I didn't know he's lucky to be alive."

Erin wrapped her arm around his waist. "He's lucky to have you."

"Thanks," he said slowly. "Can I get you two anything—coffee, tea, soda?"

"We're good," they both said.

"Come on then, he's in the den."

They walked through the formal dining room and their newly

remodeled kitchen to the den, which had once been an enclosed porch.

Erin hoped the gasp that escaped when she first saw JJ wasn't audible, but Gary's sad glance told her it had been. JJ was propped up on a couch, two pillows behind him. His right arm was in a cast up to the elbow, but that wasn't what had shocked her. The right side of his face was so swollen and discolored that if she hadn't known she was looking at JJ she wouldn't have recognized him. There was a large, purplish lump on the left side of his forehead, and an equally large bump on the top of his shaved head.

She hurried over, stopping short when she realized there was nowhere she could touch without fear of hurting him. "Oh my God, JJ. I'm so sorry," she said, trying to keep her emotions under control.

"Hey, girl. It's okay. The docs tell me I'm going to be fine. Fortunately, there doesn't appear to be any permanent damage."

"We should never have gotten you involved in this. Oh, God." This time she couldn't stop tears from forming in the corners of her eyes.

"Listen, you," JJ began. "Nobody forced me to do anything. You both told me you were dealing with some dangerous people. I'm just so glad to see you alive. I thought for sure they were going to kill you. Come here."

He reached up with his left arm, put his hand behind her head, and gently pulled her close. "I can't tell you how good it is to see you," he whispered, giving her a kiss on the cheek.

"You feel up to telling us what the hell happened?" Swish asked.

"Yeah, sit," he said, nodding toward the two white club chairs on the other side of the room. When they did, he began to narrate, describing how they were waiting for him and the resulting fight. He stopped and looked over at both of them, a pained expression on his face.

"After the third guy had grabbed me from behind, I took some serious licks. I was dazed, man. And that's when the guy with the nightstick said to me, 'Either you tell us where Rojas is or your friend McCabe is dead. Your call, cowboy. You decide if she lives or dies.' I'm sorry," he said haltingly, "but I guess he could tell that what he said had stunned me, because he then said, 'Seriously, you tell us what we need, she lives. But if not, after we kill you, we make a phone call, and she's toast.' I honestly think I would have told him if there hadn't been a banging on the door at the other end of my office. Apparently, the custodian who cleans the building at night had heard the commotion. He was screaming, 'Mr. Johnson, open up. What's going on? I called the police. They're on their way.' Later, I found out he lied about calling the police, but it made the guy with the nightstick try to finish me off. I blocked it. And then I just went crazy at that point because"—he looked over at Erin—"I thought they were going to kill you. I know I nailed nightstick guy in the balls with a good kick, and I may have broken the arm of the guy with the slapper before they took off.

"I screamed for Joe, the custodian, and he used his pass key to get in. As soon as he saw me, he called the police. I guess at that point I passed out, because I don't remember anything until I woke up in the hospital. Somehow I got hold of Swish and I got the cops to call Cranford PD, and, well . . ."

Erin went over and knelt in front of him by the couch. "It's okay, JJ. I'm okay. I just feel horrible that we put you in this position."

# CHAPTER 29

*January 1, 2009*

ERIN RESTED HER HEAD AGAINST MARK'S CHEST, LOST IN A POST HOL-
iday funk, made more intense by how things had played out with
his family.

Thanksgiving had always been the holiday Erin enjoyed the
most. Simple and centered on food and family, there was none of
the madness that came with the Christmas season: shopping,
wrapping, holiday parties. But Erin's joy in celebrating Thanksgiving had taken a major detour after she transitioned. For two
years following her transition she had spent Thanksgiving alone,
rejected by her father and brother. Two years ago, against Erin's
better judgment, her mother had convinced her to come for
Thanksgiving dinner. By then, her brother Sean's attitude toward
her had softened due to the efforts of his sons and Liz. But the
day had turned into an unmitigated disaster when her father refused to deal with her as Erin. It had taken someone trying to kill
her right before Christmas of that year to make her father realize
just how devastated he'd be to lose her.

Last year, with the disaster of the previous year still fresh, things
had been better. Her father's attitude had started to mellow. He
still had trouble dealing with the fact that Erin was dating Mark,
but they had all shared Thanksgiving dinner and it had been the
first time in three years that she had enjoyed the holiday.

At least as far as her family went, this year's Thanksgiving had been the happiest she'd had in a while. Her dad appeared to have accepted having Mark around, even if Erin suspected it was more because Mark was a jock than anything else. Her father still struggled with the fact that Erin was dating a man, but he was polite, and the rest of Erin's family welcomed Mark with open arms.

Unfortunately, Mark's mother had sided with his brothers and told him that Erin was not welcome at her house, and so he had stayed away. He and Erin had spent time with his sister, Molly, and her partner, Robin, but while Mark's excommunication from the rest of his family gnawed at Erin, there was little she could do about it.

"I'm sorry," she said softly.

"Why? You have nothing to be sorry about," Mark replied.

"If it weren't for me, you would have been able to spend the holidays with your family."

"You're assuming I would've rather been with my family than with you. Which, in case you're wondering, would be incorrect." He kissed the top of her head. "Stop blaming yourself for my family."

She looked up at him. "It's hard because I know I'm the reason you're ostracized."

"No. The reason I'm ostracized is because my brothers are idiots."

"Okay," she said, not disagreeing with his assessment of his brothers. "But I feel for your mom. Your dad died only a few years ago, and she relies on her children. I'm sure she feels stuck in the middle."

He hugged her tighter. "I know. I feel for her too. It wasn't the same not seeing her over the holidays, but I hope that with time it'll get better. Like it did with your family."

"I hope so," she said wistfully, her family's struggles still lingering in her memory.

"So, I've been thinking. You have a trial coming up in a couple of months, and you need to focus on that," Mark said.

Ann's trial was set for February 23, 2009, less than two months away.

"And I have a suggestion," he continued. "My place in Clark is bigger than this place. Plus, I have an office that you can use. Why don't you move in with me?"

She lifted her eyes so she could see his face. "Are you serious?"

"What kind of question is that? Of course I'm serious. I love you and would like to spend more time with you."

"I don't know, Mark. This place is only two blocks away from my office."

He snorted. "You're too much. You're supposed to say, 'I love you too.'"

She blushed. "I'm sorry. I do love you."

"Would you please stop apologizing? I got over my issues with you a couple of years ago. It's about time you got over your issues with you."

"Have you been talking to my mom?"

"No," he said. "What's your mom got to do with this?"

"I don't know. Just sounds like what she's been preaching."

"Well, your mom is a really smart woman," he said with a goofy grin. "Besides, if you moved in with me you wouldn't be alone. Let's face it, I don't feel great knowing people willing to kill you know where you live. My neighborhood is quiet. Not to mention a good place to run."

She didn't say anything. He slid down in the bed until his face was even with hers. "Hey, what are you worried about? Let's see how it works out. If you don't like it, you can always come back here." He kissed her gently on her lips. "Let's give it a try."

She put her arm behind his head and kissed him. "Thank you," she said. "For sticking with me and loving me."

He pulled her on top of him and wrapped his arms around her. "I wish you loved yourself as much as I love you," he whispered.

"I'm trying," she said. "I'm really trying."

Erin poured more coffee for her and her mom. Even after her mom started to feel better, Erin had continued to go over and share Sunday brunch and help her out with some of the cleaning and laundry.

"So how do you feel about Mark's suggestion?" her mother asked.

"Excited, scared—I don't know. I mean, I'm thirty-seven years old. It's not like I'm some teenager moving in with her boyfriend. It should be no big deal. Normal couples do it all the time."

Her mother gave her a funny look.

"What?" Erin said.

"I think you just answered your own question about why you're scared."

"I don't follow," Erin said.

"Why would you use the phrase 'normal couples' in reference to other people?"

Erin was at a loss.

"You're a beautiful woman," her mother said, "but there are still times when you don't see yourself that way. I know that your relationship with Mark got off to a bumpy start, but it's clear now to anyone with eyes that he's madly in love with you. And despite the fact that I think you're very much in love with him, you seem to be afraid to admit that to yourself. Why? Because that self-doubt lingers about whether anyone, especially a very good-looking heterosexual guy, could ever love you. You still don't see yourself as part of a normal couple. You still don't believe you're worthy of his love."

The sting of what her mother said caused Erin to wince. She stared at her mother. "I'm trying," she finally said.

"I know you are," her mother replied.

"If I move in, do you think Dad's head will explode?" Erin asked.

"Probably. But that's only because on some level he still thinks of you as his son."

"Wait. So you think that if I had been a gay guy Dad would have had just as much of a problem with me?"

Her mother chuckled. "Of course he would have. He's not exactly progressive on LGBT issues. Don't you see that's exactly what's happening now? You're his son, who's dating a guy."

"Oh, Mom. That's exactly why Mark has so much trouble with his family! They see me as a guy, so that makes Mark gay."

"And what I'm saying is that maybe a lot of your self-doubt comes from the fact that even you sometimes fall into the same trap and don't always fully accept yourself as a woman. You've allowed yourself to be defined by all those people who have called trans people frauds, freaks, or delusional. As a result, you see yourself as some kind of second-class woman. And so you're shocked when a guy finds you attractive. And I think part of you is still surprised that you find a guy attractive."

Erin sat there in stunned silence.

"Erin McCabe, you are one hell of a woman, and it's about time you started believing that about yourself. You seem to have found a good and kind man who loves you and accepts you. I've said this to you before, but the hell with what anyone else thinks about you or about Mark. Embrace your life as a woman—it's who you've always been."

Erin slowly got up and walked around the table. She leaned over and gave her mother a hug. "Thank you," she said, her voice choked with emotion. "I don't know what I'd do without you."

# CHAPTER 30

*February 9, 2009*

WHY DID I ADMIT KILLING HIM? PERCHED ON HER BUNK, ANN HAD her back up against the wall. The cinder blocks were cool and she turned so the left side of her face was resting against them, hoping that the coolness might ease the throbbing in her head as she mulled what her chances would be at trial.

With the trial now only two weeks away, the path to a not guilty verdict appeared to be shrinking all the time. *If I had just kept my mouth shut, I'd at least have a chance.* But the truth was, she knew why she confessed, even if she hadn't been completely honest with Erin. *I was afraid,* she'd told Erin. *I hoped that if I told them what they wanted to hear, they'd let me go.*

No. The reality was much more complex—it was the shock of learning the truth and the sudden desire to do her best to conceal that truth in order to protect someone she could only imagine had suffered as much as she had. When they had played the recording of the shooting, Parsons's voice had been a chilling reminder of the nightmare she'd lived through for years. But when she heard the second voice, the one that had called Parsons "Daddy," that had stunned her. She asked them to play it a second time, and that's when she knew: not only that it was Terry Gore who had murdered Parsons, but it was suddenly clear who Terry Gore really was. In that moment, Ann had put together the voice, the words on the recording, everything she'd learned from her girlfriend, and suddenly it all fit together. Terry Gore was Ann Parsons—*the* Ann Parsons. And despite the sting of betrayal, Ann had decided she needed to protect Terry/Ann because she had done what Ann had wanted to do every day for the last eleven years: kill the monster.

Sitting across from the detectives in the interrogation room, Ann had wanted to be part of the murder, because unwittingly she had been. The visit to the house in Westfield because Terry wanted to see where someone famous lived, then the tour of the house, and finally the overnight stay were all part of the plan, even if Ann had been clueless at the time. "I did it" had just tumbled out of her mouth, an acknowledgment that she had indeed been part of killing the monster. No, she could never turn on Terry/Ann. She wanted to hug Terry/Ann and thank her, not implicate her. The die was cast; she'd rather spend the rest of her life in prison than betray Terry/Ann because, for the first time in eleven years, she was free. The nightmares still came, but when she woke up, she knew he wasn't going to come into her room and rape her or abuse her. No, he was dead. He couldn't hurt her anymore. And although she didn't believe in God—how could a god allow monsters like him to exist—there was part of her that hoped she was wrong because the thought of him spending every day tortured in hell made the one she inhabited on earth a little more bearable.

Only now, as her trial loomed, was her "confession" coming back to haunt her. Erin and Duane had warned her that the chances of having the judge suppress her confession or bar the recording of the murder from being played before the jury were slim, but losing both motions back to back still stung. Then yesterday the judge had ruled that he wasn't going to allow their forensic voice expert to testify before the jury on whether the voice on the recording of Parsons's murder belonged to Ann after Willis had skillfully gotten the expert to admit how poor the recording was in general. Based on the expert's testimony that he'd have to filter out certain sound ranges to obtain a usable sample, Spiegel had ruled that the testimony was not sufficiently scientifically reliable to be admitted.

Erin and Duane had desperately wanted to add her brother to their witness list. They told Ann that it was her best defense, proving everything she had told them. But if they did, there'd be no way the judge could legally keep his contact information from the prosecutor. In Ann's mind that was tantamount to signing her brother's death warrant. How could she live with herself if she was found not guilty but it came at the expense of her brother's life? He was a good kid. He actually had a future ahead of him. Strange, in her mind he was still nine—just like he was the last time she walked him home from school. When she had told him she had to leave, he had cried and begged her not to go. But she told him she'd write and call. It had taken her a while, but she had kept her promise, only to realize her contact with him had allowed Parsons to discover she had a brother.

What would happen to David if she was convicted? He couldn't spend the rest of his life hiding in a halfway house. According to Erin, David was already tired of being hidden away. And as much as she wanted to believe they'd leave him alone if she was convicted, it was far more likely that they would kill him. Trying to protect him had been the reason she had pled guilty in the first place—DeCovnie's assurances that David would receive Ann's inheritance and that he'd be taken care of. *Why, after eleven years of listening to DeCovnie lie to me, had I suddenly believed her? I was such a fool.* It was bad enough she had screwed up her own life; now she was about to take her brother down with her.

No, they'd never let her brother live; Carl Shamey's "suicide" was proof enough. A few weeks after the holidays, Shamey had been found dead in his cell at Rikers Island, an internal corrections department report finding it to be a suicide.

Ann hadn't known Shamey well, but he, along with Max Gallagher, was close to Parsons and Hiller, and if the two of them weren't the decision makers, they certainly were the loyal lieutenants. They literally knew where the bodies were buried. One thing Ann was fairly certain of, maybe it looked like Shamey had committed suicide, but it wasn't suicide. They had killed him. Why she hadn't suffered the same fate remained a mystery. There must be something that they thought she knew that kept her alive, but what it was, she didn't have a clue.

Her only hope to save her brother was to expose Parsons and the rest of them as the hideous abusers they were. Even though Erin agreed it was the right strategy, she had warned Ann that it might also convince the jury she had a motive to kill. Of course, there was still a chance that the jury might find her not guilty even if they believed she killed him—jury nullification, Erin had called it. What Ann hoped was that her testimony would inspire other victims to come forward and speak out. Especially against DeCovnie, she thought. There had to be a special place in hell for a woman who would lure kids into that vipers' nest.

With only two weeks to go before the start of the trial, Erin stood at the conference room table, which was covered with every document pertaining to Ann's case. She had to keep herself focused, immersing herself in the facts of the case so there'd be no surprises come trial. Her task was made more difficult because she was sure that Ann knew more than she was telling them. But, at this point, there was little Erin could do; she had cajoled, she had badgered, she had even warned Ann that she was hurting her own chances, but so far nothing had moved Ann to open up. They also hadn't been able to find anything concrete linking Parsons and his cohorts to the child pornography business. Ann was certain that they made a fortune, but without any admissible evidence, there'd be nothing to rely on to bolster Ann's claims.

While Erin concentrated on anticipating the state's case against their client, Swish was working on developing the facts for Ann's defense case. One major hole was that Swish had been unable to locate foster care records for Felipe Rojas, the name Ann had been given at birth, even though the Florida Department of Children and Families did have records for Ann's brother, David.

The one piece of luck they'd had was that because Shamey's arrest had created an active attempted murder investigation, the

NYPD had obtained the cell tower information for the calls made on Ann's burner phone. The three outgoing calls were relayed through a tower in Hoboken, consistent with Ann's story. The one incoming call connected to a tower on the Scotch Plains/Westfield border.

It was seven o'clock when Swish stuck his head into the conference room. "Hey, what do you say we call it a night?"

Erin looked up from the paperwork and smiled. "Nah. I'm still reviewing reports. You go ahead."

He exhaled. "Come on, E. I know things have been quiet for the last few months, but I don't like to see you here alone. Go home. Mark is there. I'll feel better to know you aren't alone."

In the time since the judge allowed Ann to withdraw her plea, things had been relatively calm. After Shamey's arrest, as best Erin and Duane could tell they were no longer being followed, and no one had come after Erin, JJ, or Rojas. JJ was slowly recovering from his injuries. He was still doing some physical therapy for his right arm, and while he hadn't been able to return yet to playing in the adult basketball league, he and Mark, who was the freshman boys' basketball coach at Westfield High School, would play one-on-one in the gym after practice.

"Swish, we work in Cranford. I think we're safe."

Swish gave her a skeptical look. "Get real, girl. It's got nothing to do with how safe this town is. It has to do with the fact that we get involved in cases where we become targets."

"Actually, *we* haven't become targets, just me," she replied with a chuckle. "Go figure."

"You're a pain in the ass, you know that?"

"Yeah, I know. Stubborn too. Go home to your pregnant wife and son and I'll be okay. I'll text you when I get to Mark's."

It was eight thirty by the time Erin looked at her watch. She decided to re-review one last report, the interview of Aaron Tinsley, the IT consultant who had found the rootkit on Parsons's computer. Tinsley had given the statement on April 25, 2008, two weeks after the murder. Tinsley described being sent out by his boss to look at Parsons's computers because Parsons thought he might have a virus, only to discover a rootkit hidden in an update to encryption software that had been installed about six months earlier. Erin could almost hear the pride in Tinsley's words as he described the moment he found it, then went on to say how angry Parsons had become when he found out his computer was infected. He immediately sent Tinsley out to buy new computers, new hard drives, and new encryption software.

Erin took the report and put it back in the manila folder and labeled it "April 25, 2008 Statement of Aaron Tinsley." She was about to put it in the pile of things unimportant to her cross-examination or to the defense case when she remembered something that sent her frantically searching for another report, this one from April 18, 2008. Then she looked at the signature. It was as if the tumblers of a lock had suddenly aligned and the mystery was unlocked.

*Holy shit!*

Conroy leaned back against the banquette in the dimly lit back corner of 110 Fifth, his favorite restaurant. When Luigi had called him with the news, he had decided to celebrate, so he had invited Luigi to dinner. Famous for its haute cuisine, 110 Fifth was owned by one of Martin's clients, so he was always well cared for. Now, as he relaxed, for the first time in weeks he felt things were heading in the right direction.

"Will there be anything else, Mr. Conroy?" his waiter asked.

"A Courvoisier XO, Vincent," Conroy replied. "I'm celebrating."

"Of course. I'll bring it right out."

It had taken months of surveillance by SIS on Jamal Johnson, but it had finally paid off. Rojas had been working in the office of a halfway house run by one of Johnson's friends. He smiled. Luigi's plan for getting Rojas arrested was simple, but elegant. Equally good news was that SIS was also close to finding the real Ann Parsons. Luigi had described her as very smart and very cunning. She had been hard to track down. They had started with people who knew her in middle school and her freshman year in

high school when she lived in Westchester, New York. All of them
had lost touch with her when her father had sold the house and
moved to New Jersey. But they'd found one who remembered
that Ann had an uncle in Upstate New York. As SIS dug deeper, it
turned out that Dennis Butler, Ann's birth father, had a brother,
Ray, in Rochester, New York, who worked for Social Security. They
had sent two female investigators up to Rochester to talk to him.
Their cover story was that they were working for Ann's defense
team and were trying to find out if he had any information that
could help with her case. He had seemed surprised when they
told him that Ann had been charged with murder, insisting he
hadn't seen her since her mother passed away. But when they had
played him a tape of the murder, his face had belied that he was
hiding something. Something big.

Working on a hunch, Luigi's people had put together a data-
base of all girls between the ages of twelve and sixteen who had
died in Rochester around the time Ann had disappeared, working on the theory that once Ann ran away, she had made her way
to Rochester and her uncle had helped her by providing her with
a new identity.

"Here you go, Mr. Conroy," Vincent said, placing the cognac
on the table. "Enjoy."

"Thank you, Vincent," he said as he picked up the glass and
raised it in a salute.

The final bonus tonight was that McCabe was living with someone, which meant he no longer had to go after her directly. Like
Ann and her brother, he could go after the person McCabe loved.
She'd protect him at all cost. He took a sip of his cognac. Willis
had assured him that once the trial was over, he would give Conroy the information on the laptop. With that, and the other half
of the information he had, he'd empty the offshore accounts and
be gone before Arthur and Cassandra even suspected what he'd
done. Yes, indeed. Life was good.

She had called him as soon as she had checked everything
three times, each time confirming her crazy-ass theory.

With trembling hands, she placed the April 25, 2008, statement of Aaron Tinsley on the table in front of Swish, and then put the Computer Crimes report of April 18, 2008, next to it.

Swish picked up Tinsley's statement and read it, then took the second report and reviewed it. He suddenly looked up.

"Wait," he said. "The date on the Computer Crimes report is April 18, 2008. Tinsley's statement isn't until a week later. How could Computer Crimes have known on April eighteenth that there was a rootkit on Parsons's desktop computer? This doesn't make sense."

Erin nodded. "This is where it gets really crazy," she said. "Take a look at who signed the Computer Crimes report."

Swish looked down at the report. "Detective Sybil Lucas," he said, before his head snapped up again. "Lucas?" he said. "You don't think . . ."

"I do," she said. "Remember Mackey never met or spoke with Luke, so he just assumed it was a guy. But how else could she have known that the rootkit was there? It took Tinsley all day to find it, and he was an expert hacker; she has it in a report the day the desktop computer is seized. Swish, Detective Sybil Lucas of the Union County Prosecutor's Office is Luke. She had Mackey install the rootkit on Parsons's computers."

"But why?" Swish asked, the confusion evident in his voice. "You're talking about a detective in the prosecutor's office. I mean . . ." his voice trailed off, until it was nothing.

# CHAPTER 31

*E*RIN STUDIED THE SIXTEEN PEOPLE SITTING IN THE JURY BOX. OF THE sixteen, twelve would become the jurors who would ultimately decide Ann's fate. The other four were alternates, selected in the event that they lost jurors during the trial due to illness or unforeseen circumstances. The dilemma was, she wouldn't know who the alternates were until right before the jury retired to deliberate, when the court clerk randomly selected the jurors who would become the alternates. The alternates could be the four Erin liked the most, or it could be the four she liked the least. Which made it tricky when deciding who, if anyone, to challenge.

Starting on Monday morning, Judge Spiegel had painstakingly questioned each prospective juror and had already ruled on all the challenges for cause that Erin and Willis had raised. Prior to the questioning of the prospective jurors by the judge, Erin had been successful in convincing Judge Siegel to ask the jurors about their attitudes toward LGBTQ individuals, and, in particular, transgender people. Willis had objected, but Erin had persuaded the judge that Ann couldn't get a fair trial if a potential juror was biased against trans people, especially since Erin's status as a transgender woman was easy to discover by an Internet search. Most of the prospective jurors had said it wouldn't impact them, but the judge had removed those who did for cause.

Now it was crunch time. The sixteen jurors ranged in age from twenty-two to sixty-seven, and there were eight men and eight women. Eight were Caucasian (five men and three women), four were Hispanic (one man and three women), and there were two men and two women of color. Erin turned and looked over her shoulder at the remaining pool of about twenty potential jurors sitting in the courtroom. She had already used nineteen of her twenty peremptory challenges, which allowed her to remove a juror without giving a reason. She was down to her last one, which she always hated to use, given that the next juror in the box might be worse than the one she'd just knocked out.

Spiegel looked down at her from the bench. "Ms. McCabe?"

Decision time. She rose to her feet, turned to her left so she was looking directly at the sixteen jurors, and said, "Your Honor, the jury is acceptable to the defense."

"Mr. Willis?"

"The jury is acceptable to the state, Judge," he said, only half rising.

Two hours later, Erin faced the jury again, this time with her opening statement. She was superstitious, so she wore her "lucky" black pinstripe pantsuit, with a white blouse. Willis had just spent the last hour telling the jury the evidence that the state would present against Ann. After dramatically holding up Charles Parsons's will showing that Ann stood to inherit $10 million from the estate of her father, he had related how there were no signs of forced entry and that Ann had been recorded murdering Charles Parsons, thanks to a secret recording device in Parsons's laptop. Willis also had related that Ann's fingerprints were on the murder weapon. And, saving the best for last, Ann had confessed to the murder upon hearing the recording.

Erin had listened intently, looking for any openings she could exploit: a misstatement, or a promise to produce evidence that might ultimately never materialize—but Willis knew what he was doing.

Although she had prepared and rehearsed, Erin had learned early in her career to deliver an opening statement from her heart, not from a piece of paper. And as much as she wanted to, she couldn't promise the jury that Ann would testify. While that was the plan, too much could happen in the course of a trial, and she never wanted to be confronted during summation with an unfulfilled promise.

This also meant that she couldn't tell the jury about the abuse Ann had suffered at the hands of Parsons. Without Ann, there was no one to tell that story. For now, she'd need to be vague and offer the jury some alternative scenarios.

"Ladies and gentlemen," Erin began, standing behind the table where Ann and Swish were sitting. "It is my honor to represent Ann Parsons in this case."

She took a few steps to her right so she was standing directly behind Ann, drawing the jurors' attention to Ann, who was dressed in a conservative beige pantsuit and a mauve silk blouse. She wanted the jury to see Ann as a scared young woman, not as the conniving murderer Willis had just portrayed her to be.

"You've just heard Mr. Willis tell you that the state has an airtight case against Ann," she continued. "And if you listen only to him, it does appear that he has evidence that Ann murdered Charles Parsons. But the state's evidence is not as solid as Mr. Willis would have you believe. No, during the course of the trial you will learn that the state's case is an illusion. It may appear solid, but when you try to touch it and see what it's really made of, you'll discover there's nothing there. It's simply not real.

"Ladies and gentlemen, the way a criminal trial works is the state gets to put on its evidence first. Mr. Willis will put on his witnesses. Mr. Willis will tell you that each witness is a piece of a jigsaw puzzle, and that when he's done, you'll see a picture, just like on the cover of the jigsaw puzzle box—a picture that he says will show that my client is a murderer. But all I ask, all that Ann asks, is that you wait before you decide. Wait until you have all the pieces of the puzzle, not just the ones that Mr. Willis gives you, before you decide. It's your job, ladies and gentlemen, to look at all the puzzle pieces. The pieces that the prosecutor will present, and the pieces I will present. And when you look at the full picture, with all the pieces assembled, I'm confident the finished picture will look markedly different from the one Mr. Willis described. The final picture will haunt you, but not because it shows that Ann murdered Charles Parsons. It will haunt you because of the injustice that has been done to Ann. It will haunt you because you will know that Ann is not a murderer. It will haunt you because you will realize this case wasn't about a search for the truth or justice—it was about winning at all costs, even if an innocent woman went to jail."

Erin went on to discuss the evidence that would show Ann was in Hoboken at the time of the murder and how a cell phone she used confirmed her location. She told the jury to listen carefully to the recording, to compare Ann's voice there with the one on her interrogation. And she reminded the jury that the defense did not have to prove anything—it was the prosecutor's job to convince them beyond a reasonable doubt that Ann had murdered Charles Parsons. As she walked in front of the jury box, she made sure that she looked at each of the jurors as she passed. She wanted to connect with them. She wanted them to see her confidence, to know that she could look them in the eye and say Ann did not commit this crime.

"Ladies and gentlemen, as you look at Ann, she is innocent. She is presumed innocent throughout this trial. When you walk into the jury room to deliberate at the end of the case, she is still presumed innocent. Don't assume that the state, with all its power and resources, got it right and that they wouldn't have accused Ann unless she was guilty. The prosecution is made up of human beings, and human beings make mistakes. I am confident that at the end of this case, after you've heard all of the evidence, you will be satisfied that the prosecution has made a horrible mistake, because the evidence will show that Ann did not kill Charles Parsons. Thank you."

Erin slowly walked back to counsel table and took her seat next to Ann.

"Mr. Willis, is the state ready to call its first witness?"

"Yes, Your Honor. The state calls Detective Sergeant Edward Kluska."

The courtroom deputy opened the heavy doors that led out to the hallway and called Kluska's name. Erin had asked for the witnesses to be sequestered, which required them to remain outside the courtroom, to prevent them from hearing what the other witnesses testified to and potentially changing their testimony to conform to witnesses who had come before them.

Kluska was the perfect witness for the prosecution to start with because he would set the table for everything that followed. As Willis went through his direct examination of Kluska, Erin had to admit that, even though Willis could be an arrogant asshole, he was a good lawyer. His questions were clear and succinct as he took Kluska through the crime scene and the investigation that followed. Willis established why the detectives on the scene originally believed Parsons's death was a suicide. Willis then had Kluska explain why he had questioned that determination: the lack of any gunpowder residue on his hand; two sets of fingerprints on the murder weapon; the lack of back spatter—then, finally, the discovery of the recording and Ann's confession.

When Kluska answered Willis's last question, Willis made a dramatic turn so he was facing the jury. "No further questions, Your Honor."

Rising to her feet, Erin couldn't help being struck by the irony of cross-examining Kluska on a case he had secretly brought to her. Unlike the last time she had seen him in the Liberty Tavern, Kluska had cleaned up nicely. His beard was trimmed, and in a sports coat, shirt, and tie he seemed less physically intimidating. As she stepped forward, Kluska sat stone-faced, waiting for her first question.

"Good afternoon, Detective," she said, standing in front of the witness box.

"Good afternoon," Kluska replied brusquely.

"Detective, you are not an expert on fingerprints, back spatter, or recordings, correct?"

"No, I'm not."

"In your direct examination, you mentioned a recording that occurred in the room where the murder took place. Is that correct?"

"Yes."

"The ladies and gentlemen of the jury haven't heard that recording yet, but, if I understand your testimony, one of the things that led you to suspect my client was involved was a reference by Charles Parsons on the recording to the person speaking as his daughter. Am I correct?"

"Yes."

"Detective, what investigation did you do to determine whether my client—this woman," Erin said as she walked behind Ann, "is Mr. Parsons's daughter?"

Kluska looked momentarily perplexed. "Well . . . actually your client is his adopted daughter."

"I don't believe that changes anything legally, but let me rephrase the question. What investigation did you do to determine if my client was actually Mr. Parsons's *adopted* daughter?"

Erin saw Kluska's face twitch as he attempted to maintain his calm demeanor. "I'm not sure I understand your question, counsel. Mr. Parsons married your client's mother. Charles Parsons adopted her. Her name is Ann Parsons. She lived with him until she moved out following her college graduation."

"So, the answer to my question, Detective, is that you did no investigation. You just assumed based on the information you just testified to that my client was Mr. Parsons's adopted daughter. Is that correct?"

Erin turned so she was facing Willis. She looked back over her shoulder at Kluska. "Am I correct, Detective—you assumed?"

Willis shot up. "I object, Your Honor. Is counsel actually contending her client is not Mr. Parsons's daughter?"

Before Erin could say anything, Spiegel interjected, "Mr. Willis, I don't think it's appropriate for me to ask counsel what her defense is. I see nothing objectionable about the question. Your objection is overruled. You may answer the question, Detective."

Kluska's look had morphed into a glare. "I did no other investigation."

"So you assumed—correct?"

"Yes," Kluska answered begrudgingly.

"Thank you," Erin said with a gentle smile. "And you also did not investigate to see if Mr. Parsons had any other children, did you?"

Kluska inhaled. "No, we did not."

"In fact, you've never heard my client refer to Mr. Parsons as her father, have you?"

"No. I haven't."

"One last thing, Detective. You mention in your direct testimony a confession. Again, I realize the jury hasn't seen what you refer to as a confession, but in that interrogation of my client, one of the detectives, Detective Burke, told my client there was video of her leaving the house the night Parsons was murdered. Am I correct?"

"Yes," Kluska replied.

"That statement was a lie, wasn't it? There was no video of my client leaving the house."

"Objection!" Willis screamed.

"Reframe the question, counsel," Spiegel said calmly.

Erin smiled politely. "Detective Kluska, the statement by Detective Burke was not true. There were and are no videos of my client leaving the house on the night of the murder, isn't that correct?"

"You're correct."

"Thank you, Detective," Erin said, and started the process of returning to her seat. "That's all I have at this time, Your Honor, but I may want to recall Detective Kluska during my case in chief, so I would request he remain sequestered." As she sat, she couldn't help but notice Kluska glaring at her.

Willis quickly stood and placed both hands on counsel table and leaned forward. "Has Ann Parsons, the defendant sitting at counsel table, ever told you that Charles Parsons was not her father?"

Erin stood quickly. "Objection, Your Honor. Mr. Willis should know better. My client has no obligation to make any statements to the police."

Spiegel looked down at both of them. "Ms. McCabe, you are correct. Mr. Willis should know better and your objection is sustained. But I also caution you about speaking objections in front of the jury. You should know better as well."

Erin nodded slightly. "My apologies, Judge."

Spiegel turned toward the jury. "Ladies and gentlemen, you will disregard the last question by Assistant Prosecutor Willis. Ms. Parsons is under no obligation to talk to Detective Kluska, or any member of law enforcement. You may continue, Mr. Willis," Spiegel said evenly.

Willis turned and looked at Erin, his face flushed with anger. "Detective, at any time during your investigation, or as you sit here today, did you or do you have any reason to believe the defendant is not the adopted daughter of Charles Parsons?"

"No, I didn't, and no, I don't," Kluska responded.

"Detective, is there anything improper in telling a suspect something that is not accurate in the process of interrogation?"

"No. It's a well-recognized interrogation technique."

"Nothing further," Willis said.

Kluska went to stand, but Erin rose to her feet. "A couple more questions, Detective," she said, trying not to let her smile show. Taking a few steps forward, she watched as Kluska slowly lowered himself back into his witness chair.

"Detective, when you are personally interrogating someone, do you ever provide inaccurate information to the person you're questioning?"

She could almost see Kluska's mind flash back to seven years ago, when he'd had to answer the same question. In that case, Erin had made the rookie mistake of asking a question she didn't know the answer to and Kluska had burned her. She had confronted Kluska about providing false information to a suspect during interrogation. Now, watching his body language on the stand, Erin suspected that Kluska remembered his testimony from the earlier case, just as she had.

"No. I do not."

"Why?" Erin asked, her voice serene despite having just violated one of the cardinal rules of cross-examination: Never ask a witness why because it allows them to explain their answer.

Kluska's chest expanded as he took a deep breath. "Because I prefer not to risk having a suspect's statement challenged as being coerced or involuntary based on the fact that I provided inaccurate information."

"So, you prefer to be honest with those people you question, correct?"

"Yes."

"Thank you, Detective Sergeant Kluska," she said, using his full rank for the first time. "Nothing further, Your Honor."

As she walked back to counsel table, she hoped that her cross-examination had planted a seed in the jury's mind about whether or not Ann was Charles Parsons's daughter. If she had, that question would linger no matter what Willis put in front of them. Plan A was to answer that question when Ann took the stand, but just in case, she had come up with a plan B. She just hoped she didn't have to use it because plan B had a downside big enough to land Ann in prison for the rest of her life.

Later, as Duane and Erin walked to their cars, he said, "What do you expect for tomorrow?"

"You mean with Detective Lucas?" she asked.

"Yeah. What do you think will happen?"

"I suspect Spiegel won't let me go far, given she's only there for chain of custody. But at least I'll finally get to meet Luke, who cost Mackey his life."

# CHAPTER 32

*I*N AN EFFORT TO KEEP TRACK OF THE TRIAL IN REAL TIME, MARTIN
had decided that he wanted Preston Harrison in the courtroom
every day.

"Talk to me, Preston," Martin barked when Preston called in.

"They're taking their lunch break now. So far, Willis put on a
Westfield cop who was at the scene, the medical examiner, the
head of the Forensics Unit on gunpowder residue, and what the
lack of any back spatter evidence means."

"How was McCabe's cross?"

"She had none."

There was silence for several seconds. "At this rate, when do
you think Willis finishes?"

"Hard to tell. I assume McCabe will cross-examine Cassandra
and the witnesses concerning the recording of the murder and
the confession—so maybe sometime late tomorrow afternoon. If
not, Friday isn't a trial day, so then Monday."

"Okay, got it. Keep me posted."

Martin clicked off. "Looks like we need to implement tomorrow afternoon," he said to the other men in the room. Arthur was
standing looking out the window at the Waldorf. Sitting in the
corner was Arthur's pugnacious attorney, Liam Fletcher, whom
he had brought along as his second. Fletcher had grown up in the
Dorchester section of Boston, and despite having made his way

through law school at night, his disposition was shaped by the street gang he had grown up with. He and Arthur had met when Fletcher represented a gang member with ties to Arthur's gambling operations. Arthur had been so impressed by Fletcher's willingness to do anything—literally anything—to get his client off that he continued to refer clients to him. Now, fifteen years later, he handled all the "legal" work for Arthur's various enterprises. With Martin's pronouncement, they both leveled him with a look.

"We can't have any fuckups this time," Martin said to Arthur.

"You want to talk fuckups?" Arthur shot back. "If you had followed my advice, there'd be no trial because there'd be no defendant. But you were too squeamish to eliminate Ms. Parsons."

Martin pushed his chair back from his desk and adjusted his French cuffs. "There are times you can be a fucking idiot. We still don't know where Charles's hard drives are, and need I remind you, it would not be a good thing for you if those videos ever see the light of day."

Arthur took a step forward, his face growing red.

"For Christ's sake, knock it off," Fletcher said. "Let's focus on the work at hand."

Martin allowed his shoulders to relax and moved his head in a circular motion, trying to relieve the kink in his neck, taken aback by Fletcher's unusual foray into neutrality. "You're right. Let's deal with the present."

"Good. So go over the plan one more time," Fletcher said as Arthur took a seat in the corner of the room.

Martin nodded. "Rojas works in the office of the halfway house. One of the residents of the halfway house is going to provoke him into an altercation large enough that a nine-one-one call will be made. At that point, the responding officer will get a hit on the warrant we issued and he'll be arrested. We anticipate that word of Rojas's arrest will get back to Jamal Johnson, whose friend runs the facility, so we'll have to act quickly to have the warrant resolved before he gets to the police station. Once it's established that Mr. Rojas is not the person who is the subject of the arrest warrant, he will be released. When he's released, Arthur's people, posing as friends of Mr. Johnson, will be waiting to help him."

"After that?" Fletcher asked.

"We'll put him on ice until the trial's over. We need to make sure that Ann knows he's our guest and that he's alive," Arthur said. "Hopefully, that ensures she does what we want."

"Where you taking him?"

"The warehouse over on Trumbull Street in Elizabeth. Where we shot the videos," Arthur replied.

"Why there?" Fletcher asked.

A small snort escaped from Arthur's nose. "All the production equipment is still there. Perhaps Mr. Rojas will eventually get to be the star of a snuff film."

"You still planning on taking McCabe's boyfriend?" Fletcher asked Arthur.

"Yes. It's one of those rare occasions that Martin and I agree, especially since Cassandra testifies tomorrow." He looked in Martin's direction. "Isn't that right, Martin?"

Martin nodded. "Yes. I'm all in favor of having an insurance policy. So, will you do a double feature?" he asked with a grin.

"I think costars will be fine," Arthur replied.


"Detective Ridge," Erin began, walking toward the witness stand. "You testified that you found two latent fingerprints belonging to my client on the handgun that was used to shoot Mr. Parsons."

"That's correct," he stated.

"And you indicated that there were other fingerprints on the weapon that were so badly smudged they could not be identified. Is that correct?"

"It is," he replied.

"You stated that the two prints you found came from what we would commonly call the ring finger and pinky of Ms. Parsons's right hand, correct?"

"Correct."

"And these prints were located near the bottom of the handle of the gun."

"Yes."

"And if I understand your testimony, the smudged fingerprints were found farther up the handle of the gun."

"That's true."

"Isn't it possible that the fingerprints farther up the gun handle were smudged because someone held the gun after my client touched it?"

Ridge gave her a condescending smile. "Anything is possible, counsel."

"So it's possible that someone wearing a glove held the weapon after my client touched it."

"Again, counsel, anything is possible."

"But it is correct, you have no idea when or how those prints were smudged?"

"That's correct."

"When did my client touch the weapon?"

"I have no way of knowing that."

"Fingerprints can last on a surface for years, isn't that correct, Detective Ridge?"

"Yes."

"So, as you sit here today, you cannot testify as to when my client touched the weapon. It could have been days, weeks, months, or years before Mr. Parsons was shot?"

"That's correct."

Erin began to walk back toward counsel table. She paused and turned to face Detective Ridge. "You found Charles Parsons's fingerprints on the weapon as well, correct?"

"Yes. That's accurate."

"And one of his fingerprints, the one from his index finger, was found on the trigger, correct?"

"That's correct."

"Thank you, Detective. No further questions, Your Honor."

Erin retook her seat and looked down the table at Swish. They both knew who the next witness was and Erin was anxious to finally put a face to "Luke." When she heard the door to the courtroom swing open, Erin shifted in her seat so she could get a better look as Detective Sybil Lucas made her way down the aisle. About five foot five with close-cropped black hair, Sybil Lucas carried herself like she was still in the marines. She wore gray slacks, with a black jacket over a white turtleneck. As she took her seat in the witness chair, her eyes never wandered from Assistant Prosecutor Willis.

After going through her credentials, Willis walked up to her and handed her an envelope. "Detective, I'm handing you an envelope that has been marked as State Exhibit 5 for identification. Is that your signature on the second line?"

"Yes, it is, sir," she responded formally.

"What is that envelope?" Willis asked.

"We use it for chain-of-custody purposes, sir. In other words, Detective Burke, whose signature is above mine, confiscated a computer. In the computer was a small device. When he brought the computer to my lab at the prosecutor's office, he removed the device, put it in this envelope, sealed it, and signed it with the date and time. When I took the device out, I also put on the date and time and then signed it. That way we know that no one has had the piece of evidence in their possession unless they've signed for it."

"What, if anything, did you do with the device?" Willis inquired.

"When Detective Burke gave the device to me, he thought it was a flash drive with information on it. As soon as I examined it, however, I knew it was a recording device. So I immediately contacted Detective Barry Josephs, who works with wiretaps, and he took it from there. As you can see, his signature appears under mine."

"Did you ever do anything else with the device?"

"No, sir."

"Nothing further," Willis said, returning to his seat.

Erin walked to the witness stand with a piece of paper in her hand. "Detective Lucas, let me show you what has been marked as Exhibit D-1, which is a copy of your report from April 18, 2008. Take a look at that please."

Willis slowly stood. "I object to this, Your Honor. This is well beyond the scope of direct, which was for the limited purpose of chain of custody."

Spiegel looked down at Erin. "Counsel, does the document you handed the witness deal with the chain of custody of the recording device?"

"No, Judge," Erin responded. "It involves something else, something that I believe the detective has knowledge of."

"Does it go to Detective Lucas's credibility?"

"No, Your Honor."

"Then I'll sustain the objection," Spiegel replied.

"In that case, Your Honor, I'll reserve my right to recall Detective Lucas on the defense case. No further questions."

As Erin walked up to the witness stand to retrieve the copy of the report, she made sure to look Detective Lucas squarely in the eye. If nothing else, Erin wanted Lucas to suspect that she knew she was Luke. Willis's objection had the added benefit of making the jury think that Willis was trying to keep something important from them.

"Thank you, Detective," Erin said, taking the document from Lucas's outstretched hand.

As she made her way back to counsel table, Erin's mind drifted back to the panic in Justin's eyes and Detective Lucas's role in his untimely death. Why was Lucas involved in placing the rootkit on Parsons's computer? What was the connection? As Lucas stepped down from the witness chair and headed for the aisle to leave the courtroom, Erin glanced at Ann. Her head bowed, she was staring at the notepad in front of her. Erin turned to get another look at Lucas, who refused to look in Erin's direction, her eyes focused on the courtroom door. Erin quickly looked at Ann, then back at Lucas one last time. *Is it possible?* Erin wondered.

Kluska hovered over her desk. "So you're really leaving us?" he asked.

Sybil Lucas looked up and gave him a sad smile. "Yeah, Ed. I need a bit of a break. You know, I went straight from the marines to here. Think I need to unwind a bit."

"Have anything special planned?" he asked.

"Nah. Just chill. Maybe do some traveling. Lie on a beach some-where and do nothing. Be an irresponsible twenty-something," she offered.

"Well, I know when you put in your papers you said your last day would be a week from Friday, but I heard through the grapevine that McCabe said she's going to recall you. So you may need to hang around a little longer."

Sybil chuckled. "I think that was just her being dramatic for the jury. She's got no reason to recall me, and even if she did, the trial will be over next week. I'll be fine. Besides, you're sequestered, you're not supposed to know what happened."

Kluska made a face. "I heard Willis bitching about the fact that McCabe has asked for permission to be able to recall witnesses—me and now you."

"Like I said, I'm not worried. Still plan on this Friday being my last day in the office and using my last week of vacation next week."

"That's good," Kluska said, slowly nodding. "That's good," he repeated, almost to himself.

Sybil was beginning to feel a little uncomfortable with Kluska's behavior. It's not like they knew each other so well that he should be all choked up about her leaving.

"Listen," he said. "I got a call from a detective I know in Homi-cide in Essex County who saw a couple of articles in the paper about the trial. He's got a case, almost a year old now, involving the murder of one of McCabe's former clients. What made him reach out was that when they had pulled the victim's phone records, one of the numbers he had called was listed to Charles Parsons. When he took a statement from McCabe, she told him that she had met with her client a couple of days before he showed up dead, and he was in a panic over installing some soft-ware on computers of some rich and powerful people—software that may have contained a computer virus. He assumed we had seized Parsons's computers as part of our investigation and wanted to know if there were any viruses on them."

It was easy for her to mask any reaction because once Kluska started she knew he was talking about Mackey. Justin's death still haunted her—she should have done more to protect him. She had never envisioned he would pay the ultimate price once her rootkit was discovered. She had committed an unforgivable mistake—she had underestimated Parsons's brutality.

She opened a manila file folder, rooted through it, and picked out a piece of paper. "Ed," she said, offering him the document, "you know I found a rootkit on Parsons's desktop computer. It's in my report."

"Yeah," he said. "I remember that now. The guy in Essex also said the dead guy was working with a guy named Luke. He asked me if we found anything on Parsons's computers about a Luke."

She knew then that he was testing her, but what he knew or suspected was still unclear. "Ed, remember all Parsons's e-mails were encrypted, and all other information was either deleted or transferred to a hard drive we don't have."

"Right," he mumbled. "So . . . we don't have anything helpful for me to give Peters."

Sybil shrugged. "Sorry, Ed. Wish I could be more help."

He stood there for several more seconds. Then he offered her his hand. "You take care of yourself. Maybe after you recharge the batteries, you'll want to come back," he said as they shook hands.

"Thanks, Ed. Who knows? Maybe I'll get tired of being an irresponsible twenty-something and decide to be a responsible adult again," she said with a small snort. "I appreciate you taking the time to stop by."

"Yep, no problem." Kluska gave her one last nod and made his way down the hallway.

She watched him walk away, allowing her to return her focus to the task at hand. Disappearing this time would be harder than it had been in 1997. Security was much tighter post-9/11, and even back then, it had taken her uncle's willingness to break the law to help her secure a new identity. Once she had described what Parsons had done to her, it had taken everything she had to convince her aunt and uncle not to go to the police for fear of Parsons's retribution. Reluctantly, her uncle had provided her with the dead girl's Social Security number and a copy of her birth certificate. Then they sent her to live with her aunt's relatives in Minnesota.

After she had been in Minnesota for six months, her aunt and uncle had visited to let her know that Parsons had moved to New Jersey with his "daughter" Ann. At that point, whatever thoughts she had of trying to live a normal life disappeared. Parsons had to be stopped. She was sure that he was doing to the imposter exactly what he had done to her and to countless others. From that point on, her life had become focused on one goal: killing him. After finishing high school under her new identity, she'd joined the marines solely because they could train her in what she needed: computers and how to kill.

The die was cast—once the enormity of what she had done became known, she'd be a hunted woman. She hoped Ann's lawyers would be able to get her off, but that wasn't her problem. Her problem was to get out of Dodge before either the law or the rest of them caught up with her.

# CHAPTER 33

*E*RIN TOOK THE MEASURE OF CASSANDRA DeCOVNIE. IN HER ST. John's gray crepe tweed dress with an open-front matching jacket that fit like it had been made for her, she was a study in sophistication. She held her head erect, her posture perfect as she sat in the witness box. Her jewelry was expensive, but at the same time understated. Erin assumed that DeCovnie, like most witnesses, had received some "coaching" concerning how she should dress, and comport herself on the witness stand. So as Willis questioned her about her long business association and friendship with Parsons, Erin wasn't surprised to see DeCovnie dab her eyes with a tissue, and continue to do so as she recounted how it was that she had discovered Parsons's body and what the scene looked like when she arrived. Erin had to admit DeCovnie's performance was effective and not overdone.

Willis then moved on to playing the recording of the murder to have her identify the voices on the tape. As the recording played, Erin kept her eyes focused on the jury. She wanted to gauge their reactions.

*Look, you . . . came for. . . . I'll probably spend the rest of my life . . . jail. I . . . think you'd enjoy that . . . than killing me.*

*Boom.*

Several of the jurors lurched back in their seats as the sound of the gunshot echoed in the courtroom. DeCovnie let out a slight gasp.

Willis, who had been standing off to the side as the tape played, stepped forward. "Ms. DeCovnie, how long did you know Charles Parsons?"

"Almost thirty years," she responded.

"Can you identify his voice?"

"I can," she answered.

"Do you know the defendant, Ann Parsons?" Willis asked.

"I do."

"For how long have you known Ann Parsons?"

"I guess it's been almost twenty years since her mother was married to Charles," she replied.

"Can you identify her voice if you heard it?"

"Yes."

"How many voices did you hear on the recording the jury just heard?"

"Two."

"And did you recognize who was speaking?"

"Yes, I did," she replied.

"And whose voices did you recognize?"

"The male voice was Charles . . . I mean Charles Parsons. And the other voice was Ann Parsons."

"Thank you. No further questions."

Erin slowly walked over so she was standing near the jury box, forcing DeCovnie to look directly at the jurors. "How many times have you heard that tape prior to just now?" Erin asked.

DeCovnie began turning the gold bracelet on her right arm. "Several times," she finally said.

"What does 'several' mean, Ms. DeCovnie? Two, six, twenty—approximately how many times did someone for the prosecutor's office play that recording for you?"

"I don't remember exactly—maybe five," she said, her tone defensive.

"In the almost one year since Charles Parsons's murder, you've only heard that tape five times?"

"I guess it could have been more," DeCovnie responded tightly.

"I don't want you to guess, Ms. DeCovnie. I'm just trying to ascertain how many times you've heard that recording."

"I'm not sure," she said.

"The first time you heard it was when you were with Detective Burke and Mr. Willis, correct?"

DeCovnie fiddled with her bracelet and stole a glance in Willis's direction. "I believe so."

"And when they played it for you, did they tell you who was on the tape?"

She hesitated. "No. I believe they asked me if I recognized the voices."

"And when they played it for you the first time, this was before Ann was arrested, correct?"

"Yes, I believe it was."

"And according to Detective Burke's report of your interview on that occasion," Erin said, holding a document in her hand, "you told Detective Burke and Mr. Willis that the man's voice was definitely Charles's, but you couldn't be certain as to who the other voice was. Do you recall that?"

"Later, when they played it for me again, I recognized the second voice as Ann's."

Erin took several steps closer to the witness stand, still holding the document, and gave DeCovnie a hard stare. "We'll get there, Ms. DeCovnie. But please answer my question. When they played the recording for you the first time, you did not identify Ann as the second voice. Isn't that true?"

"Yes."

"And when they played it for you the next time, they had already arrested Ann. Isn't that correct?"

"Yes. I believe she had been arrested."

"When they played it for you the second time, didn't they ask you if that was Ann's voice?" Erin asked, this time waving the document in her hand.

"They may have, I don't remember."

"Ms. DeCovnie, isn't it true that when they interviewed you after Ann was arrested and played the recording, they said, 'That's Ann Parsons's voice, isn't it?'?"

DeCovnie shifted in her seat. "I don't recall what they asked me."

"Ms. DeCovnie, I'm going to hand you Detective Burke's report. You can read it in its entirety if you like, but in particular I want you to read the second through fourth paragraphs on page three. Please take your time."

DeCovnie took the report from Erin, put on reading glasses, and began to review the report. After about a minute, she looked up and said, "Okay."

"Does that refresh your recollection that the second time you heard the recording, after Ann was arrested, Detective Burke suggested to you that it was Ann's voice?"

"Objection," Willis said, rising to his feet.

Spiegel paused. "I'll allow it."

DeCovnie looked up at the judge. "I'm sorry, what's the question?"

The judge motioned to the court reporter to read the question back.

"Yes. That's what he asked me."

"He didn't ask you, Ms. DeCovnie—he *suggested* to you it was Ann. Isn't that correct?"

"I suppose," she replied, looking down at her hands.

"You suppose, Ms. DeCovnie? Doesn't Detective Burke state in his report, 'I asked Ms. DeCovnie if the other voice on the recording was Ann Parsons's'? Isn't that what he said to you?"

"Yes. That's what he said. All right—" she said, her tone showing her annoyance and, for the first time, a crack in her composure.

"When they played the recording for you the first time, did you have trouble understanding what was being said?"

"Yes. It does cut in and out," she replied, a calmness returning to her tone.

"And when they played it for you the second time and then subsequent times, didn't they provide you with a transcript of what the prosecutor's office said was on the recording?"

She glared at Erin. "They gave me a transcript at some point. I don't remember if it was the second time or not."

"Would you refer to Detective Burke's report again, page three, last paragraph, and see if that refreshes your recollection as to whether that's when they gave you the transcript?" Erin asked without even looking at the report.

"I see that. Yes, that's when I saw a transcript."

Erin smiled, wanting DeCovnie to know who was in control. "Ms. DeCovnie, right before we hear the sound of the gun, would you agree with me that Charles Parsons says, 'I'll probably spend the rest of my life,' then there's something that's inaudible, then the word 'jail'?"

"Yes, that could be what he says."

"Do you know why Charles Parsons would say something about spending the rest of his life in jail?"

"No. There's no reason he would say that," she answered quickly.

"But he did, correct?"

"It sounds like that's what he says."

Erin turned and walked back to the far end of the jury box, looking at the jurors as she passed, who were all watching DeCovnie closely. "Do you know of any activities that Mr. Parsons was involved in that could have resulted in him going to jail?"

"Absolutely not," DeCovnie replied emphatically. "There was no reason for him to be worried about going to jail."

Erin took another document out of a file folder. "Ms. DeCovnie, when did you first meet Felipe Rojas?"

"Objection!" Willis shouted as he jumped to his feet.

Spiegel hesitated, appearing to ponder his course. "I'll see counsel at sidebar." Once they approached the bench on the side farthest from the jury, he asked, "What's the objection, Mr. Willis?"

"Judge, she hasn't laid a proper foundation. She hasn't established that Ms. DeCovnie even knows who this Rojas person is, not to mention it has nothing to do with the direct examination."

Spiegel turned to look at Erin.

"Judge, it's cross-examination and this will ultimately go to Ms. DeCovnie's credibility."

Spiegel removed his reading glasses and rubbed his eyes. "I'm going to overrule the objection. However, let me ask you this, Ms.

McCabe. I have the sense that this will be a wide-ranging cross-examination. Am I correct?"

"You are, Judge," Erin replied.

"And this is all going to her credibility, correct?" Spiegel asked.

"Yes, Judge," Erin replied.

"This morning, you mentioned outside the presence of the jury that we would need to have an evidentiary hearing to determine the admissibility of some of the areas you want to cross-examine Ms. DeCovnie on. So, in terms of the continuity of the trial, and since I cannot weigh the credibility of witnesses at the end of the state's case in deciding a motion for judgment of acquittal, I'd like to suggest that you limit your cross now. If I don't grant your motion to dismiss the state's case, we can then have the evidentiary hearing and I will allow you to recall Ms. DeCovnie as a hostile witness so you may continue to ask leading questions."

"Judge, that's fine, but I would like to finish the line of questioning that I've started."

"Of course," Spiegel replied.

When Erin and Willis had returned to their places, Judge Spiegel turned to the court reporter. "Please read the last question back to Ms. DeCovnie. I have overruled the objection."

After the question was read, DeCovnie looked at Erin. "I don't believe I know any such person, Ms. McCabe."

"Really. Let me see if I can refresh your recollection," Erin suggested as she moved in behind Ann at counsel table so DeCovnie was staring directly at her. "It would have been about eleven years ago, and Felipe Rojas would have been about fourteen at the time and you introduced him to Charles Parsons. Does that help you recall meeting Felipe Rojas, Ms. DeCovnie?"

"No, I'm afraid it doesn't," DeCovnie said, pursing her lips and rubbing her hands. "I don't know anyone by that name."

"How about David Rojas? Do you know a David Rojas?"

"No. That name is not familiar."

"Ms. DeCovnie, you were named the executrix of Mr. Parsons's will, correct?"

"I was."

"And how large is Mr. Parsons's estate, approximately?"

"Around one hundred million dollars."

"As executrix you will make approximately one million dollars in fees, correct?"

"Yes."

"Does the one million dollars figure include money that Mr. Parsons held in bank accounts outside the United States?"

DeCovnie shifted in her seat and fiddled with the ring on her left hand. "I don't . . . I'm unaware of any such accounts."

"You never heard Mr. Parsons discuss offshore bank accounts?"

"Not that I can recall."

"Your Honor, based on your ruling, I'll end here now and re-call Ms. DeCovnie later."

Willis stood up. "Ms. DeCovnie, counsel asked you about your commission as executrix. Do you know how much Ann Parsons stands to inherit under her father's will?"

DeCovnie smiled with a bit of triumph. "Yes, I do. Ten million dollars and a condo in Jersey City."

"And what is the value of the condo in Jersey City, if you know?"

"It's been appraised at nine hundred thousand dollars."

"Thank you," Willis said, lowering himself back into his seat.

Erin looked up at DeCovnie. "The bequest that you just re-ferred to states: 'To my adopted daughter, Ann Parsons, I leave the sum of ten million dollars, and if she is living there at the time of my death, I also leave her my condominium in Jersey City,' cor-rect?"

"Yes."

"Nothing further, Judge."

Spiegel looked over at Willis to see if he had any redirect ex-amination. When Willis indicated that he had no additional ques-tions, Spiegel turned to DeCovnie. "Ms. DeCovnie, I am allowing Ms. McCabe to recall you as a witness. Based on that, I want you back here Monday morning in case you are needed. In the in-terim, please do not speak to anyone about your testimony, in-

cluding any of the lawyers or their staff, or in the case of the prosecutor's office, with any of the employees of that office. Do you
understand my instructions?"

"Yes, Judge."

As soon as Cassandra was in the limo taking her back to Parsons's brownstone on East Sixty-Eighth Street, she tried to call
Conroy. Frustrated when he didn't answer, she texted him.

**we need to act. mccabe knows too much. used ann's real name. I
have to return as a witness.**

As she silently stewed, the limo headed toward the Lincoln
Tunnel. This was not going as planned. They had counted on
Ann keeping her real identity secret so she would have a chance
to inherit. But McCabe knew her real name, Felipe Rojas, which
also meant that McCabe knew about her role in making Felipe
available to Parsons. There was a hell of a lot of money at stake,
but none of it would do her any good if she spent the rest of her
life in jail. Maybe she should think about disappearing for a
while. Her phone vibrated and she flipped it open.

**in a meeting. things under control. we get rojas and the boyfriend
this afternoon. waiting for confirmation on real ann but she should
be dealt with by tomorrow. all good.**

She closed her phone, trying to convince herself that things
*were* under control. Not for the first time, she cursed herself for
getting caught in Charles's web. She was only thirty at the time,
yet her career as a model was nearing an end when she'd met Parsons at Studio 54, where he was a regular. He was tall, well built,
and very handsome. Even though he was five years her junior, he
was already a star on Wall Street with an apartment on the Upper
East Side. He liked to party and was a regular at the famous disco.
Although the club was notorious for its restrictive entry policy, between his spending habits and willingness to share his cocaine, he
never had any trouble getting one of the banquettes located near
the bar.

She soon became a regular in his entourage at the club and

found herself immediately attracted to him. One night, after hours of drugs and booze, he'd invited her back to his apartment. She had chalked up his inability to perform to the drugs and alcohol, but he had later confessed that he found himself attracted to younger women and men. Initially startled that at thirty he considered her old, it was only after she started working with him that she came to understand that "younger" meant teenagers or younger.

So many times over the years she had asked herself why she hadn't fled his gravitational pull then, but the answer was easy: As her modeling assignments slowed, then stopped, he offered her everything that had been part of her life since she started modeling at eighteen: money, glamour, and an entrée into the celebrity scene. At first, she just helped him plan parties, but it slowly evolved until she was finding young women and men to invite. She had initially convinced herself that he wasn't doing anything wrong, but soon the truth had become inescapable . . . and yet she had allowed it to continue. Even now, it wasn't her conscience calling her to task; it was the fear of prison—the fear of losing the money, the glamour, the celebrity. Could she truly count on Martin to make everything right? Maybe it was time for her to cut her ties and take care of herself. But that would mean walking away from a third of the $550 million in the offshore accounts she had just denied knowing about.

*Hold on a little longer. Maybe Martin's right this time.*

Sybil examined the texts between DeCovnie and Conroy. She had no trouble deciphering who the "real Ann" was, but who were Rojas and the boyfriend? Based on DeCovnie's text, it certainly appeared that McCabe was going to reveal that Ann wasn't really Ann Parsons as part of the defense, and Sybil had to give McCabe credit for going all in. It was risky, especially if Ann didn't testify, but if she did, not only could she be acquitted, Conroy and the rest could find themselves on the wrong end of an investigation.

As Sybil ran different scenarios through her head, it suddenly dawned on her that they recognized the risk and were in the process of stopping Ann from testifying. She wondered if the boyfriend might be referring to McCabe's boyfriend, as she knew it had nothing to do with Ann.

She stopped herself. Why did she even care? Besides, even if she wanted to do something, how could she? This was happening this afternoon.

She now had what she needed; it was time to get out of town.

# CHAPTER 34

*A*FTER DECOVNIE'S TESTIMONY, WILLIS CALLED DETECTIVE CHRIS Burke. Burke had been the lead detective on the investigation, reporting to Kluska, who was in command. Burke testified about the discovery of what turned out to be the recording device in Parsons's laptop and Ann's confession. Erin was forced to admire that Willis had timed his direct examination perfectly. He had started the video of Ann's interrogation so that the ending, where Ann said she "did it," coincided with the court's recess for lunch, ensuring that the jury would chew on Ann's confession as they ate.

After lunch, Willis walked Burke through the tape. Knowing that Erin would attack Burke for telling Ann they had her on video when they really didn't, Willis questioned Burke about why he had done that, trying to defuse any leverage Erin might have.

Erin did the best she could cross-examining Burke, considering she couldn't make the video go away. All she could do was put the best possible spin on it. Burke admitted that they never were able to elicit any of the details of the crime from Ann—when she went to the house; what Parsons meant when he said, "You got what you came for"; why he would spend the rest of his life in jail; why she did it—even though they had tried. Even the "I did it" Ann had uttered was vague. Finally, Erin zeroed in on the fact that Ann had told them she had been in a bar in Hoboken and had repeatedly denied any involvement. It was only after Detective Burke gave her false information that she had offered her vague "I did it."

Finally, she took him through his meetings with DeCovnie and had Burke admit that the first time DeCovnie heard the recording she hadn't identified Ann's voice. It was only after Ann was arrested and Burke had played it for her again and asked the question, "Is that Ann's voice?" that DeCovnie had answered in the affirmative.

When Burke's testimony was concluded the judge adjourned for the day. It had been a long week, and as Erin and Duane walked toward the parking garage they were dragging more than their trial bags behind them.

"How you feeling?" Duane asked.

"Exhausted," Erin said with a weak smile. "Glad there's no trial tomorrow because Spiegel has his sentencing hearings. Gives us a little time to gear up for next week."

"Yeah, I'm meeting with Connie Irving tomorrow to prep her," Duane said.

"Good. I'm still thinking we do Marsha Kramer first, then Irving, then the NYC cop on the cell phone towers, then Ann, and then we make a decision on whether I need to recall DeCovnie. Maybe we won't need her, but there's a part of me that would hate to pass up an opportunity to go after her again," Erin said.

"Sounds like a plan," Duane responded. He reached into the inside breast pocket of his suit, removed his vibrating cell phone, and flipped it open. "Hi, Cheryl," he answered, then stopped dead in his tracks. He motioned for Erin to stop too, and hit the speaker button on his phone. "Cheryl, Erin's right here. We're together. We're walking toward our cars. What's the matter?"

"I'm sorry," Cheryl said, her voice sounding panicked. "I just got the strangest phone call from an unknown number and I didn't know what to do."

"What was it?" Duane asked.

"It was a woman's voice. She said, 'This is very important. Get hold of McCabe and Swisher and tell them Luke called. Tell them that I intercepted a message from the bad guys. I'm not sure exactly what it means, but the message is, 'We get Rojas and the boyfriend this afternoon.' Make sure they get that message now. It's urgent. And tell them there's a mole in the prosecutor's office. Everything gets back to the bad guys.' She then asked me to read it back to her, which I did, and then she said, 'I repeat, it's urgent.'"

Duane and Erin stood there staring at each other. "Read the message again," Erin said.

"We get Rojas and the boyfriend this afternoon," Cheryl repeated.

Erin's eyes went wide. "They know where David is," she said to Duane.

"Fuck," he said. "Thanks, Cheryl. You did good. Please stay at the office in case we need you. Can you do that?"

"Yes," she answered, the confusion and fear evident in her tone.

"Great. One of us will get back to you."

"Call JJ," Erin said as soon as Duane hung up. "He's got to get hold of his buddy at the halfway house."

Duane reached out and put his hand on her shoulder. "E, the boyfriend could mean Mark."

"Shit," she said. "They get David to control Ann; they get Mark to control me."

"Listen, we need to move quickly. I'll call JJ, you call Mark," Duane said.

After grabbing her BlackBerry out of her purse, she hit his number on speed dial, cursing when it rang four times and then went to voice mail. "Mark, it's Erin. It's urgent. Call me immediately. You're in danger. Call me."

She looked up and heard Swish leaving a message for JJ. She checked her watch: 4:50 p.m. It was fewer than ten miles to Westfield High School, but with rush-hour traffic, who knew how long it would take to get there. Mark was probably finishing up basketball practice. "Do you have the number for the halfway house?"

"Yeah," he said. "I'll call and warn them. You take care of Mark."

"I think Mark is probably still at school," she said hopefully. "I'm going to call Westfield PD and tell them to head to the school. Let's keep each other posted."

They both started running toward their cars, Duane dialing the halfway house as he ran.

She threw her things into her car and dialed 411, asking for the number of the Westfield Police Department while screeching out of the parking garage. As she guided her Miata down Jersey Avenue, she waited for the number to connect.

"Westfield Police Department, Sergeant Bernard, how can I help you?"

"Sergeant, my name is Erin McCabe. I'm an attorney currently trying a murder case in Elizabeth. I just received information that my boyfriend, Mark Simpson, who is a teacher at Westfield High, may be the target of a kidnapping attempt. Can you please send an officer to the high school to find Mr. Simpson and make sure he's all right? I'm on my way there now."

There was a moment of silence before Bernard said, "What makes you think your boyfriend is going to be kidnapped?"

Erin could tell by his tone that he was not taking her seriously. "My office received an anonymous call. As I told you, I'm involved in a murder case, and there are some bad people involved."

"Are you an assistant prosecutor, Ms. McCabe?"

"No," she almost screamed, her frustration mounting. "I represent the defendant."

"Wait. Is it the Parsons murder case? That's the one where the daughter killed her father? That happened here—in town."

"Yes, Sergeant. That's the case. Can you please get someone to the high school?"

"Look. Maybe this is your first big case, Ms. McCabe," he suggested with a tinge of sarcasm, "but defendants do all kinds of crazy stuff to try and get a mistrial. I'm sure your client just had one of her friends call your office to try and get the case delayed."

Erin thought her head was going to explode, but she reminded herself not to call Bernard a fucking idiot. "Please, humor me,

Sergeant. This is not my first murder trial. Mr. Simpson is the freshman boys' basketball coach. Just send a car over to check on him. If I'm wrong, you sent a car to the high school for nothing. But if I'm right, you could be saving his life."

She heard him sigh. "Thank you for that advice, Ms. McCabe. I'll get someone over there as soon as I can," he said, his voice dripping with condescension.

"Would you take my number please and have the officer call me if there are any problems?"

"Sure," he said.

After giving the sergeant her number, Erin hung up and immediately called Duane.

"They arrested David," he said first thing. "I'm on my way to Newark's Second Precinct headquarters now."

"Arrested!" she shouted. "For what?"

"According to Bob, who runs the halfway house, one of the residents assaulted David, and when the police came and ran a check on David, as is procedure, it came back that there was a warrant for a David Rojas out of Florida. So they arrested him too."

"Shit, how many David Rojases do you think there are in Florida?"

"I don't know, but I'm hoping I can get him bailed out. I was able to get hold of JJ. He had just left Mark at the high school ten minutes ago. They were playing a little one-on-one after the freshmen practice. JJ is going to meet me at the station. How did you make out?"

She leaned on her horn as she flew by a truck double-parked on First Avenue in Roselle. "I ran into an asshole at Westfield PD. He said he'd send someone, but I'm not sure if it'll be this decade. I think I'm less than fifteen minutes away."

"JJ said that he probably has his cell phone in his gym bag. Call the main office and see if you can get anyone."

"Good idea," she said. "Stay in touch."

It was already after five when she tried the school's main number, and after six rings, she was connected to a general message, which advised that if she knew the four-digit extension of the person she was calling she could dial it at any time. Trying to dial the first four letters of a person's name as she weaved through traffic was nearly impossible. When she finally got through to the principal, Karen Dixon, all she received was the generic "I'm either on the phone or away from my desk, please feel free to leave me a message and I'll get back to you as soon as I can" message. Once again Erin fumbled with her phone, trying to find the right numbers to connect with Dixon's secretary. Looking up to try to keep an eye on the car in front of her, she suddenly noticed it was coming to a stop and she slammed on her brakes, skidding to a halt, inches from the rear bumper of the startled driver in front of her.

"Hi, you've reached Mary Beth Clarke in the Guidance Department. I'm sorry . . ."

*Damn it.* She slammed the Miata into first gear and took off traveling down the left-hand-turn-only lane before cutting back into the travel lane. She looked around, hoping that a cop would see her erratic driving and try to pull her over. *Why is there never a cop around when you need one?*

She tried Mark's cell phone again—still no answer—then checked the clock on her dashboard: 5:20 p.m. There was still a little daylight left, but it was cold and overcast, which made it seem later. She continued to weave her little sports car in and out of traffic, drawing irate horn blasts in the process.

Finally, there was the school. Turning into the teachers' lot she noticed a black Ford Explorer with its flashers going parked behind Mark's car. *An unmarked car,* she thought with a sigh of relief and quickly told herself that having mentally castigated Sergeant Bernard, she now owed him a mental apology.

As she got closer, she could see two uniformed officers talking to Mark. She pulled into an empty parking space a few spots down, grabbed her purse, and hurriedly hopped out of her car.

She took in the scene as she approached the Explorer. Looking in the open door of the vehicle, she suddenly sensed something was off. She shifted her focus from the Explorer to the scene in front of her, studying the two officers questioning Mark, her mind shifted. She hadn't counted on this. She could tell from Mark's expression that he was surprised to see her, but before he could say anything, one of the officers turned around. "Excuse me, miss," he said. "Please go back to your car."

She kept walking toward them, her pace quickening as she let her hand slip into her purse, putting her hand on what she was going to need. "Please, officers, you have to help me. There's a man following me and he has a gun."

The officers exchanged uneasy glances as she continued to close the distance between them.

"Please, you have to help me," she pleaded.

"Lady, I said back off," the officer said, reaching for his holstered weapon.

"Erin?" Mark said, causing the officer to glance in his direction.

Erin took two more quick steps, then paused. After almost a lifetime of playing soccer and two years of taking Krav Maga classes, she executed her kick to the officer's groin with such precision that her instructor would have been proud. The fact that she was wearing heels with pointed toes only made it that much more effective. Before the other officer could even react, she swung her purse, catching him square on the side of the head. As he staggered, she held the pepper spray she had pulled from her purse and sprayed his face. She then aimed at the first officer, who was writhing on the ground, and hit him flush in his face with the spray as well.

"Come on!" she screamed at Mark. "They're not cops. I'll explain later."

They both dashed for her car. As soon as he was in, she threw it into reverse and flew back out of the parking area.

Her heart was pounding and her hands started to shake. Out of the corner of her eye, she saw Mark staring at her. He looked as stunned as she felt. "You either just saved my life or we're about to become the new Bonnie and Clyde," he said.

"Only one way to find out," she said, a tremble in her voice. "Heading to police headquarters now."

# CHAPTER 35

"*I*'M SURPRISED YOU'RE STILL MY FRIEND," ERIN SAID ONCE CORRINE returned to the kitchen after putting Austin to bed. Corrine made her way to the refrigerator and poured a glass of water. At five foot two, with a close-cropped Afro, she was a beautiful woman who moved with a grace that belied her six-month's pregnant body.

Duane was in the home office making phone calls, and Mark, JJ and a couple of guys they played basketball with had gone to Mark's house to pick up some clothes and toiletries for him and Erin. They had decided to stay with Duane and Corrine tonight just to be safe.

"I always seem to be getting your husband involved in cases where people try to kill us or others we know," she said.

Corrine's smile accentuated her high cheekbones. "Hey, he was an FBI agent when we got married. It's not like I ever thought he was going to be a patent attorney," Corrine said as she guided herself into one of the kitchen chairs. "Besides, girl, it seems like you're the one always wearing a target on your back. Seriously, are you okay?"

Erin took a deep breath and exhaled slowly. "Honestly, no. I still sometimes get flashbacks from Sharise's case," she said with a shudder. "Now I'm going to have to deal with the fact that I almost got my boyfriend kidnapped. Not to mention we received a message that if our client ever wants to see her brother alive again, she has to agree not to testify. So, no, I feel like I'm about to fall apart."

Corrine reached across the kitchen table and took Erin's hand. "Listen to me, Erin McCabe. You saved your boyfriend's life today, and between you and my husband, I'm confident you'll find a way to save your client too."

"Thanks," Erin said. "I wish I shared your confidence." She continued, "What about you guys? I worry about you and Austin. No one is safe with these people."

"Yeah, we've talked about it a lot. Duane's upset and worried. He really wants us to go stay with my parents for a while. We'll see. I hate to leave while you guys are on trial, but I also don't want us to be a distraction because he's worried about our safety."

They sat there in silence for a few moments. "How you feeling?" Erin asked, trying to change the subject.

"Not too bad. I'm a little tired. But that could just be from chasing after a four-year-old."

"How's Austin adjusting to Mommy being pregnant?"

Cori laughed. "I don't think he's too excited about having a baby brother or sister. Although he is fascinated by the fact that there's a baby in Mommy's belly."

"Yeah, I'm not sure Sean ever forgave my mother and father for having me," Erin said with a chuckle.

"Hey," Duane said as he walked into the kitchen and poured himself a cup of coffee. "Ben says hello," he said, referring to Ben Silver.

"What did he have to say?" Erin asked.

"Ben's going to reach out to Ed Champion, the acting U.S. attorney, tonight to see if there's any chance we could meet with him or Abhay Petel, the Newark FBI office's special agent in charge. I explained to Ben that this can't leak, so that's why he's going right to the top."

"So, tell me what happened when you got to the precinct," Erin said.

Duane pulled out a chair and sat down next to Corrine. "When

I got to the front desk and told the officer why I was there, he checked his computer and said David had been released fifteen minutes earlier after it became clear the warrant was for a different David Rojas. When I asked if he knew where David had gone, he just looked at me like I was crazy and said, 'Out the front door. After that, buddy, I don't have a clue.' So I went outside and looked around and then I called Bob at the halfway house, who told me he hadn't heard anything from David. Then just before six, Cheryl got the call saying they had David."

Duane studied Erin. "What about you? From the little I heard you had quite the evening. How'd you figure out that they weren't real cops?"

"A little luck, a little paranoia, pants and shoes," Erin replied.

"Pants and shoes?" Duane and Corrine replied in unison.

Erin looked sheepishly at both of them. "Yeah, like I said, most of it was dumb luck." She paused to sip her tea. "When I first saw the Explorer, I was relieved. I figured it was an unmarked car that had been sent over as a result of my call. But as I got out and started walking, it dawned on me that all it had were the blinking emergency flashers. Most of the unmarked cars I've seen either have LED lights somewhere that flash or built-in lights in the rear window and front grill that flash to let you know it's a cop car. This didn't have any of those." Erin hesitated as the scene slowly replayed in her head. "Then, as I walked by the car, the driver's door was open and I noticed the interior didn't look like a police vehicle. There was no computer, which they all have now, and more importantly, there was no radio. So at that point my antenna went up and my paranoia kicked in. As I started to get closer to the two of them, I noticed their uniforms."

Looking at Duane, she could see his confusion. "Remember the other day when Officer Palladino from Westfield PD testified?"

Duane nodded.

"Well, because I sit on the aisle, I see the witnesses as they walk to the witness stand and, then again, when they walk back out of the courtroom. The other day in court, I happened to notice how well shined his shoes were as he walked by—I mean you could probably see your reflection in them. I also noticed that his pants had a yellow stripe down the outside of each leg. As I approached these two guys, I noticed their shoes weren't shined, in fact their shoes were different from each other's, and their uniform pants didn't have a gold stripe. From there, I just made a leap of faith. Fortunately, I guessed right, or you'd be bailing me out of the county jail for assaulting two police officers."

Duane gave a little snort. "What did Sergeant Bernard say when you got to headquarters?"

"He was belligerent at first, but when I explained why we were there, his eyes went wide and he called dispatch to have all units check in—I think he was convinced that I had just assaulted two of his officers. When everyone who was on the road checked in, he immediately realized he had screwed up and sent two units to the high school. Of course, by the time the units he sent actually got there, the imposters were long gone. I had the license plate number, and not surprisingly, it turned out to be stolen. Just as we were leaving, Bernard got a call from Plainfield PD that the Explorer had been found abandoned on East Seventh Street."

Corrine began the slow process of standing. "I think you two need some time to figure what your next steps are. When Mark and JJ get back, let me know and I'll get you two settled in."

Erin stood, walked over, and gave her a hug. "Thank you so much for everything. I don't know what I'd do without you guys."

"You just be careful," Corrine said. "I can't have anything happening to you."

After Corrine had left, Erin fell back into her chair. "What are we going to do? Ann will never testify now."

"Ask Spiegel for a delay of trial?" Duane said.

"How can we?" Erin replied. "Remember what Lucas said—there's a mole in the prosecutor's office. Whoever that is will get word to whoever has David."

Duane swirled the coffee in his cup and nodded in agreement. "Even if there wasn't a mole, it's not like Spiegel could keep the delay a secret."

"True," Erin said. "So that means we either find David before Ann is scheduled to testify, or she doesn't and we hope the jury is understanding."

Duane closed his eyes. When he looked up there was a sadness behind his eyes that Erin never remembered seeing before. "I hate to say this, but regardless of what Ann does, the chances of David surviving are slim and none. They'll probably keep him alive to try and force her hand, but after that . . ."

Erin pursed her lips. "You were in the FBI. Assuming you and Ben can get them involved, what are the chances they can find him over the weekend?"

"Don't know. They'll have access to a lot of surveillance cameras, especially around police headquarters. Hopefully, they'll identify who picked him up."

"Yeah, let's try and stay positive," Erin said, although she could hear the lack of conviction in her own voice.

"Hey," Duane said.

"What?"

"You know you probably saved Mark's life," he said. "I'm glad you had the courage to act on your hunch. If you'd played it differently you could have both wound up dead."

"People keep telling me that, but seems to me he was only in the crosshairs because of me," Erin responded. "Speaking of which, I'm worried about you, Corrine, and Austin. They came for me, and now they tried to get Mark. I'm worried they'll come for you guys too."

Duane sighed, his face betraying the worry he'd been trying to hide. "Cori and I talked about her going to stay with her folks in Virginia, but right now she really doesn't want to pack up and leave. We do have a state-of-the-art home security system and, back when I was with the FBI, Cori got a gun permit and has a Glock. Truth be told, she's probably a better shot than I am. I've also made friends with a couple of Scotch Plains cops, and I know they're keeping an eye out for us."

"Would it help if I added my voice to yours in suggesting to Corrine she'd be safer at her folks'?"

"Maybe. I think I almost have her convinced, so it might not hurt for you to say something. Thanks."

Duane got up and poured more coffee into his cup. "What do you make of Lucas warning us?" he asked, changing the subject.

"Yeah. I haven't figured Lucas out yet, but it's pretty clear who my guardian angel was."

Duane leaned up against the kitchen counter, sipping his coffee. "I guess so."

"I don't fucking believe it!" Conroy screamed into the phone. "I told you not to fuck this up. Fucking McCabe beats the shit out of two of your hired thugs. Are you fucking kidding me?"

"Jesus Christ, Martin. What the hell do you want from me? We got Rojas."

"Arthur, the only reason your fucking goons got Rojas is because I set it up. Unfortunately, I didn't set up grabbing McCabe's boyfriend."

"For Christ's sake, don't blame me. Someone had to tip her off. Otherwise why'd she go straight to the high school from the courthouse? It makes no fucking sense."

Conroy momentarily wavered in his attack. What Arthur said made him pause. Why did McCabe leave the courthouse and go straight to the high school? They had followed her all week and she always went back to the office. And if she had been tipped off, who could have done it? Only he, Arthur, and Liam had known the plan.

"If you're right, and someone tipped her off, who the hell could it have been? It doesn't make sense," he finally said.

"Maybe next time you'll do your thinking before you blame me for fucking things up."

Conroy didn't rise to Arthur's bait. "I need to think this through. If we have a leak, it needs to be plugged immediately. In the meantime, make the call to McCabe's office and have Rojas leave the message. I'll make sure Willis knows to get word to us if anything unusual happens. There's no trial tomorrow, but if McCabe tries to delay, we'll need to move on to plan B."

"Fine."

# CHAPTER 36

*T*HE TEARS SLOWLY MADE THEIR WAY DOWN THE SIDE OF ANN'S FACE, weaving slightly as if following some predetermined course. "They win," Ann said, her voice a hoarse whisper through her tears. "I can't testify. It's over."

Ann had walked into the attorney visiting room that morning excited to prepare for her turn on the witness stand, but it had taken only one look at Erin's face for her to know that something was terribly wrong.

Erin had stopped at the office before heading to the jail and heard the message that had been left on her voice mail. It contained both a plea from David and a warning from whoever was holding him: If they went to the police or if Ann testified at trial, David's life would be over. After Erin explained to Ann what had happened, and the message that had been left on her voice mail, Ann had been crushed.

Erin tried to offer some hope. Even though she wasn't sure if it was true, Erin told Ann that Duane was meeting with people in the highest echelons of the U.S. attorney's office and the FBI to see if they'd be willing to get involved and explaining to them why they couldn't enlist local law enforcement. She ultimately convinced Ann that they still had to prepare as if Ann would take the witness stand on Tuesday.

Ann answered Erin's questions as best she could, but the preparation fell apart as soon as Erin took on the role of Ted Willis and began cross-examination. After only a few questions, Ann broke down and refused to go on.

"Ann, I'm sorry. I really am," Erin said. "I truly hope we can find your brother and save him."

Ann's look conveyed her anguish. "You know you can't save him. You know they've won. No matter what I do, they'll kill David. We both know that. I've sentenced my brother to death. My innocent brother, whose only crime was being related to me, so regardless, they've won. They've broken me."

Erin bit her lower lip and looked down at the table that separated them. "You told me once," Erin said, "that it wasn't the wall that imprisoned you, it was the fact that you couldn't fight back. Ann, you may be right. They may well kill David regardless of what you do—but you *can* still fight back. You can still try and stop them from winning. Don't give up without a fight."

Ann's eyes narrowed. "I bet you wouldn't be so quick with your speeches if they'd grabbed your boyfriend. I'd be willing to bet you'd do whatever they asked you to do, even if the chances were next to zero. So don't preach to me. We both know it's a crock of shit. And if you hadn't convinced me to withdraw my plea, David wouldn't be in this mess. So fuck you, Erin McCabe. Fuck you!"

Ann's words stung. They came from a place of anguish that Erin knew she wasn't privy to. What would she do or say if Mark's life hung in the balance? No, Ann was right. Had Mark been taken, Erin would do whatever was necessary to try to save him.

"Ann," she said softly. "I won't pretend that I know how you feel, or what you're going through. I don't. I do know that you'd trade your life for your brother's in a heartbeat. But you can't— it's not an option. I know it's really hard for you to hear this, but even if you allow yourself to be convicted, they're not going to spare his life. Look what they did to Carl, and he was one of their own."

Ann's mask of anger was now sliding into a look of hopelessness. Still, Erin continued.

"Your choices really come down to being convicted and going to jail for a murder you didn't commit, or fighting back and hoping that the truth will come out." Erin hesitated. "In either case, unless we can find David, the chances are they will kill him. On the other hand, if you tell your story, and let the world hear the horrors these people are capable of, maybe, just maybe, they can be stopped from destroying anyone else's life."

After a long silence, Ann looked up. "Please go," she said. "I want to go back to my cell."

When Erin got to the office, Cheryl was in the copy room, making copies of the exhibits Erin would need for Monday. Cheryl had been with Erin since shortly after Erin had started her own firm about six years ago. At the time Cheryl was a nineteen-year-old student at Union County College, and Erin couldn't afford to hire a full-time secretary. It had turned out to be a perfect fit, and no one was happier than Erin when they'd been able to hire Cheryl full-time after she'd received her associate's degree.

Hearing the noise from the copy room, Erin made her way there. "I'm here. Don't want to startle you," Erin called out before she reached the doorway.

"Thanks for the warning," Cheryl replied.

Erin walked into the room and gave Cheryl a hug. "You okay?" Erin asked.

Cheryl leaned back against the copier, shaking her head. "Thanks. Yeah, I'm okay. It was a little unsettling last night, but I'm fine."

"Thank you for what you did yesterday," Erin said. "Your getting the message to us as quickly as you did made a difference."

"Well, that's good to know," Cheryl responded with a small smile. "Can I ask what the message meant? It sounded pretty scary."

Erin hesitated. "Let's just say that some people are trying to make sure Ann gets convicted and went after her brother and Mark yesterday. Fortunately, they didn't get Mark, but they did abduct Ann's brother."

"Wait! Mark, as in your Mark?" Cheryl asked.

Erin nodded.

"Is he okay?"

"Yeah," Erin said, and it was mostly true.

She and Mark had been up late talking through what had happened, Erin apologizing for putting him in harm's way, and Mark thankful that she had managed to save his life. He had recounted that when he came out into the parking lot, the Explorer was parked behind his car with its flashers on. As he approached his car, the two "police officers" got out of the Explorer and asked if he was Mark Simpson. When he said he was, they told him that they had a complaint from a female student and they wanted him to accompany them to the station so they could talk to him about it. Needless to say, he was shocked and told them there must be some mistake. "Look, maybe it's all a misunderstanding," one of them said. "Just come with us to the station, and we'll see if we can clear this all up." Mark wasn't sure why, but he said to them, "Well, maybe I'd better call my lawyer first." With that, the officer with the clipboard threw it on the front seat of the Explorer and said, "Okay, well I was hoping we could do this the easy way, but it looks like we'll have to arrest you." Mark was totally baffled by what was happening and took a step back when he saw Erin's car pulling into the parking lot. As they had lain in the bed in Duane and Corrine's spare bedroom, holding each other, the realization of how close they had come to Mark being abducted had started to sink in, and Erin had buried her face in his chest, thankful he was alive.

"You okay?" Cheryl asked, startling Erin back to the present.

"What? Yeah. Just exhausted. It was a long night. Thanks. I'll be in the conference room. Let Swish know when he gets back."

For nearly an hour Erin worked on what she needed to cover on her direct examination of Ann. She forced herself to believe that Ann would testify, even though it seemed like a remote possibility.

"How you doing?"

Erin looked up to see Swish standing in the doorway to the conference room.

His face did not convey good news.

"It's what we feared. The feds won't get involved unless it's an interstate kidnapping. They suggested we contact Essex County, since we believe David was taken from outside police headquarters in Newark."

Erin exhaled, deflated by Duane's news. "What do we do now? Based on my conversation with Ann this morning, if we don't save David by Tuesday, there's very little chance she'll testify. She made me promise we wouldn't go to the police or ask for a mistrial because she's afraid that will guarantee they'll kill him." She rested her head in her hands, trying to come up with an option.

"I have a thought, but I don't know if it has any merit," Duane said slowly.

"Go for it," Erin said.

"Detective Sybil Lucas," Duane said.

Erin tried to guess where he was going with this, but perhaps she was too exhausted; the pieces didn't line up like they usually did.

"We know that Detective Lucas is Luke," he explained. "We also know that she must still be able to tap into some communications from Parsons's group, because she called to warn us."

"Okay, but she's a witness in the case who works for the Union County Prosecutor's Office. It's not like we can just pick up the phone and call her."

"Why not?" Duane asked.

"I'm sorry," Erin replied. "As I just said, she's a witness who works in the prosecutor's office—the same office we can't inform because there's a mole."

"First of all, she's not the mole—remember she was the one who warned us. More importantly, David's life is at stake. Not sure about you, but I'd be willing to go to the ethics committee and defend breaking some rules to try and save his life."

For the first time in days, Erin actually smiled. "Then I'm with you. Let's break some rules. What do you have in mind?"

"Let's try starting with a phone call."

"What do we want her to get for us?"

"Location, location, location—we need to know where David is."

He closed the conference room door and moved the phone so it was centered between them.

"Just be careful. We have to assume we're being recorded," Swish reminded her.

"Got it," Erin replied. Then, almost as an afterthought, added, "You're going to record it too, right?"

With a small grin Duane laid his recorder on the table and turned it on. The call went through the automated switchboard and they used the names directory to find her extension. After the second ring she picked up. "Detective Lucas."

"Hello, Detective, this is Erin McCabe and I'm here with my partner, Duane Swisher. We need to talk to you for a moment."

Lucas let out a nervous chuckle. "This is a little unusual, Ms. McCabe. I'm a sequestered witness in a case you're trying. I don't think I should be speaking with you."

"Detective, we have no intention of talking to you about your testimony," Erin began. "We're calling to thank you for calling our office yesterday. You probably saved my boyfriend's life." Erin paused. "And, even though I don't know how you did it, I suspect you were responsible for saving my life a few months back as well."

There was a long pause, then: "I don't know what you're talking about, Ms. McCabe. I never saved your life and I never called your office."

Erin's tone shifted. *At this point, what the hell.*

"Let me cut through the BS, Luke. We know who you are. We know you called here yesterday. We're calling because we need your help. As I said, your call probably saved my boyfriend's life; he was the 'boyfriend' referenced in the message. Unfortunately, the other person referenced, 'Rojas,' was not as fortunate; he was abducted. We have been warned if we go to the authorities, David Rojas, who is Ann Parsons's brother, will be murdered. We think you can help us find him before it's too late. That's why we're calling."

There was silence on the phone. Finally, after about five seconds, Erin asked, "Are you still there?"

"Yes," was Lucas's muffled reply.

"We need your help."

"Even if I wanted to, I resigned. My last official day is next Friday, but today is my last day in the office."

"Listen, we don't need you in your official capacity. We need you for your extracurricular activities."

"I don't know," Lucas replied. "Let me think about it. Call me at 856-555-0137 in thirty minutes."

The line went dead.

Erin and Swish looked at each other.

"Well, at least she didn't say no," Erin said. "But assuming she can find the location, we still have to rescue him. Without the cops."

Duane's smile told her that he was already ahead of her. "There are two guys I know, Rick Adams and Alex Fredericks, who were NYPD narcotics detectives. We became friends through a Black law enforcement group. They left NYPD a few years ago and set up their own private investigation agency. Let me reach out to them."

"Sounds like a plan," Erin responded.

Thirty minutes later they called the number Lucas had given them.

"I don't know how I can help you," she said as soon as she answered.

"We need to know where they're holding David. We think you could help us find that out," Erin replied.

"I don't know," Lucas said, clearly uncertain. "I only have one source left and let's just say it's not getting much use. I don't think I can help you."

It was out of Erin's mouth before she could stop herself. "Detective, about a year ago you fucked up, and as a result, Justin Mackey was killed. You can't bring him back, but you can help us save David Rojas's life and in the process maybe help save Ann Parsons as well."

When her statement was met with nothing but the buzz of static, Erin wondered if she had overplayed her hand.

"That's not fair," Lucas said, her voice tight. "I didn't kill Mackey. Besides, I already evened the score on that one."

Erin's eyes went wide with the realization of what Luke had just confirmed for her, but that would have to wait.

"Just get us a location," she pressed. "That's all we're asking for."

"Even if I can get it, it won't be until Monday. What's your cell phone number, Ms. McCabe?"

"Wait," Duane interjected. "Take mine. It's likely that Erin will be in court or with Ann when you reach out."

"Fine," Lucas said. "One way or another, you'll hear from me by five p.m. on Monday. That's the best I can do."

"Thank you," they said in unison.

"And just so you know, Ms. McCabe," Lucas said after a beat, "I do think about Mackey's death. You're right. I fucked up. But like you said, I can't undo it—I really wish I could."

The line disconnected. Duane reached over and shut off his recorder.

"Let me reach out to Rick and Alex and make sure they can be available Monday," he said. "Assuming she comes up with anything."

"Assuming she even tries," Erin added.

"I think she will," Duane responded. "Hey—what do you think Lucas meant when she said she already evened the score on Mackey's murder?"

Erin's head nodded slightly. "This is going to sound crazy, but I think I know. See if this works."

# CHAPTER 37

Ann stared blankly at Erin, her eyes puffy and her face drawn. Erin could tell that between the stress of trial and the fear of spending the rest of her life in prison Ann had lost a significant amount of weight since the judge had allowed her to withdraw her plea. "It'll never work," Ann said, shaking her head. "They're vicious. They'll kill David as soon as they sense anything is wrong."

"Ann, we've been through this. They'll kill David regardless. We have to try and save him. It's his only hope."

"But why did you go to her? She's a detective."

Erin locked eyes with Ann. "Ann, stop. You know why I went to her." Erin tilted her head to the side. "When did you find out? Did you know from the start or was it only after you saw her take the witness stand?"

Ann closed her eyes and seemed to deflate. "When I saw her take the stand," she said, her voice quivering. "When I heard the recording of the murder, I recognized the voice. That's when I figured out that the woman I knew as Terry Gore was really Ann Parsons and that she had killed him. But it wasn't until I saw Detective Lucas take the stand that I realized Lucas and Ann were one and the same."

"Why didn't you tell me?" Erin asked.

Ann's face looked pained. "You don't understand. I could

never betray her. She did what I always wanted to do. She eliminated the monster. I should have done it, but I never had the courage. She did. I won't . . ." She stopped. "I *can't* testify against her."

Erin paused. There'd be no way to keep Willis from cross-examining Ann on her dates with "Terry Gore," and he was much too good a lawyer for Erin to hope he wouldn't. When he did, Ann would have to reveal Detective Lucas's real identity—unless Ann lied under oath, which was something Erin couldn't ethically advise her to do. The rule was sacrosanct: A lawyer could never advise a client to commit perjury. The rule seemed so simple and easy. A trial was a quest to find the truth. If lawyers were allowed to encourage their clients to lie, the system would break down.

But sometimes, reality was not so simple or easy. Erin understood Ann's refusal to implicate Lucas, especially since, like her client, Parsons and his cohorts had probably abused Lucas as well. But, if Ann didn't testify . . . *Damn,* Erin thought, *it always comes back to Ann telling her story as the key to getting a jury to believe she is innocent.*

Erin folded her hands, as if in prayer. "Ann, I need for you to listen very carefully to what I'm about to tell you." Erin stopped, making sure Ann was focused on her. "A lawyer can never advise a client to lie under oath. That's called suborning perjury. In addition to being unethical, it's a crime. So I can't tell you to lie. Do you understand that?"

Ann nodded.

"Okay. I also can't ask you any questions where I know your answer will be a lie. So assuming you testify, I can't ask you any questions about whether you know who murdered Parsons, or whether you know where Terry Gore is or who she is." Erin stopped, wanting to make sure she chose her words carefully. "However, no matter what I do, Willis will surely grill you on those subjects. You understand that?"

Again, Ann nodded.

"So, here's the thing. If you lie when you respond to his questions, I'm not obligated to stop you. And as long as I believe that you're going to tell the truth, there's nothing I have to do before you testify. So if you do happen to testify in this case, I'm going to give you the advice that I give to every client: Tell the truth." Erin pursed her lips. "Do you understand what I've told you?"

Ann's eyes were sad, but appreciative. "I do," she said softly. "I do." She leaned forward. "But the only way I'm getting up on the witness stand is if I know my brother is safe. Do *you* understand *me*?"

Erin nodded. No sense in having the fight now. Tuesday morning would come soon enough.

"My, isn't this a rare treat," Arthur purred on the other end of the phone. "To hear from Martin Conroy on a Saturday. Why am I so blessed?"

"Luigi has found Ann Parsons."

"Excellent. So where is she and when do we eliminate her?" Arthur said.

"I wish it were that simple. Wait until you hear this: Ann Parsons is a detective in the Union County Prosecutor's Office going by the name Sybil Lucas. She works in the Computer Crimes section. She appeared as a witness in the trial."

"Un-fucking believable," Arthur muttered. "Why is it that everything involved in this case is so goddamn complicated? I don't like killing cops. It brings too much scrutiny."

"I agree," Conroy said. "That's why I have a suggestion."

"I'm listening."

"The important thing to see is whether she has the hard drives. Agreed?"

"Yes," Arthur replied.

"Good. According to Luigi, she lives in an apartment in Hillside, which has its fair share of crime, and she's on a dead-end street that backs up to a park, right off of a busy local highway called Route 22. My suggestion is that we send a team in, and then make it look like she walked in on a couple of druggies. Tearing the place apart looking for the hard drives would make it look consistent with a robbery. We don't want her death to look too gruesome, but if in addition to their pillaging your team wanted to engage in a little rape, I wouldn't be upset."

"I would have thought you would have gone for a more hands-on approach. You know, abduct her, bring her to Elizabeth, watch her suffer before she dies."

"While I appreciate your desire for some sadistic pleasure, Arthur, given her position in the prosecutor's office, I don't want to take any unnecessary risks."

"Fine. Give me the address. Will send a team tonight to do some reconnaissance, then will execute tomorrow night."

"Good. I think we're starting to see the light at the end of the tunnel."

"Let's hope so. I think we're all ready to collect our money and move on."


When Sybil left the office on Friday, her plan had been to go to Newark Airport and disappear. She had set everything up to happen after she was gone. The hard drives were stored in her desk drawer with a note to Kluska, all waiting to be discovered when they cleaned out her desk after her last day. And even if something happened to her, she felt like she could trust Kluska to do the right thing. Willis was a snake, but Kluska was a cop's cop. She could count on him.

And yet, here she was.

It had been apparent to her the day she testified that when McCabe handed her the computer report McCabe had figured out she was Luke—the person McCabe held responsible for Mackey's death. But for McCabe to actually call her and ask for help had been a shock. So had McCabe's forcefulness in arguing she owed it to Justin to help save Rojas. When she spoke to McCabe the second time, she was just going to humor her, put her off so she could put her plan into effect. But something McCabe said struck a nerve. It wasn't just that she owed it to Justin, it was the realization that she really could help them save Rojas's life.

And then there was Ann. She had purposely avoided looking at her when she testified, but she could feel Ann's eyes boring into her, could feel her sudden realization that the woman Ann knew as Terry Gore was really a detective in the Union County Prosecutor's Office. She wondered whether Ann had figured it all out—

that Terry Gore was really Ann Parsons and that she was the one who had murdered Parsons. Yeah, Ann had to know. She was an intelligent woman and there were just too many clues: the interest in her "celebrity" father; the overnight stay at the house in Westfield; standing her up the night of the murder; and, then, disappearing. Which meant that Ann's silence was her way of protecting Sybil. Protecting her because of their shared horrors. Protecting her even if it meant going to prison for the rest of her life.

As those thoughts had percolated, Sybil had driven past the airport and come here instead. Walking into the lion's den, so to speak. Maybe it was a death wish. It wouldn't be the first time she had tempted death; she had come close a few times in Fallujah.

*No*, she told herself. It wasn't a death wish—it was a reality check. If they managed to find her this time, they'd sure as hell find her again no matter where she went. Better to wind up dead than spend the rest of her life looking over her shoulder. Plus, she wasn't sure she could enjoy life knowing that Ann was rotting in a prison cell. Might as well make her stand now—if everything went south, so be it.

She looked at the package sitting on the desk. Wrapped neatly in brown paper, it looked very professional, like it was from a law office. Sure, Conroy would be careful, run it through his IT department, but they'd need to be really good to find the microphone or the GPS tracker. She gave a little chuckle. Kind of ironic that she had gotten the idea for the microphone from Parsons's little recording device. She didn't expect to get all the information she needed from those, but his desire to access the accounts would provide her with what she needed. And maybe, just maybe, they could save Rojas.

She removed the curly blond wig, threw it on the chair, and wandered over to the window to look out on the lights of New York City. *Not too shabby, staying at the Waldorf.* She could get used to first-class living.

She allowed her gaze to focus on the building across the street: 300 Park Avenue. There on the fortieth floor were the offices of O'Toole & Conroy. The hunt was on, and she was both the hunted and the hunter. But she had decided to use that to her advantage. She knew she was being hunted, but they didn't know that she was hunting them. It would be over soon. And like any good hunter, she had the advantage of being in the spot where they'd be least likely to look—right under their noses.

"You don't normally call me on a Sunday morning," Conroy said. "It must be important."

"It is," Arthur replied. "Like everything else that's happened since Charles was murdered, it appears that finding Ann has turned into a fucking shit show. The information Luigi got you is, as the saying goes, a day late and a dollar short. In this case, literally a day late."

"Arthur, what are you talking about?"

"I sent several men over last night to check out where she lived, and how we could get in and eliminate her. While they were there, they noticed an apartment for rent sign on the front yard of the property. This morning they called the number on the sign to inquire about the apartment. Turns out Ms. Parsons moved out of her apartment on Friday. She's gone."

"I don't fucking believe it," Conroy spat out, followed by a growl of frustration. "I'll get Luigi back on it. She works in the prosecutor's office, for Christ's sake. It shouldn't be too hard to find out where she's moved to."

"Let's hope so," Arthur said.

After Martin hung up, he immediately dialed Luigi's private cell. "Yes, Martin."

"She's disappeared, and we need to find her immediately."

"What do you mean? I gave you everything."

"She moved."

"*Marone*," Luigi said under his breath. "I'll get right on it."

# CHAPTER 38

MARTIN PICKED UP THE PHONE AND DIALED HIS SECRETARY'S EX-tension. "Angela, where did the package on my desk come from?"

"A courier brought it around eight this morning," she replied.

"Did they say who it was from, or leave a delivery receipt?"

"No, Mr. Conroy. The courier said it was concerning the Parsons estate. Is there something wrong?" she asked.

"No," he said staring at the hard drive he'd just removed. "Thank you."

As he hung up, he reread the note that had been taped to the hard drive. *Here's part of what you've been looking for. Let Rojas go and you'll get the rest.*

Could this really be Charles's hard drive and, if it was, who sent it to him? Clearly, it had to be someone connected to Ann. Who else would know about Rojas?

Quickly, he called Angela back and asked her to order a security scan. This was working out better than he could have designed. If he could access Charles's parts of the passwords to each of the accounts, he could safely transfer all of the money and play dumb with the others.

Fifteen minutes later, he watched as some geeky-looking guy from the firm's IT department hooked the hard drive up to his laptop and ran some diagnostics. After about five minutes, he looked up with an awkward grin. "It's clean, Mr. Conroy."

"Thank you."

Conroy put the hard drive into his leather satchel and walked out of his office. "Angela, I'm going to a meeting; if anything comes up, please call my cell."

"Certainly, Mr. Conroy," she replied.

The trip to his brownstone on E. Nineteenth Street was a relatively quick cab ride straight down Park Avenue. He was breathing heavily from anticipation as he fumbled with the lock. He threw his topcoat on the chair and made his way into his home office. *IT said it's clean, but after what happened to Charles, I can't be too careful.*

Once his desktop was up and running, he took his laptop out of his satchel and made sure there was no Internet connection. Then he plugged the hard drive up to his laptop and waited for the icon showing it was available to access. When it did, it contained two file folders.

*What? Two? There should be fifty-five.*

He moved his cursor over to one of the icons, opened it, and then decrypted it, revealing a combination of six letters and numbers.

*Excellent.* He and Charles had agreed to and stored their respective portions of the passwords knowing that without both halves it was worthless to anyone. He quickly copied them down, removed a paper from his breast coat pocket, and wrote down the numbers that made up his half of the password.

Swiveling in his desk chair, he opened the website for Nevis Trust Company on his desktop. When he entered the full password on the associated account, a hyperlink was supplied.

He took a deep breath and clicked on the link. ACCOUNT INFORMATION appeared and he let out a sigh of relief. Then he clicked on OPEN ACCOUNT.

THIS ACCOUNT HAS BEEN TEMPORARILY LOCKED.

"What the fuck!" he yelled.

His BlackBerry vibrated in his pocket. He grabbed it and looked at the text message from an unknown number.

**This phone number is associated with an account that is temporarily locked. If you believe the account has been locked in error, please click the attached link to allow access to the account.**

He clicked the link and waited.

A second text message appeared: **We apologize, but remote access is temporarily unavailable. Please contact the bank for further details.**

"Goddamn it!" he screamed. What the hell was he supposed to do when he contacted the bank? They had the tightest security in the world. There was no way they'd give him access with a phone call. He quickly tried the second of the two accounts on the hard drive, with the same result.

He pushed the chair back from the desk and started pacing his office. *Don't panic,* he thought. The passwords worked. He had gotten into the account. There's a glitch somewhere. His cell phone vibrated and there was a text message from a number he didn't recognize.

**did you get the package I left you?**

He stared at the text. **what package? who is this?** he typed.

**don't be stupid. we can negotiate, or you can remain locked out of your precious accounts. did you get it?**

**yes.**

**good. I have the original hard drive with parsons's portion of the passwords for all fifty-five accounts. I also have the other hard drives. when you're ready to trade them and account access for rojas, let me know.**

**who is this?** he typed, knowing the answer before he hit SEND.

**you know who it is you sick fuck. you and parsons abused me enough as a child. let me know when you're ready to deal.**

*You bitch. When I find you you're going to die a slow, painful death.*

He dialed quickly. "I have a lead for you," Conroy said as soon as Luigi answered.

"Go ahead."

"Use your sources to locate where this cell phone connected," Conroy said. "492-555-0137. She just texted me."

There was a long silence. "Martin," Luigi finally said, "she works in Computer Crimes. She's an expert. She could easily have blocked her number, so she has to know her location can be traced. I don't like it."

"I don't care. Find her."

\* \* \*

Everything was going according to plan.

Once Conroy had grabbed a cab outside his office, she had followed suit, giving him a two-minute head start so she'd be able to track the package and tell her cab driver where to go. Once she saw what building he was in, she had set up shop here, in an espresso shop right around the corner.

While she waited for the mocha latte, she put on her headphones. Although there was little to hear other than him typing away, she waited patiently. And there it was—the "what the fuck" she hoped meant he had come upon the account's temporarily locked page. When she had finally cracked their codes and gained control of the accounts and done what she needed to do, she had locked each of them. She had put Charles's passwords for two of the accounts onto the hard drive that she had delivered to Conroy—enough to make him try to access them. Now was the point where she hoped his greed would blind him.

She fired off a text to his number, which she had intercepted from DeCovnie: **This phone number is associated with an account that is temporarily locked. If you believe the account has been locked in error, please click the attached link to allow access to the account.**

BlackBerrys were impossible to hack, which meant she needed him to install her software onto his phone. She waited, holding her breath. And then, like a fish looking at a shiny lure, he took the bait. As soon as he clicked the embedded link, she had him. The spyware he'd just downloaded wasn't as robust as what she had Mackey install on Parsons's computers, but it should give her what she needed: the ability to monitor his texts, track his phone, and, if she was lucky, listen in on his calls.

She waited until the download was complete, then sent the second text telling him to contact the bank. Now the question was, would he do something that would give her what she needed on Rojas? All she could do was wait.

# CHAPTER 39

DURING THE LUNCH BREAK ON MONDAY, ERIN STAYED WITH ANN IN the prisoner holding area. Both were silent, almost robotic—neither had any appetite. It was just the two of them today. Duane was meeting up with Rick and Alex at their office, hoping to hear from Lucas.

Willis had started the morning with a few minor witnesses before wrapping up with Detective Dotson. Erin had hammered away on Dotson during her cross-examination, pointing out that Ann had never said the words *I shot my father*, just moved her head when Dotson had said them.

When Erin finished her cross, Willis rested the prosecution's case right before lunch.

Halfway through lunch, Erin returned to the empty courtroom and reviewed her notes for the start of Ann's defense case. Erin's usual trial jitters were on overdrive. How could she concentrate with everything that was going on—David's life on the line, Duane potentially risking his life to save David, and not knowing whether Ann would testify or not? Usually she had the ability to compartmentalize, but this was beyond the pale.

Erin gave one more check of her BlackBerry before the sheriff's officers brought Ann back into the courtroom. Ann's expectant look was met by Erin's frown—no word.

Erin started the afternoon by making a motion to dismiss the case, something that defense lawyers did routinely. Just as routinely, judges deny them, and Judge Spiegel quickly dispatched Erin's motion.

Erin's first witness was Marsha Kramer, who testified that after Parsons had been murdered, Ann had given her a cell phone to hold on to. Knowing that Willis would exploit it, Erin brought out in her own questioning that Ann had asked Kramer to throw the phone away should Ann be arrested.

Willis's cross was quick and effective. He brought out that Kramer thought Ann was nervous on the day of the arrest, and even though Erin had already asked her about it, Willis had Kramer repeat Ann's instructions for Kramer to throw the phone away should anything happen to Ann. Willis ended his cross by asking Kramer why she hadn't. Her answer that she was afraid that she could be charged with tampering with evidence if she threw it away only served to put an exclamation point on Willis's cross.

To Erin's surprise, when they went to sidebar to discuss that Duane would be needed to complete the chain-of-custody testimony as to how Ms. Irving obtained the phone, Willis agreed to stipulate that the phone Irving examined was the same phone Duane had obtained from Kramer, making Duane's testimony unnecessary.

Connie Irving's testimony had been the subject of a pretrial hearing as to whether she would be allowed to testify about the attempted robbery of the cell phone right after Duane had brought it to her. Erin had argued that the testimony would establish that there were people who were trying to prevent Ann from mounting her best defense, but after listening to the arguments, the judge had barred the testimony concerning the robbery attempt. He ruled that its connection to Ann's defense was relevant, but that was outweighed by the potential to confuse the jury since there was no definitive proof the robbery attempt was connected to silencing Ann.

Irving testified that there were only two numbers ever called on this phone: One was called every Sunday afternoon at around four p.m., like clockwork, and the other was called randomly. Irving told the jury the second number had been called three times the night Parsons was murdered, between seven thirty and nine. She also testified that there was one incoming call from an unknown number at nine forty on the night of the murder.

The only point Willis made on cross was that Irving had no way of knowing who had the phone or made any of the calls on the night of the murder.

The final witness of the day was New York City Police detective William Hake. Erin walked him through how cell phones connected to cell towers, and the information that law enforcement could gather to that effect. Hake testified that all the calls made from the cell phone were relayed through a tower in Hoboken. The one incoming call connected to a tower on the Scotch Plains/Westfield border.

As Erin feared, Willis's cross was concise and effective. As he had done with Irving, Willis had Hake admit he did not know who had made the calls. Willis then brought out an exhibit that had been previously marked, which was a blowup of a map showing where Parsons's house was in Westfield. Willis had Hake place an *X* on the map to show where the tower was that the incoming call had connected through. The jury could easily see how close the cell tower was to the scene of the murder.

After Judge Spiegel sent the jury home, he leaned back in his chair and asked, "Ms. McCabe, does the defense intend to have any additional witnesses for tomorrow?"

Erin rose. "At this point, Your Honor, I have to confer with my client as to whether or not she will take the stand. I also may wish to recall Ms. DeCovnie. But again, I'd like to speak with my client before making any final decisions." Erin looked down at her watch. "Judge, it's four p.m. As you know, attorney visiting hours at the jail end at four and resume at six. Could I have permission from the court to visit with my client in the holding area?"

"How long do you need, Ms. McCabe? Remember, the sheriff's officers have to have her back so that she can be included in the jail's daily count."

"I understand, Judge. How's forty-five minutes?"

Spiegel looked down at the sheriff's officer who oversaw his courtroom, who nodded to the judge. "That's fine, Ms. McCabe. I'll see everyone tomorrow morning at nine."

After the judge left the bench, Erin grabbed her BlackBerry—still no messages. She looked at Ann and shook her head.

When they were alone in the holding area, Ann sank down into one of the chairs. She put her handcuffed wrists on the table and laid her head on her arms and sobbed.

"It's only four," Erin said. "Lucas said she'd reach out by five. There's still time."

Ann lifted her head up. "You don't believe that any more than I do. I should never . . . I should . . . I should have kept the deal."

"Ann," Erin said. "Don't give up. There were no surprises this afternoon. We established what we needed to for the jury to have a reasonable doubt."

Ann's laugh was derisive. "If I was on the jury, I'd be convinced that we were both in on it. Me and whoever was on the other end of that call."

In the silence that followed, Erin tried to come up with a persuasive argument for why Ann's perception was wrong, but she couldn't. The best she could offer Ann was her plan B in the event Ann didn't testify. Erin had to be able to give the jury something to find reasonable doubt. Erin's plan was that she'd remind the jury of Ann's statements to Burke and Dotson, before anyone knew Ann had a burner phone, that she had called her date three times from a bar in Hoboken. And now that they had the phone, Ann's statements were confirmed. That plus DeCovnie's rehearsed testimony concerning the voice on the recording being Ann's might be enough.

"Obviously, it would be much easier to convince the jury that's not the case if you testify," Erin suggested.

Ann's expression grew defiant. "I told you, unless David is sitting in the back of the courtroom tomorrow when I walk in, I'm not testifying."

"Ann, do you really think they're going to spare your brother's life if you don't testify?"

Her defiance melted away until all that was left was a profound look of sadness. "No, I don't," she whispered. "But I couldn't live with myself if I thought there was a chance I could have saved him by staying silent."

"I know this is hard. It's hard for me to even say this. But it's not about your brother anymore. If you don't testify, these monsters will still be roaming free to prey on other innocent kids. I know you admire the real Ann because she did what you couldn't bring yourself to do: stop Parsons by ending his life. Now you have a chance to stop all of them—legally—by telling your story. You can help expose these people for who they really are. Please think about that."

When she left the holding area, Erin collected her briefcase and purse only to find she had two missed calls from Duane.

"What's going on?" she said when he answered.

"We heard from Lucas, but it was just to tell us that she was still working on it," Duane explained.

"Okay. Well it's not good news, but at least she was in touch."

"Agreed," he said. "How'd it go today?"

"On the whole, we did what we had to do, but I think Willis still came out ahead on points. He's good. No theatrics this time around."

"How's Ann?"

"A mess," Erin replied. "But why wouldn't she be? Her brother's life is hanging by a thread and she's convinced she should have just kept her plea deal."

"You don't sound too good either," Duane said.

Erin let out a small humph. "Had a rough day in the office, I just told my client that she should testify even if it results in her brother being killed, and I'm worried that my partner is putting himself in harm's way. Other than that, life's grand."

"I'll be okay. I trained for this."

"Yeah, well let me remind you, Rambo, your training was a few years ago."

"Like riding a bike," he replied.

"Bikes have changed a lot since you learned to ride."

"Got it," Duane replied.

"Please keep me posted," she said.

"I will. But listen, it may be a long night and you have a big day tomorrow. I suggest at some point you give your phone to Mark and let him monitor things. You need to get some sleep."

"Okay. We'll see. But please be careful. You have a family to think about," she said, her voice pleading with him.

"Trust me, I'll be careful," he responded. "I promise."

# CHAPTER 40

CONROY SCREAMED A FLURRY OF OBSCENITIES AS HE FRANTICALLY walked from room to room of his brownstone, trying to come up with a plan. It was 5:00 p.m. and there were too many moving pieces. Luigi was still working on finding Lucas. Preston had called to let him know that McCabe hadn't revealed if Ann was going to testify, but if she did, it would be tomorrow. He was waiting to hear back from Damien Hobson, a lawyer he and Charles had used in Nevis, who was going to try to determine why the accounts were locked. But he knew that if Sybil/Ann truly held the key to unlocking them, he was fucked. He was loath to tell Arthur, Liam, or Cassandra about the hard drive he had received, but knowing that Arthur planned on killing Rojas tomorrow or as soon as the defense rested, regardless of whether Ann testified or not, he might have no choice but to tell them.

His BlackBerry rang and he grabbed it. "What do you have, Luigi?" he asked.

"Martin, where are you?"

"Home. Why?"

"I'm sorry, where is home?"

"Nineteenth Street, Gramercy Park section. Why?"

"She's in your neighborhood. Obviously, we cannot pinpoint with precision, as we are not the NSA. But she is nearby."

"What the fuck," Conroy said, then tried to focus. "There are a couple of coffee shops and a Barnes & Noble nearby."

"Martin, even if I had the people in place, which I don't, it would be . . . difficult, at best, to try and find her right now."

Conroy pulled the phone away from his face and stared at it. "Then I'll find her," he said in disgust before abruptly ending the call.

He brought up her last text message. **how do I know you can deliver what I want?** he typed.

His phone rang almost as soon as he sent the text, briefly confusing him. He then realized he had an incoming call from Damien Hobson.

"Good afternoon, Martin. You'll be happy to know that we used our connections and the bank was able to tell me that the account is locked because someone tried to access the accounts repeatedly using the wrong password."

"But, Damien, I had the correct password and when I entered the password the account link had displayed but when I clicked on the link, it wouldn't allow me to access the account information."

There was a slight pause. "Yes, Martin. That is consistent with what I was told."

"Well, how can I get access?" Conroy asked. "Timing is critical."

"Ahh, well that is a problem. For the bank to unlock the account, you must be here in person."

"Oh for Christ's sake. Thank you for your help. I'll be down soon." If all the accounts were locked because she entered the wrong passwords multiple times, it meant she hadn't gotten into the accounts yet. The money was still there. It also meant that if he got hold of Charles's original hard drive, he'd be the only one with the complete passwords. A smile slowly formed on his lips. *This might be perfect*, he thought.

He dialed and waited. "Yeah," Arthur said.

"Ann contacted me. The original Ann."

"She contacted you?" Arthur asked.

"Indeed, she did. She's looking to trade the hard drives in exchange for the release of Rojas."

"Do you think she has them?"

"It would make sense. After all, if she killed Charles, she may well have taken them then."

"What do you suggest?"

"Make her prove she's got them, and if she does, arrange a trade—only not the kind she'll be expecting."

Sybil sat in the corner of the Barnes & Noble looking at Conroy's text. She brought up a photo she had taken of the four hard drives and sent it to him. She followed with a text saying, **send me a picture of rojas—I need proof he's still alive.**

She was trying to trap him; he was trying to trap her. It was a life-and-death chess match. But she had an advantage: She could see and hear everything he did on his phone.

An hour later, a picture arrived of a man holding a copy of the day's *New York Post*. It was at that point she realized how stupid she had been. She didn't even know what Rojas looked like. Thankfully, when she sent the picture to Duane Swisher, he verified it was Rojas.

**when and where** she texted Conroy.

**2am. 96 trumbull elizabeth. you should remember the place your father took you there all the time. you were a real movie star back then**

A shudder ran through her body as she read his text. Things had happened to her, horrible things, but fortunately, most of them were locked away. Sometimes, however, the memories exploded. There was the night in Fallujah when the truck in front of hers hit an IED and someone, she presumed an Iraqi insurgent, had dragged her into an alley. She didn't remember much, but when they found her, the insurgent's throat was slit from ear to ear, and she was holding his severed manhood in her hand. No one from the platoon had turned her in, but rumors slowly spread through the platoon and everyone gave her a wide berth after that. A week later her lieutenant had come to ask if she was okay. She had looked at him and smiled and said, "Couldn't be better, lieutenant." She probably should have been given a medical discharge, but nothing ever happened.

*Let it go. This isn't your fight. Get the word to Swisher and move on. You did your part.*

She could suddenly smell him. The cigar—Parsons always smelled like cigars. It was dark when they led her into the room. It looked like a bedroom, but they were in a building, a warehouse. There was a camera. People were laughing. Oh God, not again. Please not again.

"Miss. Miss. Are you all right?"

She looked up, startled. "I'm sorry. What?"

A middle-aged woman was standing over her. "Are you okay? You were saying, 'No, no.' It sounded like someone was hurting you."

Sybil chewed on her lower lip. "I'm okay." She gave the woman a weak smile. "Thank you. I'll be okay."

Sybil looked at her watch. She had to get back to the office to grab what she needed, and then go.

Erin pulled into the driveway of Mark's house, which at the moment was also hosting Duane as its guest. Cori and Austin had gone to stay with her family in Fredericksburg, while the three of them had returned here—safety in numbers.

Before she got out of the car, she checked her phone to see if there were any updates. Apparently Lucas had sent a picture of Rojas, so at least he was still alive. She closed her eyes and inhaled deeply. Alive was good.

When she got out of the car, she noticed JJ's car parked on the street, along with a pickup she assumed belonged to one of Mark's other basketball buddies. So as she'd dragged herself and her trial bag into the house, she wasn't surprised to find Mark; JJ; and their friend Kevin Brown, a Jersey City police officer, sitting around the kitchen table. They jumped up to help her with her things.

"Thanks, guys," she said as she gave Mark a peck on the cheek.

"You look like you've had a long day, woman," JJ said. "Think it's best we be going."

Kevin nodded. "If you have any problems, let me know. One of my sergeants knows a lieutenant with Clark PD and he's on alert."

"Thanks, Kev," Erin said. "I think we're probably safe at this point, but always nice to know that the cavalry is nearby."

After JJ and Kevin left, she gave Mark another kiss.

"You okay?" he asked.

She leaned her head into his chest. "No."

"Talk to me then," he said, nudging her over to the table to take a seat.

She explained what she had learned from Swish and what a tough day it had been in court. She didn't tell him about her conversation with Ann, as she never told him about her discussions with her clients.

"How about I make us some dinner?" he offered.

"Thanks, but I'm not really hungry. I'm going to change and prepare for tomorrow." She pulled her BlackBerry out of her purse. "Do me a favor. Keep a check on this in case Swish reaches out," she said.

"Sure," he replied.

Four hours later Mark walked into the office with her phone. "It's Swish," he said.

"Hey, what's happening?" she said, her heart starting to beat faster.

"Don't want to say too much over the phone. But we have some information. Based on that it could be a long night."

"Maybe we should get law enforcement involved."

"On it," he replied.

"I don't understand," she said.

"Trust me, E. You handle the courtroom. Let me handle this. Believe me, I'm doing everything I can to bring David—and me—back in one piece."

"Please be careful. I—"

"Got to go. Don't worry if you don't hear anything for a while. This could take some time. Good luck tomorrow," he said, and then the line went dead.

"What's going on?" Mark said. She realized she had been staring at the phone.

"I don't know. There's a lot that Swish isn't telling me and I'm not sure if that's a good thing or a bad thing."

He wrapped his arms around her and pulled her close. "You two have been through a lot together. You know better than anyone that he knows what he's doing." He kissed the top of her head. "If anyone can put this together and pull it off, my money's on Swish."

# CHAPTER 41

*D*UANE CROSSED HIS ARMS ACROSS HIS CHEST, LEANING BACK IN THE corner booth at the Skyline Diner, listening as Sybil Lucas explained what had happened before they arrived. He studied the faces of Rick and Alex, trying to gauge whether or not they were buying what she was selling. Sitting across from him were FBI Special Agents Jodi Collins and Craig Kenny.

On Friday, after he and Ben had failed in their efforts to go to the top, he had reached out to Special Agent Celeste Roberts and reminded her that she had offered to help if he ever needed to get hold of the agent in charge of the Parsons investigation—now was the time. Ten minutes after Duane hung up, Collins called. She had been the lead on the Parsons investigation, and seven years after her investigation got shut down, she was still pissed. To Duane's amazement, when he called her earlier today to tell her what was in store, she had come with Kenny and two other agents in a van designed for eavesdropping.

Duane looked at Lucas. "So, what can you tell us about the people we're up against?"

"There's an attorney by the name of Martin Conroy who's calling the shots. He'll be here in person. He works closely with a guy by the name of Arthur Hiller, who will also probably be here—if there's a chance of bloodshed, Hiller will be nearby. Hiller was always Parsons's muscle, and I suspect he's doing the same for Conroy. They're total opposites. Conroy projects an air of sophistication; Hiller, on the other hand, is a vicious thug and proud of it. He makes no pretenses over who or what he is."

"I remember both of them," Collins interjected. "Damn it. If only they hadn't shut us down, they'd both be out of commission."

There was a long silence before Lucas continued. "I'm sure whoever is here will have about half a dozen guys backing them up. I wish I knew more, but Conroy's phone went dark late this afternoon. Either he had figured out I had gotten into his phone, or he had just switched to a burner to make sure there were no records to trace. But make no mistake, they don't plan on leaving any witnesses."

"Do you know the location where they have Rojas?" Rick asked her.

Lucas seemed momentarily lost in another world. "Um, yeah," she finally said. "They've been using this location since I was a kid. It's a big warehouse. In the back they had it set up so they could shoot porn videos—basically a movie set. I haven't been there in a while, but it had surveillance cameras outside and an alarm system on all the doors. If we try to go in guns blazing, they'll know we're there before we get in the door and they'll kill Rojas."

"Do you have a plan?" Duane asked.

Lucas drew in a deep breath. "I suspect as the time gets closer Conroy will call to set up the meet. I'll need all of you in place around the perimeter before I show up. I'll force Conroy to send someone out and I'll escort them back in and trade what I have for Rojas."

"What do you have?" Collins asked.

"Hard drives with financial records, bank passwords, and child porn."

"You can't give that to them!" Collins protested.

Lucas smiled. "Don't worry. I'm not stupid enough to hand over the only copy."

"What's to stop them from just rushing you when you get there?" Alex asked. "I mean, if there's as many as you think there are, you won't have a chance."

"Suicide vest," Lucas replied, opening her jacket.

"What the fuck?!" Alex screamed.

"Relax," Lucas said with a chuckle. "You don't think I intend on blowing myself up, do you?"

Duane looked at her, unsure of the answer. "Look, no offense, but this doesn't sound like a plan. You go in there alone, you're never coming out."

"Trust me, despite the vest, I'm not suicidal. I do plan on coming out and I do plan on bringing Rojas with me."

Lucas then outlined the rest of her plan and how she thought she could pull it off. After she was finished, she and Collins went to the ladies' room so Collins could put a wire on her.

When they came back to the table, Collins turned to Duane, Rick, and Alex and said, "You guys know the drill, you're not on the job anymore so we can't have you involved."

"Don't worry about us," Rick said. "We'll stay out of your way, but we're all licensed to carry, so if things go sideways, we'll be nearby." He paused. "Just make sure your guys in the truck don't take us out by mistake. I've already got two bullet holes from getting shot by one of my own, let's not make it three," he added with a smirk.

Lucas turned to Duane and handed him a receiver. "I wired myself before I even got here. You hold on to this one, you'll be able to hear everything I say. Agent Collins added a second wire so she and her team now have ears too, and I'll make sure my phone is on speaker, so this way both of you can hear everything that's going on."

While the rest of them studied some maps and some aerials of the area that Collins had brought with her and decided where to position themselves, Lucas scarfed down an order of blueberry pancakes as if the warden had come with her last meal.

At midnight Lucas received a text from an unknown number.

**if you bring anyone with you he's dead.**

She immediately typed back, **if he's dead, I destroy the hard drives and your money goes bye-bye.**

She looked up and said, "That ought to freak him out."

"Why?" Alex asked.

"They have millions stashed in offshore accounts." Then she added with a smile, "At least they did until recently."

Collins stared at her. "Why do I think you know more than you're letting on?"

Lucas eyed Collins and laughed. "Let's just say I know where it is and they don't."

It was twelve thirty when Lucas received the next text: **how do I know you can get me access?**

**I will be nearby at 1:55, call me and I'll explain**, she texted back.

Duane studied the crew he had assembled, his stomach churning as he worried they'd be outmanned and outgunned. Damn, what was he thinking? He had too much to live for at this point. His mind drifted to Cori, Austin, and his unborn child, and he wondered if he had been foolhardy in thinking he could pull this off. He closed his eyes and took a few deep breaths. He had to stay focused. The surest way to end up dead was to be distracted. *Focus.*

He looked over at Collins. "Listen, no offense, I heard what you said before about not getting involved because we're not on the job anymore, but you don't know how many people will be inside. If you and Craig go in there alone, you could wind up getting yourselves killed. The three of us know what we're doing," he said with a nod to Rick and Alex. "If in the after-action report there's an issue because civilians were involved, I'll take the fall for that. What are they going to do? They already forced me out once—they can't force me out again."

Collins stole a glance at Kenny, who nodded. "Thanks," she said. "Just be careful."

"You too," Duane replied with a tight smile.

At one a.m., everyone but Lucas and the two agents in the van headed out and parked three blocks away from the building, making their way on foot to the perimeter of the warehouse. At 1:55 Lucas pulled into the parking lot in the van.

From where Duane was, he could see her in the van. She was parked in the open lot, under a light. She seemed like such an easy target he prayed they wouldn't just take her out as she sat there. He adjusted his earpiece and waited. Five minutes later he heard Lucas's cell phone ring.

"Who's with you?" Lucas asked when she answered.

"What do you mean?"

"I mean who the hell is with you, fuck face? Arthur, Cassandra—I need a body."

"Arthur."

"Good. I always hated Arthur. So, here's the deal, Martin. I learned a lot serving my country in Iraq. One of the things I learned was how to make a very effective homemade suicide vest. I happen to have one on now. In my coat, next to the suicide vest is the hard drive with all your precious financial information. In my left hand I will be holding a triggering device. If I take my finger off the triggering device, I explode and with me goes your precious hard drive. So, if I step out of this van and get shot, I explode and so does five hundred and fifty million dollars."

"You wouldn't blow yourself up."

She laughed. "Do you really want to test that theory, Martin?"

There were seconds of silence.

"I'll take it from your silence, you don't. So here's what you are going to do. You're going to send Arthur out to say hello to me. I'm sure he'll be happy to see me after all these years. Arthur will stop ten feet in front of the van, and then I will get out and escort Arthur back to the building. Of course, out of an abundance of caution, I will hold a gun to Arthur's head. You may want to tell him not to try and swat it away. The last person who did that to me unfortunately wound up very dead."

Lucas paused. "Arthur and I will walk inside together. You will show me David so I know he's alive. I will let you have the hard drive and you can then hook it up and satisfy yourself all the passwords are there. Once you do that, we will all walk back to my van. David and I will get in the van with you standing next to the door. Before I drive away, I will throw the other three hard drives with your precious child porn out the window. We will then drive away and you will be a rich man."

"How do I know you won't kill Arthur or me?"

"Because as much as I want to meet both of you in hell, it's more important to me to save David's life."

As Duane listened to her, there was a part of him that thought it actually might work. Then after she hung up from Conroy, Lucas started talking directly to him.

"So, Mr. Swisher, in the event this goes bad, there are a couple of things you need to know. . . ."

After she was finished Duane heard her phone buzz. "Domino's, pick up or delivery," she answered.

"Listen, bitch, Arthur is coming out. I have a gun pointed at Rojas's head. If you try anything stupid, he dies."

"I look forward to seeing you again, Martin."

Slowly a man walked out of the building. As he walked toward the van, Sybil jumped out holding something in her left hand. From where he was, Duane could hear her scream, "Stop!" She must have hit redial on her phone because Duane heard Conroy answer.

"You think I'm stupid. I don't know who this moron is, but it's not Hiller. Send out Hiller or your money goes up in smoke."

A couple of minutes later a second individual walked out of the building. As he walked toward her, Sybil put her phone in her pocket and took out her weapon. "Let the games begin," she said and started walking toward Hiller.

"Hello, Arthur," she said as she approached him. "You don't look happy to see me. Stop and turn around." She walked up to him and pointed the gun at the back of his head. "I have to admit there's part of me that would really like to blow your head off, just like I did Charles's. Okay, let's go," she said, and they began walking toward the building.

Duane watched as they disappeared into the building, and as she did, all his feelings that her plan might work disappeared with her.

About thirty seconds after Lucas went into the building, Duane heard her on his receiver say, "Where's David?"

Conroy's voice was faint, leading Duane to assume he was keeping his distance.

As Duane watched, Collins and Kenny started working their way along the perimeter of the building heading toward the door Sybil and Hiller had just entered. Alex and Rick looked at Duane and without saying a word they also started making a move toward the door.

"Show me the hard drive," Duane heard someone say in his earpiece.

"Remember, if I take my finger off the triggering device, we all go up in smoke," Lucas replied.

"Got it," a voice said.

"Okay, Martin, satisfy yourself it's real and then you, David, and me walk out together and I give you the other drives."

Collins and Kenny approached the door from one side of the building as Duane, Rick, and Alex approached from the other. Suddenly there was an "oomph" in Duane's earpiece followed by a gunshot.

At that point all hell broke loose. Collins and Kenny bolted through the door, with Duane and the others right behind them. Kenny screamed, "FBI, drop your guns!" when another shot rang out.

Duane heard Lucas screaming and the voices of two men. Several more shots were fired before Duane got to the point where he could see what was going on. Amid the chaos, he saw two men taking Sybil out a side door. As Duane ran after them, everything went black.

As Erin lay there alone, her mind was racing. What was happening with Swish? Would he be okay? If they didn't know by morning, would Ann testify, and if she did, how would she hold up? And as hard as those questions were, the second guessing hammering away at her was even harder. Maybe she should have just left well enough alone. How would she live with herself if David was murdered and Ann went to prison for life—or if something happened to Swish?

She woke with a start at 5:40 a.m., unsure when she'd fallen asleep. She immediately rushed to the guest bedroom, where she found Mark sitting in the chair by the bed. He was still in his T-shirt and jeans from the night before and clearly had not slept all night. He looked up at her, with a mixture of exhaustion and confusion.

"What?" she said.

"About forty-five minutes ago you got a call from a two-one-two area code. When I answered, the reception was so bad I couldn't make out anything the person was saying. Then, about thirty minutes ago you got a text from the same two-one-two area code number that said, 'tdrthey.' I texted back saying, 'what?' but I haven't heard."

She walked over and took her phone and stared at the message.

"You guys have a secret code?" Mark asked.

"No," she said tightly. "We don't."

*Think, think, think.*

She took her phone and dialed Swish's number. It went straight to voice mail. "Hey, it's me. Please give me a call."

She handed her phone back to Mark. "Can you do me a favor? I have to hop in the shower and start getting ready. If whoever sent this is like Swish, who still has a flip phone, for them to send a text, they have to use the numbers on the keypad and hit it enough times to get the right letter. Let's assume it's dark wherever they are or they were rushed. Let's try and figure out what they meant to say." She paused and thought for a moment. "I think we have to assume they had the right numbers, just that they entered it incorrectly. Otherwise, the possibilities will be endless."

He gave her a small nod. "Go shower and I'll figure out whatever it was they were trying to tell you."

# CHAPTER 42

"GOOD MORNING, COUNSEL," JUDGE SPIEGEL SAID, TAKING HIS seat on the bench. "Before I bring the jury in, let's do some housekeeping. Ms. McCabe, do you have additional witnesses to call?"

Erin rose. "Yes, Judge. My client will be taking the stand, and after that, I plan on recalling Ms. DeCovnie."

"Your client is aware that she does not have to testify, correct?"

"She is, Your Honor. Her decision to testify is knowing and voluntary."

Erin looked down at Ann, wondering if she might change her mind yet again. When they had met at 8:30 a.m. in the holding area, Ann was crushed that there was no definitive word about David. Erin explained that she had received a text around 5:15 a.m. that she believed was supposed to say, "testify," and that although she couldn't be certain she believed it was from one of the guys with Swish. Unfortunately, despite calling Swish's number and the mysterious 212 number all morning, she hadn't been able to reach anyone to find out what was going on.

As their discussion went back and forth, Erin asked the judge's clerk for more time because they were still discussing how they were going to proceed. Finally, Ann turned to Erin and said suddenly, "If you were me, what would you do?"

"You know that's not a fair question," Erin had responded. "It's not my brother's life that hangs in the balance."

"So, put yourself in my shoes. You have a brother."

Erin considered Ann's question. "I do have a brother. And, just like you, I know my first instinct would be to do whatever I could to try and save his life." She stopped, allowing her eyes to lock on to Ann's. "But I'm lucky. I've never been abused. And I don't personally know—or at least I don't think I know—anyone who is continuing to exploit and abuse children for want of someone willing to speak out. So I can't honestly say if I'd be willing to risk my brother's life to try and stop the abuse of innocent people. I don't know. So whatever you decide to do, I won't second-guess you."

Ann closed her eyes and wrapped her hands behind her head. "Thank you," she said. "Thank you for being honest enough to say you don't know what you'd do."

Neither of them said anything. Then there was a knock on the cell door. They looked up and the judge's courtroom deputy was standing in the door. "The judge would like to get going. Are you almost ready?"

"We still need about ten more minutes," Erin responded. "Please ask the judge for another ten minutes."

Ann chewed on her lower lip. "If he's dead and I don't testify, he died for nothing. At least if I testify, maybe . . . maybe some good will come of it. Either way, I'm not sure I'll be able to go on, so I may as well take the shot at taking them down with me." Ann inhaled and then exhaled through her lips. "Let's go. I'm going to testify."

Ann now stood in the witness box and swore to tell the truth, the whole truth, and nothing but the truth.

"State your full name for the record, spelling your last name," the clerk intoned.

"Ann Parsons: p-a-r-s-o-n-s," she said.

"Ms. Parsons, you may have a seat," Judge Spiegel said softly.

"Good morning, Ann," Erin began, purposely using her first name to humanize her to the jury.

"Good morning," Ann replied.

"Ann, you've just stated your name for the record. Is that the name that appears on your birth certificate?"

"No, it's not," Ann responded.

"What is the name on your birth certificate?"

"Felipe Rojas," Ann answered.

There was a murmur in the courtroom. Erin had positioned herself so she could see some of the jurors and Willis out of the corner of her eye. The jurors whom she could see looked perplexed; Willis looked gobsmacked.

"Ann, Felipe Rojas sounds like a name that would be given to a child assigned male at birth. Were you assigned male at birth?"

"I was."

"Where were you born?"

"In Villa Gesell, Argentina," Ann replied, her voice a little shaky.

"When did you come to the United States?"

"When I was three. My mother, Maria Rojas, and father, Felipe Rojas, came here and I came with them."

"Do you have any siblings?"

"Yes . . ." Ann hesitated and exhaled. "I have a brother, David Rojas, who is five years younger than me."

"Are your parents still alive?"

"My mother is deceased. She hemorrhaged after giving birth to my brother and died. I don't know about my father. He was deported when I was seven, and I haven't heard from him since I was twelve."

"Are you a U.S. citizen or a green card holder?"

"No. I am undocumented."

Again, Erin could hear whispering among the spectators sitting behind her.

"After your mother passed away, where did you live?"

"With my aunt and uncle. My mother's sister, Sofia, and my uncle, Jose. They lived in Miami."

"How long did you live with them?"

"Until I was twelve, and then they were arrested and deported as well."

"What happened to you and your brother after they were arrested?"

"I was originally detained, but almost immediately released to child services. My brother, who was born here, is a U.S. citizen. We were both put into foster care."

"Were you and your brother together?"

"No. We were placed with different families. But we were able to stay in touch, because I would walk him home to his foster parents after school." Ann's face seemed to brighten just for a moment at the memory. "He was lucky; his foster parents were wonderful people who took very good care of him."

"And how were your foster parents?"

Ann's eyes momentarily closed, as if to avoid the memories the question evoked. "I was not so lucky. When I was twelve, I was very effeminate, and so my foster father used to verbally abuse me. After I had been living there for about six months, he started to physically abuse me as well."

"When you say he verbally abused you, what do you mean?"

"He'd call me names. He'd call me a *maricon*, which in Spanish means 'fag.' He'd tell me I was a faggot and I'd burn in hell for all eternity. He would tell me he hoped I would get AIDS and die. Things like that."

"And the physical abuse—what did that consist of?"

"At first he would just slap me. Then he started hitting me with his belt, telling me he was going to make a man of me. And toward the end, he'd lock me in my room for several days without food."

"At twelve did you know what a fag or faggot meant?"

"Yes. As I said, I was an effeminate child and everyone assumed I was gay. I had been teased and bullied about it since I was about eight."

"Were you in fact gay?"

Ann showed a small grin. "Well, I guess it depends. I wasn't attracted to boys; I was attracted to girls. But I also knew that, even though I had boy parts, I wasn't a boy. In my head, I've always known that I was a girl. So, in that sense, I was and am gay—I'm a lesbian."

"How long did you live with your foster parents?"

"Until I was fourteen."

"And what happened then?"

"I ran away from home."

"Where did you go?"

"I found about a hundred and fifty dollars in a jar in my foster parents' bedroom. I took the money, went to the bus terminal in Miami, and bought a ticket to New York City. It cost me forty-two dollars."

"What happened when you got to New York?"

Ann lowered her head. "I was approached by a man at the bus terminal who said I looked hungry and asked if I wanted something to eat. I was starved, so I said yes. After he bought me a hamburger, he made me expose myself while he masturbated." She stopped and took a small sip of water from a cup that Erin offered her. "From there, I found my way to a shelter for homeless kids. While I was staying there, another girl mentioned there were these guys who were making videos of kids and they had a nice house where they threw parties. So, one day a few of us went with her."

"Did you meet anyone at the party?"

"Yes. I met Cassandra DeCovnie."

"Did anything happen as a result of you meeting Ms. DeCovnie?"

"Yes. She asked me if I was transgender. At the time, I didn't even know what that meant. She could see I was confused, so she told me that it meant someone who was born with boy parts but knew they were a girl. I guess my eyes must have lit up when she told me that, because it was the first time someone had described me. When I told her yes, she smiled and said she could help me."

"What happened?"

"We left the party together and she took me to another house. She came back a few hours later with some girls' clothes and she and this other woman helped me to get dressed and they put some makeup on me. When they showed me what I looked like, I started crying—I was so happy. Then Ms. DeCovnie told me that we should go to her friend's house so I could thank him for the clothes. She told me if he liked me he might even buy me more."

"Did you go with her?"

"Of course. I was so young and naïve. I was just out of my mind with joy. I felt like I had gone to heaven. Finally, there was someone who saw that I was a girl."

"Where did you go?"

"A huge mansion in Westchester County that belonged to Charles Parsons."

"What happened when you got there?"

"Parsons and DeCovnie hugged, and then he looked at me and said, 'And is this the person you were telling me about? My, you are a sexy little thing.' I didn't know what he meant, so I just smiled and said thank you."

"What happened next?"

"He looked at DeCovnie and said, 'Well, I know you have to run. Thank you. I'll talk to you later.' DeCovnie gave him a kiss on the cheek and then turned to me. 'You make sure you're a good girl, and be sure to thank Mr. Parsons,' she said, and then she left. Parsons asked me my name. And I remember I felt embarrassed, but I didn't want to lie, so I told him Felipe. And I'll never forget how he smiled at me then. 'You're much too pretty to be Felipe. From now on your name is Ann,' he said."

"What did he do next?"

"He took my hand and led me through the living room and then up some stairs to a bedroom, where he closed the door. Then he began taking off his clothes. He was a big man, and his chest and arms were covered in coarse black hairs. His smile was gone. Now his look was different. I didn't know what it was at the time, but now I know it was pure lust. He told me to start taking off my clothes. When I hesitated, he screamed at me. When I was standing there in just my new bra and panties, he told me to stop. He then said that I was going to thank him for saving me from the trash heap of life. That if I did what he wanted I would be taken care of. But if I didn't, or if I ever told anyone what we did, he would step on me like the little cockroach I was." Tears were rolling down Ann's cheeks and a small sob punctuated her pause.

"What did he do next?"

"He made me perform oral sex on him. When it was over, he

said I could stay as long as I did what I was told. He said if I did well I would be his daughter. If I didn't do well, he'd kill me just like he'd killed her."

Erin then took Ann through the years of sexual abuse Parsons inflicted on her. Sometimes he allowed a few of his friends to join, but mostly it was Parsons. Shortly after Ann moved into his house, Parsons had a doctor he knew prescribe female hormones for her. Parsons also told her that he had friends in Miami who had destroyed all records of Felipe Rojas. As far as the world was concerned, she was Ann Parsons. Ann testified that he often took videos of what he did to her, and on several occasions told her that she was a "star" on some of his porn sites. He told her that there were a lot of men who enjoyed girls like her. He finally stopped abusing her when she was twenty-one, after she had undergone gender confirmation surgery. He told her that now that she was an adult woman, she no longer turned him on.

"Ann, you described a man who sexually abused you for years. Did you ever want to kill him?"

"Every day," she replied, closing her eyes. "Every day I prayed for the courage to kill him."

"Did you kill him?" Erin asked.

Ann hung her head, as if ashamed. "No, I didn't. I wish I had, but I didn't do it."

"Ann, the jury has heard a recording of the shooting of Charles Parsons. Is that your voice on the recording?"

"No, it's not."

"The person in the recording uses the word *Daddy* in referring to Parsons. Did you ever refer to him as 'Daddy'?"

"Never."

"The prosecution's fingerprint expert testified your fingerprints were on the weapon used to shoot Mr. Parsons. Do you know how your fingerprints came to be on the weapon?"

"Yes," Ann responded. "As long as I knew him, he kept a gun in his night table drawer. There were a few occasions over the years when he'd take his gun out and threaten me with it, so I knew where he kept it. About six months before he died, I went to the house in Westfield when I knew he wasn't there to pick up some of my things. When I went past his bedroom, I saw the camera set up, so I knew he was making movies with someone I assumed was a minor. I was so furious with myself for not stopping him, I went to the night table and took out the gun. I put it up to my head and tried to pull the trigger. But I couldn't. I only realized later that I couldn't pull the trigger because the safety was on."

"You were trying to kill yourself?"

"Yes," she replied with a catch in her voice. "I blamed myself for the fact that he was abusing someone else."

"Objection," Willis said quickly, rising to his feet.

Judge Spiegel turned toward Ann. "Ms. Parsons, during the incident you're describing now, when you were in the house in Westfield, you did not observe Mr. Parsons abuse anyone else, is that fair to say?"

"Yes, Judge. I misspoke. I don't know for a fact if he was abusing anyone. I did what I did because I assumed he was, not because I knew he was."

"Thank you, Ms. Parsons," Spiegel said. "You may continue, Ms. McCabe."

Erin moved back toward counsel table.

"Other than the occasion just described, did you ever hold any gun owned by Mr. Parsons?"

"One other time, between my junior and senior years in high school."

"Tell the jury what happened on that occasion."

"It was summer vacation, and between him and his friends they were abusing me every day. One day when he was out, I went to his room and took his gun out of the drawer. It was a different gun at the time. My plan was to shoot him when he came home."

"What happened?"

"I had never held a gun before and it was really heavy. As I held it, I realized that I'd probably either not be able to do it, or I wouldn't be successful, so I put the gun back, went into the bathroom, and tried to kill myself by taking a handful of his sleeping pills. Fortunately or unfortunately, he came home early, found me, and had me taken to the hospital."

"Ann, the jury has seen an interrogation where you say you did it, then you appear to nod when asked if you killed your father. You have also seen it. Do you have an explanation of why you said you did it, and why you nodded?"

"Yes. When they played the recording of the shooting, I recognized the voice of the other person on the recording. It belonged to a woman I was dating at the time, who told me her name was Terry Gore. And when I heard her voice, I realized I had inadvertently helped her, because I had taken her to the house a few days before the murder. Hearing her on the recording, I was overwhelmed with emotion; I was amazed she had killed him. Something I wish I had done. So 'I did it' just came out, because I wanted to take responsibility, even though I hadn't done it."

"How long did you date Ms. Gore?"

"About two and a half months."

"Did you ever tell Ms. Gore you wanted Parsons dead?

"Never."

"Did you ever discuss killing Parsons with Ms. Gore?"

"Never."

"Where were you the night Parsons was shot?"

"In the Rusty Nail, a bar in Hoboken, waiting to meet Ms. Gore."

"Did you know where Ms. Gore was while you were waiting in the bar?"

"No. I thought she was at work."

"And when did you first realize Ms. Gore was involved in shooting Charles Parsons?"

"When Detectives Burke and Dotson played the recording of the shooting and I recognized her voice."

When Erin finished her direct examination, the judge directed that they'd take a fifteen-minute break. As the jurors got up to file out, Erin noticed two of the female jurors putting tissues back in their purses. A few others looked at Ann with small reassuring smiles as they passed the witness box.

As soon as the judge left the bench, Erin grabbed her purse, digging for her BlackBerry. When she turned it on there were no messages from Swish. *Damn.*

When she looked up, Mark was standing at the railing that separated the spectators from the attorneys and parties. At first, the sight of him in the courtroom was so unexpected and out of place, it was like walking into a surprise party and needing several seconds to comprehend what was happening.

"What are you doing here?" she asked.

"JJ called me at school and asked me to come."

"Why?" she asked, still trying to find her equilibrium.

"He received a message from an FBI agent that he wanted you to get."

Erin stiffened. "Okay?"

"Swish and David are in the hospital."

Erin exhaled. "Oh shit! How . . . are they okay?"

"JJ didn't know. The agent just said that's where they were."

"What hospital?" Erin asked.

"University in Newark," Mark replied.

Erin's mind raced. University was one of three Level 1 trauma hospitals in the state. Where had they been? What happened? Why University? This wasn't good.

"There was one other part, but neither JJ nor I knew what it meant."

"Okay," she responded tentatively.

"Lucas missing—feared dead," he said.

Erin closed her eyes. Sybil Lucas had saved her life, Mark's life, and maybe had helped save David Rojas's life as well. And having just listened to Ann's testimony, Erin knew that Sybil had endured the same type of abuse, if not worse, before she disappeared at fourteen.

Erin didn't believe in capital punishment, but she couldn't help but feel that Sybil's retribution on Charles Parsons was justified.

# CHAPTER 43

*E*RIN ASKED MARK TO GO TO THE HOSPITAL AND FIND OUT FIRSTHAND how Swish and David were doing. Then, she met with Ann in the holding area.

"David's alive," Erin said when Ann looked up at her expectantly. "He's in the hospital. I'm sorry, but I don't have any information on what his condition is. I can say that the information comes from an FBI agent, so that means that David was rescued."

Ann's eyes pleaded for information Erin didn't have. "Does Duane know how he is?" she finally asked.

Erin swallowed her emotions. "I don't know. The message was Duane is in the hospital too. I don't know how he is either."

The silence filled the room. "Ann, your testimony is more important now than ever. We don't know how your brother is, but we know they don't have him anymore. Focus on that and focus on your testimony. You can do this. Do it for David."

In the hour that followed, Willis relentlessly cross-examined Ann, picking out the threads that he wanted to sew together for the jury during his summation.

"Over the last eleven years you never told anyone that Mr. Parsons sexually abused you. Isn't that true?" Willis demanded.

"That's true," Ann responded.

"You attended Westfield High School for four years and you never told anyone that you were being abused, correct?"

"It's true I never told anyone, but I only attended Westfield for three years. After I tried to commit suicide, I was homeschooled my senior year."

"Mr. Parsons paid your tuition to attend Rutgers, correct?"

"He did."

"And while you attended college, a college that Mr. Parsons paid for, you never complained to anyone that you were abused, correct?"

"Correct."

"This Terry Gore, whom you claim is the one who actually murdered Mr. Parsons, do you know where she is?"

"No."

"Have you tried to find her?"

"My attorneys have," she replied.

"Did they find her?"

"As far as I know, no one has been able to find Terry Gore," she responded carefully.

"The cell phone that you used to communicate with Terry Gore was a disposable phone, correct?"

"Correct."

"You had a regular cell phone, correct?"

"Yes."

"The number you called the night of the murder also belonged to a disposable phone, did it not?"

"Yes."

"The cell phone that you used to communicate with Terry Gore the night Charles Parsons was murdered is the one you gave to Marsha Kramer and told her to destroy, correct?"

"Yes."

Erin could tell Willis was getting to the end. As before, he was precise with his questions, leaving any explanation for Erin to handle. Erin waited, suspecting what was next.

"If I understand your testimony, you contend that Charles Parsons murdered the real Ann Parsons?"

"No," Ann said. "I testified that he told me he killed her. For all I know, that's just one more lie he told me."

"When you were arrested and fingerprinted, your fingerprints confirmed that you were Ann Parsons, correct?"

"No. They confirmed that they matched my fingerprints that were already on file with law enforcement because I needed to be fingerprinted at work. When I was fingerprinted, it was as Ann Parsons."

"You claim your name at birth was Felipe Rojas."

"Yes," she said.

"Do you have a copy of your birth certificate?"

"No, Mr. Willis. I don't."

"And you contend that Mr. Parsons told you that all records concerning Felipe Rojas were destroyed?"

"Yes. That's what he told me."

"Did you make that story up before or after you concocted the story about being Felipe Rojas?"

"I never concocted any story, Mr. Willis. What I've said here today is the truth."

"Really," Willis shot back. "So, let me get this straight. There's no record of Felipe Rojas, everyone knows you as Ann Parsons, your fingerprints come back to Ann Parsons, Ms. DeCovnie testified she never heard of a Felipe Rojas, and there's no one to verify your story. The jury just has to take your word for it."

When Erin heard the question, she winced. Adding the last phrase about verification was the only mistake Willis had made. Erin held her breath, wondering how Ann would respond.

"Actually, my brother can verify who I am," Ann replied.

*This is going to be a problem,* Erin thought. The jury couldn't see Willis's face, but Erin could, and his anger was building.

Willis looked up at the judge. "Could we have a sidebar conference, Your Honor?"

Judge Spiegel rose and moved to the side of his bench farthest from the jury.

"Judge, there is a major issue based on the witness's last answer. She claims there is someone, her brother, who can verify who she is, but there is no witness matching that description provided by the defendant in her list of witnesses. As Your Honor is aware, the defendant was required to provide her witness list approximately two months ago and there's no David Rojas on her list."

Spiegel shifted his focus to Erin.

"Judge, for reasons I will be happy to explain in detail," she said, "the defense had no intention of calling Mr. Rojas. However, it now appears that Mr. Willis has opened the door to that testimony."

"Is Mr. Rojas available, Ms. McCabe?" Spiegel asked.

"Judge, at this point, the limited information I have is that both Mr. Swisher and Mr. Rojas are in the hospital. So I need to determine Mr. Rojas's condition before I can answer that question."

Spiegel squinted at Erin. "It seems like there's a lot there to unpack, Ms. McCabe. Tell you what I'm going to do. I'm going to send the jury to lunch. Then I'm going to meet with counsel in chambers, but our meeting will be on the record. Ms. McCabe, I will tell you that I'm troubled that Mr. Rojas was not disclosed as a potential witness, and that your failure to disclose his information, whether intentional or not, has caused Mr. Willis to ask a question that you are now claiming opened the door to a witness you never disclosed."

They gathered in chambers and Erin explained why David Rojas was not on the witness list. She tried to tread carefully because she was afraid the judge would have a difficult time accepting that they feared if the information on David Rojas was disclosed to the prosecution his life would be in jeopardy. Instead she indicated that after all Ann had been through, she feared for his safety, which, based on the fact that he had been kidnapped, showed her concerns were justified.

"Here's my problem, Ms. McCabe," the judge said when she finished. "While I have no reason to think that what you told us is not the truth as you know it, there is no factual record to support what you have told us. More importantly, even assuming that you were justified in not putting Mr. Rojas's name on the witness list, I cannot allow you to use your nondisclosure as a means to argue that Mr. Willis opened the door for you to bring Mr. Rojas in as a witness." Spiegel turned his chair so he was facing Willis. "My inclination is not to declare a mistrial, but to tell the jury to disregard the last answer. What is your position?"

Willis glared at Erin. "Judge, I can't help but think this was all intentional on Ms. McCabe's part. Her story with all this cloak-and-dagger nonsense concerning Mr. Rojas strikes me as the wild fantasy of a desperate lawyer, who should be severely sanctioned for what she did." Willis turned his attention back to Spiegel. "No, Judge, I don't want a mistrial. I want this case to go to the jury, and hopefully they will convict the defendant."

"May I respond to Mr. Willis's accusations, Judge?"

"No, Ms. McCabe. It won't be necessary. For the record, Mr. Willis, I don't agree with your accusations. While I've ruled that it is unfair to take advantage of you not knowing about a potential witness, that doesn't mean that what Ms. McCabe has put on the record aren't the facts as she believes them. I have no reason to doubt Ms. McCabe's veracity. I've also had the benefit of hearing Ms. Parsons's testimony and she has made a compelling witness on her own behalf. What the jury will do, I don't know. But I want the record to be clear that I do not find that Ms. McCabe did anything intentionally improper, and I find that there are no reasons to impose any sanctions."

Spiegel stood up from his desk.

"Thank you both," he said. "We will resume at one thirty."

When Erin walked back into the courtroom, the sheriff's officers had already taken Ann to the holding area for lunch. She fished her phone out of her purse and checked. There was a message from Mark: **swish concussion but expected to be ok—rojas in surgery—on my way back.**

They began the afternoon session with the judge giving the jury an instruction to disregard the last answer that Ann had given. Erin always found it strange that the law assumed that jurors were somehow superhuman and could defy human nature and pretend that they didn't hear something they had clearly heard. What was even stranger was that there were actually times when they did exactly that.

Willis stood to finish his cross-examination. "Ms. Parsons, you are transgendered, correct?"

"I'm a transgender woman. The word *transgender* is an adjective, not a noun."

"Whatever," Willis said dismissively. "You testified that Mr. Parsons took you to a doctor and at age fourteen you started taking female hormones. That's what you wanted, correct—to take hormones?"

"Yes."

"And Mr. Parsons helped you with that, correct?"

"Yes."

"And he paid for you to have sex change surgery too, correct?"

"It's called gender confirmation surgery, but yes, he paid for it."

"He paid for everything for you, correct?"

"Correct."

"You live in a condo owned by Charles Parsons. Is that correct?"

"Yes, it is."

"And you heard Ms. DeCovnie testify earlier in the trial that the condo has a value of approximately nine hundred thousand dollars. Do you agree with that estimate?"

"Yes."

"And under Charles Parsons's will, you stand to inherit ten million dollars, plus the condo, isn't that true?"

"No," Ann replied.

"That's not true, Ms. Parsons?"

"No. It's not. The will leaves the condo and ten million dollars to Mr. Parsons's adopted daughter, Ann Parsons. I'm not his daughter."

"Prior to being arrested for his murder, did you ever notify Ms. DeCovnie, or any lawyers representing the estate, that you were not Mr. Parsons's daughter so you were not entitled to receive anything from his estate?"

"No."

"After his death, did you ever offer to move out of the condo?"

"No."

"Isn't it true that before you were arrested it was your intent to keep the condo and the ten million dollars?"

"Yes, it was," Ann replied almost defiantly.

"Thank you. Nothing further."

Erin stood and slowly positioned herself at the end of the jury box so that in looking at her Ann was also looking directly at the jurors.

"Ann, let me pick up where Mr. Willis finished. Why didn't you ever tell Ms. DeCovnie that you weren't Parsons's adopted daughter?"

"Because she knew. She was the one who found me and brought me to him when I was fourteen. She knew who I was."

"Why would you have taken the ten million dollars if you are not his daughter?"

"Because for years he had abused me, raped me, sodomized me, threatened me, and used me as part of his child pornography business. I felt I was entitled to damages for what he had done to me," she said, her anger on full display.

"And why in all the years that you lived with Mr. Parsons did you never tell anyone he was abusing you?"

Ann took a deep breath and then exhaled. "Because he repeatedly told me he'd kill me if I did, and because he made a point of saying he was rich and powerful while I was nothing but an undocumented trannie whore no one would believe. Later, after he found out I had a brother, he threatened he'd have my brother killed if I told anyone."

"Did you believe he was capable of carrying out the threats he made against you?"

"Yes," she said, chewing on her lower lip.

"Mr. Willis questioned you about your use of a disposable phone. Why did you use a disposable phone?"

"Initially to be able to call my brother. Mr. Parsons owned the regular cell phone I used, so he could see everyone I called on the bill. Since I didn't want him to know I was calling my brother, I purchased a disposable phone."

"Why did you use the disposable phone to call Terry Gore?"

"Same reason. I didn't want him to know I was seeing someone."

"Thank you," Erin said. "No further questions."

As she turned to walk back to counsel table, she saw Mark sitting in the audience. She didn't know why he smiled at her, but it was reassuring nonetheless. She was about to sit down when the door to the courtroom swung open and in walked Duane Abraham Swisher. His head was wrapped in a bandage, and the left side of his face appeared bruised and swollen, but after pausing momentarily in the rear of the courtroom, he slowly made his way down the aisle, pushed open the gate that provided access to counsel table, and stood next to Erin.

"I apologize to the court and the jury for being late," he said without any hint of irony.

Spiegel hadn't taken his eyes off of Duane since he walked in the door. "Ladies and gentlemen," he said, "we're going to take a fifteen-minute recess."

As was custom, everyone stood as the jury filed out. When they were safely away, Spiegel asked, "Mr. Swisher, are you okay?"

"Never better, Judge," Swish replied.

Spiegel shook his head. "Glad to hear that," he said. "Ms. McCabe, is it still your intention to call Ms. DeCovnie as your next witness?"

"It is, Your Honor."

"Thank you. The court is in recess," Spiegel said as he walked off the bench.

Before Erin could say anything, Duane held his finger up to his lips. "Not now," he said, then sat down next to Ann. "Your brother is safe and he's going to be okay. During the rescue, he was shot on the right side of the chest, but fortunately it went pretty much straight through him. I stayed at the hospital until he was out of surgery, and the doctors believe he'll be as good as new in a month or two."

Ann began sobbing. "He's okay?"

"He's okay," Duane said reassuringly.

Ann went to throw her arms around him but stopped. "I don't

want to hurt you," she said, clasping his hand. "Thank you. From the bottom of my heart, thank you."

Erin leaned over and gave Ann a hug. "It's all good," Erin whispered.

As she was hugging Ann, she raised her eyes to Swish. The grin he'd been wearing since the moment he walked into the courtroom hadn't faded. Totally perplexed by his demeanor, Erin mouthed, "What's going on?"

"It's about to get interesting," he said cryptically.

# CHAPTER 44

*I*T WAS THREE THIRTY P.M. WHEN ERIN FINISHED HER QUESTIONING OF DeCovnie. Erin had taken DeCovnie through her career as a model, meeting Parsons socially, and then her time working for him. Erin established how DeCovnie was paid over $250,000 a year by Parsons's company, yet her only apparent role was to plan the infrequent parties he liked to throw in New York City and Miami Beach. She denied knowing that Parsons abused minors, that she secured minors for him, or any awareness that he made and sold child pornography. Once again, she vehemently denied knowing anyone named Felipe Rojas and insisted that the Ann Parsons sitting at counsel table was Charles's adopted daughter resulting from his marriage to Ann's mother. During her questioning, Erin watched each of the jurors, and most seemed to be taking a very jaundiced view of DeCovnie's denials.

When Erin was finished with DeCovnie, Willis had no cross. Erin then asked to be allowed to approach sidebar.

"Judge, I know this is a little unusual, especially since it's already three thirty, but Mr. Swisher has provided me with some new information. I'd like to recall Detective Sergeant Kluska to the stand. However, to avoid any issues that could potentially cause Mr. Willis to demand a mistrial, I'd like to have Detective Kluska initially testify outside the presence of the jury."

Spiegel turned his gaze to Willis, who shifted uneasily from one foot to the other.

"Judge, I don't know what game Ms. McCabe is playing," Willis said, his annoyance evident, "but if she wants to voir dire Detective Sergeant Kluska outside the presence of the jury, I don't have any objection—other than it's a waste of our time."

"Why don't I just let the jury go for the day?" Spiegel asked.

"Judge, I think for reasons that will be obvious, if you are going to permit the jury to hear Detective Kluska's testimony, I'd like it to happen today, since the jury just heard Ms. DeCovnie's testimony."

"All right. Let's see what happens," Spiegel replied.

When they returned to counsel table, Spiegel told the jury that he needed to take care of some legal matters outside of their presence, but he wanted to see how long the hearing was going to take before he sent them home for the day.

After the jury retired, the bailiff went into the hallway and called Detective Sergeant Kluska. Kluska entered the courtroom with a box and made his way to the witness stand. To everyone's surprise, Duane slowly stood up, steadying himself by placing his hands on counsel table.

"Good afternoon, Detective," Duane began.

"Good afternoon," Kluska replied, his tone and demeanor noticeably different from the first time he'd appeared on the witness stand.

"Detective, when you came in, you were carrying a box. What's in the box?"

"Four external computer hard drives."

"And where were the hard drives before you took possession of them?"

"In the bottom drawer of a desk belonging to Detective Sybil Lucas."

"What made you look in Detective Lucas's desk drawer?"

"This morning at about nine hundred hours—sorry, nine o'clock a.m.—I received a call from FBI Special Agent Jodi Collins, who requested that I look in Detective Lucas's drawer, as it had been reported to her that there were four external computer hard drives there."

"Did she tell you who had advised her of that?"

"She did. She told me it was Detective Lucas."

"Did she tell you when she had received this information from Detective Lucas?"

"She did. She said at approximately two a.m."

"Did Agent Collins indicate anything about the circumstances of Detective Lucas's statement?"

"Yes. She said Lucas was about to walk into a warehouse where there were a number of people with weapons. Detective Lucas wasn't sure she would make it out alive."

"After you located the hard drives, what, if anything, did you do?"

"I consulted with Agent Collins and we discussed the best course of conduct concerning the hard drives. As a result of that discussion I took them to FBI headquarters in Newark."

"What happened there?"

"They were logged in as evidence. A duplicate copy of each hard drive was made, and experts from that office reviewed their contents."

"Did you see any of this content?"

"After their experts reviewed it, I was shown excerpts."

"And what was on the excerpts you were shown?"

"One drive contained what appeared to be financial information and lists of customers. The excerpts I saw from the other contained child pornography."

"Do you know if anyone is prepared to testify concerning the content of the hard drives?"

"It's my understanding the FBI can have the agents available as early as tomorrow."

"In reviewing the content of the drives, did the agents observe anything that is relevant to this case?"

"Yes. In one of the excerpts I was shown, one of the adults who appears is clearly Charles Parsons."

"You saw Mr. Parsons in one of the excerpts you were shown?"

"I did."

"And did that excerpt contain child pornography?"

"Unfortunately, it did."

"Do you know why these hard drives were in Detective Lucas's drawer?"

"Agent Collins advised me that Detective Lucas told her that she had taken them from the Parsons residence the night he died."

"Why was she at the Parsons residence?"

"Again, according to Agent Collins, Detective Lucas told her that she went there to retrieve the hard drives and to kill Mr. Parsons."

There were murmurs amongst the spectators in the courtroom.

"And what would be Detective Lucas's motivation to do something like that?"

"She told Agent Collins that her real name was Ann Parsons."

The cacophony of noise that erupted caused Judge Spiegel to rap his gavel gently on the bench. "Quiet, please. You may continue, Mr. Swisher."

"And where is Detective Lucas now, if you know?" Duane asked.

"According to Agent Collins, Detective Lucas was abducted last night when she participated in an effort to secure the release of David Rojas, who had been kidnapped. Apparently, during the course of the FBI raid, two of the suspects took her away at gunpoint. At this point, there is an all-points bulletin out for her and her kidnappers."

"Judge, subject to Mr. Willis's cross-examination, the defense would like to have the detective and Agent Collins testify to these facts before the jury," Duane said.

"Judge, this is outrageous!" Willis said, leaping to his feet. "There is no reason for me to cross-examine Detective Kluska. This is nothing but the rankest of hearsay. There is no way to authenticate these hard drives, there is no chain of custody, and we have no way of knowing if they have been altered. None of this is admissible."

"I'll see counsel in chambers," Spiegel said.

As Erin stood, Duane slumped back into his chair and closed his eyes.

"Are you okay?" she said.

"Still a little woozy," he replied.

She quickly sat down next to him. "Do you want me to have them call for an EMT?"

"Nah. I'll be okay. Just needed to sit for a minute."

"You sure you're okay?"

"Yeah," he said. "Once the room stops spinning, I'll be fine," he added.

"God, I was worried about you. I don't think I've ever been happier to see someone as when you opened the courtroom door," she said, taking in the full measure of her partner.

"Happy to be here," he replied with a mix of a grin and a grimace.

"And great job," she added.

"Thanks. Let's go see what the judge is going to do. Just do all the talking. I'm exhausted."

Spiegel motioned to the chairs around his desk when Willis, Erin, and Duane walked into his chambers. "I agree with Mr. Willis that there are so many issues with Detective Kluska's testimony and the hard drives that it could be a bar exam evidence essay question," Spiegel said as soon as they sat down.

Erin leaned forward, ready to respond, but the judge held up his hand.

"That said, how can I ignore what is going on here? If Detective Kluska, or, I guess more importantly, if Agent Collins can come to court tomorrow to testify, how can I preclude that testimony? I agree with you, Mr. Willis, that the statements Agent Collins attributes to Detective Lucas are hearsay, but those statements appear to fall within the hearsay exception for statements made against penal interest and in anticipation of death."

"But, Judge, we have no way of knowing if what's on the hard drives is authentic. That evidence has to be excluded."

The judge's eyes narrowed. "Mr. Willis, I understand this may be a lot to digest, but isn't your job to see that justice is done, not to obtain a conviction at all costs? All of what Detective Kluska just testified to is consistent with the defendant's testimony. If in fact

Mr. Parsons is shown in the video, isn't that self-authenticating? If you need time to have them analyzed by experts to ensure they haven't been altered or edited, I have no problem delaying the trial for a few days so you can do so. Likewise, if you want to brief the issues on admissibility, I'll give you time. But my sense is that if I don't admit this evidence now, and the jury was to convict the defendant, I'd have to grant a new trial. Why allow that to happen?"

"Judge, if you're going to allow it, I'd like the opportunity to go to the appellate division on an emergent application. I'm sorry, but I vehemently disagree with the court."

The judge's intercom suddenly buzzed. "Yes, Toni?"

"Prosecutor Picaro for you."

The judge looked down at his phone and none of the lines were blinking. "On the phone?"

"I'm sorry, no. He's here in the outer office. He'd like to see you with counsel on the Parsons case."

Spiegel looked at them and shrugged. "Oh. Okay, send him in."

They all stood as Union County prosecutor Dale Picaro walked into the room.

"Good afternoon, Mr. Prosecutor. To what do we owe the pleasure of your company?" Spiegel offered with a smile, gesturing for him to take a seat in an empty chair.

"Good afternoon, Judge."

When he turned to greet counsel, his eyebrows shot up upon seeing Duane's condition. It took a few seconds for him to recover.

"Judge, I have been briefed by my office on what Detective Sergeant Kluska testified to in court. I've also had the opportunity to speak at length with the special agent in charge of the Newark FBI office, Abhay Petel. In addition to the items testified to by Detective Kluska, Detective Lucas's desk drawer also contained a detailed account of her involvement in this matter, starting with her having a rootkit installed on Charles Parsons's computer as well as those of several other individuals. Our computer people have advised me that Detective Lucas also left a hard drive with the e-mails, text messages, and documents that she obtained by using this rootkit. While there will be lots of evidentiary issues in the future, as the prosecutor, I cannot ignore that Detective Lucas has left behind enough corroborating evidence that my office is convinced that Ann Parsons, or, more correctly, the Ann Parsons who is currently on trial, did not murder Charles Parsons. When we leave chambers, I am prepared to go on the record and ask the court to dismiss the charges."

His gaze flickered to Erin for a moment before returning to the judge.

"The only reservation I will make is that while we are unaware of any evidence suggesting that Ms. Parsons conspired or aided or abetted the killing of Mr. Parsons if that evidence were to come to light, we would consider whether she should be charged with those offenses. However, this case is over. I will be holding a press conference later, and announcing that the U.S. attorney's office will be pursuing human trafficking charges against Ms. DeCovnie and others."

Spiegel looked at Picaro. "Thank you, Mr. Prosecutor, you just made my day much easier." He turned to look at the gathered counsel. "After the dismissal, I plan on speaking with the jurors. Any objections?"

"No, Your Honor," Erin and Duane replied.

"Mr. Willis?" the judge asked.

"No objection," he replied sullenly.

"Tom, I need to see you in my office after we're done here," the prosecutor said, his tone less than friendly.

As Erin made her way back into the courtroom, she couldn't dim her broad smile.

"What?" Ann said, her eyes wide with anticipation. "Tell me, what's going on?"

Duane looked at Erin. "Please, it's all yours," he said to her.

"It's over, Ann. They're dismissing the charges. You won," Erin said.

"What?" Ann squeaked. "Over?"

Erin and Duane nodded.

"Oh my God—it's over," Ann said, suddenly choking back tears.

"All rise," the clerk announced as Spiegel bounded onto the bench. "Mr. Prosecutor, I understand you have an application to make."

Picaro rose and placed on the record the dismissal of the murder charge against Ann, just as he had indicated in chambers. When he was finished, Spiegel looked over at Ann, who was standing between Duane and Erin.

"Ms. Parsons, based on the application of the prosecutor, I hereby grant his application and dismiss the charges against you. You are free to go. On a personal note, I am sorry for what you've had to endure and I know survivors can sometimes feel guilty and blame themselves for what happened. I hope you won't do that. I admire the courage you have displayed throughout your young life, and I wish you well. For the record, Indictment 08-00527 is hereby dismissed. As I indicated in chambers, I am going to speak to the jury and then release them. Thank you, counsel."

Ann threw her arms around Erin. "How can I ever thank you?"

"There's no need to," Erin replied. "You were the one who made it happen."

Ann then turned to Duane and gently touched the side of his face without bruises. "I don't know what happened, but I can never repay you for saving my brother's life."

Duane smiled. "Glad it worked out. Plus, for one night, I got to be back with my agents at the Bureau."

Erin looked across the courtroom. "Excuse me for a minute," she said, then made her way to the table where Tom Willis was packing up his stuff. She extended her hand. "Tom, you tried an excellent case."

He looked at her hand, then at her, before grabbing his trial bag off the chair and walking out of the courtroom.

"I apologize for Mr. Willis."

She turned to see Prosecutor Picaro standing there, his hand extended.

She took his hand and clasped it between both of hers. "Thanks, Mr. Prosecutor."

"Cut the Mr. Prosecutor crap," he responded and then smiled. "It's good to see you again, Erin. It's been a few years," he said. "I heard you did a good job in this one. Glad things worked out."

"Thank you, Dale, and thank you for doing the right thing," she said.

"I think it's part of my job," he said with a wink. "Got to run. I have a press conference to give."

Erin had one other person to thank. "Hello, Detective Sergeant Kluska," she said. "Good to see you."

"Nice job, counselor."

"Thank you," she said with a small grin. "Maybe when things die down a bit, I can buy you a club soda and we can compare notes."

"I try to avoid defense attorneys," he said with a hint of a grin.

"That's not what I hear," she said, then motioned in the direction of Picaro, who was walking out of the courtroom. "Unless I misread things, the boss doesn't seem too happy with Mr. Willis."

"How are you at keeping secrets?" he asked.

She gave him an "are you kidding me" look. "I don't know, Ed, how am I at keeping secrets?"

He chuckled. "Rumor has it that Tom may have been supplementing his income by conveying information to the Parsons estate. He may not have broken the law, but he certainly violated the office rules and regulations. At least that's the rumor," he said with a wink.

Erin reached out and shook his hand. "Seriously, Ed, thank you. You saved her life."

"Don't get all mushy on me, McCabe. I just put the wheels in motion. Everybody else did the rest."

"Right," she said. "You did a good thing, Ed, and I for one won't forget it."

"Whatever," he said with a grin.

"Excuse me, everyone," the bailiff said. "The jury will be coming out. Please take your places."

As the jurors filed by, several of them quietly said congratulations as they passed Ann. Juror number eleven paused in front of them.

"I want you to know that you and you"—she pointed to Erin and Ann—"have changed my life. I used to think all of you BLT people were crazy. But you two made me realize you're just like all of us. Thank you."

When the last of the jurors had left, Judge Spiegel waved for Erin and Duane to approach.

"I thought you'd both want to know that if the case had gone to the jury today, you would have gotten a not guilty verdict in about a half an hour. I'm not sure if Willis had anything for a rebuttal case, but you two did a great job. Congratulations."

He looked over at Ann, who was talking with some people who were still milling about. "She's a courageous young woman. It took a lot of guts to go to trial." Then he looked at Erin. "It also took a lot of guts to recommend going to trial. Kudos to you both." He reached out and shook each of their hands. "And, Mr. Swisher, perhaps at the next bar meeting you can tell me what the hell happened to you."

"Will do, Judge."

Once Spiegel gave them a nod and headed back into chambers, Erin looked at her partner. "I hope I don't have to wait until a bar meeting to find out what the hell happened." She reached up and gave him a hug. "But thank God you're okay. And thank you for whatever you did."

Erin and Swish made their way over to where Mark was standing with JJ and Kevin. As she did, she took Ann by the hand. "There's some people I'd like you to meet."

After the guys exchanged high-fives with Swish and each of them gave Erin a hug, they looked to Ann.

"Ann, this is Mark, a.k.a. the boyfriend. This is JJ, who flew down to Florida to bring your brother back, and got in a major brawl keeping his whereabouts secret. And this is Kevin—he's our own personal police bodyguard."

Ann started crying, hugged them all in turn, and thanked them profusely.

Erin touched JJ's arm. "I hate to impose, but I was wondering if I could ask you for another favor."

"No imposition. What do you need?" JJ asked.

"I need to walk across the street with Ann so she can collect her personal belongings, and then I'm sure she'd love to go to the hospital to see her brother. Can you help her out?"

"No problem," JJ said.

Then Erin turned to Kevin. "Kev, Ann's been incarcerated for almost a year. She lives in a condo in Jersey City. Do you think you could meet her there after she leaves the hospital and make sure it's safe? There are some folks who won't be happy the case is over."

"Done," he said. "Happy to check it out. I'll also make sure a car drives by periodically to ensure everything's okay."

Erin turned to Swish. "How did you get here from the hospital?"

"Taxi."

"So I'll drive you back to Mark's. The condition you're in, you shouldn't be alone."

"Not to worry. I called Cori from the hospital and she and her parents were driving up from Fredericksburg. They should be there by now. All I need is a lift to Scotch Plains."

She turned to Mark. "How about while I get Ann situated you take Swish home and then maybe pick up some takeout. Thai and Sam Adams might be good," she said, at last feeling free of the stress that had been haunting her these past weeks.

He leaned over and kissed her. "Sounds like a plan," he said.

She looked around the courtroom, trying to take it in and savor the moment. Tomorrow there'd be another case to work on and today's victory would be old news. There was so little time to enjoy the wins, whereas the defeats seemed to linger and haunt her. She smiled and turned to Ann.

"You ready to go check out of your current accommodations?" Erin said.

"Yeah. It'll be nice to sleep in a real bed."

"Excuse me, but can you and your client speak with me for a moment?"

Erin looked up to see Rich Rudolph from the *Newark Journal.*

"Would love to get some reactions from all three of you on the dismissal and everything that took place today," he continued. "I've been covering the courts for over ten years and today was one of the most fascinating days I can remember. Not sure I've seen anything like it." He paused, then as his smile grew he said, "I seem to remember someone telling me that when the trial was over everyone would know Ann was innocent—sounds like she got it right!"

Erin looked at Duane and shrugged as if to say, "It's nice to be right."

Later, as Erin laid curled up with Mark on the couch, all of the emotions of the last few weeks spilled over. "You could have gotten killed because of me."

"But I didn't—because of you," he replied.

"I don't know, Mark, I seem to bring nothing but trouble to your life."

"Don't start," he said, gently lifting her head so she was looking at him. "There isn't anyone I'd rather be with than you. I love you, Erin McCabe," he said as he wrapped his arms tightly around her. "I would gladly give my life for you. But I'd be even happier to spend the rest of my life with you."

As she stared back at him, the implications of what he had just said suddenly landed and she felt her face flush. What was she so afraid of? She loved him. But maybe that was it. She had loved once before and it had ended badly. She understood why it had. Lauren was straight; she wanted to be with a man and Erin no longer filled that role. But even though she intellectually understood why it happened, it hadn't prevented her from being crushed. It wasn't lost on her that on some level she'd always love Lauren—her first love. And in that moment it suddenly crossed her mind that perhaps she wasn't a heterosexual woman, maybe she was bisexual—a thought that had never entered her mind before. Yet, she had no doubt that had Lauren been willing to stay with her, she would never have wanted anyone else. But here she was, looking into the eyes of a man who loved her, and still she held back. Why? Was it his family, her feeling of being unlovable because she was trans, or the fear of being crushed again? Whatever it was, with one sentence he had forced her to look at her fears for what they were—her fears, not his.

"I love you too," she whispered, sure of her love, but very unsure of where it would lead.

# CHAPTER 45

ALTHOUGH ERIN HAD SPOKEN WITH HER MOTHER ON THE PHONE while the trial was in progress, it wasn't the same as their breakfasts, so she was excited to finally see her again. When she walked into the diner, her mother jumped up and hugged her longer than usual. When they separated, Peg held her at arm's length, looking her up and down.

"What?" Erin said.

"I don't know. I just want to make sure you're in one piece," her mother said. "You've lost weight."

"It's my new diet sensation—called stressful trial. Works every time." Erin flipped her hands up as if to say, "Ta-da!" "How about you? Look at the new do. I like the punk look," she said, referring to her mother's short hair, as they both slid into opposite sides of the booth.

"I don't care what it looks like as long as I'm not wearing a wig."

"Seriously, how are you feeling?"

"I'm good," her mother said. "My scans are good. I feel like I have energy again." She paused and smiled. "I really am starting to feel normal again, physically, mentally, and emotionally."

After the waitress brought them coffee and took their order, Peg reached down and held up yesterday's newspaper, where the dismissal of the charges and the news of the federal human trafficking investigation were on the front page. "Congratulations! Even your father commented on the fact that you won."

"Thanks," Erin said.

Her mother opened the paper to page twelve, where there was a picture of Erin, Duane, and Ann on the courthouse steps next to the continued story. "Nice picture of you and your client, but Swish looks like he's gone a few rounds with Muhammad Ali." Peg cocked her head to the side. "What happened? And don't you dare tell me he walked into a door."

"It's a long story, Mom. Let's just say, Swish is lucky to be alive, and should never have left the hospital on Tuesday to come to court."

"Listen, Ms. McCabe, it's time you came clean and told your poor old mother what the hell is going on. Yesterday I get a call from a friend of mine who happens to be the guidance counselor at Westfield High. You know we guidance counselors stick together, and she asks me what happened with my daughter and Mark Simpson in the parking lot of Westfield High the other day. Apparently, the rumor going around school was that my daughter beat up two Westfield police officers."

Erin winced and looked down into her coffee. "Funny how those rumors take on a life of their own. If it's any consolation, they weren't cops."

"No. It's no consolation."

Realizing that her mother would be relentless, Erin explained about the fake police and the attempt to abduct Mark, and the successful abduction of David, their client's brother.

Her mother stared at her. "Don't you ever have any normal cases?"

"All the time," Erin said with a grin. "But they aren't on the front page of the paper."

As soon as Erin walked into the office, Cheryl jumped up and hugged her.

"Oh my God, you two are amazing. You must have about sixty messages. Your voice mail box apparently filled up Tuesday night, so all day yesterday and this morning I've been taking messages. You've been getting calls from newspapers, cable news, you name it. Also a few lawyers who called to say they represent potential victims of Parsons and are looking to talk to you and Ann." Cheryl bent down and retrieved a stack of paper messages and handed them to Erin.

"Thanks," Erin said, glancing at the messages. "Is Swish in?"

"Yeah, he's in his office." Cheryl hesitated, her exuberance fading. "Is Swish okay? He looks pretty banged up."

"I think so," she said. *I hope so.*

She made her way down the hallway towards his office. "Hey there," she said, standing in his office doorway. "How you feeling?"

"Like I just went a few rounds with Muhammad Ali." There were dark circles under his eyes, and the bandage that had been wrapped around his head had been removed, revealing a lump the size of a small walnut over his left eye and several stitches next to his left ear.

She raised an eyebrow. "I swear there are times you and my mother communicate by mental telepathy."

He gave her a puzzled look. "Say what?"

"Nothing," she said, before dropping into a seat. "So let's start with the easy part—how severe is the concussion?"

"Moderate to severe," he responded with a grimace.

"I'm surprised they let you out of the hospital on Tuesday."

"They didn't," he replied. "I signed myself out against medical advice."

She was going to ask why, but she already knew the answer to that question. "Lucas. Have you heard anything about Lucas? What happened to her?"

He reacted as if her question caused his head to throb. "The short answer is no, I haven't heard anything. Between the Bureau and the prosecutor's office, everyone is doing everything they can to try and find her."

Erin frowned, knowing that she had goaded Lucas into helping to save David, perhaps at the cost of her life. "So, what happened between when we last spoke Monday night and you showed up in court? You had heard something from Lucas and hinted you were reaching out to law enforcement."

Duane allowed himself to drift back. He explained that he, Rick, and Alex had gathered at the office Monday afternoon.

Around four p.m. Lucas sent word she was still working on getting the location where David was being held. She also let them know that she was setting up a swap, David in exchange for hard drives the people holding David wanted. None of them felt great about the exchange idea, but, since Lucas was the only one in touch with whoever had David, she was calling the shots. At that point, Duane reached out to Collins to let her know what was happening.

Duane explained the meeting at the diner and the lead-up to the rescue, going over what Kluska had testified to in court.

"There were also some things that didn't come out in court," he said, motioning in the direction of the tape recorder sitting on his desk. "Before I left the hospital to come to court, Agent Collins gave me a copy of the wire recording the agents in the van had made just in case we needed it for the hearing. This is the part when we were all in place and waiting outside the building and suddenly Lucas started talking, but this time she was talking to Collins and me."

He reached over to the tape recorder and hit play. "So, Mr. Swisher, in the event this goes bad, there are a couple of things you need to know. Tell Detective Kluska that in my bottom desk drawer are the real hard drives. The one taped to my chest with the financial information is a copy of what they want, but as I mentioned, there's no money for them to get.

"Yes, Agent Collins, I did take their money—all five hundred and fifty million dollars. Tell Kluska there is also a full confession as to how I shot Charles Parsons. I made my confession in anticipation of being killed tonight, so hopefully it's not hearsay. Ann Parsons, at least the Ann Parsons who is on trial, is completely innocent. I used her to gain access to the house, which allowed me to learn the security alarm code. And while to this day I'm not sure I would have pulled the trigger, I was holding the gun against Parsons's temple when he tried to knock it away—that didn't work out real well for him. And, Agent Collins, before you judge me too harshly, Charles Parson started sexually abusing me when I was six. A couple of years later when my pediatrician told my mother that he believed I was being abused, she confronted Parsons. I heard them screaming at each other that night. The next day both my mother and the pediatrician died—her, *falling* down a set of steps, and the doctor killed by a hit-and-run driver. Since you're an agent, I suspect you don't believe in those kinds of coincidences any more than I do. With my mother gone, he continued to abuse me, including making pornographic films of me, until I ran away at fourteen. Lest you think he acted alone, Conroy, Hiller, and others also took advantage of me for years." Duane hit pause. "It was strange. What she described had happened to her was horrific, yet, as you can hear on the tape, she said it devoid of any emotion. It was as if she were talking about someone else. Maybe she had to do that to survive, but . . ."

After a long pause he described the scene in the parking lot, Lucas walking into the building with her gun pointed at Hiller's head and them slowly getting into position to follow her into the building.

"I didn't know what happened at the time. All I heard was 'oomph,' and the sound of a gunshot. David later told me that one of the guys working with Conroy had tackled Lucas from behind, but as he did, her gun went off, killing Hiller instantly. Apparently Conroy believed she was bluffing about the suicide vest, but even if she wasn't, Conroy now had the hard drive, and the way the guy hit her from behind, Lucas went down on her stomach with the guy sprawled across her as they hit the ground, so if there had been an explosion, Lucas would have taken the brunt of it and the guy on top of her would have taken the rest.

"At that point all hell broke loose. Collins and Kenny bolted through the door, with us only seconds behind them. I could hear Kenny yelling, 'FBI, drop your guns,' when another shot rang out. Again, from what David told me at the hospital, that was when he was shot. Conroy had screamed at one of his men, 'Kill him.' The guy had turned and shot David, hitting him on the right side of his chest.

"I could hear Sybil screaming and the voices of two men, one I presumed to be Conroy, the other the guy who tackled her. Several shots were fired before Alex, Rick, and I got there. It was a chaotic scene, but from where I was I saw two men taking Sybil out a side door. I immediately took off for the door. Unbeknownst to me, there was a third guy hidden in the shadows, and as I was running by where he was he caught me on the side of the head with something, not sure what it was, but Rick told me he thought it was a two-by-four. I went sprawling. I don't think I was out for too long, because I was aware that there were still shots being fired. By the time I staggered to my feet and got to the door, all I saw was a vehicle heading out of the lot and down the street. I managed to get back inside and Alex found me. Between Collins, Kenny, Alex, and Rick they had subdued the three other guys that had been with Conroy. Two of them had superficial wounds and, miraculously, no one else had been shot. I made my way over to David and he had a classic sucking chest wound. I immediately put pressure on it and called for help. Fortunately, as soon as the two agents in the van had heard the first gunshot, they had put out an 'officer down' call, thinking it had been Lucas who had been shot.

"Elizabeth PD was there in about five minutes, and it was shortly after they arrived that I passed out. When I came to, I was in the ER. That's when I told Alex to text you for Ann to testify. They sent me for a CT scan and told me I had a concussion. Alex and Rick filled me in on what had happened after I passed out. They also told me that David was in surgery, but the initial indications were that he would make it. I waited at the hospital until he was out of recovery, and then—well you know the rest."

Erin looked at her partner, shaking her head, trying to process everything he told her. Her heart ached for what Lucas had been through. At the same time, her admiration for Duane's courage and resolve caused her to get up, go around his desk and, in the gentlest way possible, hug him. "You're amazing," she said holding him in her embrace.

The phone buzzed. "Duane, Erin, it's Special Agent Collins from the FBI."

"Thanks, Cheryl. Put her through," Duane said.

"Duane, how's the head?" Agent Collins said as soon as she beeped through.

"Getting better," he said with a grimace.

"Glad to hear that. I'm calling because I have an update that involves Detective Sybil Lucas."

They looked at each other, fearing the worst. "Go ahead," Duane said.

"The bodies of two men have been found in the trunk of a car at Newark Airport. The preliminary identification indicates they are Martin Conroy and Sergei Mollusca, who was a reputed soldier in the Russian mob. I should also mention that based on finger-prints, it appears that Mr. Mollusca was at the warehouse two nights ago."

They shared a surprised look. "Causes of death?" Duane asked.

"Mollusca was shot once in the chest. It appears Conroy died of a broken neck."

"And Sybil?" Duane asked.

"No sign of her. We're checking all flights that have gone out in the last two days, but so far nothing."

"Thanks," Duane said.

# CHAPTER 46

*I*N THE WEEK FOLLOWING THE END OF THE CASE, ERIN WAS IN REGULAR contact with Ann. Her brother continued to recover and the doctors were hoping he could be discharged from the hospital by Friday. Erin had also spoken with Lucy Nichols, an assistant U.S. attorney, who was going to be handling the human trafficking case. Liam Fletcher had been arrested at Logan Airport in Boston, trying to get on a flight out of the country. Nichols had indicated that because Ann was a human trafficking victim, the U.S. attorney's office would be able to assist Ann in obtaining a green card and legally changing her name if that was something Ann wanted.

After Erin had insisted, Swish had agreed to take a few days off to recover from his concussion. Now back at work, he seemed no worse for the wear. They were sitting in Erin's office going over their case list and trying to figure out what needed to be done when Cheryl buzzed. "Detective Sergeant Kluska on line two."

Erin made a face indicating she didn't have a clue as to why he was calling. After a brief greeting, he snorted.

"Obviously you haven't looked at your e-mails recently. Take a look," Kluska said.

Erin opened her e-mail. There were the usual spam e-mails, a few she could see were work related, and then one from lucas.sybil@county.union.po.state.nj.gov. She motioned to Swish to take a look.

"I see it," she said to Kluska.

"Read it," he said, and hung up.

Erin opened the e-mail and printed two copies, one of which she handed to Swish.

Hello All

If you are reading this it likely means I'm dead. I programmed this to be sent at 11 a.m. on my official last day of work, knowing that if I were alive, I could cancel it from being sent. Unfortunately for me, since you're reading this, apparently things did not go as I planned.

I hope that by now the hard drives and my statement that I left in my desk drawer have been discovered. I also hope that as a result, the charges against Ann for murdering Charles Parsons have been dropped. If they haven't, they should be—I did it.

So, here's the other piece of the puzzle. As a result of the rootkit I had Justin Mackey install, I learned Parsons, Conroy, Hiller, and DeCovnie had taken the profits from their child pornography and trafficking businesses and placed them into offshore accounts. As of the time of Parsons's death, they had approximately $550 million in accounts in Nevis. I will spare you the gory details, but those accounts have been emptied—yes, by me. Since it appears that I have not survived to disperse the funds at my leisure, I have set up wire transfers that will be triggered at noon today.

I understand that these funds are the product of illegal activities, and therefore there will be those in law enforcement who will argue all the money should be confiscated and forfeited. I am hopeful that, when those of you in authority see what I have done, you will allow my allocation of the funds to stand. I have allocated the funds as follows:

$210m to the IRS for federal income taxes;
$60m for NYC & NYS income taxes;
$40m for NJ income taxes;

$200m to fund a victims' compensation fund for those abused
   by Parsons et al.;
$5m for Justin Mackey's mother—Ms. McCabe can explain this
   one to everyone for me;
$15m for Ann Parsons, aka F. Rojas;
$5m to be held in trust to cover the legal fees for representing
   Felipe/Ann and Mrs. Mackey, and to pay counsel fees for
   other victims;
$15m for me—I know I'm dead, but I made private
   arrangements for that money; they abused me for eight
   years and killed my mother. I deserve it.

In terms of the victims' compensation fund, I have set it up in
an account at Chase Bank. For money to be withdrawn and paid
to a victim of Parsons et al., the payment needs to be approved
by the agreement of the prosecutor of Union County, the U.S.
attorney for NJ, and either of the partners at McCabe &
Swisher; or, alternatively, by order of a judge after considering
any objections to the payment. I know it's cumbersome, but I
want to make sure the money goes to real victims and I trust
that between the prosecutor, U.S. attorney, and McCabe and/or
Swisher they'll get it right.
   I won't try and justify everything I've done. I have certainly
colored outside the lines. That said, my only regret is that I cost
Justin Mackey his life. I went to my grave incredibly guilty over
that mistake. Otherwise, I did what I set out to do—I stopped
the monsters and stripped them of their booty.

Sybil Lucas, aka Ann Parsons

Erin glanced at the list of people the e-mail had been sent to:
her, Duane, Prosecutor Picaro, acting U.S. attorney Ed Champion, Ed Kluska, and FBI Special Agent in Charge Abhay Petel.
   "Wow," Erin said. "That's pretty amazing."
   "You think the authorities will do what she wanted with the
money?" Swish asked.

"I don't think they'll have a choice. I mean, how do you think they'd look in the press if they tried to take two hundred million dollars away from victims of sexual abuse? And it's not like they can prevent us from going to the press." Erin looked down at the copy of the e-mail. "So do you think Sybil is really dead?" she asked with a certain air of incredulity.

Swish looked at her, his small grin unmasking any professed uncertainty. "The agent in me says no. There's no body, the people who took her are dead, and this whole thing with the money is set up perfectly to cover her tracks. I mean, who's going to be looking for a person who just gave away all but fifteen million of over five hundred and fifty million dollars? If you're in law enforcement, why do you want to find her? To prosecute her for killing the person who started abusing her when she was six and killed her mother? I know I wouldn't want to prosecute that case. All I can say is that dead or alive, Sybil Lucas did good by a lot of people. I hope she made it out alive."

"Amen," Erin added.

# CHAPTER 47

*Three months later*

MARIA ROJAS LOOKED AT HER PASSPORT AS SHE TOOK IT FROM THE customs agent. Between Erin and Lucy Nichols, they had been successful in getting her a green card and a legal name change. She had chosen Maria in honor of her mother. She had met extensively with Nichols and FBI Agent Collins, and between Maria's testimony and the evidence on the hard drives, the government had built an overwhelming case. The final nail came after Liam Fletcher was arrested and DeCovnie began cooperating with the government, transforming the case into a multipronged human trafficking investigation.

The press surrounding the dismissal of the criminal charges and the arrests that followed had sparked a number of lawsuits, including one class action that already had over thirty alleged victims of Parsons and his cohorts. Maria had been thrilled to see the Parsons estate being sued. After Erin and Duane had threatened to go to the press, the authorities had decided not to challenge the allocation of the money. In Maria's case, it meant she was a wealthy woman. She had moved out of the condo that Parsons had owned and bought a brownstone on Sixth Street in Jersey City.

Now, after two weeks vacationing with her brother in Aruba, who had flown home, she had flown on to Mozambique. Making her way through the airport, she saw her walking toward her. They both stopped a few feet from each other. Mozambique seemed to be agreeing with her. Her hair was a little longer and she was well tanned.

"What name are you going by these days?" Maria asked.

"Abigail Rogers," she replied. "But most people call me Abby. How about you?"

"Maria. Maria Rojas. And thank you for inviting me."

"Figured it was the least I could do. Besides, I don't know if you'll believe me, but I really did enjoy being with you. You know, before . . ."

Maria smiled. "I suspect I'll have some trust issues for a while about that."

"I can't imagine why," she said with a sardonic grin.

"But in the end, you saved my brother's life and helped end the case against me. So I can't complain too much."

"Kind of the least I could do under the circumstances. I did kind of fuck up your life."

"No, Syb . . . Abby. You saved my life. Thank you."

They stepped forward at the same time then, folding into each other's embrace.

"I'm so glad you're alive," Maria whispered. "When Duane told me what happened the night you all rescued David, everyone was convinced Conroy was going to kill you."

"Yeah, I was convinced I was a goner too. Fortunately, when they threw me in the backseat of the car, I still had my backup weapon in a waist holster that was behind me. When Conroy's gorilla jumped in the backseat, I already had my hand on my weapon. I was able to draw and fire, hitting him in the heart. When Conroy turned to see what happened, I took him by the head and snapped his neck. I was able to hop in the front seat and stop the car before we hit anything. Fortunately, we were in an industrial neighborhood at two in the morning so no one saw anything. Putting them in the trunk and leaving them in the airport was just payback for what they had done to a guy who worked for me—McCabe's client, Mackey. Payback's a bitch."

Neither of them said anything for the longest time.

"Would you like to see my place?" Abby finally asked.

Maria laughed. "Guess that would be a good idea, since that's where I thought I was staying. How far away is it?"

"About a hundred miles. But as you'll soon see, one of the blessings or curses of Mozambique, depending on your point of view, is there are very few paved roads. So a hundred miles will take us about three hours. But when you see the house on the ocean I've rented, I think you'll like it."

"Why Mozambique?" Maria asked.

"It's inexpensive. It has a great climate and beautiful beaches. Oh, and no extradition treaty with the United States," she added with a wry smile before reaching down to take Maria's hand. "Let's get your luggage. It's time to get reacquainted."

Erin carried her shoes in one hand as she and Mark walked hand in hand along the beach, the rumble of the waves crashing on the shoreline providing a perfect soundtrack. The ocean breeze had forced her to throw a light sweater on over her sundress. There was no moon, so the stars dominated the night sky. They had enjoyed the beginning of Memorial Day weekend lounging on the beach, followed by a wonderful seafood dinner at one of their favorite restaurants in Asbury Park, and now they were enjoying a leisurely barefoot stroll along the ocean on their way back to her condo.

"I could get used to this," Mark said. "I really like Bradley."

"Yeah, I love it down here," Erin replied with a sigh. "Maybe someday I'll convince Swish that we need a Monmouth County office—Freehold or Red Bank would be perfect."

"How are the Swishers doing?" Mark asked.

"Corrine and the baby are doing good. Swish says they're lucky; Alysha is already sleeping for four hours at a clip at night. And Austin seems to be adjusting to his baby sister pretty well. Hopefully, later in the summer we'll be able to get them down here."

"That would be nice," he said, his tone flat.

She looked over at him. "Is everything all right? You seem like you have something on your mind."

"I do, actually."

"What's the matter?" she asked.

"Nothing's the matter, but . . . well, we've been living together for over five months now, and it seems like every time I try to bring up the future, you avoid the subject."

Her shoulders slumped. "You're right," she said.

"So what should I take from that? Do we have a future?"

"Mark, this is hard for me. I'm thirty-seven years old and I spent more than thirty of those years loathing myself and convinced that no one could ever love me for who I was—for who I am. And then, when I did accept myself, and told the world this is who I am, my worst fears were realized. Other than my mom, my family rejected me. My marriage fell apart and most of my friends deserted me. So I guess when it came to us, I've always been waiting for the other shoe to drop—for you to realize I'm not worthy of your love."

He went to speak, but she suddenly stopped walking. "No," she said, holding her finger up to his lips. "It's best if I finish."

She drew in a deep breath. "The last three months, since the trial ended, I can't remember a happier time in my life. I'm not big on clichés like 'soul mate' or 'you complete me.' You're you, and I'm me—we're different people. But you've done something for me that I didn't think was possible. I think most of my life I've had a hole in me that made it impossible for me to love me, and, as a result, it made it just as impossible for me to accept that someone else could love me, just for being me. Somehow you found a way in and you patched that hole."

She stood on her tiptoes, reaching her arms out and wrapping them around his neck, pulling him close.

"Thank you, Mark Simpson. You have done something even more important than loving me. You have allowed me to love me. Whatever happens in our future, I will be forever grateful to you for that. I love you." She moved so her face was level with his and kissed him deeply and passionately on his lips.

When they broke their embrace, he kissed her on the forehead. "Thank you," he said with a grin that she had come to love so much.

They slowly began walking again. "So let's talk about our future," she said as the cold waters of the receding wave washed over their toes.

# ACKNOWLEDGMENTS

Somehow you managed to find your way to the acknowledgments page of the book. Maybe you've read the whole book, or maybe you just aimlessly opened the book to this page hoping that you'd be on the last page of the story and get to read how it ends without having to read everything else in between—sorry, you need to go back a few more pages for the end. Assuming you're here because you finished the book—thank you. Let's be honest, books don't mean anything unless someone reads them. So I can thank everyone who helped make this book happen, but if there's no one who reads it, it doesn't matter. So to my readers, thank you for investing your precious time in reading (or listening to) this story I created. I hope you've enjoyed it as much as I enjoyed creating it.

Like most works of fiction, the characters in this novel are made up. There is one character, however, who is loosely based on a real person—Erin's mom, Peg McCabe, who is an homage to my mom, Alice Gigl. My mom was an amazing woman, who like Erin's mom didn't understand anything about what it meant to be transgender when I came out to her. But like Peg, my mom found her way to continue to love me as only a mother could love their child. Unfortunately, my mom never got to see my first novel, *By Way of Sorrow*, published because she passed away in December 2020. I miss her every day. This book is dedicated to her and her memory. Thank you, Mom, for everything.

I owe so much to my agent, Carrie Pestrito, at Laura Dail Literary Agency, who somehow managed to get me, an unpublished nobody, a two-book deal. I know this book wouldn't exist without her. Likewise, to my wonderful editor at Kensington Books, John Scognamiglio, who took a chance on doing a series featuring a transgender protagonist, written by an unknown author. John, you are the best.

Similarly, I want to thank all the people at Kensington Books who have worked so hard to make this novel the best book it could be. In particular, I want to thank Holly Fairbank for catching all of my mistakes—and trust me, there were a lot! Also, to all the folks at Kensington who work behind the scenes to publicize and help promote my books. I am so grateful to have such a great team working with me.

As I did with my first novel, I owe a major debt to Andrea Robinson, an independent editor, whom Carrie recommended to me. I know that when I sent Andrea the original draft of this manuscript she was incredibly generous with her thoughts, suggestions, and edits. I know writers thank their editors all the time for their contributions, but in my case it really is true—Andrea's input made this a much better book. Thank you.

To my son Colin, writer and computer engineer, thank you for your sage advice on some of the technical aspects of the story. Likewise, to Lynn Centonze, a former police chief, for her advice on the law enforcement aspects—if I still managed to get things wrong, blame me, not them. And to my most faithful reader, Lori Becker, your encouragement and kind words always seem to come at exactly the right time to pick me up and keep me going. Lori read so many drafts of this book she can probably recite it from memory.

To Jan, my best friend and mother of our children—I literally wouldn't be here but for you. Thank you. To our sons, Tim and Colin; our daughter, Kate; granddaughters, Alice, Caroline, Madison, and Gwen; and daughters-in-law, Carly and Stephine, you get thanks for just being you. I love all of you more than you'll ever know. To the rest of my family and my friends (especially Joyce, Lynn, and Donna), whom I often told I couldn't make some event or get-together because I needed to write, thank you for your patience and understanding. But at least here's the proof—I really was writing!

Finally, to everyone in the LGBTQ+ community and especially those in the trans and nonbinary communities, thank you for your inspiration.